AN EDGE OF DARKNESS NOVEL

PSYCHOTIC OBSESSION

LEIGH RIVERS

AN EDGE OF DARKNESS NOVEL

PSYCHOTIC OBSESSION

LEIGH RIVERS

PLAYLIST

Cray - eat your heart out
Amber Run - I Found
Daughter - Medicine
Artemas - wet dreams
Sleep Token - The Offering
Psycho - pieces of me
2WEI - Toxic
DPR IAN - Nerves
Muse - Madness
Skeler - Two to the Chest
Cray - Mr Brightside
€CHO€D 4W4Y - I wanna be your lover

Find the playlist on Leigh's Spotify

CONTENT WARNING

Stalking, extremely possessive behavior, murder, kidnapping, drugging, trauma, mental health, pregnancy, child death (not detailed), abuse, unreliable narrative, dubious consent, non-consent, and mental abuse.

If you haven't come from *The Edge of Darkness* Trilogy, please be aware that this interconnected standalone is a dark and dangerous love story and not a romance. There is no happy ending for Aria and Tobias within this book.

If you have come from the trilogy, please keep in mind that this is set over twenty years before and Tobias is not the same version of himself. He's unhinged, dangerous, and extremely toxic.

For those who crave darkness yet hide in the light.
You can come out now.
Tobias is home.

PROLOGUE
ARIA

There's one thing controlling everything and anything in life, an emotion so strong, it can completely debilitate us. It overwhelms all our senses while we turn a blind eye to the toxicity surrounding us.

Love.

I always saw it as some romantic word to describe appreciation, loyalty, passion, a healthy relationship that could lead to marriage and children. Movies and novels always paint it so perfectly, and some people are lucky enough to find that type of love.

In reality, it's not all sunshine and roses.

I had absolutely no idea it could drive someone so insane–that the raw emotion between two lovers could result in complete and utter carnage.

That it could rip apart your identity.

I didn't know what it felt like to live as a vessel while the world around me continued to spin. Yet I could see it in his eyes many times, those deep, penetrating, innocently intoxicating blues burning into my psyche with each slow, carefully controlled thrust.

With a mixture of seduction and false promises from that

four-letter word, he would fuck me into oblivion, taking over every inch of my body as I submitted to him.

He wanted to own me.

And I let him–as long as I was able to own him too.

He was mine and I was his.

Being in a toxic relationship is pretty bad.

Being in love with a psychopath is way worse.

Love is dangerous.

Trust is a weakness.

Possession is a toxic game.

The devil himself delved into my mind and whispered he was everything I ever needed, wanted, craved, and I listened.

He loved me, just in his own screwed up, deranged way. I was everything to him, but that led to me being pulled onto the goddamn stage with the bastard himself. He tormented me while everyone else judged our relationship the way he wanted.

They were blind. We all were.

Everything between us was going well–or so I thought. When his mask dropped, the tell-tale signs of control grew stronger. The destruction wreaked by his mind games messed with me in ways I struggle to explain.

Physically, he would never lay a finger on me, but mentally, he destroyed my soul.

His twisted thoughts led to so much devastation, such unforgivable consequences.

Did Tobias Mitchell care?

No.

Unless it involved me...nothing else mattered to him.

1

ARIA

The elevators are broken.

As I stand here with a box already causing my knees to shake from its weight, I scowl at the *not in service* signs. The yellow and red-striped stickers are stuck to all the elevators. I need to take the stairs. God dammit.

I could cry.

Do you know how many floors I have to climb until I reach my temporary office here in the States?

Eight.

My poor legs.

I struggle to open the door to the stairway. Thankfully, my colleague and best friend, Gabriella, catches up to me. "I'll get it," she offers, waving her hand out for me to go in first. "You could have waited for me." She flips her long, bouncy blonde hair over her shoulder.

"You were taking forever in the queue."

"I needed my morning coffee," she responds with a shrug, walking ahead while I still struggle with the box. "I go every morning, Aria."

"You have a coffee machine in your office."

She shrugs again. "The barista is hot."

I roll my eyes. She has given that excuse every morning since we arrived four days ago.

By the time we reach the eighth floor, I'm wheezing, in desperate need of an inhaler as my hands press the base of my spine to relieve some of the painful pressure. I don't know how many times I stopped to drop the box and catch my breath, but Gabs seems like she could go another eight floors. I guess she does work out every day, unlike me.

Despite being from Scotland, I grew up here in America, having moved away when I was a young teen and returned to study. Gabs has been my roommate since college, and we've never really been able to separate since. I've spent years putting up with her wild ways, and I'm still going.

I follow her into her office, practically gasping for breath as I settle the box on her desk and drop into her chair.

"How many are coming to the meeting?" Gabriella asks.

"Seven, maybe," I reply. "I managed to convince a specialist from London to come speak about the case. Oh, and two from Delaware showed interest and wanted to attend."

She whistles. "You did good. No one would take the case for over a year until you joined the team. It's been a blessing to have you with us instead of down in the labs. You thrive more up here."

The transfer had been a big step for me, but I was honestly one genetic test away from blowing up the entire lab. Day after day, it was the same. I wanted more. I wanted to make a difference on the frontline. Gabriella told me there was a position opening up for a clinical scientist with experience in genetics, and I'd been in the labs for too long. I applied, and somehow, I managed to impress them enough to land the job.

It has been hard, don't get me wrong–the change of scenery and the workload caught me off guard. But I'm here, and just like Gabriella said, I'm thriving.

When I took over the Ivy Dermot case, we had travelled across the world to discuss possible trials for her unknown illness, or to at least find a diagnosis, but after dozens of failures, a doctor here in the States invited us to see if Ivy would be a match for them.

"Okay, we have three minutes," she says, staring at her watch. She claps once. "You ready?"

I shake myself, taking a long, deep breath. No, I'm definitely not ready.

"I'm ready," I lie.

My best friend can see right through me.

She grasps my wrists, holding them up to her chest. "You've got this. You're smart. You're professional. You care. Don't think about them all being older, or that they have more experience. You fight for what you believe in and don't allow anyone to talk down to you because of your age. You understand? Your research is spot on, you've done everything properly, and I'll be surprised if it gets refused."

I nod once.

But the lump in my throat is growing. I swallow it down, reminding myself of that beautiful smile from the most precious girl in the world.

I need to do this for her.

All the specialists are way older than me, and it can be daunting and nerve-wracking, especially when they try to dominate the room and talk down to me.

The conference room is blindingly bright, so much so, I struggle not to screw my eyes shut. Floor-to-ceiling windows span two walls of the corner room.

We sit at a large, dark, oval-shaped table, paperwork covering nearly every inch of the wood.

No one looks at us as we take our seats.

No one speaks, not even when the doctors and students walk in and greet those they already know. Across from us, two others drop down into their seats. Young men, maybe around their mid-twenties like me and Gabriella. They're well-dressed and look confident. One of them pushes his glasses up the bridge of his nose while reading from a sheet of paper, and I have to look away before anyone thinks I'm staring.

I cross my legs at the knees, placing my folder in front of me and opening to the front page.

"Did you bring all of the—" Gabriella stops as soon as the door opens, silence filling the room.

The specialist doctor we were waiting for enters in powerful strides that make my spine tingle. To say I'm terrified is an understatement, but I can't show it.

I clear my throat, grabbing everyone's attention. This is the third time I've stood in a meeting like this and fought for this child's life. Maybe this meeting will actually be positive and I won't be shut down for not having their same level of experience.

"Thank you for coming today," I announce, painting a confident smile on my face.

I begin by discussing with a few of the staff about other patients here in the hospital, how their treatment has impacted their quality of life and my exact reason for reaching out.

I try to keep my chin up, my back straight the same as Gabs', as I address the doctor at the head of the table, Doctor Blythe. He wants to say a few words regarding my research, and my palms sweat as he stands from his seat.

He clears his throat to grab everyone's attention. "This is quite a peculiar case we've been looking into for some time. Remarkable work you've done here." I remain passive, waiting for the blow to land like I've been expecting. He tells the room of my work, my achievements in such a short time, and nods to me before taking his seat again. "I believe each of you have statements to make over the next few days before Miss Dermot's arrival."

Wait, no.

"Oh, sorry," I say before he can continue. Everyone looks at me. "Aren't we looking into the information before instructing the patient to travel here? It would seem unnecessary if she were to come all the way from Scotland, only to be told the trials aren't compatible with what she needs? She's currently wheelchair-bound, and arrangements need to be made regarding her stay."

Dr. Blythe nods. "I know that. Please have the patient

brought here by Friday. I've had a specialist look into her case, and he believes there is a strong match."

"They think she is compatible?"

"Yes," is all he says in reply, his eyes challenging me.

I sit back on my chair, crossing my legs under the table as Gabriella shifts beside me.

As usual, I'm the last to know. I'm relieved but pissed I've been here for four days and not once did he email me or come to my office to tell me specialists agree on a match.

Blythe continues, "I have asked two assistants to join the team." He points to the two young men across from us, both their heads buried in their notes. "Mr. Mitchell and Mr. Lapsley have been part of my team for three years, researching genetic mutations and pathogenic variations."

The one with pale eyes lifts his head, giving a nervous wave. The other keeps reading his paperwork as if there isn't a room full of professionals discussing a little girl's life. He licks the tip of his thumb to turn the page, dark brows furrowed deep behind the frames of his glasses.

"In front of you, if you haven't looked through them yet, are all the details needed. A copy of the enrollment, the specifics of the trial, the possible costs, side notes, and a section for your own, if needed. And Aria..." His eyes find mine over his glasses. "As you are the one who set this up and the listed primary worker on her case, I'd like to speak with you tomorrow at noon, just to go over some extra details."

To take control, you mean. Which is fine–he is more experienced, with a good twenty years on me. I'm just a girl in my early twenties, still breaking my way into the field, but my age shouldn't make me feel useless the way it does when people talk down to me.

"Thank you," I reply with an enthusiastic smile, ensuring I make eye contact with each person in the room–except the guy in front, still fully focused on his paperwork.

"Everyone, if there are any concerns or any questions, you are

9

welcome to direct them to Aria, as she likely knows more information on the patient than anyone."

The doctor from Great Ormond across from me clears his throat and stacks his pages. "How long have you been working on this case? From what I've heard, you're very new to the department, a lab worker only two years ago. Am I correct? You're certainly one of the youngest I've worked with."

Sigh.

Being in my twenties sucks sometimes.

Gabriella is the same age as me, and she never gets comments like that.

But I refuse to back down, especially with this case.

"My age is of no concern," I reply in the gentlest tone, trying not to piss anyone off. "I—"

"Shouldn't we have someone more qualified in charge?"

I smile at the doctor who just interrupted me. "Thank you for showing concern. I've been in this department for a little over two years, and yes, before that, I was a geneticist down in the labs. I take my role very seriously. I've done my own research for my patient, have spoken with her family numerous times about finding equipment at home, ease of travelling, anything to help her. There's only so much available in our country, so we are limited unless we can organize a transfer. That's why I have reached out to others, why we were in Germany six months ago and then attended meetings at the Bambino Gesù in Rome. Ivy Dermot is a mystery, but I believe all mysteries can be solved."

I feel Gabriella smiling beside me.

When they all nod, I relax, resting both palms over Ivy's main file.

"I look forward to working with you all and hopefully finding a diagnosis and quality treatment plan for Ivy. As Dr. Blythe said, if you have questions, I will be happy to answer them."

I feel another lump building in my throat, this one threatening to suffocate me. As a professional, it is highly recommended not to form a bond with patients.

But I struggled to separate myself.

I overstepped two months ago and appeared at Ivy's family's door with flowers and a present for her eighth birthday. She'd smiled the whole time and cried when I left. She always gets excited when we have appointments, the beaming grin alone enough for me to continue fighting for her. Her seizures aren't as intense now that I've gotten her on different medication, and most days, she can stay awake for longer than a few hours. But her body—her muscles—are slowly deteriorating, her undiagnosed sickness whittling her away, and I want to stop it, or at least make life easier for her.

I glance up and see the hands of one of the assistants. He's still flicking through Ivy's file, deep in concentration, and as my heart starts to slow from the unwanted adrenaline, I stare at his fingers, the thickness of them, the blunt nails, the bands on his wrist.

When the meeting finishes, it's late, the sun vanishing, replaced by the moon shining through the floor-to-ceiling windows lining the wall. Most of the staff leave without looking at me; others give me a nod. Gabriella rests a hand on my shoulder and tells me I did well and that she'll see me at the hotel we're staying at nearby.

It's about ten minutes away, and as much as I hate walking around by myself, I have too much left to do before I call it a night. Now that I know Ivy will be transferred here, I need to ensure all the staff needed are on board and that her family is aware of what happens next.

I'm the last to exit the conference room by the time I check over all the documents again before I start sending emails. I throw my bag over my shoulder, tucking loose strands of hair behind my ear.

Lifting the dreaded heavy cardboard box full of paperwork, I make my way out of the room. I don't get far as my foot hits an outstretched leg—a man sitting with his back to the wall with papers in his hand.

Tumbling not so gracefully, I land face-first on the marble floor, paperwork and bag scattering everywhere.

"Oh, fuck! I'm so sorry," the man says in panic, quickly

scrambling from the floor and holding his hand out for me to grab. In his panicked tone, he adds, "Here, let me help you."

Intense, unexplainable shocks run up my wrist as I take his hand, his palm soft and warm. Not looking up while I get to my knees, attempting to save myself from more embarrassment, I try to stack all the paperwork back into the box and nearly give myself a papercut.

I see him in my peripheral lowering to the floor, also gathering the papers. When I lift my bag, mortification lashes through me as my phone, lip balm, purse, and tampon topple out.

If one more embarrassing or bad thing happens today, I'll cry.

I let out an annoyed huff, wiping my forehead, still on my knees staring at everything for a minute in silence.

The mystery man sets a pile into the box, and I can tell all the documents are mixed up.

My eye twitches.

"Are you—"

I cut him off. "You should really sit on the seats or in an office; I could have been a patient," I snap.

The air nearly leaves my lungs as I glare at him, his soft smile the first thing I notice. He's clean-shaven, with penetratingly vibrant blue eyes and long lashes to match his dark hair and brows. Now that I'm staring, his smile drops, and his perfect white teeth bite down on the plumper part of his bottom lip.

"Are you okay?" he asks with a hint of humor.

I drag my eyes away. "Sorry. I'm just tired, and today's been a bit much."

Squatting, he leans his elbows on his thighs, sleeves rolled up to reveal he's wearing a watch and charity bands, and he isn't heavily tattooed like my ex. "Sorry I tripped you," he apologizes, handing me my phone and lipstick, probably refusing to lift my tampon. "You're the Scottish doctor, aren't you? Why do you have an American accent?"

"I grew up here then moved."

"Ah," he replies. "A quick escape to the highlands."

I hum a response, rubbing my elbow that's aching from the fall.

He continues by asking with a tilted head, "Are you hurt, Doctor?"

"I'm fine. And no one calls me that. It's just Aria."

"Aria," he repeats, like he's testing the way my name sounds on his tongue, tasting each syllable.

I don't know why, but he sounds intrigued. I also don't know why I like his voice, or that he's not a stuck up asshole like most of the people I've had to work with.

Then, he smiles. "Doctor sounds better."

I scowl at him.

His shirt pulls taut along his chest as he straightens, offering me his hand once again. It's then I realize I'm gawking at him with my lips parted, nerves prickling in me.

Why am I nervous? Worse, why am I nervous at work?

"You're one of the assistants," I state the obvious. "You're working on the Ivy Dermot case too."

His dimples dent in deep as he grins again, and I nearly buckle at the knees. As he steps back, grabbing his bag and throwing it over his shoulder, his parting words reach my ears.

"I am, but a pretty little thing like you can call me Tobias."

2

ARIA

A pretty little thing like you.

Um, excuse me? I don't mind flirtatious advances, but not at work. It's unprofessional and...and... No. Just no. I'm certain my cheeks are still red from our unfortunate event that resulted in me crashing to the ground yesterday. Unless they're beaming because of what he said? The way he looked at me? No, Tobias can go flirt with a broken lamp for all I care.

"Why are you growling at my boobs?"

My eyes lift up to Gabs' face. I must've been in a daze, wondering why I'm so bothered by such a small incident. "Oh, sorry, Gabs. My head's a bit all over the place."

"Still hung up on Toby?"

"Tobias," I correct, rolling my eyes, hating that I'd told her what happened and dealing with her comments all morning. "And no. I'm thinking about what we're having for dinner later."

She clicks her tongue. "Sure. Then you won't mind if I invite both the assistants along tomorrow?"

"You wouldn't," I say.

She cocks a brow as if to say *I totally would.*

And the scariest part? I believe her. She knows more than anyone how much I don't like to mix my work life with my personal life, so asking the assistants to join is a rule I refuse to break. We're going to a club because she wants to see the band playing, and I, against my own wishes, agreed to join her. Our day off usually consists of me sitting on the hotel bed with my laptop, so maybe a breather will help the nerves I feel about Ivy's arrival.

But inviting them isn't going to help me relax. The total opposite, actually.

"Don't you dare." I grit my teeth in a bid to show how angry I am without raising my voice, but it doesn't faze her. I'm not the slightest bit intimidating, not with my small height compared to her towering form. "You know I hate mixing work."

She shrugs, her eyes going back to her computer. "You have a meeting in ten minutes with Blythe. Maybe Toby will trip you up again."

"Don't start," I say. "It was an accident." I sigh. "And for crying out loud, his name is Tobias."

She snorts. My best friend may be professional around others, but when it's just us, her fun, playful side comes out. I think that's why we fit so well together. She calls me the grump, whereas she is the life and soul of every party we attend. She vowed to make me as wild as her one day.

I think I've done well with letting her have all the wild.

Gabs seems to find my unlucky topple over Tobias hilarious. My first mistake was telling her, though my second and most important was becoming her friend in the first place.

Earlier, she had nudged me with her elbow and winked in his direction when he walked by our meeting room, and then again when he was in the ward's kitchen, studying his tablet intensely.

She even intentionally asked me to grab coffee when she saw him venturing for his own hot drink. It's ridiculous. She's ridiculous. He's ridiculous. Who flirts with someone they just met and tripped up?

Don't get me wrong, it's not that he isn't hot. I just don't have time for romance or distractions, especially with my ex still very much in the picture. We're technically friends–our breakup was abrupt and I'm still coming to terms with it, but I need space from him until I can figure my own life out.

The meeting with the doctor goes quickly. We discuss Ivy's likes, dislikes, her sensory issues, and ways to make her feel comfortable here. Once we go over her medical history one last time, he tells me he has assigned me an assistant to help with the workload heading my way.

When the door opens, I glance in its direction as a tall figure steps in, and my gaze darts away when Tobias joins us.

Why is he here? Please don't tell me—

"Tobias will be assisting for the next few weeks. He's a hard worker and a fast learner."

Tobias smiles as he closes the door, a melting smile that makes me look straight ahead, trying not to show my traitorous blush as he sits down beside me.

"Good afternoon, Doctor," Tobias says in a low tone, legs parted so wide, our knees nearly touch. With an elbow on the armrest, he glances at me. "It's a pleasure to have the opportunity to work with you."

I give him a tight smile, but deep inside, I'm screaming.

He can't be another Kaleb. He *cannot*.

When I was in college and on a break from Ewan for months, I was literally obsessed with him. Two years older, hot, the bad boy with a big brain. He asked me for help on a paper he was struggling with, so I met up with him at a coffee shop, then again at his house, and again, and again, until we fell into bed. Let's just say when I found out he had a girlfriend, I raised hell at him for weeks before swearing off anyone in my field. The dread heavy in my gut when I got back together with Ewan and had to tell him about my fling made me sick. I was always honest and open with my ex.

If we get back together again, which I'm still unsure of, my conscience will push me to tell Ewan about Tobias, and nobody wants that.

Which means I need to put a stop to the crawling heat

currently wrapping around the apex of my legs. His voice is so deep, so arousing, I can barely think straight.

Once the meeting is over and he's still calling me doctor, I ask Tobias to follow me down to the labs. When we meet with one of the seniors, we begin discussing the most recent tests performed on Ivy and what we plan on doing next now that she has been accepted for a new medical trial.

As I talk, Tobias watches me intently.

He listens with his arms crossed, biceps tensing under his shirt, nodding at everything I say.

He puts on a pair of thick, black framed glasses and takes notes while asking all the right questions, and I must admit, I'm impressed. I think I smile once, maybe twice, when he asks someone about a specific technique.

I learn, whilst sitting in the cafeteria on the third floor, that his full name is Tobias Mitchell. He's twenty-six and is allergic to cats. Devouring a sandwich, he asks me if I'll need his number to contact him about Ivy's case outside of work.

For once in my life, I don't hesitate. In fact, I probably say *yes* far too quickly.

"Call me so I can save yours," he tells me.

And I do, happily.

In this moment, I feel myself inwardly sighing as Gabriella appears in the cafeteria, waving like a lunatic. But thankfully, Doctor Shique, another specialist who flew over from Scotland with us, appears behind her, ushering her towards another table with a file in his hands.

From where I'm sitting, I can see Tobias' screen as he saves my number as "Doctor Miller".

He just lost ten points.

I narrow my eyes at him as he looks down at his phone.

"Do you have set shifts here, or has Blythe given you the go-ahead to come as you please?"

"Say that again." He tilts his head in confusion. "You talk so fast."

"What is your schedule?" I clarify, speaking a little slower.

"Ah, eight till eight, but I can rearrange it earlier or later if that doesn't work for you?"

I shake my head. "That works fine. Are you staying near the hospital?"

"My house is about fifty minutes away."

I sip my drink. "Do you drive?"

"I do. I usually pick Justin up on the way here."

"Is he the other assistant?" I ask, knowing he has been assigned to Gabriella. Which, in all honesty, I feel bad for him. She might be fun on the outside, but she's a bossy bitch and extremely demanding when it comes to work. It suits her, gets her to where she wants to be with her workload, so I just wave it off whenever she's being moody.

"I was actually supposed to be your colleague's assistant, but Justin insisted he would work better with her."

I snort. She will eat him alive.

By the time we finish and my shift comes to an end, I say goodbye to everyone and head to the hotel.

Gabs won't be back for a few hours–she has a date she matched with on her dating app, so the chances of her coming home at all are slim to none.

I bathe in the hotel bathtub and relax with music playing, reading a book. I'm fully immersed in my fictional world when the first message comes through.

TOBIASWORK

> I want to apologize again for tripping you the other day. I was looking at a test Ivy Dermot had a few months back. Is it possible to call and discuss it with you?

ME

> Which one? We can look over her files tomorrow.

His reply comes through while I dry myself with a towel and settle into bed.

TOBIASWORK

> She had Pharmacogenetic tests done in April.
> Was that for the seizure medication you had
> her put on?

I'm starting to think he's just trying to talk to me. This isn't even slightly necessary, definitely something that can be discussed during work hours. I entertain him by replying with a yes, and then I place my phone on its charging station.

It's nearly ten, and I'm usually asleep by now, but each time my phone dings, I pounce for it. For the next two hours, it's a back and forth discussion about tests and trials that have already been looked at. When I finally tell him this should be something we should be talking about in a meeting or in my temporary office, he quickly apologizes, followed by a "goodnight, Doctor".

ME

> If you call me doctor one more time, I will
> make your position as my assistant hell.

TOBIASWORK

> Oh, really? Is that a threat?

My bottom lip traps between my teeth as I reread the words. This isn't professional at all, right? If someone were to read these messages, they'd assume there was some sort of flirting going on. A shot of excitement runs up my spine at the thought, but I shake my head and reply.

ME

> Yes. I wouldn't get on my bad side, Tobias.

TOBIASWORK

> Sounds like a challenge, Doctor.

I send a smiley emoji so he knows I'm not too serious, slapping myself on the forehead when I realize it definitely is flirting.

When he replies with a wink, I toss my phone to the floor with a groan.

As soon as we get into work the following morning, Gabriella has made plans for us tonight.

Tobias sits on his phone most of the day instead of helping me, and every time I ask him to look at something, he apologizes and rushes out of the room.

I understand emergencies, but a little communication helps a lot.

I'm left to do all the paperwork, all the phone calls, and my assistant seems to have vanished off the face of the Earth.

Not the flirty one in the messages at all. He seems stressed and anxious. He fidgets, runs his hands through his hair, and stares at the same page for nearly two hours on the opposite side of my desk. He simply hums when I ask if everything is okay.

When Gabs comes in and says it's time to go, he gets to his feet and doesn't spare either of us a glance as he leaves the room.

Gabriella raises a brow. "What's up his ass?"

3

TOBIAS

My hands shake as I stare down at my phone. The words still aren't registering, because what the fuck do I do with this information?

Eye flicking up to the door, I pull the latch again, making sure to double check the lock is definitely in place. I don't need anyone walking in here and seeing the shit I'm looking at. They'll report me for stalking, and then I'll likely lose my job. Right now, after setting my eyes on her, that's not something I'm willing to risk.

Besides, this isn't stalking. This is me simply wanting to know more information about someone without their knowledge. It's not a crime to do some research, even if my demands were probably threatening when the asshole said he could only get her address, date of birth, and what kind of car she drives back in her hometown.

No. I needed more.

And now, I kind of regret it.

The email came through a few hours ago, and ever since I scanned the message, my heart has been racing dangerously fast. I contemplated, or still am contemplating, crashing her night with her friend. They're going to a club to see some band—I'd overheard Gabriella talking about it.

The more I think about it, maybe Justin and I need to blow off some steam.

It's decided, then. We're going.

Taking an annoyed breath because the voice in my head is getting erratic, I glance down at the screen once more.

Name: Aria Miller.
Age: Twenty-seven
DOB: May 8th.

My left eye twitches. I've only ever fucked one person, and she was older than me. What if the fact I'm only twenty-six puts her off me? What if she likes being with someone older or the same age? She didn't seem too bothered when I told her my age before.

Her birthday is in May, so we have a month where we're the same age at least. Maybe I can approach her in April and there won't be an issue.

I shake my head and continue reading.

Birthplace: California. Moved to Scotland as a teenager-never picked up the accent.
Occupation: Clinical scientist-it seems she is quite dedicated and works more hours than she should, potentially to catch up to those who are either above her or to outdo her peers.
Family: No known siblings, aunts, uncles, or cousins. Parents are alive and married. Grandfather is deceased. Grandmother is alive. Only seems to have one friend who she recently moved in with, Gabriella McGhee.
Romantic relations: Ewan McElroy, aged 27, father to Jason McElroy, aged 10. In a relationship for 8 years?

My jaw clenches as I reread the last one. Who the fuck is Ewan? Does she have a kid with this guy? Does she care about him?

I'd wanted these details. I wanted to know everything about this girl.

Everything from her eye and hair color, to where she buys her coffee in the morning, to what perfume she wears and her weight at birth.

I frown at the bottom line again. A question mark next to the duration of their relationship. Does that mean it's unclear? Maybe they were together less time and it might not even be a big deal. Is she single then? Taken? Do I care?

This guy was able to get all this information on her, but not if she's still fucking this Ewan. It's probably the most important piece. If she does have a kid, that's fine. I can handle kids. They are tolerable. But if she belongs to someone else, that just isn't going to work for me.

Will it stop me from staring at her? Following her back to her hotel? Hunting for her schedule to see when she takes her breaks so I end up on the same one as her? Nope. Still gonna do that.

Gulping, I blow out a breath and think.

I could just ask her if she's single or if she has someone waiting on her back home. Maybe I can slip it in when we're discussing schedules or if she brings up how hot it is here when Scotland will be cold and raining for the hundredth time.

I type back an email telling him to go deeper into her romantic relations and to send me shit on this Ewan. He quickly replies to confirm he'll do just that.

I release a sigh and close my eyes, sliding my phone into my back pocket.

What the fuck is going on with me? I met her days ago, and now I'm hiring people to dig into her personal life, and for what?

Because I think she's pretty?

Yes. Because she *is* pretty. Probably the only girl I've taken an interest in. My nerves around her are my first warning sign, but the deep, intense need to claim her over her little fucking desk is my biggest red flag that I need to calm down and take this as slowly and carefully as possible so I don't scare her off.

Blowing out a breath, I check myself in the bathroom mirror and adjust my glasses before going back out into the ward to find my doctor.

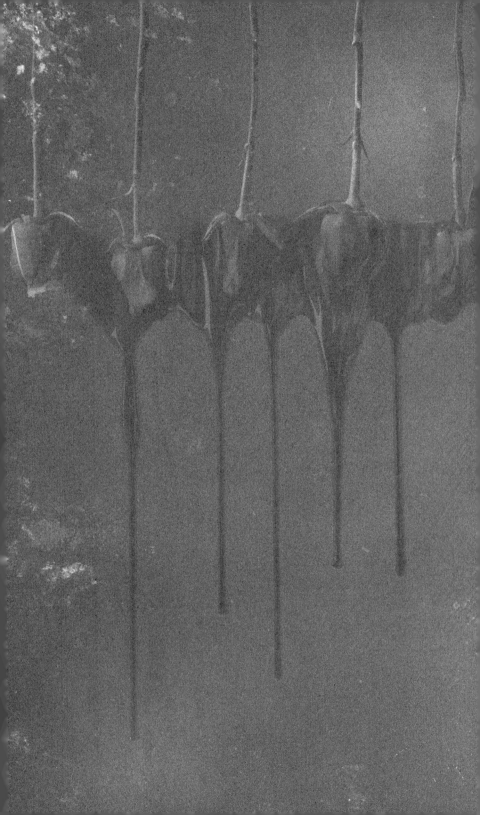

4

ARIA

Gabriella has always been a bit of a party animal. She can down drink after drink and never get drunk, stay up until early morning and still look perfect.

But when we decided to go out tonight, I truly believed it would be a relaxed, de-stressing night, considering we're in America for work. Alas, she never fails to prove me wrong, because I'm currently watching someone effortlessly swing on a pole, music nearly blowing my eardrums out from how close Gabriella has us sitting to the speakers.

The band she came here to see canceled last minute, but she decided to make use of her night anyway.

I keep my glass of water close—I don't know anyone here, and I refuse to get roofied. Not only because I'd likely die, but I also need to be up early tomorrow for another meeting with Dr. Blythe.

I fix my glasses onto my head, pulling some of my hair from my face and looking around the club. The strobe lights will likely give me a migraine soon–the base from the music is literally shaking the booth beneath my ass, and I'm starting to realize how much of a moody party-pooper I'm being.

"You're frowning so hard, Aria," Gabs says in my ear, loud

enough for me to hear over the music. "At least have one drink to lighten your mood. Please."

I roll my eyes but laugh. "I'll end up drunk on the floor and late for work tomorrow if I have as much as a sniff of alcohol."

"Lightweight," she mutters.

I flinch back as she lifts her glass to my face, my nostrils filling with the smell of her pink gin. "See?" she says. "You sniffed, and you're still sober and moody."

"Saturday," I tell her. "Then I'm all yours."

"Has Ewan been blowing up your phone?" she asks, letting her eyes scan the room.

I shake my head. "I asked him for space, and he's giving me it."

"Well...what's the best way to get over someone who cheated on you?"

My shoulders slouch. "You know I'm not going to sleep with someone else. We only just broke up. Besides, he cheated on me six years ago, not recently." Despite me only just finding out about the betrayal, it still hurt enough for me to walk away. All those years of lies just slapped me across the face.

"I don't care if he cheated on you two hundred years ago and you just found out. He's a snake and doesn't deserve you. When the right person shows up, or more like trip you up, and you embarrass yourself by hitting his foot with your tampon, you'll be ready to be fucked within an inch of your life and forget all about that cheating sleeze-bag."

"What about Jason?"

"That's something you need to talk to Ewan about, when you're ready. I know you've basically raised him, but how will it work if you're no longer dating his dad?"

All I do is shrug and chew my lip.

She narrows her eyes behind me. "Isn't that the extremely hot and extremely off-limits assistant you hit with said tampon?"

"I didn't hit him with my tampon," I retort then click on to what she just said.

I turn in my seat, my eyes landing on Tobias and Gabriella's assistant, Justin. They're standing at the bar, the latter talking to a girl while Tobias' eyes are cast down to his phone screen, one hand in his pocket. He looks impatient, agitated, and god dammit, he's hot. Definitely the type I would go for if I was swiping for a date online.

Not that I know. I'd been dating Ewan since I was a teenager, and this is the second break we've taken. The thought of my ex has me swallowing and ignoring the urge to call him to break my own rule.

Ewan has been trying to get back together–I'd asked him to leave me alone so I can think about things.

But I can't go back to someone who was unfaithful, regardless of me finding out years later and raising his kid.

I take a deep breath and look away from our assistants. "Did you invite them when I said not to?"

Her eyes widen. "God, no. I wouldn't do that to you!"

My gaze narrows as I search her face. "I believe you."

"How did they know we were here, though?" Gabriella asks. "Ohhhh, what if he's secretly a party boy and gets drunk off his ass while screwing everyone in sight?"

I shake my head but don't look back at them. "It's the closest club. They probably always come here." Then I laugh. "I honestly can't imagine Tobias being like that. He seems too serious."

"You could totally test him."

Frowning, I stare at my best friend. "Meaning?"

She winks and finishes her glass, smiling over at the pair and getting their attention. I want to tell her to stop, that we don't need their company, but she's already waving at them and muttering into my ear that she's going for another drink.

I know she's going straight to Justin, though, and I tut to myself, pulling my phone out to check the time.

I'm being a total grump and I know it. Gabriella knows it. The assistants know it, and the couple getting handy in the corner booth know it.

I'm sure he's fingering her while she tugs his zipper down and grabs his—

"Stop staring," Tobias whispers in my ear before he takes the seat beside me in the booth. Now that he's so close, I can see him clearly. He's dressed in pants and a shirt that hugs every single muscle, and he smells nice–leather, I think, and a hint of something minty. I get a closer look at his bands–some for charities, two for mental health in teens, and one for a girl called Lucy.

If my memory serves me right, we have a patient on the ward with that name, and she's currently fighting an aggressive form of cancer. Tobias spends a lot of time in her room–either reading a book to her, watching some kiddie TV show, or he's helping her parents take fingerprints and hand casts. It was her birthday last month, and there are polaroids on her wall with him in a few.

"I'm sorry about today," Tobias says, leaning into me so I can hear him over the thundering bass. "My mother is in town and staying at my place, and she wouldn't leave me alone all day." His warm breath tickles my neck as his hand rests on the back of the booth, his fingers gently touching my shoulder. A shiver runs down my spine; it's such a traitorous feeling, but I don't try to pull away from his touch. It's kind of nice.

I'm certain the music gets even louder, the bass harder, and my heart is racing so fast, I feel like I might go into cardiac arrest.

His thigh is pressed up against mine, his legs parted, one hand resting on the table, his finger tapping the wood.

I should shift to the side. I should push him away from me. But I'm not–my assistant's body is touching mine, and I'm not revolted.

I'm most likely looking too much into this. He's just a large man in a small booth, and I need to get a grip on my life.

"I'll make it up to you," he continues, his tone deep and...

God, his tone actually seems a bit teasing, almost flirtatious. Or is it the alcohol? Is he drunk? Why do I want to flirt back?

Screw it.

"You better," I say with narrowed eyes before smiling up at him. "Because if not, I'll find someone else."

I poke at his chest, and he snatches my wrist. Electricity rushes up my arm, heating my cheeks at the intense look in his eyes and the touch of his skin against my own.

"Is that right?" he asks, making my heart skip so fast, I stop breathing at his closeness. "Doctor Miller, don't underestimate me. I'll be the best assistant you've ever had."

"So far, I'm not impressed," I joke, raising a brow as I move back a little.

His fingers tighten around my wrist, and he pulls me closer to him. "I'll impress you. Don't worry. You tell me what it is you want, and I'll give it to you."

Shakily, I reply, "Are you still talking about work?"

His shoulder raises in a shrug.

"You can't flirt with me," I say, hating my words. "It's unprofessional and goes against the hospital's policy."

"Hmm," he hums, trying to stop his smirk and failing as he releases my wrist.

Then, he goes quiet, and I nervously shift to the side to put what minimal space I can between us.

Half an hour later, Tobias and I are still in silence as we watch the crowd. Justin is talking to my friend, and I know he's trying to get with her. It's written all over his face with the way he keeps licking his lips, watching her mouth, the way his hand slides under the table to grab her thigh. She enjoys it. Her cheeks heat and she keeps doing that fake, flirty laugh while dropping her head onto his shoulder.

Something about Justin sends alarm bells blaring in my head, but I don't quite know why.

Gabriella taps my shin with the pointed toe of her shoe, and I frown at how red her eyes are. "Come to the bathroom with me!"

She stumbles as she gets to her feet, latching onto my arm as we head to the bathroom.

5

TOBIAS

Fucking Justin.

The asshole nearly ruined my plan and blew my goddamn cover. I knew the second I told him where I wanted to go—a club full of strobes, lasers, and half naked people —he knew exactly why. I don't go to these types of places, so he fucking put two and two together and realized my new obsession. He saw the way I'd been staring at Aria at work, how many times I checked my messages throughout the day, seeing absolutely nothing from her chat box.

I wanted to reach out first, but I searched online that if you lay it on heavy, it can be uncomfortable and come across like I'm a creep.

I'm not a creep—I just like the look of Dr. Aria Miller.

She hates when I call her that, but I don't care. I like the way her nose scrunches when the name leaves my mouth, or how her lips purse, her eyes flashing with anger and annoyance. I almost want her to slap me.

It would be amazing. Imagine having her hand on my cheek? I'd be dreaming.

"Fuck, dude. She's hammered."

I look up from my phone to see my doctor's friend, Gabriella, falling around the dance floor as they try to get to the bathroom. Aria is worried. She's trying to get her to walk straight. I almost want to go get a bottle of water for her drunk ass, but that involves leaving my seat and missing the view of her walking towards me on her way back to the booth.

Her friend is supposed to be here for work, and she's drinking like that? I'm sure she hasn't had that many drinks, but then I freeze and grip my phone so hard, I'm shocked it doesn't crack.

I look at Justin, and he winks at me when he realizes I caught him. "Easy night, am I right?"

My left eye twitches at his words. I knew he was a scumbag, but to roofie a girl he's trying to get with is a new low. I grit my teeth as Aria stresses more, her eyes lifting to me momentarily before vanishing through the women's room door.

If her friend wasn't so fucked up right now, I'd have her attention. It's hopeful thinking, but I know she'd be over here, and I'd either have my arm behind her on the booth or she'd be giving me some sort of attitude for drinking alcohol when we have work tomorrow.

I'm not. My glass is filled with water. I don't drink.

It messes with my medication, and I like to be in full control without putting a blocker on my psyche. It's one thing my father was heavy on with me before he died. He was the only one who understood me and the way my mind worked, because I was exactly like him. Mom hated him for encouraging me to embrace my true self.

My true self meant being obsessed with one thing at a time and making it my entire life. When I was a kid, that was cars. Actually, one specific car. It was a red toy Ferrari that caught my attention in a store one day, and my entire room ended up covered in different sizes of it.

It seems the older I get, the more...intensely this obsessive personality trait is becoming, though this is the first time I've been obsessed with a person.

A girl.

Someone who I just happen to be an assistant for while she's here temporarily.

Gabriella is whispering something to Aria on their way back, who rolls her eyes and shakes her head, dragging her friend to the booth. Justin smiles at me.

"Time to shine," he says. "Wish me luck?"

"Why would I wish you luck when you drugged her? You're weak and pathetic."

He laughs. "That's why we are best friends."

It's not. I tolerate him most of the time. I met him during a group therapy session when we were eighteen, and he kind of latched onto me. Since I'm a loner, he's the only guy I talk to. Getting him into the same job as me was hard, considering my stepfather hates him, but it was a deal breaker if I had to come into this on my own.

But Justin is definitely trying to fuck with me right now, because he's attempting to hide his smirk as he calls out Aria's name the closer she and her friend get to us.

I watch Aria's eye lift to him, and she tilts her head as he gets up and gestures for her to sit on his side of the booth. Her lips are moving as she says something to him, and I feel itchy with the way he leans on the table and smiles at her while secretly planning to fuck Gabriella.

Thankfully, Gabriella moves my doctor aside and drops down beside Justin.

My skin tingles as a presence sits beside me, and I'm so fucking drawn to her scent, her naked leg one slight movement away from touching me, her blonde hair flowing down her back...

Damn. I am so fucked for this girl, and I've only just met her.

I pull out my phone to try to distract myself from dropping my hand to her thigh and demanding she let me lick every fucking hole available to me.

ME

Keep Justin away from your friend.

Without lifting my eyes to watch her, I see the three bubbles pop up as she types back.

> **DOCTOR MILLER**
>
> Are you jealous? You don't seem the type.

> **ME**
>
> I'm not, and I'm not jealous. He'll just try to fuck her, and we don't need that kind of awkwardness at work when he ghosts her after it.

> **DOCTOR MILLER**
>
> Good point. I'm going to call a cab and take her home.

> **ME**
>
> Don't bother. I'll drive you back to your hotel.

I don't give her a chance to type back—my phone slides into my pocket, and I take one last drink of my glass of water.

Wanting to crack open his jaw, I mouth to Justin, "back off the doctors."

He laughs. "The fuck?" he mouths back. "I'm not claiming yours."

I stare at him, losing my patience. He laughs again and lifts his hands.

My phone vibrates in my pocket, and I turn to Aria, seeing her click her screen off and give me a nervous smile.

Checking it, I see she sent me another message.

> **DOCTOR MILLER**
>
> Can we leave now?

WATCHING her sleep should be illegal.

She has no right to be as beautiful as she is, so fucking addictive to be around. I can't even leave her hotel room. Her friend is sleeping in the bathtub, Justin is asleep on the floor, and my little doctor is tucked up in bed, looking fresh and adorable.

She groans gently while she dreams, her brows furrowing while she turns her head away from me. The sound alone is enough to make my dick hard, which is wrong. I shouldn't be turned on by her. She's off limits, technically in charge of me at work, and I don't have an attraction to people.

It was always something I thought was wrong with me. I was homeschooled, so I didn't experience the same upbringing as the likes of Justin, who fucked everything with a pulse. I didn't go to a prom, homecoming, or have a group of friends who helped each other get laid. It was a miracle I even lost my virginity at the age of twenty-three.

I shake my head and refuse to think about that one time I was drunk. The only time I was *ever* drunk, because me and alcohol don't mix. I'd end up with someone fifteen years older than me again and used as a toy because her husband was sleeping around on her.

I've never been interested in sex, never felt attraction.

So why am I staring at this girl and feeling the need to protect her at the same time as needing to shove my cock so far down her throat, she stops breathing?

Fuck.

Repress.

There's movement in the bathroom, and I look over to see Justin leaning against the doorway, rubbing his eyes. "You let me sleep on the fucking floor?"

"You passed out while trying to fuck the other doctor, and I was busy."

"Busy staring at her like a weirdo?"

Yeah. I guess, in a way, he's right.

I don't reply, turning back to watch her again. Even without any makeup on, like at work, she's beautiful, and my heart beats faster when she stretches and arches her back, knocking the duvet down past her chest.

Her nipples are hard.

Justin will see.

"Leave," I tell him. "Go back to the car. I'll be down in a minute."

"You're a bossy motherfucker, do you know that?" he retorts, shaking his head as he leans back into the bathroom, grabs his coat, and vanishes from the hotel room.

My conscience is telling me to wake her up, but the voice in my head has other ideas. Since I never usually let my inner self take the reins, I give in to temptation and move carefully across the bed, settling beside her and gently gliding the pad of my thumb across her mouth as slowly as possible.

She licks her lips and I pause, my eyes widening at the wet touch against my skin.

Did she just...lick me?

My dick hardens as I run my forefinger and thumb together, my breathing heavy as I look down at *my* doctor.

I chew my inner cheek and watch her, pondering if I should leave or not. She'll freak out if she wakes up and sees me here. I'm sure I put enough sleep meds in her water to keep her unconscious a little while longer, same with her friend and Justin. It's a miracle he's awake right now.

As soon as we got Gabriella to the hotel, I got to work on my plan. I didn't want to leave, and my doctor was adamant everyone had to get out of the room so she could sleep. So, I helped her along with my own meds, a strong prescription that usually knocks me out within ten minutes.

Who knew spiking bottles of water from the hotel's vending machine would make my plan run so smoothly?

All I want to do is look at her right now. I can study her features, touch her mouth and eyelids and nose, and not worry about her screaming at me to get away or people telling me I'm overstepping.

When I know she's still in a deep sleep and her friend is still passed out in the tub, I lean in, keeping my eyes on her face as I run the pads of my fingers down her throat, feeling her pulse racing, matching the tempo of my heart.

The touch is innocent in a way, but fuck me, my cock is jumping in my pants, begging for me to stroke it. Her face stays the same, although I can see her pulse speeding up in her throat as I lower my head and kiss the tip of her nose.

Then, I drag my mouth down, feeling her breath against my lips.

Can I make out with her while she's asleep?

Is that wrong?

Against the law?

I inwardly punch myself in the dick, because of course it is.

However, I don't move. I keep my mouth an inch from hers and press my fingers to her pulse, slightly gripping the expanse of her throat.

Her breathing picks up, and she parts her lips in her sleep while I try not to blow my load from this alone. I've never done this before, and I'm sure it's a rule breaker if I ever want this girl to marry me.

Good thing she'll never find out, but by the way she's whimpering in her sleep, her nipples tightening against the material of her shirt, it might be a kink. Might not be. I could possibly bring it up to her years down the line and ask if she likes somnophilia.

Maybe she'll let me fuck her while she's passed out.

My phone buzzes in my pocket, but I ignore it, knowing it'll either be my mom or Justin. They can wait. I'm currently in fucking heaven while I touch my doctor without her knowing.

It's definitely wrong, but it feels more right than anything else.

Her back arches a little, a soft moan falling from her lips when I let myself have this and capture her bottom lip between my teeth, my mouth watering, needing to taste everything.

I release her flesh and let it snap back into place, my eyes dropping to the way her hips rise.

"Keep going," she whimpers. "K-keep going."

Fuck.

My cock is sore from how hard it strains in my pants. Maybe I should wake her and ask if she wants to have sex? Would she care if I told her I've only had sex once? Will she laugh at my inexperience?

I've never given a fuck until this moment.

"Aria?"

The sound of her friend calling her name has me yanking myself away and rushing to the door, wanting to strangle Gabriella for ruining my fucking moment.

I hear her climbing out of the tub and take that as my sign to unfortunately abandon my plan. With one more glance at my doctor, a frown on her face even though she's still asleep, I quietly leave.

My back presses to the door when I close it, my heart nearly bounding out my fucking ribcage.

Why the fuck did that feel so good?

6

TOBIAS

She talks to herself a lot. I don't think she realizes it, but whenever she's working on her laptop, walking back to her hotel, or even when she's deep in her head and staring at the wall with a blank expression, her lips move, as if she's having a conversation with herself.

I'm desperate to know what she's saying, desperate to know if any of the words passing those perfect lips are about me.

Maybe she was awake the other night and liked the feel of my fingers on her skin, or the way I tasted on her tongue when she licked my finger.

I almost want to ask her if she remembers, and if so, would she want me to do it again while she's awake and conscious?

Aria smiles at the cashier, accepting her groceries while Gabriella talks on the phone to Justin. I know this because he's right beside me in my car, pretending he's in his apartment. He laughs at something unlikely to be funny then tells her he'll see her tomorrow night before hanging up.

I frown and turn to him. "Tomorrow night?"

He lifts his hand for a high five. "Guess who just bagged a date?"

Refusing to respond to his hand gesture, I scowl deeper

before I turn back to look at my doctor giving the exact same expression as me. She's not happy about the arrangement either, and I wonder if it's because Justin is an idiot, or if she's completely against workplace romances.

There's a possibility she's not single, but I'm still working on those details. Ewan, her soon-to-be ex forever, needs to stay out of my fucking way while I try to pry into his life. Unfortunately, he already blocked my guy from his email account after a successful hacking, so what I know so far is that he's a father after getting someone pregnant when he was sixteen, a homeowner—annoyingly with Aria—and a construction worker in Scotland, born and bred.

On social media, Aria only posts views from her bedroom window or some sort of quote about life, and Ewan's page is covered with pictures and posts about his kid.

She's in some of the pictures, including one from four months ago of the three of them on vacation in Spain. The more I look into them, the more I feel like I could hurt this fucking Ewan asshole.

Stopping myself when I feel the spiral start to hit, I grip my steering wheel and watch her disappear around the corner. Justin huffs and slouches then grins at me again. "See? I told you following them was a good idea."

Although I loved his idea, I'm not going to admit that to him. "It's creepy."

Tutting, he pops a piece of gum in his mouth, and my eyes burn into him when he drops the wrapper in the center console. "Gabriella said they're heading back to their hotel then going to the movies. What if I found out which movie they're going to see and we just so happen to be there to see it too?"

This guy is a goddamn fool, but even I can't say no to that plan.

Firing up the engine of my black McLaren, I intentionally take the wrong turn so I drive past her hotel, catching a glimpse of her blonde hair and perky ass through the hotel's revolving doors.

What the fuck is happening to me?

There has never been a time in my life where I've been so focused on a person, *ever*. Yet the second she fell over my legs outside the meeting room and our eyes clashed, it was like everything in my life meant nothing.

Love at first sight? Potentially. I already know I'm different, that I feel things differently, but the medication and therapy I've been on for years has had a huge impact on how I control myself. I have alarms on my phone so I never forget to take my medication, and not only do I have reminders pop up for sessions, my mother also calls me.

I wish she wouldn't. Her constant checking up on me and demanding my stepfather push himself into my life at work is tiring and makes me feel like a teenager still. She was always keeping me in metaphorical bubble wrap, as if the world wouldn't be kind enough to me.

Somehow, she still tries to act that way in my adulthood.

Pulling onto the narrow street where Justin lives, I slow to a stop and let him out, waving him off with one finger from the steering wheel when he tells me we'll make a plan for tonight.

I already have one forming in my head, one that doesn't involve a third or fourth participant. However, as much as I hate going to work on my days off, I did tell Lucy I'd stop by, since she's just about to start her last round of chemo.

I'll go there first and then start my night of watching Aria.

Despite my mind being bad to me, I'm a good person. I know I am. I like helping people. I like working in the hospital and watching kids I've entertained get better. Usually, when I know they're terminal and don't have long left, my stepdad forces me to work in another ward or stay away from the patients in case it triggers something in me.

So I've yet to lose a patient I've bonded with.

I know Lucy is dying, and I know he'll try to make me leave, but not only do I want to stay by her side and make her happy, moving to another part of the hospital also means leaving my doctor.

I'll stay there. And when the time comes to say goodbye to

Lucy, I'll hold it together for the sake of my obsession with Aria Miller.

By the time I get changed out of my workout clothes and drive to the hospital, the sun is starting to set, and the sky opens as rain pours.

I shake off my hair once I take shelter in the hospital's main entrance, grab some stuff from the vending machines, and head to the ward.

Once I'm in the elevator, a hand stops it from closing, and my stepfather walks in. He doesn't smile at me or greet me; he just sighs and stands beside me.

"Your mother has been calling you for the past hour," he says. "You didn't go to therapy today."

My eye twitches at his tone, but I stare forward and ignore him.

I didn't go because Justin wanted to watch Gabriella and Aria, so I skipped for the first time ever.

"Remember what we agreed to. You only work here if you abide by the rules she set. Take your meds, attend therapy, no fighting, and stay out of trouble with the cops."

Silence is all he's met with. I want to shove my fist down his throat most days, but he did get me this position, and he did decide to marry my mother and make us filthy rich, so I try not to argue.

But my patience is slowly slipping.

The elevator doors open, and a nurse walks in. "Good evening, Doctor Blythe."

He grins at her, and I try not to roll my eyes at his façade of being a jolly, nice guy. Despite changing my life, he's a fucking asshole with a complex and a deep desire for control.

Being the president of numerous scientific research centers will do that. I still have no idea why the fuck he kept his position in this hospital when he has more money than sense, but Mom said he likes his job.

Asshole.

As soon as I get into Lucy's room, I find her trying to read a book. She looks up at me and smiles. "You came!"

"Of course I did, little one," I say, sitting beside her bed. "How are you feeling?"

"Sick," she replies, her smile dropping. "My mom said she wouldn't be back for a few days because they're going on vacation."

My jaw tenses, but I force a half-smile. "Good thing you've got me. What are we watching?"

The excited teen slowly takes the remote, her hand shaking as she turns on the TV and finds the show she has been making me watch with her.

We talk for the first ten minutes before we zone in on the screen, and when Justin texts me about tonight's plan, I turn off my phone.

7

ARIA

Today is the day Ivy arrives.

The nurses and doctors here have arranged everything, so as soon as the transport pulls in, she'll be in perfect hands. As far as I'm aware, only her mother is coming, and they've set her up in a hotel nearby at the same time as ensuring she has somewhere to sleep in Ivy's room.

When I walk past one of the patient's rooms, one who is still waiting to be transferred to hospice, I pause when I hear a deep voice.

"Did you ever listen to the book?"

Without looking in, I pretend to read notes by the door.

"It was giving me a headache. My ears are sensitive."

"Ah," Tobias replies. "What if I read it to you, or are you going to argue with me about how to pronounce words again?"

The girl—Lucy—huffs. "You were saying the dragon's name wrong for ten chapters straight."

A smile creeps onto my face at the way Tobias deeply chuckles. Then, my eyes lift to see Gabriella watching me, her eyebrow raised.

"Did you hear me?"

Blinking, I shake my head. "Sorry. What?"

"Ivy's plane just landed. The nurses are ready. What do you want to do? Go back to the hotel and sleep those bags off, or go for some food and catch a movie?"

"We were at the movie theatre yesterday," I reply. "Besides, I'll probably pass out ten minutes into the movie."

I'm struggling to get a good night's sleep in the hotel bed. That, and the fact I may have been doom scrolling for any trace of Tobias on the internet.

It seems my lovely assistant has an aversion to social media, because he's nonexistent.

I don't usually look up coworkers online, but after the potential flirting in the club and how I know when he walks into a room without looking, I've become intrigued.

She clicks her tongue and looks behind me. I turn to see Tobias gently closing the door, pushing his glasses up the bridge of his nose.

He must be tired too. After me and Gabby's girl date, I came back here to look through paperwork and call some of my colleagues back in Scotland for further advice. He was in Lucy's room—she was asleep, and he just sat there, like he always does.

If I hadn't gone in with some coffee and asked him to give me a hand with something, I doubt he would have left. With her mother not here, she doesn't like to be alone, and it seems Tobias doesn't like the idea of her lying in the ward, awaiting more answers about her disease without any company.

I like his heart.

Wordlessly, he lowers his head in greeting before he goes straight to the exit. Dr. Blythe stops him with a hand to his chest to whisper something into his ear, and Tobias lifts his head with a scowl.

His jaw tenses as he replies, but since he's gritting his words through his teeth, I've no idea what he's saying, or why there seems to be tension between the pair.

"Can we at least grab food?" Gabriella asks, stepping into my line of sight. "I think burgers, or maybe pizza."

"Pizza," I agree. "Then we go back to the hotel and sleep. I have to—"

"Pizza sounds good!"

Justin interrupts us, and I want to roll my eyes at the blush creeping onto Gabriella's face. Instead of telling him absolutely not, she invites him along and tells him to meet us at seven outside a diner not far from where we're staying.

I love her, but I might strangle her right now, along with her assistant. She needs to stop giving him "take me to bed and fuck me in every position possible" eyes. Without warning, a presence comes up behind me, and Justin grins before he opens his mouth again.

"You're off soon, right? Pizza with the bosses?"

"Are you going?" Tobias asks me, and I pause; I'm pretty sure I've just turned paler than pale as I look around us.

I point to my chest. "Me?"

"I'm looking at you, aren't I?"

"Will my presence deter you from going or something?"

He smirks and averts his eyes with a shrug. "Or something."

"So..." Justin gestures to Tobias. "Yeah?"

A hum, and he does the same as me, staying silent while they make the plans. They invite two nurses who politely decline, leaving the four of us going for food.

It's going to look suspicious, right? Two scientists from Scotland going out for dinner with their assistants?

What if Gabriella decided to snap a picture and post it online? Will Ewan see?

A huge part of me dreads something like that, but there's also a sick part of me that wants her to post, because then he'll think I'm moving on and not sitting around with a broken heart. It's going to be hard when I get back home. I've been in Jason's life forever, and the distance is already killing me, but Ewan fucked up. I can't stay with someone who keeps a secret like that for years and acts like they're the most perfect person ever.

Let Gabriella rub it in his face.

Do I care?

Not enough to cancel and go to the hotel myself.

TWENTY MINUTES of us being at the pizza place, and Justin has been the one to talk the entire time. His voice drones on and on and on, and Gabriella eats up every word while Tobias glances at me when he thinks I'm not paying attention.

Sitting diagonal from me at the table, he fidgets, his middle finger tapping, his knee bouncing, and I wonder if he's a smoker like my mother and needs a cigarette. Her nicotine withdrawals always end up with her yelling at my dad every five seconds, eating her weight in food, or doing exactly what Tobias is doing right now.

"How did you two meet?" Gabriella asks Justin, and it grabs my attention—I've wondered this too, since they're polar opposites in every way. Their friendship makes no sense.

"Met in a therapy group when we were teenagers," he replies, nudging his elbow into Tobias, who scowls at him like he wants him to fall off a cliff and die. "His dad got him a job at the hospital and, being the great best friend he is, he got me in too."

"Stepdad," Tobias corrects.

"Whatever. We live close to each other, so he's kind of stuck with me forever. Did you know he has three motorbikes in his garage?"

I frown at the random information.

"I crashed one of them, and he beat the shit out of me. Remember? You broke my arm and kicked me down your apartment stairs."

Huffing, Tobias stands from his chair and doesn't announce his departure as he heads straight for the bathroom.

"He's quite moody," Gabriella says. "Does he loosen up when he's drunk?"

"He doesn't get drunk. Think I've witnessed him drinking twice, and both times, he went home early and didn't speak to me for weeks."

My phone buzzes in my lap, my heart skipping a beat when I see who the message is from.

TOBIASWORK

He never shuts up.

ME

Neither does Gabriella.

TOBIASWORK

Want to ditch them?

ME

They'd end up on 'missing' posters all over the city.

TOBIASWORK

That's a risk I'm willing to take.

ME

They'll never let us leave.

TOBIASWORK

Give me 5.

Justin heads to the bathroom after reading a message on his phone with a furrowed brow. I assume Tobias told him to meet him out back to beat him up again if he tends to hit his friends.

The entire time they're gone, Gabriella makes a list of the pros and cons of sleeping with her coworker, and whether she can trust herself not to get attached to Justin if she does.

While she talks, I have butterflies–not because she has talked herself into her fling, but because Tobias wants to sneak away from them with me.

The confused feeling is making me want to drink until my mind is obliterated, but since I can't handle hangovers and I'm too "professional", I'm going to stay sober this whole work trip.

My phone vibrates in my hand, and it's ridiculous how quickly I flip it over and cut off Gabriella.

TOBIASWORK

Pretend you need the bathroom.

I frown and look up, not seeing him anywhere as Justin winks at a waitress and heads back to us.

ME

And go where?

He doesn't reply. He goes offline, and I chew my lip, glancing at my friend and the way she's fluttering her lashes at Justin, looking at him like she wants to devour him.

"I'm going to jump to the bathroom too," I say, and neither respond to me, too deep into their eye-fucking to pay me any attention.

And just like that, I slip my jacket on and push through the exit to the coldness outside.

"Let's go," a low voice comes from behind me, cleaning his glasses with his spectacle cloth and putting them on. "They won't notice our absence until they're done fawning over one another."

"You noticed that too?"

"Justin is like that with everyone, if you want to let your friend know he's not husband material."

I giggle as we cross the sidewalk and slip onto a path running along the side of the promenade. "Gabriella isn't much for romance and relationships either."

"What about you?"

My eyes widen as I look up at him. "Oh, um..."

He smirks and stares at the water while we walk. "Was that inappropriate?"

"If I say no, will you make me answer you?"

"Depends," he replies. "I'm not going to end up in a fist fight because I'm walking with someone's girl, am I?"

"I'm very much single, so I doubt that. Plus, this is just coworkers walking away from our other coworkers nearly screwing in front of us."

He snorts. "Yeah. I guess so."

8

TOBIAS

She's so close to me.

If I take one step to the right, my arm will touch hers. Or her shoulder, since I'm a lot taller than she is.

I wonder if her ex is tall. From my research, I know he has brown hair. I have black. He has green eyes, I have blue. He's completely covered in tattoos, and I don't have a spot of ink on my body. He's rough-looking. Muscular, with a thick stubble. He smokes, gets his hands dirty at work, and has pictures online of him at boxing sessions. Honestly, he looks like he could crush someone's skull. Even though I work out and have a good build, I'm also clean-shaven, need all my clothes to have no creases, and have an addiction to wiping my glasses every hour.

I haven't been in a fight since I was eighteen, unless I count all the times Justin has pissed me off.

We're nothing alike. If that's her taste in men, then I'm screwed.

So I guess I'll enjoy the view while it lasts.

Her hair is flowing down her back, and I have the urge to wrap the strands around my fingers and bring them to my nose to smell her shampoo. Whenever she answers one of my questions about work, she gives me eye contact, and I feel like it would be completely out of line to tell her she has beautiful blue eyes, that I want to see them roll while I—

"When did you start working at the hospital?"

I rub the back of my head, unsure how to word it. How do I tell this girl I didn't study like she did and basically got handed the position?

"A few years," I say, gulping deeply. "I started part time, and when I grew an interest, I switched to full time." I shrug and drop my hand, shoving it into my pocket to stop the fidgeting. "How about you? When did you realize you wanted to work in that field?"

I already know. Thanks to my digging, I found Gabriella's mother on social media, and she shared a "throwback" of Aria and her daughter going to college. She captioned it as *her little scientists.*

Aria is talking, but I can't think straight, because we've walked right past her hotel. If she realizes, she might cut this short. If I try to distract her from the fact we've already reached our destination, this ends, and I'm not ready.

I have all of her attention.

I like having her attention.

She rubs her hands up her arms, and I internally slap my forehead, because she's cold, and I have a jacket.

I pull it off and hand it to her, and as confusion flashes over her face, I cover her shoulders and watch it drench her body.

"You're cold."

"So the assistant is a gentleman."

If that's what you want to call someone who just met you yet knows more about you than you do and can't seem to get your face out of his head, fine, yeah, I'm a fucking gentleman.

Every organ in my body stops functioning as she lifts the collar of my jacket to her face and inhales. "What cologne is that?"

Fuck. "Tom Ford."

"I like it," she replies with a smile and smells it again. "I might need to keep your jacket forever."

I fist my hands and push both of them into my pockets, staying silent. If I don't contain them, I'll do something stupid, like grabbing her face and kissing her–which is weird, since I hate kissing. It's messy and useless, and the thought of passing saliva by touching tongues makes me uneasy.

I think I'd kiss her, though.

Part of me wants to know what her spit tastes like. I'd lick her body, suck on her tongue, and then bury my face between her—

"Gabriella always says I need to loosen up, but I think you might take the crown for that. It was a joke, Tobias." I gulp as she smiles and nudges me. "And we walked past my hotel like ten minutes ago."

"You want to walk back?" I ask, stopping, my eyes following her as she keeps going.

She shakes her head. "Nope. I'm going to check out the arcade nearby. Do you want to come?"

Where the fuck are her communication skills? She's a scientist on the frontline of cutting edge research, yet she couldn't mention when we left the restaurant that she wanted to go to an arcade?

Regardless of the sudden plan sprung on me and making my skin itch, I nod and follow her as rain starts to pour.

She tries to give me my jacket back, but I decline. My white shirt is basically see-through, and my glasses have droplets all over them, but I refuse to take it from her.

"There!" she calls out, pointing to an arcade with lights flashing outside.

In all honesty, the thought of going in there makes me want to vomit, but the light shining in her eyes has her looking full of life, a massive change from being fully invested in work. I like this shining side of her as she grabs my wrist and pulls me towards the entrance.

The touch doesn't burn like it would with someone else. I don't have the urge to snap her fingers or scrub myself with bleach until my skin turns red.

The noise is the first thing that irks me. Music plays like we're at some sort of concert, lights dimmed, everything glowing neon. She turns and smiles up at me, her teeth glowing white from the fluorescent lighting.

"It's so pretty in here." Her gaze travels around the flashing walls.

"Yeah," I reply, wanting to leave but enjoying her grabbing my wrist again and leading us towards the basketball machine.

"Don't tell Gabriella we came here, or she'll kill me."

I'd strangle her before she had the chance.

She takes forever throwing basketballs at the hoop, then tries to get me to do it with her, but I shake my head and watch our surroundings. Men are looking at her. Why wouldn't they? She's hot, in a little black dress with heels.

They don't seem to see the jacket she's wearing that practically drowns her. If that isn't a claim to keep their eyes off, I don't know what is.

She goes to the claw machine, fails, then goes to the mini casino and wastes fifty dollars, then ventures to the coin machine and gets change.

"Aren't you going to play something?"

My right eye twitches at the pinging noise of someone winning something nearby. "No."

"As my assistant, I demand you have fun."

I let out a laugh despite hating this place. "I'm not sure that falls under my job description, Doctor."

"I'll write it in. Now, play with me."

"I like this fun side of you," I say, taking the toy shotgun from her and aiming at the plastic cans lined up on the screen. I hit all of them and pass her back the gun with a smirk. "Your turn."

My anxiousness of being here lessens with every game she forces me to play, like we're teenagers on a first date or best friends hanging out.

She talks to me about my allergy to cats and how she needed glasses when she was a kid but miraculously doesn't anymore. She asks me about my childhood, and I decline to answer. She rolls her eyes at me. She does that a lot. It's rude and childish, but for some reason, I like it.

"It's late. I'll get an Uber back to my hotel. Do you live far?"

"I'll drive you," I reply, pulling my Aston Martin keys from my pocket. "I'm parked nearby."

I'm glad we're leaving. I've been socializing too much, and I feel exhausted. Plus, I don't feel myself, and I don't want to be around someone like her when I shut down.

When we reach my car, her mouth falls open at the matte black car unlocking.

"How does an assistant have a car like this?"

I tilt my head. "Are you discriminating on my job?"

"This is a quarter of a million dollar car."

I shrug. "Maybe I stole it."

"Did you?" she counters.

"No."

Her eyes widen as she goes to pull the handle, and the door slides upwards. "No way."

"I thought you were from a rich family in Scotland? Why does a butterfly door shock you so much?"

Her hand flies to her hip. "My parents are rich, not me. And they drove Rolls Royces, not super sporty cars that look like they belong on a race track."

Aria drops into the passenger seat and searches for the seatbelt. Two minutes go by before I let out a breath and lean forward, trying not to inhale her scent like a creep while I reach for the seat belt behind her. She doesn't move, doesn't breathe, and my gaze lifts to her as I yank the material from being trapped in the door.

"How do you know I'm from a rich family?"

Shit.

I researched you. I paid someone to get information. I stalked your entire presence online, including your ex, your best friend, and her family, and found articles on your family online. I even know your address, the car you drive when you aren't walking to work, and what classes you took in college.

I gulp. "It was a wild guess."

She stares at me as I click in her belt and move away, needing to put space between us before I do something stupid, like kidnap her. The thought of taking her back to my apartment and locking her in my room with me sounds like a dream. She'd be scared to start with, but then she might get Stockholm syndrome and fall in love with me.

I blink and turn on the engine, my hands shaking as I grip the steering wheel. What would she do if she knew how badly I was prying into her life?

She bristles as I pull out of the parking space, her fingers digging into the leather seat. The radio isn't playing and she isn't talking, and I feel nervous energy filling the car.

Swallowing, I glance at her while at a stop light. "Still wet?"

Her eyes widen. "What?"

"From the rain," I clarify, noticing the way she's clenching her thighs as I speed up. "It was raining."

Her lips move, but it takes her a second to close her mouth and shake her head.

I've made it awkward. I asked if she was wet, and she thought I meant something else, and now she thinks I'm a weirdo. Fucking perfect, Tobias. Well done, you fucking idiot.

Silence passes between us again, and then she finally speaks.

"My mother was always strict when it came to their money. I was to earn my way into the world without having any luxury, even though she was born into wealth too. As soon as I was old enough, I went away to study. I got a job and a car that was hardly road legal, and she watched me struggle."

I keep driving. I keep listening.

"I guess it was a good way to teach me, but even when I was struggling to pay rent and wearing the same sneakers for three years, she never helped me. So no, I wouldn't say I was rich. Even now, I rent an apartment with my best friend because I can't afford a place on my own. Which is ridiculous, because I have a mortgage with—"

She stops, her head moving to the side to stare out of the window. "Never mind."

"You have a mortgage yet you rent?"

She nods but doesn't look at me. She's upset.

I feel the urge to kill that fucking ex of hers. He hurt her. He must have. Did he hit her? Yell at her? Break her heart? Cheat? Lie? Manipulate?

"If it makes you feel any better, I come from a rich family who give me everything, and it's not as lavish a lifestyle as you think. They hang everything over my head and threaten to cut me off if I ever step out of line like I'm still eighteen." I let out a derisive laugh. "I have my own income now, but they never let me forget it."

"People suck."

I nod and then tilt my head toward the sidewalk of the hotel entrance.

"Gabriella texted and said she was going to Justin's place," she tells me, staring at her phone. "He's okay, right? I don't need to worry about her?"

"The worst he'll do is fuck her and move his interest elsewhere."

For some reason, she doesn't frown. "Gabriella will likely do the same."

All of a sudden, I wonder if she has been sleeping with people after breaking up with her ex. How many? Who? Does she like them? Does she still talk to them?

"I felt younger tonight," she says, slowly taking off her seatbelt. "I've been so focused on work for so long, I forgot to enjoy myself. Thank you."

I hated every second. The only reason I endured the arcade was for her. When she was pouting every time she didn't win on the crane machine, I wanted to smash it to smithereens and give her every prize.

Aria slips off my jacket and leaves it in the seat as she climbs out of my car. I try not to stare at her ass, but my eyes fail me. One day, I'll have my tongue buried inside her as she screams my name.

Aria stands by the revolving door and turns to me. "Did we get tricked into a double date?"

I smile and shake my head. "Justin isn't that good."

With that, she blushes. Fucking *blushes*. Because of me. I made her blush.

"So this wasn't a date." It wasn't a question, though I'm not sure she'd like my answer. It wasn't *supposed* to be a date. I just wanted to get the fuck away from Justin–her taking me to the arcade then me driving her back here just...happened.

"Of course not," I reply. "Workplace rules and all that stuff, remember?"

She playfully narrows her eyes then giggles, and the sound hits me right in the goddamn chest like a brick. I wish I recorded that sound to lull me to sleep, since I struggle to get more than two hours each night.

My mind isn't too kind to me when it's supposed to be quiet.

"Goodnight, Tobias."

I lower my head, fingers gripping the steering wheel. "Doctor."

She rolls her eyes and laughs as she turns around and pushes through the revolving door.

As soon as she vanishes, I blow out a breath and rub the back of my head.

I think I just died and went to heaven.

By the time I get home, I'm already itching to send Aria a message. I have no idea what I'll say, but anything is better than nothing.

I'm sure there's some sort of rule to this. Do I wait a few hours? A day? Act like nothing happened at work tomorrow?

But nothing did happen, at least I don't think.

I had my first date. I don't give a fuck if she tries to say it wasn't–it was for me.

Pulling out my phone, I check my notifications.

Apart from my mom asking me to call her back and a reminder for my next session with my therapist, there's nothing new. Nothing from *her*.

My jaw tightens as I grind my teeth, checking her social media and expecting one of her life quotes to pop up.

Nothing.

Her last post was a week ago, sharing a story about a fundraiser for cancer.

I exit her page and open up my emails, asking my contact if he has any new information for me. The last I heard, he found out she's on the pill that has been prescribed to her for years.

Now, I wait.

I toss my keys on the kitchen counter and start my night time routine. My medicine cabinet is fully stocked, and each pill that keeps me grounded slides down my throat with a cold glass of water.

My phone dings, and I huff when I see who the message is from.

JUSTIN

I know you're into Aria, so I'm telling you as a friend not to bother. She's fresh out of a relationship and doesn't sleep around. Apparently, she keeps running back to the asshole. You want a quick fuck? I can ask Gabriella if she wants an extra dick.

JUSTIN

Or I could watch you both. Whichever you prefer.

ME

Fuck off.

She keeps running back to him. My doctor won't be running back to fucking anyone if I can help it.

I stare at my empty glass, white knuckling the countertop as a message finally comes through from Aria.

DOCTOR MILLER

Hey. So one of the receptionists from our ward saw me getting out of your car and asked me if something was going on. It was fun tonight, but we should keep things strictly work-related so no one gets the wrong impression. I'll speak to Gabriella too.

The glass smashes as I launch it against the wall.

9

ARIA

Despite how well we got on and the miniscule flirting, Tobias hasn't been at work for two days, so I've had to run around with barely any breaks. I'd sent him a text last night to make sure he was okay and wasn't sick, but all I got back was an "I'm fine", so I've resorted to pretending I don't have an assistant while running two hundred tasks at a time.

My work email has been busy. A lot of my research back home has been updated, so I'm trying to stay on top of everything.

When I told Tobias about the receptionist catching us, I didn't think it was a big thing. Could that be why he has been off? He's embarrassed people might think something is going on between us?

We were two work colleagues at the arcade. That's all.

To my surprise, two hours earlier than he was supposed to start, Tobias walks into the office in silence and drops onto the chair in front of his desk.

His jaw holds a lot of tension, his eyes burning into his laptop as he sets it down and opens it. The typing is aggressive, and he huffs, checking his phone and shoving it back into his pocket.

"Everything okay?"

He simply hums in response and keeps his focus on the screen.

Tobias is usually quiet, but there's something else going on. His right eye keeps twitching, and he looks mad. My automatic reaction, being the sentimental person I am, is to comfort him, but that would be out of line. He's my assistant, and I need to start seeing him that way. Even though I enjoyed myself the other night, even though I liked spending time with him, I remind myself I'm here for work.

Without meaning to, I keep looking up at him from my laptop, his glasses reflecting his screen. If I focus enough, I can make out he's in his emails. Then, I shake my head and internally slap myself at the invasion of privacy as I get back to my own notes.

I check my notepad full of information Dr. Blythe sent me on two more patients he wants me to look into. I need to make sure my knowledge is sufficient enough to get involved, since America and Scotland are vastly different when it comes to research.

One of my main reasons for getting Ivy over here was because we have more space for research and trials in the States. Although the cost is higher, they have a lot more options for children like Ivy.

I want to ask Tobias if something is accurate, but I don't feel like I can. His brow is furrowed, and his leg shaking the table from how much he's bouncing his knee.

What's making things awkward is that not only has he sat in silence for the next hour, but he has been ignoring his phone. It rang four times before he turned it off and tossed it onto the table.

"Do you want to talk about it?"

"No."

"Why weren't you here yesterday?" I ask. "We had quite a busy day of planning."

His shoulder raises. "I had to take the day off."

My head tilts with curiosity. He doesn't seem sick. "How come?"

His eyes lift from the papers. "Since when do we ask personal questions?"

"Since you're sitting there in silence as if someone broke your favorite toy."

"Close," he replies. "Coffee?"

Confused at his sudden mood swing, I frown at him and tilt my head. "Huh?"

"Do you want coffee?" he asks and laughs, his smile momentarily clouding my mind.

"Oh, yeah. Thanks."

He nods and walks out of the room. I hear him greeting someone as he closes the door before disappearing from my view.

I lean back on my chair, staring at the ceiling with heaviness behind my eyes. Coffee might help, or maybe a week-long nap–or maybe an assistant who doesn't give me whiplash.

The blaring of my phone has me sighing as I note the caller ID.

I answer after staring for too long. He hasn't tried to call in a while, and it could be something serious.

"Hello?"

"Don't hang up," Ewan says, a pleading tone in his voice. "I just need five minutes, and then I'll leave you alone."

"What's wrong?"

"When do you fly back home?" he asks, machinery clanking in the background. He's on the site he has been stuck working for over a year. "Can we talk when you do?"

The door opens, and Tobias walks in with two coffee cups just as I sigh and say, "Ewan, please don't do this right now."

"Just...just talk to me, Aria. You've completely cut me off instead of talking about this."

My eyes close. "I don't know what's left to talk about. You cheated, and then you lied about it. You called me a paranoid psychopath, only to be proved wrong."

"I cheated years ago. *Years* ago. I'm not that guy anymore. I only lied because I was scared you'd leave me."

I let out a snort. "Right. It hardly matters now."

"Can we at least talk when you get home? What are we doing about Jason?"

A knife lodges in my chest at the thought of the little boy I've raised since he was a few months old. "I don't know."

Cutting Ewan out of my life also means cutting Jason out of it. I love them both. They were my family. But his dad did me wrong, and now I'm stuck on where to stand.

Will it mess with Jason's head if a woman who has nothing to do with him is in his life? His bio mom is absent, and he always had me. But now...now, I don't know what to do. I don't know what is right for him.

"It might confuse him if we aren't together anymore and I'm still in his life."

Ewan sighs deeply. "Please, Aria. I haven't cheated since. I haven't done a single thing to step out of line."

"You lied three times. I gave you *three* chances to own up."

Gulping, I can tell he's running his hand through his hair. "What about the house? The car? The caravan? Our entire lives?"

"I'll deal with it all when I'm home." I open an email, scanning the words. "I need to go. I'm far too busy to have this conversation."

"You've been living with Gabriella since way before we split up. I know I fucked it all, but were you unhappy before? Is that why we weren't getting along? Tell me so I can fix this."

"I'm unhappy because my boyfriend since I was a teenager cheated, lied about it, and then tried to gaslight me. There's nothing else to discuss. We'll figure out how to move forward without hurting Jason in the process."

"I was eighteen, Aria."

"I'm going now."

"Aria," he pleads. "Let me fix this."

"Goodbye, Ewan."

Once I hang up, I let out a heavy breath. I'm trying not to be heartless. I get it was years ago, and we're totally different people now, but he lied when I asked. That hurt me the most.

A huge part of me is yelling at myself to grow up and get over it, but I need to breathe and think.

I reach for my laptop, but a voice has me pausing.

"Who is Ewan?" Tobias asks, setting coffee on my desk and standing across from me. "You look pissed."

"Since when do we ask personal questions?" I use his words against him, proud of myself, but he doesn't seem to like it.

He sucks on his teeth and rolls his jaw before he brings his attention back to the paperwork in front of him. His fingertips press into the pages, and I know he isn't taking any of the words in.

Why does he look like he's about to explode?

Closing my laptop, I watch him. "Did you see the part where we basically get pushed aside?"

He frowns and looks up. "What do you mean?"

I stand and walk to him, noticing how he straightens at my close proximity, and when my shoulder presses against his chest as I lean down to the pages, he doesn't back up enough to break contact. I shuffle through his papers until I find the one I'm looking for and point to the paragraph.

"Right there," I say, pausing my breathing as he leans over my shoulder to look, his hands on the table on each side of me.

He completely towers over me, enveloping me with his form. And he smells good. *Really* good. So good, those traitorous butterflies show their faces and make me internally shiver.

Large hands curl into fists as his knuckles rest on the table, and he reads from the paragraph. "So basically, we sit around and evaluate their notes?"

I nod, my voice shaking as I reply, "Yes."

"Hmm. I mean, I get why. We aren't in the care department, and we definitely aren't nurses or doctors." I hear the smile in voice–the one and only time he'll ever say I'm not a doctor despite using it as a...pet name?

Oh, God. Does he have a pet name for me?

I gulp and lower my eyes to his wrist. Apart from the thick

veins, he has no tattoos visible, and I trace over about ten charity bands. I pinch the bright pink one, tilting my head.

"How old is Lucy?"

"Just turned fifteen," he replies deeply, tipping his chin so his mouth is near my ear as I trace another band. "That's for a canine foster center. They've recently opened up a larger facility and lowered their euthanasia ratio."

"That's good."

He hums. We stay like this, in this questionable position, as I go through each band and he explains them all. From animals to children to farms, he contributes to them all. He either helps out or donates when he can. He also helps out at food banks, which, for some reason, warms a cold part of my heart. He's caring.

Tobias surprises me. He doesn't look the type to be so gentle–he looks like he would beat up an old lady for staring at him too long.

"Are you done, Doctor?" he whispers in my ear.

My smile falters, my fingers lingering before I realize I'm touching his skin, tracing the veins on his forearm showing from the rolled up sleeves. I pull my hand away. "I'm sorry. That was inappropriate."

"Turn around."

My heart rate spikes at his demand as I curl my fingers into my palm.

Wetting my lips, I glance over my shoulder to see his hooded gaze. "What?"

"Turn around," he repeats. "Now."

My body follows his command until I'm facing him, trapped between Tobias and the table, his arms on each side, keeping me barricaded.

Briefly, my eyes flicker to the closed door, the blinds thankfully already drawn from the important meeting earlier. I look back at him, my chest rising and falling, matching his own.

"What are you doing?"

"If I kissed you right now, would you think it was inappropriate?"

I pause, my mouth instantly watering with how serious and raw his tone is. All my issues back home vanish, and I feel the sudden urge to cross the boundary with my assistant.

"So yesterday was a date," I say, pushing back into the table but still stuck between two immovable objects.

Tobias shrugs. "What would you say if I said yes?"

"That you tricked me," I reply, swallowing, warmth gathering deep within me at how much I want him to kiss me. "It goes against the rules of the workplace."

"If we get caught." The glint in his eyes through the lens of his glasses and his teeth peeking out from his parted lips have me nearly melting, but I hold myself together and push his arm out of the way.

I go to move around him, but he captures my wrist and spins me to face him. He's completely unfazed as his fingertips glide across my jaw, brushing his fingers into my hairline behind my ear.

"You still didn't answer me. If I kissed you right now..." He leans down, nose nudging my own, and every rule goes out the window as I let him keep going. "Would it be..." He lowers his voice to a soft whisper against my lips. "Inappropriate?"

Yes. It would be. But after my ex on the phone, being pushed aside on Ivy's case, and my friend vanishing to sleep with Justin, I give in to temptation.

Before he can make the final move, I close my eyes and press my mouth to his, feeling his slight intake of air as he sinks into the kiss.

A thousand voices scream at me to stop as Tobias parts my lips with his and kisses me hard, walking me back into the wall.

Air forces its way out of my lungs on a moan as his fingers wrap around my throat and tighten while he pushes his tongue against my own.

"Aria?" a voice comes from the door.

I try to shove Tobias in the chest, but he holds me in place, smiling against my lips when the handle rattles.

He locked the door.

He knew this was going to happen.

He planned it.

When I press my palm to his chest again, he steps back, both of us panting.

Tobias licks his lips, staring down at me like he wants to devour me.

The person at the door disappears, and I take it as my cue to run.

I'm out the door and into the bathroom in seconds, slamming the cubical shut and finally taking a deep breath. My lips tingle as I trace my fingertips over them, and I try not to smile and fail.

Kissing Tobias felt good–more than good. It felt forbidden, like if we got caught, everything would blow up. We would be in so much trouble if someone saw us. Why does that thought make me hot?

I cover my mouth as the bathroom door opens, heavy footsteps filling the emptiness. I know it's him. I can feel him all over me, all around me.

My phone buzzes in my cardigan pocket, and I pull it out with a racing heart.

TOBIASWORK

Open the door, Doctor.

Shaking, I type back.

ME

Why?

TOBIASWORK

I wasn't finished.

Two seconds pass. Five. Ten. My heart has stopped, my brain buzzing. Against my better judgment, I reach for the lock, shaking fingers sliding back the latch.

And he's on me.

Large hands. Thick arms with wrists covered in charity bands. A shirt white as snow with not a single crease. As soon as his mouth lands on mine, I fall apart, whimpering into his mouth as our tongues move together, swallowing each other as he slams the door shut and closes us into the cubicle.

It's so wrong yet so right. I fist his hair and knock his glasses off, hearing them clatter on the floor as his teeth graze my bottom lip.

With his hand on my throat, not squeezing but providing enough pressure to show dominance, he pushes me back enough to disconnect the kiss. "You have no idea what you're getting yourself into."

I gasp when he reaches down and grabs between my thighs through the thin material of my skirt, his hot breath on my neck making it almost impossible to think straight.

"You like that?"

My heart hammers in my chest—or maybe it's his against my chest. I don't know anymore. He's everywhere but nowhere, and that's not enough. His fingers press into my skin as he draws the sensitive spot beneath my ear into his mouth, sucking.

"Answer me. Do you like it when I do this?"

I nod erratically and absently roll my hips forward, panting, needing more despite being in the hospital bathroom.

His teeth sink into my bottom lip again, and I can tell he's losing control. Of what, I'm not sure. Why? I'm not sure either. His cock is hard, pressing into me while he's tugging my bottom lip until it snaps back into place, making my breath hitch. I'm completely stuck in this daze that is *him*.

He hums. "This taste," he says quietly as he licks his lips. "I like it."

He adds more pressure, and I whimper as his attentive fingers press firmer against my clit despite how tight my pencil skirt is.

The bathroom door opens, and I hear two of the nurses talking. Tobias covers my mouth and nose to stop any sound as he circles his fingers, watching with a hooded gaze as my eyes slowly roll to the back of my skull. My lungs burn for air, my hips move, and I cry into his palm when his fingers speed up their circles.

"Good girl," he breathes. "Be a good little doctor and stay quiet for me."

The nurses do their thing as Tobias releases my mouth, allowing me to breathe for a few intakes before he's crushing his lips to mine again.

He pulls his mouth away, snatching my jaw and pressing the back of my head to the bathroom stall. "I'm still not finished."

Releasing me, he steps back, both of us panting, lips swollen from the fierce kiss that shouldn't make my body ignite.

I watch him leave the stall as he picks his glasses up from the floor, cleaning them on the edge of his shirt I must've pulled from his pants at some point.

Tobias vanishes then, the bathroom door closing, and I allow myself to breathe, to slide down the wall of the cubicle to the floor and close my eyes.

Between my legs tingles with the sensation of his touch, the loss, the need for more. So many thoughts are running wild in my head, but all I can focus on is one.

He said he wasn't finished yet.

10

TOBIAS

My hands are fucking shaking so much, I can barely hold my glasses properly as I incessantly try to wipe the already spotless lenses clean.

I don't have anyone to tell. I don't have someone to call for advice. My head is spinning, and all I can think of is Aria and what she's doing, how she's feeling, if she's full of regret.

Maybe she's already on her way back to Scotland.

I pull out my phone and check when the next flights are, swearing to myself when I see there's some every day.

She can't leave.

We have so much left to explore, and she's deep in my system, burrowed into my fucking skin. I'm not ready to push her out yet. I don't know what the fuck is wrong with me, why I've grown some weird obsession with her. It has never happened before, so why her? Why now?

She's technically off-limits. Not only am I her assistant, but apparently, she keeps running back to her ex, so why would I even try to pursue anything?

Because she's beautiful.

And she has a nice smile.

Also, she's the only person who doesn't make me uncomfortable.

I'm so fucking drawn to her, like she's a drug and I'm fully addicted. I could stare at her all day, taste her goddamn mouth and feel her soft skin under my hand as I lift her into me and kiss her until our lips turn blue.

Fuck. I kissed Aria. She kissed me. We kissed, and I still don't feel satisfied. I need more from her before she leaves.

If I'm confused by a feeling and unable to handle it, I speak with my therapist, but I don't want him to know about Aria. The fewer people who know she exists, the fewer threats there are of something coming between us.

They might tell me to leave her alone.

"Are you okay?"

I look up at Lucy and realize she paused the movie, the room filling with the beeps of her machine.

"We don't need to watch this," she adds.

I pocket my phone and lean forward, my elbows to my knees. "Sorry."

"You look tired," the teen says before she yawns. "So am I. Your work day ended four hours ago."

But I couldn't drive home. I couldn't think straight. When I checked on Lucy to see how she was doing, finding her sick and spiking a temp, I didn't want to leave. So, we've been watching a trilogy about vampires and werewolves.

She fell asleep a few times. She's weak, more so than usual, and it concerns me.

"I'm due back in the morning. There's no point driving all the way home."

I live nearly an hour away, and with the way my head is all over the place from Aria's touch burning into every nerve ending, I don't trust myself behind the wheel. I'd black out and crash, and then I might not see her again. She'd be gone by the time they pulled me out of a coma from my injuries.

My contact hasn't given me any new information, and it's pissing me off. He just keeps saying he's "on it", that it's limited because she doesn't have much of a presence online, nor does she do much other than work.

Like myself, she donates to charity. She likes dogs, regularly eats at a pizza place near her house, and purchases the same watermelon shampoo whenever she visits the grocery store.

Pathetic information. If I had the tools, I could find out more.

I glance over at Lucy to find her eyes are shut, having fallen back into a deep sleep from all the drugs the doctors are pumping her with, mostly for pain. I'm not sure why she hasn't been transferred to hospice yet, since this isn't the right ward for her.

Leaning back in my seat, the same one I always sit in when I keep her company, I look around the room at all the cards, deflated balloons, fake flowers, and the countless games of Xs and Os we've played. Her handwriting has gotten close to illegible now because she trembles too much. She can't even hold a pencil without dropping it.

She isn't getting any better, and it fucking kills me. I wish I could help her, find a cure for her disease, somehow stop it from eating her alive, but I'm just an assistant with no qualifications who does research with his stepfather.

My teeth grit, and I'm checking my phone again, not seeing anything from Aria.

An idea springs to life, and it takes me a few minutes to book myself a room for the night at the same hotel she's staying at. Not that I'll do anything, but maybe the proximity will stop me from sweating, desperate to hunt her down for another taste.

Lucy is still asleep when I gently close her door and speak to one of the nurses about removing the deflated balloons, and about possibly getting another doctor in to check her over. Once she agrees, I grab my jacket and head for my car.

I have missed calls and messages from Justin, probably to give me a play-by-play of how his night went with Gabriella. I'd rather burst my own eardrums and stab myself in the chest than hear whatever the fuck he has to say.

By the time I reach the hotel, my hands are still shaking, and

I've had to take my glasses off to rub my eyes. I grab my room key, thank the receptionist, and head to my floor.

Annoyingly, I'm the floor above her, but the thought of being so close has me a little at ease. I'll send her a message and ask to talk, and if she says no, I'll figure out a way into her room so I can watch her sleep.

The door closes behind me, my back against it as I pull off my glasses and press the heels of my palms into my eyes, not knowing if I need sleep, a vacation, or to hit something. This behavior is unacceptable. Since when the fuck do I get like this over a *person*?

I sit down on the bed, pace the floor, and look out the window before I send the first message.

11

ARIA

I frown at my vibrating phone just as I climb into bed.

TOBIASWORK

Can we talk?

ME

What's up?

TOBIASWORK

I'm losing my fucking mind thinking about you, and I don't know how to stop it.

My lips part at his words—I know exactly what he's talking about, because ever since I ran from the bathroom and headed straight here, I've thought about him and how much I wanted more.

I might as well be honest. Maybe we can crush this mutual fascination together. I was going to ask Gabriella for advice, but I know she'll tell me to sleep with him while I can. Once I go home, I'm going to have to sit down and discuss my relationship with Ewan and how we navigate going forward with Jason if we're no longer a couple.

I can have fun with Tobias, right? We don't even need to have sex. We could go on dates and kiss, no sexual contact. Gulping, I shake my head, because from one kiss, and I was ready to yank his pants down and suck him into my mouth.

ME

Me too.

TOBIASWORK

I'm trying to control myself, but I don't know how to, not when it comes to you.

My thighs clench together in excitement. I'm possibly playing with fire, but I don't care. Tobias came at me initially and practically offered himself up, so I'll do the same.

What's the worst that can happen?

ME

Maybe I don't want you to control yourself.

I'm a flirt right now, but I can't help it. I've felt his addictive lips on mine, felt him pressed against me, and I'm not messing around, I need more of him, to feel all of him.

TOBIASWORK

You shouldn't tease me, Doctor. I'm sorry for my behavior before, but I won't apologize for what happens next if you push me.

This doesn't need to be anything more than just sex, and I'm sure he will agree.

I did the whole friends-who-fuck thing with Kaleb, and it's safe to say I never want to do that again.

But with Tobias, I can fly back to Scotland and end it all without any worries. Me and Ewan aren't together, and even if I do ever forgive him, they'll never cross paths. They also couldn't be any different.

I stare at my screen, chewing the side of my mouth, contemplating my next words. This could go two ways: I flirt and he rejects me, or I flirt and he drives over here.

I hope for the latter as I type the reply.

ME

No strings?

Even though he hasn't replied, I hop out of bed and beeline for the bathroom, shoving the toothbrush in my mouth. I turn on the shower and freshen up, hearing my phone buzz twice on the bathroom sink. I'm not usually this nervous about something like this, and even the soap bubbles don't ease the tense muscles.

What if he says no? I will be humiliated and definitely couldn't face him again. What if he tells people in the ward that his *technically* boss tried to seduce him and offered him casual, no strings attached sex?

I may have just made a horrible mistake. What if they send me back to Scotland and take me off Ivy's case?

Then again, *he* kissed *me*, so maybe I'm being paranoid. He literally just said he can't control himself with me.

Wrapping the towel around my body, I lift my phone, closing one eye to try to shield myself from his shattering rejection. I suck in a breath and look up at my reflection in the mirror, my chest and cheeks becoming more flushed by the second.

TOBIASWORK

No strings as in...sex?

TOBIASWORK

Don't tell anyone, then. Open the door.

Staring at his message with wide eyes, I tighten the towel around my naked body. He's here already?

My heartbeat ricochets in my chest, and I check myself in the mirror one more time before walking to the door, taking a few deep breaths, and opening it.

Tobias is on me within a second. Both hands cup my cheeks,

his lips pressed against mine, completely consuming me as he kicks the door closed behind him and walks me back. "Are you sure about this?" he asks against my mouth, biting down on my bottom lip until I feel a sting.

I nod enthusiastically and open my mouth for him, our tongues moving hungrily, tilting our heads to deepen the passionate kiss.

Tobias, keeping his lips attached to mine, lifts me up by the back of my thighs, and my towel drops to the ground, completely exposing me to my assistant. He locks my legs around his waist and sits me down on the side table, letting his hands roam my entire body, rolling my peaked nipples between his fingers, igniting a fire inside me.

I feel his cock straining against his shorts, so I hook my fingers into his waistband, pulling them down and freeing his impressive length.

My eyes widen. So thick and long and perfect. My mouth waters at the sight.

"What's wrong?" Tobias asks, nudging my cheek with his nose. I shake my head and grip him in my palm. He leans his forehead against mine as I slowly work both my hands up and down his length, twisting my wrist when I reach his swollen head.

I don't flinch as one of his hands moves from my hip, pressing up between my breasts before curling around my throat, holding me in place as I continue my movements.

"I want you." His voice shakes in my ear, hot bursts of breath fanning against my neck as his fingers tighten ever so slightly. "And I know you want me too."

I smile against his lips as I kiss him lightly. "Want is a strong word."

He releases my neck, both hands grabbing at my inner thighs as he spreads my legs wide, his fingertips digging into my heated skin as I whimper.

"You want me to touch you?"

God. "Yes." I bite down on my lip, nodding. "But you can't tell anyone."

"Deal," he replies with a grunt as I keep stroking him.

He runs his palms up to the apex of my thighs and presses both thumbs against my core. Just his touch causes my eyes to roll, my spine tensing. He hums, bringing one of his thumbs between his lips before kissing me once again.

"You wanted to talk?" I say, loving the way his head falls on my shoulder as he pants against my skin.

When he doesn't reply, I run my lips up the shell of his ear, fisting his hair to keep him in place while I tighten my fingers around his cock and pump faster.

"Does that feel good?" I ask against his temple, feeling him nod, his knuckles white as he tries to control himself.

Suddenly, Tobias grabs my wrist to stop me and pulls back, his pupils fully dilated, bursts of minty breath hitting my face as his stare burns into me.

"Will you fuck me?"

He groans and closes his eyes, giving no response as he lifts me by my thighs and walks me to the bed. He drops me on my back and doesn't wait to hover above me. The flesh between his legs weighs heavily against my navel, dangerously close to my pussy.

"You're on the pill, right?"

Tilting my head at him, confused as to how he knows that, I nod. "Yeah."

"Good," he responds, pressing his lips to my neck, my mouth dropping open from the sensation between my legs. I moan as he kisses my skin, biting, sucking, before he drags his tongue up my throat, along my jaw to my mouth, shoving against my own.

"You're so fucking intoxicating," he tells me. "I'm never going to get enough of you."

He forces my legs open with his knee and settles between my thighs, but not before he moves his hand between us and slowly starts to circle my sensitive clit. I groan, aching for him to apply a little more pressure. With his teeth nipping my neck below my ear, I gasp, moaning when he pushes a finger inside me to wet it, then brings it back to circle around me again. I think I'm about to lose my mind as he alternates between sliding a finger in, pumping it, and rubbing me with a rhythm that makes me tremble beneath him, his swollen cock still pressing against my inner thigh.

"Oh God," I moan out, silenced by his mouth on me, delving his tongue inside and kissing me harder with each whimper that leaves my lips.

I feel my legs starting to tense, my spine tingling with impending euphoria until I see stars. Then, Tobias retracts his fingers from inside me and sits back, pushing his salty fingers into my mouth.

"Do you taste good?" he asks, his knuckles hitting my teeth and making me gag, my eyes instantly watering. He pulls his fingers out of my mouth and tastes them himself, groaning his approval as he kisses me again.

He pulls away, resting on his haunches as his eyes roam the length of my body.

I raise a brow. "What?"

He runs his thumb along my bottom lip, dragging it down until it springs back into place. "As I said...intoxicating." His hand slides down to grab my throat. "Beautiful," he adds as his other hand goes between my legs again, pushing two fingers inside me and making my back arch. "Addictive." He curls his fingers and lowers himself until his mouth is inches from my pussy, his fingers moving in and out slowly, driving me insane. "And now, you're all mine."

His glasses fall off as I slam my thighs shut from the intensity of his lip grazing my pussy. Tossing them aside, he parts my pussy lips with his thumbs as he runs the tip of his nose up my core.

"So many parts of you to taste, so little time," he says breathlessly, fingers digging into my flesh and fully opening my pussy to him. "You've made a terrible mistake, Doctor, because I might need to keep you trapped in my basement while I fuck every bit of sense out of you."

I whimper. "Please."

Tobias' work phone starts vibrating on the unit next to the mirror, and he grunts and grabs it, keeping his face between my legs, looking up at me as he *answers* with, "Tobias." I flinch as his tongue lashes out against my clit. "What do you need help with?"

I cover my mouth to stop the moans from slipping free as he licks me between words, and I'm stuck between wanting to slap him for doing this and wanting him to keep going.

His lips cover my clit, sucking delicately as he hums in agreement to whoever is on the phone.

"Wait, really?" he says, pulling his face away from between my legs and sitting up. "Yeah, I didn't realize the time. Are they still waiting? Okay, I'm on my way." He hangs up and throws his head back, huffing. "I'm really sorry."

"What's wrong?" I ask, sitting up and covering my nakedness with my hands.

"I told Ivy's mom I'd assist on their day out to the beach between her med switches." He pushes a lock of hair behind my ear. "I love your hair. It's so blonde and shiny. Promise me you'll never dye it."

I laugh and check my phone, feeling the intense wetness between my legs and watching Tobias pull his shorts back on.

"I'm going to come with you, if that's okay? I want to see how Ivy is doing and spend time with her, since Doctor Blythe has me doing everything but just that."

"Sure. And I'm sorry for overstepping again. I understand if it was just a spur of the moment thing."

I shrug. "I was the one who mentioned no strings. Really, though, no one can know. You need to promise not to tell a soul, not even Justin."

"Will you tell Gabriella?"

"Of course," I reply. "She's my best friend."

He nods, almost like he expected that. "I'm staying at this hotel. I'll go get dressed and meet you out front."

Why is he staying here when he lives so close to work? I don't even want to ask, because my entire body is still trembling, and I need him to leave so I can go scream into my pillow.

I fully expect him to leave without saying anything else, but he leans forward and kisses my cheek, running his palm down my back, making me swoon inside.

"I'm still not finished with you," he says against my ear, a yelp falling from my lips as he slaps my ass on the way out, closing the door behind him.

12

ARIA

After a long day at the beach, my skin is so red, it hurts. I'm not technically working, so I plan on heading straight to the hotel once Ivy gets into the car they hired. Watching Tobias fold her wheelchair in the back and buckle Ivy into her seat, I discuss with her mom about other days out we can take her on if the hospital allows it.

Her smile always lights up my day, and she giggles when I smile back. "Did you have fun today?" I ask her, placing her toy on her lap. She nods her head once in excitement. "We'll go again soon, okay?" I tuck a strand of her golden hair behind her ear and say goodbye.

"Are you going with them?" I ask Tobias, who gives Ivy the thumbs up, pulls a funny face to make her laugh, and closes her door.

He shakes his head, and I feel a smile fighting its way to the surface. "My car is at your hotel," he says. "I'll walk back with you."

I'm not really sure why I'm trying not to frown, or why I care where he goes, but I feel a pang of disappointment. "Okay," I reply in a quiet tone, dropping my eyes to my moving feet.

We could easily pick up where we left off, since we're free for the rest of the day, but I don't want to mention that unless he does first.

"Sorry about earlier," he says, walking beside me along the promenade, the sun starting to fall behind the tall buildings on our left, the warm glow reflecting on the sea on our right. "I can't miss a call on my work phone." His smile at the last word completely lights up the blue in his eyes, and I'm staring for too long before I shake it off.

"It's okay." I shrug. "Although I give you points for multi-tasking."

He laughs, wrapping his fingers around the leather strap of my bag, pulling me to him.

I almost stumble, inhaling his masculine scent, his arm wrapping around me to keep my feet steady on the ground while the other cups my face. He runs his thumb along my cheekbone, dipping his head, his nose nudging mine before his lips softly press against my own.

It's not a greedy kiss, no tongue, no gasps for air. No, it's just his mouth pressing against mine, and he still overwhelms every sane part of me. The voice in my head is yelling at me to stop kissing Tobias in public, to stand back and tell him it's wrong, completely forbidden. But as I feel a strong wave of comfort wrapping around me, around us, I ignore my inner Aria and melt against him.

As soon as my brain catches up with my actions, I pull away, nervously glancing around us at the people walking by.

"Someone might see us. Moves like that cross the line of having whatever this is be no-strings only."

Scrunching his nose, he pushes off the wall with his shoulder and once again runs his thumb down my cheek softly. "I don't care," he says with a smile, kissing the tip of my nose before walking past me and across the street to his car.

The engine of his sports car roars so loud, my bones shake, and the window rolls down, revealing him in his sunglasses, a toned arm hanging out.

Standing frozen in place, I watch him drive off, my lips still tingling and my heart beating so fast, I might pass out on the sidewalk.

"MAYBE YOU SHOULD SEND him a message explaining exactly what a fuck buddy is," Gabs says, throwing a bag of chips at my face. "Here, you need to eat something. You look ill."

I ignore her comment. I feel fine, just a little...dazed.

"Or I can just say it was a mistake and we should just stay colleagues."

Gabriella's face had lit up when I explained to her what happened in the last twenty-four hours, and she apologized for leaving me on my own in the first place. She was staying with Justin and left me in the hotel room for two days. She'd squeaked when I gave her a play by play of what happened in here too.

She's always telling me to find someone else to keep my mind off Ewan and to keep me out of his bed when I grow bored, and I piss her off for the hundredth time when I go back to him anyway. I know she means well; she isn't one to run back to her ex when she feels alone. No, she finds someone else to get under and deals with it that way.

But this thing with Justin, I don't like it. He gives me the creeps. But she must like him, because she's blushing as she tells me he's on his way to pick her up to go bowling. I know she's happy, and I don't want to dampen that by pointing out that we leave in a few weeks and to not get attached.

"Why don't you ask Toby to come over?"

I tip my head at her in disdain, scrunching my nose up at her. "No. And his name is Tobias."

"You are your own cock block, Aria. You know that, don't you? Live a little and ask the man over to fuck your temporary innocence away." She swipes on red lipstick in the mirror and puckers her lips, ruffling her curly hair. "Explain to him what no strings means while he makes you choke on his fingers again."

Giggling, I shake my head at her. I shouldn't have gone into so much detail and shocked her with that part. "I'm never telling you anything again. And *temporary innocence?* Shut up."

"Suit yourself. Don't wait up for me," she says, kissing both my cheeks before she walks out the door. "Toodles."

I roll my eyes at her, but a smile plays on my lips.

After showering and applying aftersun to the raw skin on my arms and shoulders, a dash of lotion on my burnt face, I lay in bed and swipe through my phone, staring at Ewan and Tobias' contacts, fighting with myself. Should I reply to Ewan's earlier message to call him or ask Tobias to come over to finish what he started?

I throw my phone aside, choosing option three: ignoring the world. I click on the tv, deciding to watch some action movie. I get ten minutes into it when my phone vibrates beside me.

EWAN

I miss you. Please come home. You belong here.

Love is overrated, and from experience, it makes you weak. Unless you have that epic love that consumes you more than life itself, in my opinion, it's not worth it. Maybe one day, I'll think otherwise, but for now, I'll ignore Ewan and ask Tobias what he's up to tonight.

13

TOBIAS

I'm so fucked.

I thought getting another taste of her would at least lessen this weird obsession I have with the doctor, but instead, I need more. So much fucking more. I can feel her hands in my hair, her legs wrapped around me, her taste on my tongue.

She might be in trouble, because I don't think I can stop. I'm in the hotel again, same room as before, and she already sent me a message asking what my plans are tonight. I'm trying not to barge into her room right now and fuck her against the wall.

What the hell is wrong with me? Since when have I acted this way?

When I used to screw the older woman, I was never attached–it was a bit of fun and not in the slightest serious. I never thought about her, felt her on me when she wasn't around, and I certainly did not hear her whimpers in my ear when the room was in total silence.

My mind is playing tricks on me. It happens from time to time–I play a scenario in the head and think it's real. This morning, I'd showered, got dressed, and was seconds from picking Aria up because I thought we planned something, only to check my phone to see the last messages weren't us planning a date.

My imagination can be dangerous.

I'd tossed my phone on the bed and lay down, warring with myself, trying to figure out if I hallucinated everything with Aria. But then her message came through, a little too casual for work colleagues, and I at least knew I didn't imagine the kissing and tasting.

I stare at the message I've yet to answer. I feel like I need to pump the brakes at the same time as I press the accelerator. She's leaving soon. She's not here forever, so what the fuck do I do when she gets on a flight back to Scotland?

Follow her.

No.

I screw my eyes shut and pull my glasses off, rubbing them until I see black dots in my vision.

My head spins, and instead of getting up and dealing with this hard-on or replying to my doctor, my stupid anxiety takes over, and I pass out.

14

ARIA

Ivy sleeps a lot.

Every time I go to see her, she's asleep. Doctor Blythe has informed me the medication she has been given is stronger than anything she has had before. So no more days out.

So I just stand there for a few minutes and watch her sleep, speak to her mother about how her trip has been so far and if there's anything I can help with. I squeeze her shoulder in a comforting manner and head back to my office to catch up on some emails.

Sitting at the computer, typing away, my phone rings, and I see Ewan's name for the hundredth time in the past two days. Huffing, I answer and put him on speaker, throwing my phone on the desk. "Can you please leave me alone?"

"Hi, Aria! Why do you want me to leave you alone?"

Oh, Jason. God, I'm such an asshole.

"Hey, little guy. How are you?"

He laughs at Ewan trying to grab the phone.

"My dad doesn't know I called you," he tells me, and I can tell he's running while Ewan yells at him to give him the phone. I can hear the dogs barking in the background, our two pugs Ewan refused to let me keep when we broke up.

A door closes, and I hear the latch pulled aside. "I'm okay. I just miss you. Can I come to stay at your house when you get home?"

"Did you lock yourself in the bathroom?"

"Yep. Dad hasn't let me talk to you because you're busy, but I miss you. Can you bring home American candy"

I let out a laugh. "Of course. I'm at work just now, so I'll let you know when I get back to Scotland, and I'll come pick you up."

"Okay. We miss you," he says. "Dad keeps messing up the pasta you make, but I don't want to tell him it tastes disgusting."

Laughing again, I lean back on my computer chair. "I'll make it for you when I get back, but I really need to go do some work now. Tell your dad I'll call him when I land so we can arrange a sleepover."

"Okay." He sounds sad, and it's like a knife to the chest. "I do really miss you."

Tobias walks into the room, his white shirt rolled up to his elbows, showing off his watch and charity bands. A smile tugs at the corner of his mouth as he puts a finger to his lips, sitting down in front of me.

"Yeah. I miss you too," I reply, keeping my eyes on Tobias, who's watching me intently, a brow rising at my words. "I need to go."

Before I can hang up, I hear Jason opening the door and Ewan begging him for the phone. My eyes close, and I put my hand to my forehead.

"My dad wants to talk to you."

I hear Jason 's voice echoing in the distance and Ewan taking a deep breath. "Hey."

Tobias tilts his head at me and leans forward, placing both hands on my thighs and squeezing, making me silently whine and cross my legs.

"You there?"

"Yeah."

I mouth a "stop it" to him, and he shakes his head. His hands move up to the apex of my thighs, shifting my skirt and fingering the string of my thong.

"I'm taking these off," he says quietly as he hooks his fingers under the material at my hips. "Don't make a sound, Doctor."

"Aria, please talk to me." Ewan lowers his voice to a whisper, the exhaustion evident, making sure Jason doesn't overhear him. "Do you know how much this is messing with my head? Are you going to give me the silent treatment while over there and come home and pretend everything is fine like the last time? Are we actually done? Tell me. Please."

The last time. I want to scoff at his words, because the last time, we were split up for months and I went back to him because I couldn't handle it anymore. I'm not sure why he thinks it's going to happen again or why he thinks I'm messing with his head.

"Answer him," Tobias mouths, his thumb pressing to my clit as he slides off his chair and lowers to his knees between my legs.

The sight of Tobias Mitchell on his knees for me has my toes curling–I wish I could take a picture of this moment and frame it. I'd look at it whenever I needed to get myself off once whatever this was between us ended.

He parts my legs, opening me to him, keeping his eyes on me as he closes the distance and presses a soft, wet kiss against my underwear-covered pussy.

"Please," I whimper before slapping a palm over my mouth with wide eyes. If he doesn't stop, I'm going to break so many damn rules–one, being on the phone to an ex while orgasming with someone else, and two, being in my office at work where anyone could walk in.

"Are you okay?" Ewan asks. "Did I upset you?" When I don't reply, he sighs. "Baby, I'm so fucking sorry. For everything."

A frown plays on Tobias' face before he snaps the straps of my thong, making me reach for one of his wrists to give him eyes that say *don't you dare.* He glares back, freeing himself from my grip and pocketing my underwear.

"I need to go, Ewan," I pant accidentally, eager for Tobias to move his fingers to the right a touch so I can ease this fire igniting around me. The phone slips from my hand, dropping next to Tobias' knee. He lifts it, stares at the screen, then places it on speaker.

My eyes widen, and when I try to grab it, he pulls his hand away and places it on the desk, out of my reach.

Tobias leans up on his knees, bringing his face to mine as his mouth reaches my ear. "Who's Ewan?" he whisper-hisses, pulling my earlobe between his teeth, making me pool in my seat. "The ex?"

I nod once. "Please hang up," I breathe.

Tobias doesn't listen, though—he lowers back down and places soft kisses up my inner thigh, gripping my flesh and groaning his approval when he sees how soaked I am.

"Aria?" Ewan calls out just as Tobias eases a finger inside me, my spine tingling as he twists his finger inside, shoving knuckle deep.

I moan as he sucks on my swollen clit, making the temperature in the room rise. "Oh God."

"What?" Ewan asks. "What's going on?"

I struggle to string words together to answer him, squirming in my chair as he circles his tongue and sucks again, all the while not daring to take his eyes off me. Adding another finger, he thrusts, working my clit with his mouth at the same time and making my head fall back.

My hand slides over and hangs up the phone just as a moan slips out.

With a knock at the door, he pulls away from me and sucks his fingers, sitting back on his chair, leaving me a panting mess, sweat rolling down my chest. I straighten myself up quickly and pull down my skirt, between my legs soaking and hungrily needing more.

"Come in."

Tobias raises a brow at me as I fix my hair.

Gabriella pops her head in and tells me she's going for lunch, asking if I want to come. I agree and give Tobias a sideways glance, telling her I'll see her at the reception desk before she closes the door with a knowing grin.

"You need to stop that, Tobias," I say, my words not sounding slightly threatening. I'm breathless, my cheeks are hot, and my heart rate is accelerating with the way he licks his lips. "We're at work."

He shrugs and pulls my chair towards him, pushing my legs open with his hands. I shriek when he grabs my hips and makes me straddle him, my skirt riding up over my ass where his hands grasp me. "It makes it more exciting. The thrill of being caught. Just like you with your boyfriend."

"Boyfriend?" I lean back and raise a brow at him, his handsome, unbothered face staring back. "I said he was an ex."

Smirking, his eyes trail down the length of me. "So I'm not breaking any rules if I do this?" He pulls down the front of my shirt, the buttons popping open, and dips his hand into my bra. "Or this?" he mutters as he exposes my breast, leaning in so he can roll his wet tongue around the sensitive nipple.

Against my better judgement, I moan.

His eyes don't leave mine as he looks up at me, watching me through his dark lashes, making me bite down on my bottom lip to try to stop the sounds strangling in my throat.

"We shouldn't be doing this," I eventually manage to say, my hands in his hair, wrapping the strands around my fingers as I pant. "It's—"

My words falter as his hot mouth sucks against the skin hard enough to leave red marks before he rolls his tongue around my nipple again. I sigh above him, my head lolling. I feel his hard cock through his work pants, pressing against my soaked pussy.

"Sometimes, the most forbidden and taboo moments are the best," he mumbles against my sensitive skin. "Wouldn't you agree?"

He's right—the thrill of being found in this position makes the act more intense. Anyone can walk through the door and see me straddling my assistant, his mouth on my nipple as he pushes his free hand down my back, pulling my skirt up higher so he can get a firmer grip.

He pulls away from my breast and presses his mouth against mine, both of us exhaling deeply as his fingers ease inside me, urging me to move my hips against his hand.

"Tell me, Doctor: how do I make you feel when I do this?" he speaks against my lips, biting down as he stretches me with another finger, making me cry out into his mouth as he picks up the pace, gripping my hip aggressively to move me onto his thrusting fingers. "Do you feel alive?"

"Yes," I whimper above him, leaning one hand on his lap behind me to make me grind harder, the other in his hair, pulling at the roots. With my toes curling painfully in my shoes, my spine tingles with a rush of pleasure, my legs tensing with each pulse threatening to crash through me.

I think if Gabriella walked in right now, I would keep going. Nothing is coming between me and Tobias and how hard my orgasm is building.

"You're close, Aria. So fucking close. I want to feel you come around my fingers. Show me what I do to you."

He presses his lips to mine again, angrily claiming my mouth with his tongue as his fingers synchronize with my hips rolling, his thumb rubbing my clit. I drop my head to the crook of his neck and moan his name, riding a high that hits its peak just as someone knocks at the door again.

"Hurry up, Aria," I hear Gabs grumble, and I lean back up, my mouth wide from the pleasure, my body spasming with each shuddering twitch of my orgasm.

Tobias uses his free hand to cover my mouth, his palm silencing my illicit sounds as my eyes roll, my body tightening with each spasm.

"Are you coming or not?" Gabs continues.

"Don't worry, she's there," Tobias says as my inner walls tighten repeatedly around his fingers, the waves of electricity knocking me into oblivion momentarily.

15

ARIA

"You need to actually hit them, Doctor Miller."

I swear, I've been here an hour, and I already want to murder him.

"Aria. Call me Aria, or I'll hurt you," I warn him, dodging his palm swinging towards my ass. "Nice try." I smile, throwing the bowling ball and missing yet again.

Gabriella and Justin have basically stayed in the arcade since we got here, leaving me with Tobias and his sarcastic comments about putting the guards up so I can at least hit one.

"Here, let me show you." His deep laugh vibrates the air as he steps behind me, pulling me so my back is to his hard chest, leaning down to whisper in my ear. "I hope you're good at taking directions, Doctor."

"Aria," I huff, the heat of him around me already making my cheeks hot. "Say my name, and maybe I'll actually listen to you."

"I can think of loads of ways you can make me say it," he teases, his warm breath hitting my neck as his hands drift up my sides to my shoulders, his hair-raising touch making me shiver as he works his hands down my arms, covering my hands with his. I would be lying if I said I hated it. "For now, try to at least stay out of the gutters."

He moves my arm back and leans into me more, throwing the bowling ball, and guess what? I miss again.

"You're a terrible teacher," I say, turning in his arms and pointing at his chest. He laughs, releasing me as I walk over to our glasses, taking a drink of my vodka. I watch him gulp down his water, blue eyes searing into me. "Why don't you drink?"

I must've struck a nerve, because his whole mood changes, staring down at his shoes with a frown.

"Sorry. I didn't know it was a touchy subject."

He shakes his head, forcing a smile. "Do you want to go to my place? I think they left already. This seems like a date, and I don't want you freaking out."

"I'm not freaking out," I reply, raising a brow. "I know it's not a date."

"Then what is it? I am aware the arrangement we have does not require nights together like this. Would you rather leave so I can fuck you already?"

His serious expression and words make my breath hitch, and I watch him raise his brows, waiting for my response.

My eyes scan our surroundings for anyone who could've heard him. "Do you live nearby?"

"Relatively."

Shrugging, I finish off my glass and change my shoes, lifting my leather coat. "What happened at the office cannot happen again, okay? It was inappropriate and unprofessional of us. Whenever we want to be in any way sexual, we do so outside of work. I mean it."

He sniffs, standing to tower over me. "We'll see."

TOBIAS TAKES HIS CAR, the flashy, expensive one he drives far too fast. My knuckles practically turn white as I grip the leather seat, watching him swerve through traffic.

"Do you need to drive like this?"

He laughs, a deep one that shows his perfectly straight, white teeth, his dimple denting. "It just seems like I'm driving fast because it's a powerful car."

"Sure," I say sarcastically, shaking my head as I watch the stores and bars pass, obscured by his speed.

"Aria?"

I turn to look at Tobias as he strums his fingers on the steering wheel. Goosebumps surround me as his hand reaches over to grab my inner thigh. He smirks at my whimper, fingers dangerously close to my sex.

"Give me your underwear."

The thrill powering through me right now, mixed with a little bit of nervousness, urges me to bite down on my bottom lip and fix my curled hair to one side. "You want my underwear?"

"Yes," he replies firmly. "Give me them."

A flicker of amusement takes over my face. "I don't have any on."

His jaw tenses, his hand gripping his steering wheel hard as he lets out a groan. "You shouldn't have told me that."

I cock my head to the side, chewing on the red nail of my thumb before slowly trailing my hand down to settle on his. "What are you going to do?"

He closes his eyes as if he's counting to three, accelerating as the light turns green, my back pushing into the chair from his ridiculous speed.

Trying to hold back a nervous smile, I narrow my eyes. "Tobias."

"I want you to..." He moves his hand from under mine, clasping his fingers around my wrist and pushing it between my legs to cup my heated core, a gasp falling from my lips. "I want you to finger yourself."

"You're joking," I say with a laugh, my eyes widening as he shakes his head, keeping his expression serious. "I am *not* doing that here."

He hums, looking around the busy street. "I can fix that, Doctor Miller." Tobias slows down next to a parking lot but chews his cheek and continues.

"Aria," I say, rolling my eyes and biting my thumb nail again, watching him search around us as he drives. "What are you looking for?"

He abruptly turns the car down a narrow street, making me grab the door handle before he parks somewhere relatively obscured. "Tobias!" I shriek at him, and for some reason, a massive smile takes over my face.

"I guess that's one way to make you scream my name," he says, unbuckling his seatbelt before leaning over and doing the same to mine. "Let's see how many other ways I can make you scream it."

He pushes a button in the middle of the car, making both doors shoot up, keeping the radio on that's blaring music. I watch him walk around the front of the car, looking at the buildings around us until he reaches my side.

"What are you doing?"

He leans down and circles his fingers on my wrist, pulling me out of the car and into his arms. With a heart that needs to restart and heat creeping up my spine, I gasp as Tobias presses his body against my own, pinning me to the car as his lips crash against mine.

I push one of my hands into his hair, grasping a fistful and tugging his head so it tilts to the side, kissing him harder. He grips my hips, slowly edging his fingers to the front of my dress so he can press his palm between my legs.

I whimper against his mouth as a wave of pleasure hits me, giving him the opportunity to move his tongue past my parted lips, kissing me deeper. With our mouths slanting, we find a steady rhythm of his hand pressing against me and my hips rolling against his hand.

"*This* wasn't the plan," he says against my mouth, both of us breathless, my lips tingling. I instantly miss the contact as he removes his hand and steps away from me. I frown at him, watching my assistant cross his arms, the evidence of his arousal tight against his trousers.

I raise a brow. "What? You want me to finger myself right here?"

His silence is my answer. My eyes widen as he looks from side to side, making sure we're still alone. His eyes land back on my worried face, his smug look falling. "What's wrong?"

"It's just..." I stop, looking at the ground. I *want* to do this, I really do, but I'm nervous. "I..."

I'm terrified.

I look back up at him already in front of me again. He tilts my chin with his finger, placing a soft kiss on the corner of my mouth before he trails his lips along my jawline, stopping when his hot breath is against my ear.

"I wouldn't have you do anything you're not comfortable with, Aria." He places a kiss against my heated skin, my eyes fluttering shut. "Let me help you feel relaxed. I'm new to this too."

Knowing he hasn't done any sort of public sexual activity does ease me somewhat. The fact the place is hardly lit save for the car's headlights and a flickering streetlamp a few feet away doesn't hurt either.

He nips the skins below my ear, my head falling back to give him more access, and he sucks hard enough to leave a red mark before dragging wet kisses down my throat. I cry at the contact, swirls of butterflies in my stomach bring a flush of heat to my cheeks.

I'm pooling, already feeling uncomfortable between my legs with a dire need for touch. I nearly fall apart in his arms, pleading at the feeling of his mouth moving across my collarbone, his strained cock pressing against me.

"Tobias," I beg, the need for him increasing.

He pulls back and hooks his arms under my thighs, lifting me so I wrap around him, his lips on mine again as he walks us to the front of his car. The cold metal against my back makes me wince, but the heat from Tobias' body pressed against me has me drunk on my assistant, eagerly needing him to give me some sort of release.

As if he can hear my inner thoughts screaming at him to pleasure me, he leans on one of his hands and dips his other between my legs, making my mouth fall open as his fingers slide down my slit, my wetness making it easy for him to ease two fingers inside me, pressing his thumb against my clit. "Is this what you want, Doctor Miller?"

His pupils are taking over the ocean in his eyes, his raw lips parting.

I can't stop looking at him.

I feel his fingers wrapping around my throat, soft but firm. "Aria?"

"Yes," I hiss, my eyes screwing shut as he pumps his fingers faster, curling them, making my breasts move with the force of his thrusts. My heels catch the grill of the car, and I widen my legs for him, gripping his arm to try to control myself by digging my nails into his skin, electricity spreading through me as every nerve in my body is set on fire.

He releases my throat and moves back, standing with his fingers still thrusting into me. "Your turn," he pants, turned on. "Just follow my lead."

I don't pull away as he takes my hand, and I definitely don't refuse as he removes his fingers and replaces them with my own.

"What if someone sees us?"

He looks around. "It's just me and you." His voice lowers. "If anyone sees you, I'll kill them."

It's an empty threat, but the low tone and the darkness in his gaze has me listening and believing him.

I've done this to myself plenty of times, but doing it while lying on top of a car, outside, with someone I've known for a few weeks, is completely new to me.

He notices I'm having an inner battle, barely thrusting my fingers, so he leans over me, moving them for me as his hand covers mine. "If you want to stop, just tell me, okay?"

I nod in agreement as he presses his lips to my jaw.

He moves my two fingers away from my entrance and circles them over my clit, my eyes fluttering shut. The pressure he's using against my hand, mixed with his attentive kisses to my chest, urges me to move on my own.

Watching me slowly unravel from my own touch and his wet mouth, he sinks his teeth into his bottom lip and lowers his gaze to between my legs.

"I want to fuck you."

I whimper, a warm sensation wrapping around my spine and coiling tight.

My back arches. "Tobias," I moan.

"Such a good little doctor," he groans. "A filthy fucking doctor touching herself for me." He fists my hair, tugging. "Come."

His name falls from my lips louder the faster and harder my fingers go, ignoring our surroundings, or the fact Tobias is watching me writhe beneath him by my own hand. The fire builds around me, and I know I won't last much longer, feeling Tobias' hand squeeze my throat, the other holding my hair tighter.

A strangled whimper, curling toes, tensed legs, and I'm hitting my pinnacle as he cuts off my oxygen with his fingers grasping my throat. I try to scream through my orgasm, but I choke, my vision blurring, the music playing through his car a muted buzz.

"See?" He looks at me, nudging my nose with his, the corner of his lips tugging up. "I knew you'd scream my name while finger fucking yourself," he says, crashing his lips against mine as the waves of pleasure ripping through me grow more intense, my heart thudding against my chest. Every muscle in my body spasms as I ride my high, coming on my own hand.

My orgasm brings me to the brink of passing out, panting, the sweat coating my forehead and chest. Slowly, I pull out my fingers, and before I can find something to wipe them with, Tobias grabs them and closes his lips over the digits as he cleans them with his tongue, keeping his blue eyes on me before they flicker closed, groaning his approval.

16

ARIA

"**D**id you know Doctor Blythe hasn't been at work in three days?" Gabriella tosses another chip into her mouth. "Supposedly, he's never off sick or anything."

"Yeah, I heard. He didn't sign off on Ivy's transfer either, so we need to wait until next week now."

We got the devastating news yesterday that Ivy's trials weren't going to plan. Blythe thinks it's time to send her home and not waste more money or make her anymore uncomfortable. When I sat down in the meeting, I was spoken down to when I asked for alternatives or for more time, and Tobias butted in by asking for another week, but Blythe told him to leave the office.

He has been removed as my assistant, since more cases have come in for him to help with and all I need to do is tidy up a few files and make arrangements for Ivy. Then, sadly, I need to fly back to Scotland and deal with my real life problems.

Now, Blythe and Tobias have been off work, although the latter has been messaging me nonstop, informing me he had to drive back to his mom's place to sort out a few things.

Gabriella is going out with Justin and promised she wouldn't come home, so I invited Tobias over. As soon as he accepted, I ran to the shower, washed, shaved, and tidied up.

I may or may not be wearing lace under my pajamas, and I may or may not have bought a bottle of wine for us both to drink. I know he claims he can't drink, but what harm is a few glasses in the hotel room while watching a movie?

Gabriella kisses both of my cheeks before leaving, telling me she loves me and hopes I have lots of dirty sex.

I watch TV for a bit, jumping up when I hear a knock on the door.

Tobias is dressed in light grey gym shorts and a tight black gym top, looking hotter than usual with messy hair, his chiseled jaw a lot more defined after a clean shave.

"Hey." He smirks, looking down at my bare legs and back up to my eyes. "Are you going to let me in?"

"Maybe," I tease, leaning against the door frame. "What's the password?"

He narrows his eyes at me, a smile playing on his lips as he lowers his voice to a whisper. "Let me in..." he steps closer, his mouth delicately grazing mine, "so I can eat you out."

I don't hesitate for a second. I press my lips against his, and he instantly reacts, kicking the door shut and wrapping his arms around my waist, lifting me up so my ankles can cross behind his back.

Tobias walks us to the bed, mouths devouring each other, the butterflies in my stomach going fucking crazy. My fingers twist in his hair, and he pushes his tongue past my parted lips, tilting our heads to deepen the kiss.

He doesn't carefully place me down. No, he throws me, and I nearly fall off the other side of the bed.

"You're an idiot," I laugh, but he cuts me off with his mouth on my neck and his hands pinning my arms above my head.

"Let's see if you still think that when I'm done with you," he pants, biting my bottom lip. He nudges my legs open with his knees and settles himself between my legs, his strained cock pressing against my aching center.

I wince as he bites and sucks on my neck, gripping my hair,

angling my head to the side to give him more access, his other hand on my hip, slowly moving under my waistband.

My heels dig into the back of his thighs, urging him to press harder against me.

"I'm going to fuck you into oblivion, Doctor."

The excitement goes south, and I roll my hips, moaning into his mouth as he pulls my hair.

I whimper as his fingers dip under my waistband, his hard cock pressing against my inner thigh, silencing my gasps with his mouth again as he shoves two fingers inside me.

My eyes roll.

No distractions or interruptions.

I mentally pat myself on the back when Tobias rips open my shirt to reveal the black lace, and when he pulls down my shorts and tosses them aside, I chew my lip, watching his eyes travel the length of my body.

With parted lips and a hooded gaze, Tobias leans forward, hovering above me, tongue running along his bottom lip. I watch his mouth, aching for him to kiss me again. "You have no idea how badly I want you, Doctor."

My breathing hitches, and I feel myself heating up, the hairs rising on my arms from his intense eye contact. I gulp, moving my hips up to create some contact, his hard cock rubbing right where I want him. "Then take me," I say, desperate, running my hands up the sides of his face until my fingers push into his hair, and his eyes close momentarily.

Tobias fervently crashes his lips against mine and drops his weight, gripping my hair with one hand, taking my breath away as his tongue pushes past my lips and moves against mine.

"You're mine, Doctor," he growls, nipping my bottom lip with his teeth, making me gasp when his hand cups my soaking core. "This." He applies a little pressure, and my eyes flutter closed at the sensation. "This is mine. No one else gets to touch you." I nod, my eyes rolling as he pushes the material aside and shoves a finger inside me, making me clench. "Words, Aria."

"Yours," I whisper, my mouth falling open as he pushes

another finger deep inside me, curling his fingers and slowly retracting before vigorously pushing into me again. My hands drop from his hair and I grab my own, strangled moans stuck in my throat. "God."

"Tobias," he corrects.

He shifts, pressing a kiss to my inner thigh before he looks up at me through his dark lashes. I feel the swirls of frustration already building in my spine.

My legs shake, and he pins them down at my knees, spreading them wide. A moan leaves my mouth as he presses another hot kiss higher, still keeping eye contact with me. I whimper, my head falling back.

He bites down on the flesh close to the apex of my inner thigh, and I grip his hair in a tight fist, my lip securely between my teeth with the building pleasure. His hands move under my legs to grab my hips. "I want you to share every single part of your body with me, Doctor. I want to own it."

"Take it," I moan, his hot breath blowing against my aching core, writhing beneath him. I need him to stop teasing me, to get it on with before I grab his face and forcefully face fuck him. "Please, Tobias."

"Please what?" he asks, dipping his fingers under the material on my hips, slowly pulling the black lace down before he goes back into his position between my legs. "You want me to lick your pussy, don't you?" His tongue runs just a bit to the side of my slit, my sex throbbing for him to move to the left a touch. "You were so sweet on my fingers, Doctor. Tell me what you want me to do."

"Taste me," I say, my voice hoarse, moving my hips up to his mouth. "Please, Tobias."

His tongue flattens over me, slowly gliding up my wet core, and I gasp. My toes curl from the explosive sensation of his repeated strokes, mouth falling open. The intense feeling stops suddenly, and Tobias looks up at me as he hums, his eyes shutting briefly. "So fucking good. I'm going to make you come with my mouth, and then you're going to ride my cock until you pass out. Is that what you want, Doctor?"

My fingers tighten in his hair, urging him to go back to what he was doing. I nod with a whimpered yes, sucking my bottom lip in anticipation. My eyes roll back again as soon as he closes the distance, sucking on my clit harshly, alternating between pushing his tongue into my entrance and teasing over my bundle of nerves, his thumb circling the sensitive spot while he devours me. "Tobias," I cry out, fire ripping through me as I see stars.

"You react so well to me. So fucking wet."

A string of curse words and moans leaves my mouth, my back arching with each hot lick of his tongue, every muscle contracting as he eases two fingers inside me, keeping his mouth on my clit, sucking, licking, thrusting his fingers into me as I gasp his name.

The tension in my spine heightens, and I tug on his hair, my back arching more, hips raising to meet his fingers.

"You're close, Doctor. Come for me," he commands, his fingers thrusting into me faster, harder, his lips sucking hard on my clit. My legs tense, eyes squeezing shut, a blinding orgasm hitting its peak. My walls clench around his fingers as I pulse through each spasm, ploughing into me vigorously, pushing me over the edge.

"Keep going," he orders, my strangled moans growing louder, my heart completely bounding out of my chest. "Hold on to that feeling." He sits up and presses down below my navel, pumping his fingers into me more aggressively, adding another, stretching me.

His mouth is shiny from my arousal, and he licks his lips while he watches me, his rigid cock pressed against my leg. "All fucking mine," he growls, gritting his teeth as sweat drips down his forehead.

I'm powerless, the stimulation ripping through me, my body on fire. The waves of pleasure bursting through me have me moaning and convulsing on his hand as my entire body spasms, consumed by euphoria.

I raise my head from the bed, my mouth falling open with no sound coming out, my eyes widening as Tobias keeps going, riding my orgasm until the very end.

Tobias retracts his fingers and smirks at me. I'm boneless on the bed. He leans on his side next to me, pushing the cup of my lace bra aside to run his wet fingers over my hardened nipple. The feeling makes me slam my knees together and whimper, still trying to catch my breath. Trailing his fingers from my chest, over my throat, my jaw, he runs his middle finger along my lips. "Open up," he says. "I know you like to taste yourself."

Slowly parting my lips, I groan as Tobias pushes his finger in, pressing down on my tongue. "Suck," he orders, and I comply. I hear him deeply exhale out of his nose when I start to suck, tasting myself.

He stares down at my mouth, his bottom lip between his teeth. He moves his hand away, sits up, and pulls down his shorts, the hard, impressive muscle between his legs hanging free. "I'm going to fuck your mouth now, okay?"

Tobias doesn't give me a chance to move; he sets his knees on each side of my chest, his cock in his firm grip with his other hand woven through my hair, guiding my head until the tip presses against my lips. "Open that mouth for me."

Teasing him, I smile, shaking my head before I lick the swollen crown. He groans, his grip on my hair tightening.

Growling, he gulps as my tongue runs up the underside of his cock, watching his jaw tense when I reach the tip, savoring his precum.

"So beautiful," he says, biting down on his lip and sucking it in. His head falls back when I run my tongue up his length again, tracing the thick veins until I close my mouth over him. "Fuck, Aria."

Rolling my wet tongue around the swollen tip, I suck lightly, popping it back out of my mouth once more, making him huff in frustration. I try to reach up to grab him, but he snatches my wrist, his other hand still in my hair. "No. I want you to touch yourself."

I feel the butterflies return, the ones that have me soaked between my legs. "Again?" I ask, and he nods, easing forward while my lips are parted, the tip touching my teeth. "You're impossible to please," I say against the warm flesh, opening my mouth for him once more.

"Impossible?" He tilts his head and pushes his hips forwards, inch by inch, and I swallow him until he hits the back of my throat, making my eyes water as I gag. "I'll be satisfied when you stop talking, Doctor," he growls, and I narrow my eyes as he smirks down at me.

Using the grip on my hair to control my movements, he slides his thick cock down my tongue, hitting the back of my throat with each thrust.

I continually gag, my core already needing him again. He releases my wrist, and I do as I'm told, reaching down between my legs while I suck on his head. The saltiness on my tongue makes me hum in approval, the vibrations of my mouth causing his eyes to roll.

I plunge two fingers into my wetness, making me suck harder on his crown, swirling my tongue around the head before I swallow him again. My arousal coats my fingers as I circle them over my clit. It's an erotically foreign feeling, pleasuring myself while Tobias thrusts deeper into my mouth, grunting, swearing, his eyes screwed shut as his leg muscles tense.

I spread my legs wider, using both of my hands now to touch myself, Tobias still on his knees above me, rolling his hips erratically. "Fucking... You're..." He struggles with his words, my eyes watering as I stare up at him losing control, blowing out his cheeks as his movements become sloppier, my mouth slippery with saliva.

My eyes flutter closed as I start to feel myself building, the tension in my spine returning in full force. With my thighs crashing together, I moan with him still deep in my mouth. Tobias leans back and forces my legs open, pulling my head with one last thrust, moaning my name repeatedly as his cock stays buried to the hilt, making me gargle as I feel his salty cum runs down my throat.

I lose myself then, my walls contracting around my fingers as Tobias watches me fall apart.

"It wasn't too rough, was it?"

With us both lying on our sides, facing each other, Tobias' fingertips explore my body, running up and down my ribs. I shake my head, licking my lips as I stare at his face. His dimples are deep, his eyes a light shade of blue, *almost* grey. Although his hair is a mess right now, he's still fuckable, handsome, even.

"I didn't pull your hair too hard?"

Shaking my head again, I reach up to run my fingers through his dark locks. "I liked it."

He hums deeply, rubbing a palm up and down my arm, wrapping it around my waist to pull me flush against him. He gives me a soft kiss on the lips and presses his forehead to mine. "When do you leave?"

I don't want to have this discussion with Tobias. I dodged it as much as I could. Although it has only been a few weeks, I do think I'll miss him. Why do I feel emotional at the thought of leaving?

"Next week," I say, hooking my leg over his hip. "My flight's on Thursday night."

"I tried to help," he says, tucking a strand behind my ear before running his palm up my thigh, stopping at my knee on his side. "Doctor Blythe didn't budge."

"I know. I'm sorry."

The corner of his lip tugs up, and he settles his head closer to me on the pillow. "You don't need to say sorry, Aria. It's going to suck when you go, though."

Teasingly, I lean forward and kiss the side of his throat, licking the skin until I reach his earlobe, biting down playfully. "Will you miss me?" I whisper, his body tensing as I reach down to grab his semi hard-on in a firm grip, slowly pumping him in my palm. "Because I might just miss you."

He buries his head in the crook of my neck, running his palm up my spine and grabbing the nape of my neck. When his wet kisses press against my flushed skin, I moan, feeling his lips trail up my jawline until he reaches my lips, instantly diving into a deep, passionate kiss.

I gasp as his free hand drops between my legs, pushing a finger inside me easily. I feel him throb in my hand as I bite down on his bottom lip, tugging it until it snaps back into place. "So wet for me again," he groans before shoving his tongue into my mouth, both tilting our heads to deepen the kiss. Breathlessly, he pulls back for a second. "I need you, Aria," he admits, taking deep breaths as we look into each other's eyes before roughly kissing again.

We stay in this position, consuming each other in every way possible. I'm stuck in a seductive trance I never want to break free from.

Tobias eventually shifts us so he's hovering above me, still knuckle-deep as he curls his fingers, his thumb moving side to side on my clit, making me drop incoherent words against his parted lips.

Pumping his cock in my hand, twisting my wrist when I reach the tip, I feel his head bulge as I smear his precum with my thumb.

Tobias jerks back, and I release him from my hand, looking up at him kneeling between my legs, his fingers still attacking my core. His blue eyes are burning into me, and I gulp, feeling his fingers retract from my sex, making me whimper. "I might lock you up so you can't go back to Scotland."

I giggle, but he cuts me off with his mouth, his tongue pushing past my lips to run along mine. "I might like that too," I tease, my fingers lacing in his hair. He groans against my lips, biting me playfully, and I feel his crown press against my entrance. "Don't tempt me."

The heat moves up my neck as he trails his lips up to my throat, leaving tingles in their wake. Tobias bites the skin along my jaw playfully, whispering in my ear while pressing himself against my core.

Tobias smirks when he reaches my mouth, and I gasp as he finally eases his head past my soaked entrance, only to instantly pull out again. I groan in displeasure, hooking my ankles around his calves, raising my hips to feel his head press against my clit, a surge of pleasure rushing through me as he grinds up, running the underside up my slit.

"I want you to trust me with your body," he says, leaning up on his elbows to look down at me. I chew on my lip, nodding, knotting my fingers through his hair tighter, watching his eyes flutter closed at the contact. When he looks at me again, his eyes drop to my mouth, his tongue flicking out to lick his own before crashing down on mine, consuming me more than ever before.

With Tobias' lips glued to mine, I roll my hips up, feeling the tip of his length push through my dripping sex once more. The tingling sensation runs up my spine, and I want more, *so* much more.

"Wait," Tobias breathes, pulling away from me, his hands on each side of my head, still slightly inside. "How many glasses of wine did you drink?"

I've honestly lost count of the number of times we've gotten close to actually having sex, only to be interrupted. Tobias may be confusing me more than anyone I've ever come across, but my God, I'm about to kill him. "Two," I reply bluntly, blinking. "Same as you."

I frown at him as he sits back on his heels, leaving me empty once more. "You're sober, right?"

I can't help the annoyed tone in my voice. "Tobias..."

"I just don't want to fuck you when you're drunk," he admits, lifting a shoulder. "Surely you understand that?"

"And shoving your dick in my mouth an hour ago was okay?" I reply, and he tilts his head at me.

I reach up and intertwine my fingers around his neck, my nose nudging his as his eyes close. I place a kiss against his lips before traveling to the skin below his ear. "Relax," I sigh, pulling him to me and wrapping my legs around his waist. "I'm not drunk, Tobias. I want this."

He shivers at my touch. "Say that again."

"I want this. I want you."

132

Tobias' entire control vanishes, his facial features now calm, gentle, as he runs his thumb along my cheekbone, the corner of his lips curling up, dimples denting deep. The once fierce-looking man is now staring into my soul with adoration, making butterflies go wild inside me.

"You're so beautiful, Aria. I have no idea why you're letting me anywhere near you."

My heart shouldn't be flipping right now, but it is, and I'm blushing, chewing on my inner cheek. "I could say the same to you. You should be worried about me breaking your heart."

"Yeah?"

I nod. "Yep. Especially with the way you're looking at me right now."

I'm joking, obviously, but his eyes shine through the darkness. "Hmm."

Humming, he shakes his head and kisses me once again. It's soft, and instead of crushing my mouth, hungrily devouring me, he's passionately claiming my body, making my head sink into the pillow as the underside of his cock rocks against me.

His head pressing to my entrance, he straightens his arms and looks down at me. "You're sure?"

There's no cockiness in his voice. No smirking. No boldness that he's about to fuck my brains out. If anything, he looks worried.

"You're shaking."

I slide my hands up his sides as his arms tremble, his breaths rushing out like he's nervous. "Sorry," he whispers, closing his eyes and lowering his forehead to mine. "I don't want to hurt you. And I..." He stops, annoyed with himself. "I've only done this with one person."

"We don't have to if you're not comfortable."

He shakes his head. "I want to," he replies, and my back arches as he slowly enters me. He eases in, inch by inch, until he fills me. Letting out a burst of air, he places kisses on my throat as he slides out to the tip and thrusts back into me, making me whimper and dig my fingers into his back.

Slow and deep, Tobias thrusts into me as his lips crash down on mine. The fullness, the way his hips push me further into the mattress, the feeling of his body covering mine... My breath hitches, and a gasp spills into his mouth from my own.

I whimper as my spine arches, taking him deeper and making him groan against my ear.

Slowly, Tobias rocks his hips into mine, and I can feel every inch of him filling me. With each thrust comes a warm feeling, the heat creeping up my chest and neck. My eyes stay on his as we watch each other, enjoying the feeling as our bodies finally connect, our eyes burning every time we pull away from a kiss.

"I don't want you to be afraid of me," he admits, panting against my mouth, gripping the pillow on each side of my head. His controlled movements are slow but deep, completely burying himself in me and making my heart rate rocket.

Moaning, I try to reply, but he cuts me off with his mouth once again, his tongue darting past my lips, tilting our heads while our bodies move together.

I expected him to be rough, but his nerves are palpable, and I can feel the shaking of his bones with each thrust and kiss and whimper into my ear. The fact someone like Tobias is nervous about sex pickles my brain.

But there's also something special about it. He obviously doesn't screw around, or this wouldn't be a big deal for him. He's letting himself have this, and he's doing it with me.

A warmth builds inside me, and I'm not sure if it's from the revelation that Tobias might care for me, or if it's that mixed with how good his cock feels buried inside me, swelling with each rock of our hips.

I feel my walls clenching around him, suffocating his cock each time he ploughs into me, the invisible force between us strengthening, his movements becoming harsher, quicker, more intense. "Fucking hell, Aria," he moans, burying his head into the crook of my neck, panting against the flushed skin. "So fuck-ing...fucking wet."

I can't speak, my voice strangled, my lungs gasping for air as his pace speeds up, pummeling into me erratically, forcing my eyes to roll to the back of my head. My toes curl painfully, every nerve in my body on fire.

I have no idea how I'm going to fly back to Scotland and forget this guy exists. It's like he knows every single action that will drive me crazy, every single part of my body that needs attention, effortlessly making me writhe beneath him, moaning out his name in pure ecstasy.

He knows where to put his mouth to make me soaking wet, where to grab me to make me whimper, how much pressure my throat can take under his grip, just enough to drive me into another blinding orgasm.

I feel my walls close around him, his cock buried deep, his hands gripping my hips as he perches up on his knees. He wraps an arm around the small of my back to lift my hips, the other hand swirling circles around my sensitive clit. "Come for me, Doctor," he growls, his movements quickening as he keeps his cock buried deep, pressing against a spot that sends shockwaves up my spine.

My mouth falls open, our eyes still trained on each other, his blurry form above me. "Tobias," I cry, the sensation too much to handle. "Harder," I beg, my body spasming beneath him, pulsing around his cock.

I can feel his own body tensing as he does as he's told, his fingers stopping suddenly before he grabs one of my breasts, his other hand still holding me up before he starts to ram himself inside harder, making me scream his name.

I close my eyes when he pulls out of me, spraying cum over my stomach and chest, my head hitting the pillow, panting, breathlessly trying to speak.

I watch Tobias, my lungs slowly refilling. Licking his lips, he lazily rubs his hands over my chest, smearing his cum into my skin before running his thumb along my bottom lip. I dart my tongue out and taste him, humming my approval as my eyes close.

"Do I taste good, Doctor?"

Nodding, I smile up at him, wetting my lips when he removes his thumb.

Tobias grabs a towel and drops down on the bed next to me, perched on his side as he wipes his cum off my body. "Can I see you again?"

"What do you mean? We work in the same ward."

Shaking his head, he shifts to sit on the edge of the bed, wrapping his arms around my legs and pulling me to him. He looks at me, his eyes a dark shade of blue now, nearly overtaken by his dilated pupils. "No, I mean like this," he says, kissing my hip, making those annoying butterflies appear again.

"I leave next Thursday, Tobias. Would it be wise to do that?" I ask, tilting my head at him and cupping his face in my palms. "This will end when I leave. What if we catch feelings?"

For some reason, my words annoy him. He scoffs and forces a derisive laugh.

"You really think you'd break my heart? I'd need to have one first."

17

TOBIAS

The email is staring me in the face.

My stepfather, because he's incapable of calling or sending a message, has informed me that Lucy is becoming weaker and thinks it would be a good idea to transfer.

Since Aria is leaving soon, I decline, making sure I stay as close as possible to her. I still need to find a way to keep her here, or at least pursue something with me past sexual.

She must like me. Going by my contact, apart from that asshole Ewan, she has had one other sexual partner, someone I plan on visiting one day to strangle the fucking life out of, just for looking like a prick.

He looks like Ewan. He's smart, works in the same hospital as her, and he has money. I glance up at myself in the mirror, wondering if I go ink myself up and get rid of my glasses and all my medication, if she'd consider me acceptable as her type.

When I fucked her, I didn't want to leave the room. We stayed there for two days while Gabriella slipped in for a change of clothes and disappeared again. During those forty eight hours, we had clothes on for maybe two.

I was inside her too many times to count.

She'd fallen asleep, and I'd taken pictures of her face. I know that was wrong, a violation of privacy, but I needed something for when she left.

I pull my glasses off, my vision blurring as I watch myself, inspecting my facial features. I have a strong jawline like my father, a slim nose, straight teeth, long lashes. What else do I need to do to gain her affection? To make her fall in love with me so fucking hard, she never leaves me?

I missed my therapy session yesterday, and it got rescheduled to today, but I don't plan on going then either. I've found the only cure to my mortal mind is spending time with Aria.

My doctor will make me feel better.

She just needs to understand I'm different. I can be difficult and weird and harder to deal with, but I'll try. I'll try to be normal enough to be considered her partner.

Even if I need to remove all her previous partners so she has no one to compare me to.

I check my phone to see a message from her, asking what my plans are for dressing up at work tomorrow for superhero day.

ME

Lucy wants me to be an Avenger.

To be exact, she wants me to be a shield wielding guy with supersonic speed, stronger than anyone else on the planet. He's her favorite from watching all the movies.

DOCTOR MILLER

Cute. It's my last day tomorrow if you want to do one last thing together before I leave. Maybe a movie with Justin and Gabriella?

My jaw tightens until it hurts. She's implying we won't do anything after she flies home, that this is done.

Over my dead body.

18

ARIA

Monday comes faster than I hoped, and although it's Superhero day and we all get to dress up, it's my last shift at the hospital. It's also my last time ever working with Tobias, and a part of me is devastated by that.

He is still on the same ward, but he is no longer my assistant. Yet he still comes into my office, sneaks a kiss on the cheek, brings me coffee, and texts me throughout the day about how he can't wait for the shift to be over so we can hang out.

Honestly, I feel like a teenager again with a crush, and I like it. It keeps my mind off what's waiting for me back home: impending heartache.

Although, the thought isn't as bad now that I have Tobias keeping me company. I don't miss Ewan as much, but there's always that long-lasting, lingering love, and the fact I miss him.

I'm selfish and need to stop this with Tobias, because I'm starting to like him, really like him, and I know he likes me.

We agreed to keep things going the way it is for now, but when I fly back to Scotland, we will part ways. If I'm ever back in Florida, we can meet up, maybe continue where we left off.

I agreed to one last date, a parting gift of sorts for us both—a night at a restaurant followed by the movies, probably ending in a bar somewhere. Gabriella and Justin are coming too.

I pull my phone out, rereading his message from this morning. I slept in and haven't had time to reply yet.

TOBIASWORK

Can I just lock you up so you can't leave?

ME

I'm not sure how serious you're being, so I'm going to go with no. Plus, I doubt you have any skills in doing so.

TOBIASWORK

I'm offended, Doctor. Do I need to teach you a lesson again?

My thighs clench together, remembering his lesson in the shower last night before he left. Every time I made a sound, he removed his tongue from my pussy. He wanted to show me how much more intense my orgasm could be when I'm trying to hold in every moan and every whimper.

I practically fell apart in his arms, blinded by euphoria, and he carried me to bed and kissed my cheek before leaving.

ME

Maybe.

"What are you smiling at?" Gabriella taps her knuckles on the table between us. "Oh my, Aria. You're blushing."

Quickly, I toss my phone back into my bag and look up at my best friend. "Nothing," I say, averting my gaze out the cafe window, watching all the people rushing by.

"Doctor Shique is Iron Man," Gabs snorts, showing me a picture all the morning staff took together, crowding around the reception desk wearing their chosen costumes. "Poor kids. He probably ruined Stark for them, being the miserable bastard he is."

I roll my eyes at her, smirking. "He's not too bad."

"Did you get your costume?" she asks, and I nod, wiping my mouth with a napkin.

"Did you get the red and blue hair spray?"

"Yes," I reply. "And before you say she isn't a superhero, she's Ivy's favorite." I shrug, gathering our plates to take back to the counter and thank the server. I turn back to Gabs, raising my brows. "Ready for our last day?"

"Nope," she replies, grabbing her coat and following me out the door.

DURING THE MEETING at the start of our work day, all the staff gather in the break room, discussing patients and what needs to be done. They offer a farewell and a thank you for joining them and hope we enjoy our final day on the ward.

I blush as they clap.

Gabriella is down at the labs, my temp assistant on her break, and I'm now sitting at reception, reading over Ivy's final report, chewing my thumbnail and signing on the dotted line that I'll be arranging her pick up at Glasgow airport with one of our trained staff.

"You even sprayed your hair red and blue. That's dedication," I hear a familiar voice, and my mood instantly lifts. "Have you already had lunch?" Tobias asks, leaning his elbows on the reception desk, dressed as Captain America. "You look pretty, by the way."

I turn my wrist to look at my watch. "And you look," I stop, running my eyes over his swollen muscles through the spandex suit, "hot." I shake my head to rid myself of the dirty thoughts, trying to remember we're at work. "I'm about to go on my lunch break."

"Good. I have something to show you." I tilt my head, and he looks me up and down, smiling, tapping on the reception desk once. "Give me ten minutes."

The grin stays on my face as he turns and walks away, even

while I read the rest of Ivy's file. I close the report, standing and grabbing my foam hammer, holding it to my shoulder as I walk to Ivy's room.

I tried on the netted tights with the costume, but I was far too exposed to be walking around a children's hospital ward, so I instead opted for thick black tights. "Good afternoon, Mrs. Dermot," I say, knocking on the door to see Ivy's mom packing. "Do you need a hand?"

"That would be great, Aria. Ivy's still asleep."

I look over at the little girl, her face completely relaxed and at ease. I feel my chest tighten, gulping away a lump forming. "I'm sorry. I really thought we could do something here." I fold up a pink blanket and place it in the bag.

She reaches over, her hand over mine, giving me a warm smile. "Don't apologize. You did everything you could."

Yet, I still feel like I could've done more.

I help her finish packing up most of Ivy's things, arranging the bags at the side of the room. We sit together until porters come to transport them to a hotel next to the airport.

I step out of her now-empty room and sigh.

"Ready?" I hear Tobias behind me. "I found something you might like."

I bite down on my lip as he leads me down to the basement stairway. "Where are we going?"

"Follow me," he says, his hand on the small of my back. We make it to the very bottom of the stairs, the underground area where the cleaners and drivers come in from. He looks around as we walk through the cool hallway, stone walls and flooring making it feel eerily haunted.

"You're not kidnapping me, are you?"

He laughs, looking around once more before opening a door and shoving me in. I gasp, feeling his arm wrap around my waist as he shuts the door, locking it behind him.

His mouth is on mine within seconds, inhaling deeply as his hand moves to the side of my neck. I melt into the kiss, running my hands up the suit.

He pulls away so we can catch our breath, coated in darkness. Tobias moves around, keeping his hand around my waist until he turns the light on, and I laugh, glancing around us. "A broom closet?"

"Yep." He smiles, bringing my head back to him, kissing me once more. He breaks away from it just as fast, breathless, backing me up against a table and lifting me onto it, settling between my legs. "My good doctor needs to go out with a bang, right?"

I feel myself getting wet between my legs. This feels so...*forbidden*. It is, and it's making me even more turned on.

My heart needs to figure out a way to stop beating irregularly, threatening to blow through my chest—the intensity rushing through me while Tobias kisses down my neck, slowly unbuttoning my shorts, has me starving for his touch.

"Can we really do this here?" I ask, breathlessly trying to unzip his suit at the back, watching as it drops to the floor, revealing his toned body, his powerful shoulders and back. I quickly peek at my watch as I sit on the metal table, and my eyes widen at the time. "We only have fifteen minutes."

He ignores my words, pulling my body to his and kissing me harder. One of his hands runs up my spine until he reaches my neck, clamping his palm around my nape. With each swipe of his tongue over mine, every bite on my lip, I feel myself pooling, my panties definitely soaked.

The coolness of this room is replaced with a furnace, a scorching inferno, the heat engulfing me as Tobias continues to ravage me, gripping me, tilting his head to the side to deepen the passionate kiss.

"My doctor," he drawls, leaning his forehead against mine as we both take deep breaths. "I'm going to miss staring at your ass around here."

I try to hide my smirk, but it's pointless. "Then maybe you shouldn't be looking in the first place."

Grinning, he bites his lip, running both hands up and down my sides, electricity running through me from his touch. "I can't help it; you're beautiful. I'm still clueless as to why you would even want me."

"What is that supposed to mean?" I ask, wrapping my arms around his neck tighter. "Should I not want you?"

"I'm not your type."

"And how would you know what my type is?" she counters.

He shrugs, placing a soft kiss to my lips. "If you were smart, you wouldn't let me anywhere near you."

Tilting my head, I glare at him, my eyes narrowed to slits. "I am smart."

"Debatable. Depending on how this ends, you might need to run."

The smile grows on my face. "What happens if I run from you?"

"I'll hunt you down, Doctor," he says, pushing hair behind my ear. "Because you're mine."

I let out a laugh and push his chest. "We only have fifteen minutes, Tobias," I repeat, crossing my ankles behind him to pull him back into me, the cold steel table beneath me doing absolutely fuck all to ease the fire running through my core. "Do something."

He pulls away from me, his sea blues searching my face as he ponders his next move. "Hmm," he hums, nudging my cheek with his nose so I move my head to the side, allowing him access to drag wet kisses down my throat. "Do something," he repeats. "And what exactly do you want me to do?"

I feel myself aching for him, every nerve in my body exploding from the feel of his mouth on my sensitive skin. "I...I don't know," I stutter. "Anything."

He brings his hand between us, heat rising up my spine the lower he drops it. "Do you want me to touch you?" He nibbles on my earlobe, and I can't hold in the strangled whimper any longer, nodding quickly. I can feel him smiling against my neck as he finally dips his hand between my legs and runs his finger up my slit, making my legs tense around his body.

"Always so wet for me, Doctor," he purrs in my ear, gently

gliding his finger over my entrance. He continues to spread my arousal, barely touching my clit as he glides over it.

Moving his face to mine, he bites my bottom lip, making me softly moan into his mouth with each stroke. I grit my teeth as he shoves two fingers inside of me, finding a rhythm that nearly pushes me over the edge within seconds.

"Can you feel what you do to me?" He presses his hardness against my inner thigh, groaning against my lips when I palm him through his black boxers. He drops his head to my shoulder when I dip my hand in and start to pump, twisting my wrist as I reach the tip.

Quickly, he pulls away from me, grabbing my hips and flipping me on the steel table, making me shriek in surprise. He stretches my hands out in front of me to grip the edge of the table, kissing my neck as his body leans over me.

With me bent over at the waist, he tugs down my shorts and tights to my ankles, making me pant, anticipating his touch.

He kicks my legs open wider and positions himself as I eagerly wait, trying to control my breathing, my eyes rolling at the anticipation.

I flinch as I feel something wet hit my ass, tensing all over as he pushes his thumb against my hole. My mouth drops open, and I grip the table as he eases the tip of his thumb into my ass.

"I'm not going to be gentle," he tells me, pulling his thumb out and lining his cock up with my entrance, rubbing the tip through my arousal.

Just as I feel his head pushing into me, a sound buzzes from his costume heaped on the ground. "You've got to be kidding me," he swears, keeping a grip on one of my hips as he leans over to grab his phone, pressing it to his ear, using his shoulder to keep it in place while he straightens back up behind me.

My eyes widen, looking back at him as he grabs my hip with one hand and pushes into me. "Tobias," he says, because he's incapable of simply saying "hello".

Thrusting deep, he stays in place as he hums in agreement and tells someone to transfer him over. My breath hitches as he starts to fuck me, and I'm biting down on my lip, white-knuckling the table from his fast pace.

"Don't make a fucking sound," he warns me with a punishing thrust that rattles the table, and I think my pussy contracts so tightly, I might have leaked some cum down my leg.

My brows knit together as he pulls away abruptly, and I turn to look at him. He steps back and starts to pull up his boxers, his face turning pale white.

"Fuck," he spits, hanging up and rushing to get dressed. "Lucy coded."

19

TOBIAS

Lucy is dead.

What is even the point of life when it's so easily lost?

I was supposed to spend time with her, and I cancelled, sending a nurse so I could fuck Aria in a broom closet, and now, my conscience is eating at me so fucking painfully, I want to punch something.

I need it to hurt.

Aria has messaged me a few times, asking me if I want to hang out at her hotel and help her pack before she leaves, but I can't. Not yet. I need to continue my research in loss. I'm not sure how to handle it. I've never been good at emotions. I'm always getting attached to feelings that make no sense.

Take my doctor, for example. I have no idea how I feel about her, but I know I feel something powerful.

She will know how to fix me, right?

Maybe something in my brain isn't right, and I just need to feel something more to break through the wall in my mind.

My therapist is gonna kill me. I cancelled again.

My mom has called a few times. Violetta Mitchell—now Blythe—doesn't know when to leave me the fuck alone.

Blythe, my stepdad, has emailed demanding I take time off work and come home, but I blocked the sender.

Apart from Justin, I have no one else.

Aria makes me feel good.

I need to keep her.

I will keep her.

Because she might not know it yet, but she's mine.

Her fucking friend is an asshole–when she walked in on me trashing the place after finding out Lucy was gone, she told me to back off Aria. She'd found out from Justin that I'm heavily doped up on drugs for my mental health and apparently, Aria deserves better. She won't tell her friend, but I have to end things and not ruin Aria's life.

So instead of giving in to her goddamn threat, I haven't taken my meds, and I won't. They're all already flushed down the toilet.

I'll prove to that bitch I can handle myself perfectly fucking fine, that I can be more than enough for Aria. And when Aria agrees to marry me, she isn't invited to the wedding. If I somehow get her pregnant, which would actually be terrible considering what I'm like, she isn't getting anywhere near our kids.

She's trying to ruin what we have, and I might just kill her.

If I knew how to do it without being caught, her body would already be nonexistent.

I slam my laptop shut and pace in my kitchen. I have sixteen hours until she leaves. Her flight isn't canceled, and there's nothing to keep her in America. She needs me to help her pack her suitcases, so I send a message back that I'll be over soon and get showered and dressed.

All I can think about is keeping her. Why the fuck would I want to pack her goddamn suitcases?

I might burn them, maybe steal her passport, cage her, keep her trapped in my bedroom. A plethora of ideas cross my mind, but most will result in her hating me.

I did do some more research on Stockholm syndrome, and although it sounds possible, I want her genuine love.

Think, Tobias. Think. Think. Think.

How do we keep her?

How do we take this beautiful, smart woman and make her love us?

It's all we need. Loyalty and affection and marriage and kids will all come eventually; however, I'd rather not spring young versions of myself on her, since I'm a trainwreck most days, especially now as erratic thoughts of kidnapping her are becoming more and more and more and more clear in my mind.

I could do it.

Would I?

Maybe.

Yes.

Aria meets me at the hotel entrance, not caring that we're in public as she walks right up to me and kisses my cheek. "I'm sorry about Lucy."

My chest burns with rage, but I ignore it and gesture for her to move towards the elevators.

Her hand is in mine the whole way up to her hotel room, and I measure her from behind for the size of cage I could keep her in, smiling forcefully at her when she turns around. "Stop staring at my butt."

She wishes that was what I was doing.

No, my dear, darling, beautiful doctor. I'm calculating how easy it will be to make you disappear, to keep you forever, while also making you fall for me, continue to fuck me, and smile at me the way you are right now.

My leash is gone. I don't know what it is, but I can feel myself slipping so fucking fast, and the only thing keeping me grounded is this human being with a heartbeat.

20

ARIA

Pulling up on the sidewalk across from his place, Tobias releases my thigh from his hold, turning off the engine. I lean over him to look at the three-story building.

"That's all yours?"

"Yeah," he says quietly, gulping.

I climb out to get a better look, meeting him at the bumper of his car. "I want to ask if you are some sort of drug dealer or maybe a mass murderer who steals people's money."

"Nope." Tobias taps his nose before wrapping his arms around my waist, pulling me against him. "I'm just a really good assistant."

I hum, circling my arms around his neck, kissing his lips softly. "You're a shit assistant, to be honest. All you ever did was distract me."

He snorts, shaking his head. "You distracted me."

"Whatever." I roll my eyes, a loud scream echoing around us as Tobias lifts me up and wraps my legs around his waist. He hooks my ankles behind him as he carries me across the road, pressing the key over his shoulder, the beep from the car indicating it's locked. "I can walk, you know?"

"Doctor, after tonight, you won't be able to walk for the rest of your time here. I don't plan on letting you leave my bed, not even to catch the flight."

"But Gabriella is picking me up later."

"That won't stop me from fucking your brains out," he replies.

I bite my lip to hide my grin, burying my head in his shoulder as he taps in his code to open his security gate. With me still wrapped around him, he walks us up the pathway, pressing my back against the stone wall beside the double-doored entrance, making me feel warm, comfortable, and a little turned on.

"I'll get your bags from the car later," he says, pressing his lips against mine. "But I'm bending you over the table on the other side of this door as soon as I unlock it."

"Oh, really?" I tighten my legs around his waist, the strain of his hardening cock through his shorts rubbing directly where I want him. He nods, licking his lips as he stares at mine. Tilting his head, our mouths find each other with such force, I let out a soft moan, his tongue pushing through my parting lips, hungrily claiming me. He only releases one of my thighs to fumble his keys in the door, unlocking it and dragging us inside the house.

With the lights out, darkness surrounds us, and Tobias releases me, my body sliding down his front. His hands grasp at my behind as he pushes his cock against me. Our clothes drop to the floor as we walk backwards, Tobias pulling my hair free from my ponytail and wrapping his hands in my blonde strands, claiming my mouth once more as my fingers wrap tightly in his hair.

Tobias lifts me onto the table, settling himself between my legs. Pulling my hair so he has enough access to destroy my neck with his mouth, he kisses, sucks, nipping along my collarbone as I feel his crown press against my soaking wet entrance, throbbing for him to thrust into me.

I have no idea what possesses me, but I let out a chuckle mid-pant. "This isn't exactly bending me over."

Tobias groans and flips me over, slapping my ass so hard, I yelp.

With the polished wood below me, my cheek pressed against the table, Tobias rams into me with such force, the lamp teeters before shattering across the floor.

I moan, a strangled sound that repeatedly falls from my throat with each thrust into my soaking core, making my spine tingle and my eyes roll to the back of my head.

"Is this what you want, Doctor? You want me to fuck you this way?"

I cry out as he presses a finger into my ass, pushing through the back hole while fucking my pussy so hard, I think I might explode any moment.

His hand lands on my ass again when I only reply with a nod. "Words."

"Yes," I pant. The positioning of his cock pushing into me makes it nearly impossible to not beg him to go harder, faster, deeper. The way he's fingering my tight hole, the curses dropping from his mouth as he buries himself even deeper...

I feel the building sensation at the bottom of my spine, my walls starting to close around him. "Tobias," I whimper, my legs tensing.

He pulls his finger out, and his cock gives one last thrust before he leaves my pussy empty.

"No, what are you doing?" I pant, turning to him. He smirks, grabbing the back of my head and crashing his lips to mine, taking my breath away as he lifts me up, slamming my back to the wall as he eases into my soaking entrance once more.

"Jesus," I whimper at the intense pleasure that comes with him thrusting into me, his mouth fused to mine, hands grasping at my ass.

"Not even he can save you, Doctor."

I bite down on his lip, hard enough that he hisses, and the metallic taste of Tobias' blood seeps into my mouth. "I don't need to be saved; I need you to fuck me harder." I lick my lips, probably looking like a crazy person while he pounds into me. "So do it."

Tobias's eyes darken, becoming hooded as he stares at my mouth, and he releases one of my legs so he can run his thumb along my bottom lip. He watches the red smudge with a fascinated gaze while I study him, zoned into what he's doing.

He's in a complete trance, as if he's drunk on the sight.

"I like the look of my blood on your lips."

"Then give me more," I reply, breathless, licking the blood from my lips.

His hand returns and tightens under my thighs, the touch of pain sending shocks through my body as I fist a handful of his hair, pulling it harshly until he moans into my mouth. "Fuck," he drawls, halting his movements when I suck his lip, tasting more of him. "Aria, I need—"

He doesn't finish his words; he just pounds into me faster, making the back of my head smack against the wall, my nails digging into his skin as my body starts to tremble, the fire stirring once again.

Just like before, he stops right before I come, dragging us away from the wall, sweat pouring off our naked bodies as we get halfway up the stairs. My legs are still wrapped around his waist, his cock sliding into me while he grabs the banister on the stairway.

He doesn't move this time–I do. With my hands wrapped around his neck, I use him as leverage, a way to powerfully move against him. His length stretches me, his swollen crown deep inside, hitting that sweet spot that has my body shuddering, another surge of pleasure slapping me across the face, a moan ripping from my throat, trailed by his name.

His hand pushes against the small of my back, stopping me, keeping himself buried as he reaches the top of the stairs, both of us breathless as he pushes open his bedroom door.

With barely any energy and sweat dripping from us both, Tobias lazily kisses me until the mattress meets my back. Leaning over, he keeps his mouth on mine, the cool bedding and the breeze from his slightly open balcony door soothing my heated skin.

His tongue runs along mine as we devour each other before he licks across my jaw, down my neck, sucking harshly on my collarbone, claiming me as his before I head home to Scotland.

All my senses are heightened; even the feel of his lips on my skin makes me want to cross my legs, my soaking core desperate for his cock, his fingers, anything.

"Touch me," I beg, pulling him on top of me so he settles between my legs, his cock weighing heavy on my inner thigh.

"Where?" he asks, teasing me, his nose running along my jaw, his tongue running up my throat before he grabs it, applying slight pressure, sending all my nerves into overdrive. "Do you want me to touch you here?" His palm cups my pussy, my clit throbbing. The sensation goes straight down my legs and up my spine, ready to explode as his fingers glide up my slit, pushing inside me to gather my wetness.

He removes his fingers, circling my clit slowly, keeping the trail going up my stomach, circling my nipple, making me jolt when he pinches it before ending at my mouth, easing them past my lips.

"Suck," he orders, gagging me when his knuckles hit my teeth, my eyes watering, eager for him to consume me.

I don't find it as surprising this time. Instead, I find it...appealing? Maybe it's the look in his eyes, or maybe it's the fact that he's lining himself up at my entrance while his fingers are down my throat, but either way, I love it.

I also love that he doesn't wait around, pushing in until his body smacks against mine, completely burying himself inside me with one roll of his hips.

"I want you to come with my fingers down your throat," he orders, his thumb digging into my cheek while his cock eases out of me fully, making me gargle a gasp when he fully pushes back inside, the tip hitting my sweet spot.

His fingers slip from my mouth, replaced with a desperate kiss that consumes me. The blinding white lights of my pleasure have me spiraling into a frenzy, my orgasm hitting its peak just as Tobias picks up his pace, gripping my hair and pulling so my throat is fully exposed.

He moves his lips to my neck, sucking the delicate skin as another hand moves to push two fingers past my lips again, gagging me as his teeth sink into my shoulder, intensifying my wave of euphoria. He stills on a deep moan, filling me as my heart accelerates and my breathing quickens, gasping for air when he eventually retracts his fingers.

Tobias rolls off me and lies on his back, looking over at me as we both heave for breaths, his smile gleaming, his dimples clear in the moonlight shining in from the balcony.

I grin, moving on to my side, running my fingers up his abs, tracing each impressive muscle, each ridge, right up until I reach his face. He's watching me closely.

"I like you, and I'm going to miss you," I admit. "Is that bad?"

He nods. "Very. You shouldn't tell me that."

"Why?"

"Admitting to me that you feel anything means I'm yours," he says, leaning up to press a soft, chaste kiss to my lips. "And you're mine."

"I said this would end when I left, and you didn't argue on it."

His shoulder raises. "That's before you told me you liked me."

"Tobias..." I sigh his name.

He rolls me over, dragging me against his chest. "Fine, but I get to cuddle you to sleep one last time."

I'm not sure who passes out first, but my eyes grow heavy from my post sex bliss, his arms tight around me, and I fall asleep on his chest.

21

ARIA

The airport is busy—we've been standing at the check-in for what feels like hours. Gabriella has taken to using her suitcase as a seat while I try to stay awake.

"What did you buy Jason?" Gabs nudges me once more, frowning when I don't reply. "Hello? Earth to Aria?"

"Sorry. I'm just tired," I reply, running my palm across my forehead. The air conditioning in this airport is doing nothing to stop the heat. "I'll jump into Duty Free once we go through security and see what I can find for him."

"What about a souvenir? Or maybe—"

The buzzing of my phone takes all of my attention, blocking her words out. Quickly, I unlock the screen to see messages from Tobias.

> TOBIASWORK
>
> What the fuck, Aria? You left?
>
> TOBIASWORK
>
> What did I do?
>
> TOBIASWORK
>
> Three missed calls.

Guilt takes over me. I left his place a few hours ago. Gabriella picked me up, and we came straight here. I had no idea how to say goodbye, so I wrote him a note that basically said if I ever visit again, I'll hit him up.

"Oh God." I lift the screen for Gabs to see, and she raises her brows. "What do I say back?" I ask, chewing on my bottom lip. "I didn't even wake him to say goodbye."

She shrugs, repositioning her glasses to hold her grown-out bangs from her face. "Do you still want to talk to him? I mean, I told Justin it was done before he left for work this morning, and he understood. Did you not explain to him that when you left, that was it—done?"

"It was supposed to be just sex anyway."

"When is it ever?" she asks, and we continue walking until we reach the food court, taking a seat next to one of the stores and waiting for Doctor Shique. He's always late. "It's better to be honest, Aria."

Looking down at my screen, I see five missed calls and countless messages. I read the most recent, my heart sinking.

TOBIASWORK

> I know I'm not the easiest person to be around, Aria. I can be a dick and I'm sorry. Please answer the phone so I can talk to you, I'm losing my mind here. Please tell me what I did.

I have no idea what to say to him, because he didn't actually do anything. I'm still battling in my head whether I should stay in contact, see how things go, or block him and forget this ever happened.

I like Tobias—I really like him. But there are so many issues with us being together. Plus, how do I tell him that although I feel something for him, I still feel for Ewan?

I close out his messages and pull up Ewan's, asking if he's available for a call. I need to figure out what we're doing about

Jason. I want to see him, maybe have him over for a sleepover with Gabriella so we can play board games and watch movies.

I can't help it; I've been in Jason's life for years. We grew extremely close over the years, even after Ewan and I split for good. He's not my biological child, but he's very important to me, and I couldn't imagine my life without him.

"Hello?" Ewan answers on the third ring, making me side-eye Gabs as she clicks away on her screen. I tap her shoulder and point to the store, telling her I'll be back in five minutes.

"Hi, um...I was going to get a gift for Jason. Anything in particular he would like?"

He lowers his voice to a whisper. "He's next to me. Two seconds." I hear shuffling around, beeping in my ear indicating another message from Tobias, I slide the notification bar down, seeing loads of question marks. "You don't need to bring him anything back."

Walking through one of the gift stores, I lift up a snow globe, trying to hold back a smile when I see palm trees inside, little specs of fake snow floating around in it. "It's okay. I found him something he'll love. I wanted to ask you a favor, though."

"Anything," he replies, clearing his throat and repeating the word with less desperation.

"Don't tell my mom or dad I'm coming back yet if they ask. I kind of need some time alone before I start back on Monday." Images of my parents crowding me...it's not something I can handle right now. They are both high profile scientists, and anything I do with my career never seems good enough in their eyes.

"Are you okay?" he asks when I'm unable to hide the tremble in my voice, my lip involuntarily shaking.

"Of course."

"You sound a bit off. Surely you're not still scared of flying?" He laughs, making me fight back a smile and a sob.

Thanking the cashier, I grab my receipt and lean my back against the cool airport wall, standing at the entrance of the store.

I see Gabriella as she talks on the phone, waving to Doctor Shique across the food court.

"I couldn't save her," I say, a lump forming in my throat, nearly suffocating me as I try to continue. "Trial failed. They sent Ivy home so they can just..." I look up, a lone tear escaping down my cheek, and I wipe it away with my hand. "They just want to continue to treat her symptoms."

He takes a deep breath. "I'm so sorry, Aria. I know she's important to you. Please don't hate yourself. You do more than any other specialist, and Ivy is lucky to have you."

The corner of my mouth tugs up, but my heart is shattering. "I came here for Ivy, and instead of solely focusing on her, I got too caught up with—" I stop myself. Ewan doesn't need to know everything I've been doing. "I just feel like I should've done more."

Typical Aria, looking for comfort from my ex. But right now, he seems to be the only one who can actually calm me down, listen to me without interrupting, letting me vent until my throat goes dry. I don't need him in a passionate, loving way; I need him as a friend.

"Look, Aria—"

"The plane's boarding. Let's go!" Gabriella appears beside me, cutting off whatever Ewan is about to say. "Is that Toby?"

I hang up as soon as the words leave her mouth and shake my head no, hurrying next to her as we make our way through the terminal. "It was Ewan. I was asking about Jason."

"Damn. I hope he heard me. You know, so he gives up trying to win you back."

She gives me a knowing look, and I ignore her, showing my pass to the flight attendant before walking onto the plane and taking my seat next to the window. Staring out, a strong feeling of failure floods through me, making me bite down on my lip and lean my head back against my seat.

My phone vibrates once more. Another message comes through, Tobias again.

TOBIASWORK

I'm going to fix myself. Gabriella was right. I'm not good enough for you. But I'm going to be better. Just tell me I still have a chance. I miss you.

My eyes flash over at Gabriella. "Did you say this?"

I show her the screen, and she waves her hand nonchalantly. "I was messing around."

Knowing her, she was brutal. I need to calm Tobias down before he truly does appear in Scotland.

ME

I have no idea what she said, but that's not true. The only reason this has to end is because I'm not ready for anything serious. I'm sorry.

Then, against everything within me, I block his number and cut him out of my life altogether. It's for the best. We had no chance.

I used him yet started to fall for him in the process, so this is me safeguarding myself. Besides, I need to go home and face the music of Ewan and Jason, figure out what my future holds.

Part of me dreads having to tell Ewan someone else had my time while in America, but then again, he gave his time to someone else while we were still together.

I wipe a tear slipping down my cheek and rest my head against the window.

22

ARIA

Ewan hands me Jason's school bag, leaning his elbows on the rolled-down window of my white Mercedes.

His green eyes shine in the sunlight, the stubble on his face hiding what I know is a perfect jawline. Jason climbs into the back seat and says bye to his dad while I stare forward, anxiety hitting me at what I've been doing for the last few weeks with Tobias.

I feel guilty. Although we aren't together, it still feels wrong to let another man touch me when I love someone else. I know Ewan would set the world on fire for me, so I just look like a horrible person.

He needs to know.

"I like your hair," he tells me, gesturing to the freshly dyed brown locks. "You haven't been brown since you were twenty."

I force a nervous smile. "I needed a change."

Correction, I needed Tobias out of my system, and he loved my blonde hair.

"Do I need to pick Jason up from school too?"

He shakes his head, and I nod, turning my engine on, making him step back. "Thanks again," he says, rubbing the back of his head. "I'll speak to you later?"

"Sure," I reply, and for the first time in a while, I want to speak to him. I want to see him. It could be the guilt strangling me, or maybe it's the realization I may have messed up more than him.

"Ewan?" I call out as he turns back to his work building, the small metal container next to the construction site. He's wearing old clothes, rigger boots, and a streak of oil marks down the side of his face.

"Yeah?"

The sun shines in his eyes when he reaches my car, leaning into my window once more. His forest greens have specks of hazel, rimmed with a darker shade of green, completely captivating me for a long second before I shake it off. "Gabriella is away and she usually fixes it, but the washer is jammed again. Can you do it?"

"Of course. I'll come by later."

I smile at him, the young, reckless boy I grew up with nowhere to be seen, replaced with a man, a new and improved Ewan. But that doesn't mean I forgive him or even want anything with him. I'd like to be friends. I enjoy being around him even if it's for the wrong reasons, especially when I feel a void caused by a certain someone. "I'll order food in."

"I don't want to overstep, Aria."

I huff, placing two hands on my steering wheel. "You aren't."

"But...Tobias? Gabriella told me."

I'm going to kill her.

My eyes momentarily leave his, and I look at my lap, chewing on my bottom lip. "I ended things with him." The look on his face makes me fight back a smile, something like relief washing over him, but he quickly glances away.

"I'll just come fix it and leave," he tells me, stepping back from the car. "I'll see you when I finish work."

"Thank you."

"Good luck with your presentation. You'll smash it, as always," he continues, and my eyes meet his again for a split second.

I put my car in reverse and drive away, not daring to give Ewan one last look.

Jason is in the back, headphones on, listening to whatever music he downloaded onto his dad's old phone. He smiles at me in the mirror, and I return it, driving him to the school entrance, saying goodbye, and making my way to my presentation.

23

ARIA

Peeking through the curtains lined along the side of the huge stage, I pale, seeing every chair filled, crowds of professionals waiting with notepads and pens, ready to take notes on everything I have to say.

"Okay, five minutes, and you're on, Aria," the stage director announces, fixing a microphone onto the front of my white shirt, tucking the small box into the back of my black pencil skirt. "If you need to take a break for water or a breather, just do it."

"Right," I reply, taking deep breaths. It's not like I'm not used to these, but this is the largest one I've done. I'm a confident woman, but right now, I feel like I'm going to pass out and bring up my breakfast on top of this dude's pair of shiny shoes.

Swirling water around my mouth, I make sure my throat is lubricated and ready to speak for an entire hour. I try to remember certain notes and accept that I'm going to screw it up, but I'm unable to think straight, my palms sweaty, heart beating heavily in my ears.

The lights start to dim, and the presenter walks onto the stage, thanking everyone for travelling here, giving an introduction about me–how I earned my qualifications, travelled to numerous hospitals around the world, in partnerships, and many facts that make me even more nervous not to screw this up.

Straightening, I concentrate on not tripping over my heels as I walk onto the stage, the applause from the crowd easing me somewhat as I give them a wave, shaking hands with the presenter before standing beside a large projector.

"Thank you everyone for coming today. As you already know, my name is Aria Miller, and I'm a clinical scientist working closely with multiple organizations to help research rare diseases."

I watch them all, keeping eye contact as my heart starts to race. I turn to the screen, using the clicker to change the slide.

"Today, I'm here to talk to you all about a rare disorder called Ribose-five-phosphate isomerase deficiency, or RPI deficiency for short." Clicking the next screen, I continue to explain the disorder, how only four people in a twenty-seven-year period have been diagnosed, how it affects the body, and how it's diagnosed.

I show them my recent finding; it's currently the rarest genetic disease in the world.

"This autosomal recessive disorder has no treatment, nor does it have a prognosis because it's so rare."

I scan the crowd as they all jot down notes, some nodding, some chewing their pens, some on their phones paying no attention. Those are the ones I want to launch the clicker at and glare at them for wasting my time when someone else could be here in their place, actually learning something.

It goes on for another twenty minutes, my throat going dry.

"Does anyone have any questions at the moment?" I ask, several hands raising. I accept a few questions confidently and move on.

Before I can turn to continue, one more hand raises, and I need to focus my eyes to see all the way to the back.

The blood drains from my face as the clicker hits the floor.

No, I mouth, my lips parting more each passing second before I shake off my shock.

"Yes?" I ask the person to speak up, gulping down a large,

painful lump as Tobias stands from his seat and straightens out his tie, dressed in a fitted, dark grey suit and white shirt.

I want to run off this stage and tell him to leave, but I also battle against my hormones, the mere sight of him igniting something deep within me, like I'm some sex crazed idiot.

"Am I correct in saying only children have been diagnosed with this disorder, Doctor?"

With my nails digging into my palm, I nod, struggling with my words. "That's...that's right. Only children and teenagers have been diagnosed with this...so far."

He takes his seat, a smirk on his face as I try to pull my eyes away from him, a fire building in me and I'm not sure if it's the good or the bad kind.

I lift the clicker from the floor, changing to the next screen, sweat now coating my forehead. "Um," I mumble, losing my position and words, my head scrambling.

Turning to the crowd, I try to regain some sort of composure, the crowd waiting for me to continue. I push my glasses up my nose, taking short breaths to make sure I appear calm, but inside, I'm spiraling.

"We're going to take our break now, and we will continue in..." I look down at my watch, plastering on my fakest smile when I lift my head again. "Twenty minutes."

I hurry off the stage, my mind whirling as a large hand pulls my arm at the bottom of the steps, dragging me straight into an empty room. "What's wrong? You were doing so well."

Tobias's icy blue eyes are burning into me, his brows furrowing, and I fight back the urge to slap him for nearly messing up one of the most important presentations I've ever done.

I'm still trying to process Tobias standing in front of me. I stare down at his hand on my arm, his thumb stroking up and down over the white material of my shirt.

"Why are you here?" I snap at him, moving his hand off me and crossing my arms. "And how did you know where my presentation was?"

He shrugs, tilting his head at me as I scowl at him. He narrows his eyes, looking lost. "You left and blocked me. What was I supposed to do?"

"You need to go home, Tobias."

He looks confused. "Why?"

"This," I point between us, "isn't a thing, remember? It was over when I left."

"You're mad," he huffs, standing back and pushing his hands into his pockets. "I want you to... No, I *need* you to understand me. I can't do that when you've cut me out."

If I wasn't seething with rage right now, I would hug him, tell him I missed his annoying face, kiss him until my lips feel raw. But I don't. Instead, I scowl at him until he gives me a reasonable explanation. He stands in front of me looking deflated, confused, and, if anything, hurt by my reaction.

"I missed you, Aria."

He steps forward so he's close to me once more, his cologne filling my nose, and I feel my anger starting to fade, especially when the corners of his lips curl, his dimples deep, hands gently touching my folded arms.

"I want a chance."

Delicately, his knuckles tip up my chin so I look at him, hot bursts of breath hitting my face. I blow out my cheeks, sinking into his touch. "I don't know how to do this with you. I'm not ready for a relationship."

"We don't need to be in one. We can continue our arrangement by visiting each other, fucking it out, then repeating the cycle," he replies, leaning down so his forehead rests on mine, my heart racing at an unhealthy pace. I'm trying to regulate my breathing so I don't show him he affects me in ways I wish he didn't, but I know I'm failing. "Say yes."

"I don't know," I answer honestly.

"You look beautiful, by the way." He looks at my dark hair, his right eye twitching as he curls a lock around his finger. "Suits you."

I run my tongue over my lips to wet them, looking away from his intense gaze. "Thanks." I move as he tries to lean in further, dodging his kiss. He huffs, dropping his hands to his sides and stepping back. "I need to go back on. This is important to me."

Tobias follows behind me, splitting when I reach the stairway to the front stage, giving me a look over his shoulder, telling me I've got this.

He disappears back to his chair as I take the stage once more, my eyes occasionally falling on him when I lose my thoughts–his nodding and proud facial expressions give me the confidence to wing the rest, ending the presentation with the crowd standing and clapping as I walk off.

Once I'm no longer attached to wires, I throw cold water over my face in the bathroom, staring in the mirror, intently watching my tired-looking reflection gazing back at me.

I'm not even sure what to say to Tobias. Despite my inner self screaming her head off to take him home and make him screw me, I dry my face and hands and fix my hair, letting sheer curiosity get the best of me. I head outside to meet Tobias.

He's standing at the front entrance with an umbrella for me.

I hate myself, and I hate my feelings, because I truly am happy to see him.

Tobias stares at me the entire drive back, looking away when I turn my head to him. He stays quiet, maybe thinking of a hundred ways to annoy me further, flipping the radio stations every two seconds, turning the dial on my volume to an even number.

I frown at him when he starts tapping his hand on the edge of the door, humming to the song.

He stays behind me in silence as I unlock my door, and I stand aside so he can walk in, pulling his suit jacket off and hanging it on my fancy, tree-shaped coat holder. He eyes my apartment, walking in front of me, and I watch him as he explores, running his fingers over nearly everything.

"You do look good with brown hair. Did you dye it because I said I liked the blonde?"

I look down. My exact reason for putting the hair dye on was because he liked my hair so much, and I thought it would help the emptiness inside me. Like maybe if he did reappear, he wouldn't like me, and it would be easier to walk away.

Silence follows while he walks into my kitchen, reaching his hands out to me, wanting me to stand between his legs as he pulls himself up to sit on the counter. I shake my head, sitting up on the counter opposite him.

Frustrated, he groans, running a palm down his face. "Come on, Aria. I'm trying."

"Why did you come here? It's not like you drove an hour. You live thousands of miles away." I screw my face at him, trying to show how royally fucking pissed off I am. "Then you turn up at my presentation and think it would be okay to stand to show yourself? I don't know what you expect me to say to you. I really don't think we—"

"That you missed me," he interrupts, making me narrow my eyes at him, crossing my legs at the knees. He disregards my glare, gripping the edge of the counter. "Or just tell me you aren't mad at me."

He slides off the counter, and my breath hitches, my heart picking up pace with each step he takes in my direction, his face relaxed, eyes hooded.

"I told you I missed you." He tilts his head to the side, only two strides away from me. "You blocked my number."

"For a reason. It was done," I throw back, holding my breath as he rests both hands on each side of me, leaning in slightly so I can clearly see the mixture of blues dancing in his eyes, his flawless skin, the full lips that make me want to—

"It's not done, not for me."

"You can't be serious?"

"Why tell me you liked me then? If you were going to throw me away so easily?"

"Wasn't it just sex for you?" I ask, absentmindedly resting my hands over the top of his, our touch electrifying. "I do like you, but you're pushing a boundary I've put in place."

He settles between my parted legs despite my words, and the annoying excitement starts to crawl up my inner thighs, and I revel in the feeling of him so close to me once again. "I'm changing. For you, I really am."

Sighing, I run my hands up his muscular arms, lacing my fingers at the nape of his neck.

"Give me a shot," he pleads, lowering his forehead to mine and pulling my body into his. "I'll be good for you."

I ignore him again as he narrows his eyes at me, nudging my nose with his, our lips inches apart. One slight movement, and the atmosphere will change. The room will rise in temperature, most likely ending with our clothes ripped off and scattered along the floor.

"You want me to follow up on my promise if you ignore me again, am I right?" he asks with curiosity against my mouth, and I nod slowly. His teeth graze along my jaw and stop at my ear, whispering his next words so seductively teasing, I have to stifle a moan. "Do you want me to fuck your face, Doctor?"

"Maybe something a little more..." I gasp as Tobias' fingers dig into my hips, pulling me to him harder, cock straining in his trousers. "...a little more mutual," I breathe, letting out a whimper and swallowing hard as he leaves wet kisses down the side of my throat, groaning against my heated skin when my fingers trail up, grabbing and tugging a handful of his brown strands while the other hand palms him, cock already hard enough to take me right here.

I'm in complete and utter denial, half of me wanting him to screw me senseless. The other half doesn't have a clue what is going on.

I just can't seem to get enough of him. Every single fiber of my being needs and wants him...intimately and emotionally. It feels like time should stand still when we have moments like this, staring into each other's eyes with intensity, but it passes too fast, making me wish I could be stuck in limbo with him forever.

A knock at the door has me pulling away from Tobias in a panic, completely forgetting the time and who is coming. He snaps his head in the direction of Ewan's voice, shouting that it's only him, the handle pulling down. I push him away from me, stepping out of the kitchen, and my face pales when Ewan's relaxed eyes connect with my horrified ones.

"I need to go get Jason in half an hour, so I'll be quick."

Ewan halts his words and stands still as Tobias walks out behind me, both hands on my tense shoulders. I fully expect a war, or for me to be placed between them both and demanded to choose, but when Tobias introduces himself as my boyfriend, Ewan's eyes flash to me.

"Boyfriend?"

"Who are you?" Tobias asks, making my ex's glare darken, bringing his eyes back to him.

"Her ex, Ewan."

"Any reason why you're in my girlfriend's house?"

Ewan's hands curl into fists, his teeth gritting, staring at me. "Yeah. Why am I in your house, Aria?"

I gulp. "I... The washer was broken, and I..."

Tobias decides to put his arm around my waist, smiling down at me as he kisses my cheek. I watch Ewan intently, the heartbreak he must feel right now killing my soul, making me want to tell Tobias to back off and apologize.

"I suggest you leave before I make you," Tobias warns. "And don't ever come into my girl's house again."

"Did you just threaten me?" Ewan sneers, stepping forward, making Tobias let go of me.

I'm between them instantly, shoving them both in the chest. "Stop! Just stop!"

"You have no reason to be here," Tobias spits. "Fuck off."

"Just go, Ewan," I say quietly, pleading with him with my eyes.

I feel the atmosphere getting more tense in the room, and silently, the two of them stare it out until Ewan looks between us and clears his throat.

The greens of his eyes, devastatingly full of emotions, watch me for a long second, before he shakes his head. He turns and leaves the house, causing me to release a deep breath and close my eyes, turning to Tobias and giving him a nervous smile.

"Do you see him often?"

I shrug, looking from the door to Tobias, pouting my lips as I chew the inside of my cheek. "Just when I'm seeing Jason." When Tobias stays silent, I add, "His son. We raised him together for years."

"I don't see a kid around here," he states, looking around in exaggeration. "Do you?"

I roll my eyes, shaking my head as I turn and walk into my bedroom, Tobias following close behind. "He was coming to fix the washer for me, that's all."

Abruptly, he spins me around to face him, his expression serious. "I don't share."

"I'm not anyone's to share in the first place. Book a flight home and leave my house."

His hand snatches my wrist, and instead of turning to him, I close my eyes and let out a long, heavy sigh, ready to pull free of him and stomp into my bedroom.

His silence has me stopping in my tracks though. I turn to him, and he's staring blankly at me. "Ari—" His voice cuts off, wild blinking taking over his soft expression.

I freeze my movements, watching him as his face goes completely vacant. "What's wrong?" I cup his cheeks, searching his face. He doesn't say a word as he drops to his knees in front of me. "Tobias?"

"I...I need to...to go," he stammers, his speech slurring as he attempts to get up, grabbing my arm for support.

He clambers off me messily, face paling, his jaw clenching. "Tobias, what's wrong?" I hurry after him. "Tobias?" Before he can make it to the bedroom door, he falls against the wall and collapses.

"Tobias!" I scream, my eyes wide, and I drop next to him, my heart shattering as his body begins to convulse.

24

TOBIAS

My head feels like it has been smashed in with a baseball bat.

The light of Aria's lamp burns my eyes, and I roll over onto my front to shield my blurred painful vision.

She rushes to me. "You're awake. How do you feel? You had a seizure and passed out for hours."

I groan and bury my head into the pillow.

This wasn't the fucking plan. I came here to prove myself, not seize on her floor. I could feel it coming, and I wanted to stab myself in the goddamn heart. I didn't want her to see me so weak.

And now, she has.

"Do you want to see someone?" she asks, and my ears ring from how close she is.

"Light," I croak. "Turn the light off."

She hurries to the bedside unit and bathes us in darkness, and I finally lift my head, my body stiff and sore. I haven't had one of those in years.

I blink up at Aria, my beautiful doctor. "Did I scare you?"

"Of course you did! Is this normal? Should I have called an ambulance? Do you need me to do anything right now?"

I shake my head and sit up, desperate to pull her to me. "I'm fine. It happens from time to time, but I have it under control."

My eyes trail over her bedroom, gaze landing on one of the hidden cameras I set up the week after she left me in my own bed without a goodbye.

She has no idea I've been here. Always here. Always watching. My contact helped me get to Scotland undetected, got me a rented apartment nearby. If I wasn't here while she was at work, I was watching her outside or checking up on who the fuck Ewan actually is and if I can catch him out in some shady shit.

Much to my fucking annoyance, he seems normal.

Aria touches my face, and my entire body tenses from the abruptness.

"I was worried."

Starved of her touch and being so close but unable to touch or talk to her, I sink my cheek into her palm, closing my eyes. "Fuck, I missed you."

When I look at her, her eyes are watering, her chin dimpling. "I don't know how to do this."

I don't reply, because I don't know what to say. I haven't exhausted all my options to have her as my own yet, and I'm willing to try harder.

"I know you don't want to hear this, but Ewan is special to me. His son, Jason, means the world to me. I can't bring you into that when I don't even know where my head is."

It's settled, then. I'm going to erase Ewan.

"But I'm willing to try," she adds.

Maybe I won't kill him.

Instead, I pull Aria on top of me on the bed, holding her thighs against my hips as I lie back. "Prove it," I demand. "Kiss me."

She leans down and captures my mouth, her hands on my chest keeping me in place as she takes control of the kiss. She sucks on my bottom lip, my tongue, then swallows the deep groan that rips from my chest as she grinds against my hardening cock.

I need inside her like I'm about to fucking die if I don't.

She moans as I tear the material of her leggings and her panties before slamming her down on my cock, completely sheathing myself. Fuck, she's wet, soaking, even, and her cunt strangles my cock, I might have to trap her in this position forever.

I tangle my hand in her hair and tug her head up so she watches me while I thrust into her with quick snaps. Her lips are parted in bursts of panted breaths, her eyes hooded and glazed over, and I think I might watch this later when she thinks I've left the country.

This is a violation of privacy. She has no idea I'm recording her being fucked as I rip open her shirt and toss it aside with her bra, sucking a nipple into my mouth while her pussy grips me through her building orgasm.

I need to feel the tightening, the way she pulses around my dick. I need it all. The sound of her moans. The look on her face. Forever, if at all possible.

"Come inside me," she demands, moaning so fucking loud and trembling above me as her high hits its pinnacle.

I groan on a deep thrust as I come with her, filling her with every drop until I'm fully spent.

She collapses on my chest, both of us exhausted. "It's so not okay to sleep with someone who just woke up from a seizure," she says, panting, a thin layer of sweat coating her skin.

I let out a laugh and kiss her forehead. "Probably not."

I've been feeling absent in my head lately, but right now, as my naked doctor falls asleep in my arms, I feel at peace. My mind isn't being cruel to me, things aren't dark, and I like myself.

I can do this.

25

ARIA

I'm not sure if it's because we're about to leave for the airport, but Tobias' thrusts are torturously slow, dragging his cock out of me gradually, ramming back in to fill me, the repeating, my legs shaking, toes curling with each movement.

"Faster," I moan, tugging at his hair, trying to dig my heels into his thighs to accelerate his speed. He doesn't listen, keeping his pace controlled but hard, his hands gripping my hips with his face buried in the crook of my neck.

"I need you to tell me you'll miss me," he mumbles in my ear before his lips glide along my jawline and stop at my mouth. "Will you?"

His hands trace up the length of my body, his cock buried deep as his movements halt. I gasp, the sensation of him rolling my nipple between his fingers sending waves of pleasure straight to my core.

"Yes," I reply breathlessly, attempting to grind, my hands gripping the muscles of his back.

He pushes his hips against me more, burying deeper than ever, making me moan into his mouth as his tongue delves into mine. Tobias tilts his head, passionately claiming me with his lips, swallowing each whimper as one hand drops between us. He applies pressure, dipping his fingers to where his cock is shoved into me, dragging my arousal to my clit and circling.

"Are you falling in love with me?"

My back arches, my head pushing against my pillow as he starts to ease his cock out before slamming into me, keeping his fingers on my clit. The heat around us has me sweating, and our bodies slap together, the noises echoing around the empty house.

You'd think after three hours, after an entire week of this, he would be too tired to keep going, but each time he fills me, he wants to go again. I've lost count of how many times I've fallen apart with him inside me. Each time the tension builds in my spine, I scream out Tobias' name and dig my nails into his back, dragging to leave marks.

Like now. I feel the tingling, the warmth, every single nerve ending getting ready to explode and send me into oblivion.

But that doesn't happen, because Tobias stops his movements and pulls out of me. I growl at him and perch up on my elbows, panting. "What are you doing?"

"You didn't answer me."

I roll my eyes as he sits back on his calves. He's holding his cock in a firm grip, pumping it as he watches me with a glint in his eye, biting down on his bottom lip. With his eyes dragging down my chest and stopping between my parted legs, I open them wider.

"Fuck. You are perfect."

I huff, pushing his hand away and shoving his shoulders so he falls next to me. I straddle his body, my knees on each side of him, and I sit with his cock between my legs, stroking the underside slowly with my fingers.

"I think you might be falling for me," I say with as much seduction as I can manage, pressing his length against my sensitive core, watching his jaw clench.

"I'm seconds from face fucking you, Doctor. Do I need to do that?" he replies breathlessly, bucking his hips as his swollen head glides through my soaking slit. "Because I will."

I giggle, lifting so his head is teasing my entrance, lowering myself slowly, his thick cock stretching me with each inch. My mouth drops open from the fullness, stretching me.

"Do you want me to fall in love with you?"

"Stop talking," I moan, grinding on his cock.

He says something else, but I'm too paralyzed by my impending orgasm to pay attention, so I ignore him, my head falling back as he grabs my hips and thrusts to meet my movements. Minutes pass, our groans and gasps filling the room, my bedroom windows steaming up, my hair a mess.

He grabs my throat, and I can feel his chest under my palms starting to tense, his heart racing, matching mine. He grips my hips to stop me moving as he groans through his orgasm, filling me with his cum.

We lose ourselves in each other, bodies wrapped together as we come down from our highs, both panting, sweating, our lips raw.

"I think I might," Tobias says after nearly ten minutes of me lying in his arms, him twirling my hair around his fingers. "It's hard."

"What is?" I ask, my chin resting on his chest, staring at his chiseled features.

"Nothing." He shakes his head, reaching over for his phone. "We need to go soon. Shower with me?"

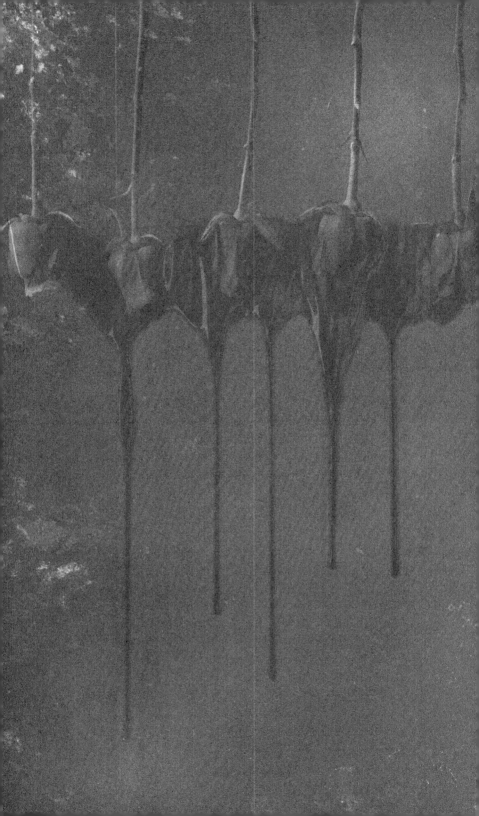

26

ARIA

"Thank God. You were non-existent while he was here," Gabs says as soon as she walks in the front door, Justin trailing behind. "Did you go to work today?"

Shamefully, I shake my head, twisting my fingers as she gives me an ugly look.

It's true. I've called in sick every day Tobias was here, missed every appointment, ignored calls that could have been important. I wanted to spend time with him before he went back home, and he said it was a good idea to turn my work phone off to de-stress.

So, I listened to him.

"Did you even call your mom back?" she continues, and all I can do is shake my head again. She looks around at our house, the cups and plates filling the sink, takeaway dishes littering the counters. Beer and wine bottles overflow in the bin, and I don't notice the foul smell until she points it out. "Okay." She drops her bags on the floor in the hallway, hands on her hips. "Justin, go sit in my room so we can clean up."

"I'm sorry, I've just been busy, and I didn't realize how bad the place is." Tobias left a few days ago, and I've felt lost. The thought of cleaning up was the last thing on my mind.

"Ewan's been trying to get a hold of you too. You were supposed to pick Jason up from school today."

My eyes widen, and my hand flies up to my mouth as I drop my body onto the armrest of the sofa. "Shit."

I've never once forgotten Jason, and my heart hurts that I did. I feel my eyes watering once more, an uncomfortable lump forming in my throat.

"I told Ewan you were busy and went and got him for you. That boy sat in the office for nearly an hour." She opens a bin bag, swiping her arms along the counter so all the rubbish falls in. "What's going on with you lately?"

I'm a monster. First, I ditch my work. Then, I close off the world to spend time with my boyfriend, and now Jason... I'm slowly letting everyone down.

"This isn't like you, Aria. You're responsible, professional, and you always put others first. What's going on? Where's your head at?"

I look at my best friend, my lip trembling. "I don't know," I sigh, dropping my head in my hands. "I think I'm just tired."

DAYS OF TEXTING BACK and forth turn into weeks of voice and video calls. Tobias is far too busy with work to visit, and I'm just off probation from taking so much time off and missing appointments. But it's my first day back, and I don't have an appointment until tomorrow.

I don't think.

My files are piling up, emails are delayed, and I sigh when I think about all the stuff I need to do before I can go home and talk to Tobias.

Oh, and who knew phone sex could actually be enjoyable? Tobias talks me through exactly what he wants me to do, begs me to send him videos, pictures, and I do...probably far too many. It has been a long two months without him, and the more time I spend away from him, the more I want him, all of him.

I wish he could be more expressive with how he feels about me. It's a massive struggle to get him to open up fully.

I gulp down my wine, emptying my fourth glass while someone is talking, but I've too zoned out to focus on what they're saying. Other than that, I've never felt better. Tobias talked me into deleting all my social media accounts, removing myself from that toxic environment. He spoke to me about not going out so much to a point that I would now rather stay at home and do work or video call with him, usually belligerently drunk.

Being drunk makes it easier without him. He said his mother used to get drunk when his father was out of town because it quietened the pain of missing the person, and he was right. I still want to see him, but my mind can't focus enough.

Seeing Jason has been a battle, only having him stay over a handful of times in the past eight weeks. I've completely blocked Ewan. There's no reason for me to have my ex's number and be in contact. For me to see Jason, I go through Ewan's mom, but recently, I haven't had much time.

I want to sit down with Ewan, work it out, fix this situation for Jason's sake, but when I suggested that to Tobias, I got my head bitten off. He's an ex, and no matter what history we have together, or how much I miss even just speaking with him, he's a threat to my relationship.

"You've gone silent on me again, Aria," the specialist on the other end of the phone repeats himself for the third time, and my eyes go wide as I sit up on my couch.

"Oh, sorry! What was the outcome?"

I hear him huffing, papers crunching. "Ivy Dermot hasn't been selected, but I think you argued enough to change their minds. Maybe give them a call and find out when the final listings are."

"Shit," I mumble, my eyes widening at my horrific language. I clamp my hand over my mouth, screwing my eyes shut. "Sorry. I'll call them now."

"Maybe get some sleep first. You've made a great statement."

We hang up, and my forehead meets the steel desk again, groaning at myself. "Fucking hell."

I struggle to sleep most nights, probably because I'm up until all hours, talking with Tobias. The time difference is a pain, and I've come close to asking him to just transfer here or vice-versa.

I've never been so off the ball with work. I can hear my worst nightmare currently walking up the hallway, and I know she's about to blow through my office and lose her—

"What the fuck, Aria?" Gabriella snaps. "Why didn't you go to the meeting?"

I frown at her, wiping hair out of my oily face. "What meeting?"

"You are unbelievable." She shuts my office door, dropping down on the chair opposite my desk. She has never looked at me the way she is now—disgusted. I prepare myself for an argument. "I think you need to take some time off work, maybe go see someone."

"I don't need to see someone."

"Aria! You are a mess." She picks up the empty wine glass and sees the bottle under my desk, her mouth dropping open. "You're drinking at work? What the fuck? And when do you ever miss any type of meeting for Ivy, or any of your patients, for that matter?"

All I do is glare at her. She's also becoming an issue in my relationship.

"My best friend never forgets this stuff, ever."

I take a deep breath, fed up with her controlling ways. "Then maybe your best friend needs you to back the hell off."

She tuts, completely disappointed in me. "I've already filed your paperwork. Pack your things and come back when you're feeling better," she tells me, standing tall. "I've been trying for weeks to get you on track, Aria. I've done everything I can as a friend to help you, but nothing I do is working. You don't speak to me at home, you never pick up my calls, and you act like I'm some sort of enemy. You're my best friend. Tell me how I can fix this?"

"Stop trying to fix something that isn't broken, Gabriella."

I watch as her eyes well up, chewing on the inside of her cheek as she nods slowly. "I know you're going through a hard time. Not seeing Jason as much and your parents demanding you go see them, it must be eating you alive, but I'm here for you. And I'm not saying it's Tobias." I glare at her as she says his name, preparing to go to war. "But ever since he has come into your life, you're not the same, Aria. He doesn't have your best interests at heart, and I think he might be manipulating and controlling you."

"Tobias is the only person there for me!" I slam my palm on my desk and stand. "He's the one talking me down when I panic for no reason. He's the one who cares about my actual feelings and knows exactly how to make me feel better. Not you, not Ewan, not Jason. Him."

She scowls at me, humming as if something registers with her. She takes a deep breath, tears rolling down her cheeks. "Okay, then I'll go stay elsewhere."

"You do that," I snap as she walks out of my office, and an email pops up telling me to go on leave for four weeks.

GABRIELLA, staying true to her word, clears out half her drawers, leaving a note on the kitchen counter.

> Aria,
> I know my best friend more than anyone on this Earth, even more than that idiot Ewan. Get some sleep, go back to the gym, and eat healthy like you always did before. I promise you it will get easier, and I will be with you every step of the way. But please, for the love of God, get that guy out of your life before he ruins it.

I'm giving you space. Get your head straight and take a bath...preferably a long one.
I love you.
G.

I reread it, unsure if she's genuine or if she's belittling me. Scrunching up the paper, I toss it in the trash, opening the fridge and grabbing one of the bottles of wine. I skip a glass, drinking straight from the bottle as I sit down on my bed, staring out my window at the busy streets, my afternoon taking a ridiculous turn.

I'm happy, I'm really happy. Gabriella needs to just back off and concentrate on her own life. Maybe it's jealousy that Justin hasn't spoken to her since leaving, or maybe she just misses having me to herself, but Tobias is my number one.

My phone dings as soon as I finish the bottle, and since I have everyone else on silent, I know it's Tobias. I bite down on my lip while I drunkenly attempt to unlock my screen, the fingerprint scanner not working.

I enter my pin instead, failing six times before opening the message.

TOBIASWORK

How's work?

Just as I begin to reply that it has been a shitty day, someone knocks on my front door. Instantly, I jump up off the bed, stumbling a little while I screw my eyes up, totally buzzed.

"Who is it?" I yell out, using the wall to lead me down the hallway.

No one replies, and I get butterflies at the possibility of Tobias being here, waiting on the other side of the door, cupping my cheeks, telling me everything is going to be okay.

I hurry, stubbing my toe on the sofa, cursing as I wobble to the front door, swinging it open with a wide smile. It drops as soon as I see who it is, and quickly, I slam the door on his worried face.

"Aria, no. Come on," Ewan says, sighing. "I just need to make sure you're okay."

"I have a boyfriend," I say, my palm slapping against the door as I lose my balance, my heart racing from fear of him, or maybe it's just my usual reaction to being near him. Either way, he needs to leave. "You need to leave, Ewan. Do you know what he will do to you if he finds out you're at my door?"

"I really couldn't give a shit what he does. I just need to know you're okay. Gabriella came to my house. We're worried about you."

"Yeah? I'm fine. You can go now." I hear him muttering something under his breath. I turn so my back is to the door, sliding down until my ass hits the wooden floor. "I don't need any of you," I whisper, my palms resting on my thighs. "I need the world to leave me alone."

"You didn't pick Jason up today either, but I don't think it's a good idea to be around him while you're like this. You need help, Aria. Let me help you."

My eyes start to water, the suffocating lump forming in my chest rendering me speechless. The room begins to spin, and at this moment, against every single emotion rocketing through me, I want to just sleep. I want all these hurtful things going through my head to stop.

"I love Jason," I say, my jaw clenching, trying to hold it together.

"I know you do, Aria."

I feel something hit against the door, the sound of his leather jacket sliding down the opposite side. "Is that what's wrong? Why did you need to hurt me?" I begin to sob, my words barely audible as the tears fall from my eyes, my body shaking as I lose control. "Why would you do that to me? We were happy, and you ruined it."

"I'm sorry, Aria. I don't know how to fix this. Please don't cry."

"You're a liar and a cheat," I spit, saliva falling from my mouth, my nose running, the room a total blur. I try to get up, but as I grab the wire to the tall lamp, it falls, and the shade smashes across the floor, shattering glass everywhere.

"What was that? Aria, let me in!" I hear him yell, pounding his fist on the wood as I completely fall apart, sobbing with my forehead on the floor, glass impaling my palm. "Aria!"

"I'm fine," I reply in a shaky voice, slowly lifting myself from the floor, grabbing the side table for leverage, my legs shaking. I can see the glass in my hand, but I don't feel any sort of pain. I don't feel anything, to be honest. "If you're here to..." I fall back against the wall, a bloody hand dragging down the white paint. "I have a boyfriend."

My vision blurs, and my body begins to retch as it attempts to bring up the contents of my empty stomach, bile spilling along the floor.

"Fuck," I hear him swear.

I drop to my knees just as Ewan kicks the door open, and I fall into his arms face first before a dark void swallows me whole.

Struggling to open my eyes, I'm met with my usual morning hangover, a bucket half full of water and vomit next to my bed. A glass of ice and a breakfast roll sits on my bedside unit, the first aid kit lying open.

I wince as I reach for the glass, my hand bandaged up. "What the hell?" I groan to myself, looking around the room and pausing when someone sits up from the chair.

"Hey," I hear Ewan's voice, and I scream, covering my fully dressed body with my blanket. He raises his hands, gulping deeply enough that I see his throat bobbing. "Woah, woah, woah, Aria. You're okay. I didn't know what else to do."

The view of him standing at the foot of my bed with messy hair and baggy eyes has me remembering last night. I gasp, my eyes widening. "What did you do to me?" I feel fear, *immense* fear building around me. My hairs raise and goosebumps cover my skin as he takes a step closer, confused at my reaction to him.

Tobias is the only one who can keep me safe, not him. He only breaks my heart.

"Aria, baby. You need to listen to me. You—"

"No! Don't call me that!" I interrupt him before he can continue, rushing to the other side of the bed as he nears, my breathing erratic. "You're dangerous. You're the threat."

Defeated, he drops his hands and backs himself up to the bay window, sitting down on the chair again. He sighs, running his tattooed hand through his dark hair. "I don't know why you think that. I've never been a threat to you."

"You make me like this," I add. "You want to hurt me."

"All I'm trying to do is help you," he replies, leaning forward so his elbows rest on his knees. "I slept on the chair beside your bed to make sure you were okay."

"You shouldn't have bothered helping me. I don't need you here."

He huffs, standing. "Then you would have choked on your own sick. Is that what you want?" I shrug at him, and he narrows his eyes. "What the fuck is going on with you?"

Shaking my head, I stare down at myself. My palm is covered in a bandage. "Did you do this?"

He nods. "You had glass in it."

The sting is welcoming, and he watches as I press my finger into my palm, wincing a little. The pain helps. I don't know what with exactly, but it helps.

"I want you to leave," I say quietly, my body shaking. A huge part of me wants him to stay, and it's fighting with the sensible part. "Because he's a threat," I say out loud.

"Aria, do you really think I'm a threat to you? I've been in love with you since we were eighteen. It's Tobias, isn't it? He's in your fucking head." Ewan runs his hand through his hair again, exasperated. I try to say no, but he cuts me off before I can. "I've never seen you like this."

"Leave," I say sternly, reaching over to grab my phone. "Leave before I call him."

He laughs in disbelief, but he doesn't find any of this funny, gripping the bottom of the bed frame. "I'm not scared of him. Maybe you should be," he says before pushing away, pulling on his jacket and shoes.

"At least he doesn't betray my trust," I reply spitefully, making him stop in his tracks at the bedroom door.

He looks at me over his shoulder, his jaw clenching. "I was a cocky teenager, Aria. I've apologized over and over again. Our relationship has nothing to do with you throwing your life away for a guy who is making you like this. You're spiraling, badly, and you need help."

Silently, I watch him leave the house, my heart nearly pounding out of my chest. The door slams shut, and I walk out, noticing Ewan has brushed up the broken glass, attempted to scrub the bloodstain on the wall, and tidied up my kitchen.

I smell air freshener and take a deep breath, closing my eyes while I try to figure out what I'm doing. "Shit," I blurt, panic striking me as I rush for my phone, unlocking it with my pin and seeing over fifty messages from Tobias.

I call him, my chest rising and falling quickly, chewing on my fingernails. He answers on the first ring, and his tone tells me he's pissed off. "What the fuck are you doing?"

"I'm sorry. I got drunk and fell asleep," I lie, unsure how to explain the last twelve hours. The tension builds in my head as he snaps at me, each word blowing through the phone having my eyes squeezing shut. Tobias stops eventually, and the tears are falling down my face as I sniffle. "I'm sorry."

He sighs down the phone. "I was worried. I nearly booked a flight to Scotland."

I frown, pulling the phone away for a second to see the time. It must be four in the morning for him. "That's a little dramatic, Tobias. I fell asleep."

"Yeah. Well, with someone like Ewan close by, I'm allowed to worry."

I agree with him silently, nodding, my eyes falling to the glass of ice and the sandwich. "I'm fine."

"Of course you're fine. Promise me you'll stay away from him. He isn't good for you."

"I promise."

27

TOBIAS

He's trying to split us up.

I should deal with him.

Right now, he's taking his son to school, and I watch him, calculating how to remove him from the equation. That asshole is the reason Aria isn't fully mine. He has a little part of her heart that should belong to me.

If he isn't in the picture, then there's no issue.

I did some research into who Jason's mom is, but annoyingly, she's not someone I can use to get Ewan away from us. I initially wanted her to seduce him, but she's on so many drugs in a psychiatric unit, she probably forgets she has a son at all.

The girl he cheated on Aria with is happily married with children, so she's out of the picture.

I have no idea why I watched him all night. I think I wanted to know if Aria would let him touch her, and if she did, I would need to deal with him. However, my girl was vomiting all night from my special concoction I'd managed to slip into her wine bottles while he made sure she didn't choke and die.

So, I watched.

And watched.

And waited.

Like I am now.

He's trying so fucking hard to take back what's already mine–he wants her all to himself. Maybe I should fuck her in front of him until he understands she's no longer his.

Having a past with him doesn't grant him access to her new life. She's under control, thriving, and I get almost all her attention, so why the fuck does he need to try and push his way in?

If I could get away with murder, I'd kill him, dump his body in a river somewhere and pretend he never existed. I could continue my life with Aria and not have to worry about being arrested or losing my doctor to some asshole who doesn't even love her.

Not the way I do.

If it's even what I feel. It's strange. Whenever I think about her, my chest gets all tight and warm, and I grow desperate to see her. I usually open the live footage and watch her gulp down glasses of wine and watch sitcoms without me.

Right now, he's at her parents' house.

I'm on my motorbike nearby, watching him stand at the entrance of the mansion as his hands fly around while he talks, her father yelling at her mother before she runs in and grabs her jacket.

Great. Now they're going to get involved. More people to potentially deal with. Getting Aria away from best friend and her ex was one thing, but her parents? That's going to be a hard task.

My first plan is to figure out how to kill someone without being caught.

Then, I'll take Aria away from here, somewhere safe, and keep her to myself forever.

28

ARIA

"Aria!" A heavy fist hammers on my front door, and I nearly drop my wine glass. The sound of my mom's voice catches me off guard. After ignoring her for weeks, I should have known this was coming. "You open this door right now, young lady!"

I roll my eyes, looking around at my messy house, the basket full of dirty laundry, the sink full of plates. Paperwork is scattered across the living room floor from trying to catch up on work despite being on leave.

"Aria!" I hear her yell my name once more. "I know you're in there."

"What do you want?" I shout back, leaning my forehead against the door before unlocking it. My mom's deep blue eyes burn into me as soon as the door swings open, and I fear she may hit me.

As usual, she's dressed in a fitted suit, her hair tied back tight enough to flatten out her wrinkles, or maybe that's the heavy makeup. I'm not sure anymore.

"No calls, no messages. You're slacking at work. If it wasn't for Ewan coming to ask us for help, I'd have no clue you were spiraling. I should have known you weren't cut out for this field."

My eyes widen, and I clench my fists, ready to pull her expensive handbag off her wrist and smack her with it. "How dare you? I'm fine."

"Look at you," she says, reaching out and flipping my knotted, greasy hair. Her eyes trace down my slim frame, clothes hanging off me. "You look like a drunk. And what in God's name is that smell?" She covers her nose with her palm, looking around the house as she walks up the hallway, stopping at the kitchen. "What's gotten into you?"

She needs to leave–Tobias is minutes from video calling me, and I haven't even set up my laptop yet.

Silently, I stare at the floor, feeling her burning glare on me. I know Mom well enough to know she will stand here, waiting until I dive into a deep hole of emotions and reveal myself to her.

She sighs, taking off her glasses and folding them closed, setting them on a takeaway dish with a grimace. "I'm going to run you a bath. I'm not leaving you alone like this."

"No! Mom, you need to go now before..." I trail off and chew my lip to silence myself.

Knitting her brows together, she regards me with a confused look. "Before...?"

"I just... I'm tired and I need to sleep."

"Well, you need to wash first." She looks me up and down with a tight-lipped smile. "I'll change your bedding while you hop in the shower."

On instinct, I grab her wrist with an iron grip, spinning her with my teeth baring. "I said no! You need to get the fuck out of my house and stop acting like Mom of the Year. We both know you're only here because Dad forced you."

Frowning deeply, she looks from my still-bandaged hand grabbing her to my twisted face. "Let go of me, Aria," she demands calmly. "I'm not a threat to you."

My brain explodes, and I let her go, stepping until my back hits the wall between my counter and table, eyes wide with fear. "Ewan is the threat. Mom, I need to protect Jason!"

"What? What in the world are you talking about?"

I shove past her, my heart racing as I quickly dig through the dirty washing for a hoodie, throwing it on and running out my front door with my mom yelling after me.

I don't dare stop, my bare feet slapping the pavement as I sprint as fast as I can, stumbling a little from my alcohol intake. The rain should be making me shiver, cold in the middle of November, but I feel nothing but the dread that Jason is in terrible danger.

Do anything necessary to save him.

The thought keeps running through my mind as I fall to my knees numerous times, the streetlights aiding me in the darkness. I feel a painful constriction crushing my chest, and I slow down my run to catch my breath, leaning my palms on my knees.

Tobias is going to lose it that I'm not there to take his call, and my phone vibrating in my pocket continually makes me cry softly at my guilt. I wipe under my nose before pulling it out and turning it off. Everyone can wait until I finish my mission—everyone needs to step back while I save his life.

Eventually reaching Ewan's front gate, I inhale a few deep breaths, my clothes completely soaked through. My hair is matted to my face, and I'm sure I have a bit of glass in the soles of my feet.

I'm scared. The repercussions of trying to rescue Jason can be worse for me, but he's my priority. Tobias has made it clear Ewan shouldn't be anywhere near me, that he is capable of anything, so why the hell would I leave Jason with him?

I crouch under his living room window, peeking in to see the TV on, Ewan sitting on the couch wearing just a pair of dark boxers, his phone pressed to his ear. If I open the front door quietly enough, I might be able to sneak in and out without being noticed.

I gulp down a lump, the taste of vodka on my tongue making me gag. I whimper, crawling over to the front door with stones digging into my knees, mud now covering my bare legs and hands.

I stand, reaching for the handle, stopping in my tracks when the lock turns and the door swings open. Ewan, in complete shock, stares at me, his gaze dropping to my bloody feet and back up to my face.

"Don't call the cops. She's here," he says to someone and hangs up. He opens the door fully and holds his hand out to me, as if I'm so fragile, a simple touch could break me.

"You're okay."

I'm not. I'm not okay.

"Come inside. You're safe here."

I'm speechless, all my hair rising as Tobias' words rattle through my mind, every single fiber of me telling me to turn and run. I can't. My feet are glued to the ground, my jaw chattering as my eyes water, feeling my knees starting to shake.

Seeing him in front of me, I feel distraught, as if my mind is against me. Tobias is right, but I don't want him to be, because he's Ewan.

I flinch as he tries to reach for me, retracting his hand and lifting them both. "Aria, breathe for me."

I had no idea I was holding my breath, my lungs burning for air.

"Aria's here?" I hear Jason yell from the hallway, and Ewan quickly grabs the door and swings it half shut so I'm out of view. "Is she coming home?"

"Go to your room, buddy."

"No, I want to see Aria!" I see his small hand on the door, attempting to pull it open. My heart is shattering into small pieces, and as soon as his head pops around to look at me, his pale green eyes connect with mine for a split second.

I fall apart. I drop to my knees, my mouth wide open as I let out a loud sob just as Ewan pulls him away, telling him sternly to go back to his room.

I hear Jason asking if I'm okay, that he wants to see me.

Hands touch my shoulder, my name on Ewan's lips, before I feel someone soft wrapping around me. They smell just like Ewan.

My body relaxes somewhat, and I sob harder.

"What am I doing?" I cry, staring at the puddle beneath me.

My faint reflection makes me sick, the sight of me revolting. "What am I doing?" I repeat just as Ewan lifts me, hooking his arms under my legs and shoulders.

"You're freezing," he says, carrying me through his warm house, the same place I used to call home. My body starts to tremble, the cold painful, every bone in my body rattling in Ewan's arms. "Did you walk here? Are you drunk? Your pupils are fucking huge," he speaks as he sits me down in front of his fire, wrapping another towel around me. "Aria, say something. Talk to me so I know you're okay."

My blurred gaze traces the room, landing on a huge canvas of Jason above the gray couch. "I need to help him," I blurt out, my face contorting as I look down at Ewan's hand running up my arms to heat me up. I hit them away, hurrying to my feet as I back away from him. "What are you doing to him?"

"What?" he asks, confused, standing slowly with his hands up. "Aria—"

"Is he hurt?" I panic, my eyes widening as the thoughts run wild in my mind.

"Hurt? No, he's in his room. What's going—"

He's lying.

"I need to get him out of here, Ewan. Help me. It isn't safe." I walk to him, gripping his forearms with a begging look. *Hurry.* "Please help me get him out of here."

"You need to stop. I'm his dad. He is safe."

"No, you hurt people and mess with their heads." I start to raise my voice, my lip trembling as I cover my mouth. "You want me to lose everything."

He kneels in front of me as I drop to the rug, rubbing both hands down his face, his tired eyes on my scraped knees. "I would never hurt you, Aria. It's not me you should be worrying about," he says, pushing my wet hair out of my face, tucking it behind my ears, the contact nearly taking my breath away. "This guy, he has his claws dug deep into you, and you're falling into a deep hole. When does Aria Miller ever let anyone run her life?"

"He doesn't."

Settling his hand over mine, he rubs his thumb over my skin. The act is small, but it's massively affecting me in ways it shouldn't.

"I'm worried about you, Aria. To me, you're a strong, independent, intelligent woman who takes bullshit from no one. I need you to remember that when you feel like you're lost." I watch him with tears streaming down my cheeks; my lips move, but no words come out. "And I'm not saying all of this because you mean so much to me. I'm saying it because it's true. A lot of people look up to you, me included."

"But..." My throat tightens, my free hand grabbing his sleeve. "I *am* lost."

"Are you? Are you sure you aren't just hiding? If you were lost, then you wouldn't know unless you were found. You told me that years ago, remember?" I stare at him, chewing the inside of my cheek. The corner of his lip curls up, and I feel some of the crippling pain lifting from my chest. "You still have clothes here. I'll put them in the bathroom so you can change."

I watch him stand and let out a heavy breath as he walks around the couch, opening a cupboard in the corner, pulling out a fresh towel. Handing it to me, he helps me up from the ground, and I stagger a little, my palm hitting the wall. "I don't like how I feel," I admit, meeting his gaze. "I don't like it. I feel sick all the time. I have butterflies."

"I know. You really need to speak to someone," he says, wrapping an arm around my waist to help me walk without falling, the closeness erasing the dark feelings and thoughts, replacing them with something calm, something that makes me let out a deep, well-needed breath.

"I'm talking to you," I reply, looking up at him. "Can I sit with you and Jason? We could watch a movie?" I ask, Ewan leading me to the bathroom, turning on the light that blinds me momentarily, sitting me down on the edge of the circular bathtub. I wince a little as he lifts my leg, pressing a cool cloth to a cut on my foot. "I just want to see him for a while. I miss him."

"I don't think that's a good idea. I'll get you dressed and take you to your parents' house. Tobias will get the wrong idea—"

"I'm not here for a quick fuck. I'm here for Jason." Interrupting him, I stare him down, watching his pale green eyes close in defeat.

"Not when you're like this, Aria. If you don't want to go to your parents', you sleep it off in the bedroom, and we'll get you to a doctor tomorrow."

He pours me a glass of water that I gulp down before handing it back to him. He's shaking just as much as I am, and I want to hold his wrists and tell him the way I feel, truly feel, but the words and thoughts and feelings are caged.

Ewan helps me up the staircase, the wall lined with family photos of us three through the years. The dogs are at my feet, excited and barking, but I can't see them. When I think about leaning down, I feel like I'm going to pass out or vomit, or both.

The bedroom we shared for years still looks the same, it only being a few months ago since I left. My favorite bedding is on, the window slightly ajar the way I like it. He tugs the duvet down and fluffs my pillow, settling another glass of water next to the bed.

"I'll bring you a bucket in case you feel sick again. Do you need anything else?"

I shake my head. "I need sleep."

He nods. "I'm going to settle Jason down. He might've overheard, and I don't want him to be worried."

My fingers twist together as I walk towards the bed, sitting on the side. He settles my phone next to the glass, giving me a warm smile before leaving.

I reach over to the table and flip my phone in my hand, wondering if I should turn it on yet. I look around at all the pictures, and my eyes land on a very small one, one we took in a booth years ago when Jason was three. We are all smiling, Jason sticking his fingers up both our noses. We all look happy.

A lump builds in my throat, and I look away.

Holding the power button down, I feel my chest tighten, waiting for the vibrating to stop so I can call Tobias.

With the phone pressed to my ear, I quietly walk down the hallway to the bathroom, taking one step at a time as Tobias answers. "Where the fuck are you?"

"Um...I went to see Jason," I reply quietly, reaching Jason's room, peeking through the space between the door frame.

I hear him huffing in irritation. "Where?"

Whispering, I keep my eyes on Jason as Ewan kneels next to his bed, running his hand through his dark locks. "Ewan's."

"Are you fucking kidding me?" His aggressive tone has me shutting my eyes momentarily, and I open them to look at Ewan, watching his soft features while he tucks in his son, kissing his forehead. "That guy is a snake, Aria. You need to run, right now."

"He's just looking out for me. I don't feel good."

Silence follows, and I pull the phone away to see if he's still there.

"Tobias?" I say his name, tiptoeing down the hallway and down the stairs, the dogs following at my feet.

"How do you feel?" he asks.

"Dizzy," I reply, my knees wobbling. "I'm leaving now."

"Yes, you fucking are. What else did he do to you? Did he touch you?"

"Of course not," I reply, and he slams his fist down on something.

"Goddammit, Aria, can't you see what he's doing to us? Did he give you something? Did you drink something?"

I lick my dry lips. "Water."

"Fuck," he spits. "He's drugged you, Aria. Get the fuck out of the house."

"Stop," I whimper. "He wouldn't do that to me."

"Wouldn't he? You broke up with him, and he's got you in his goddamn house. You drank some water and now you don't feel good."

"Stop," I whisper, a tear sliding down my cheek because there's a huge possibility he's telling the truth. Why would Tobias lie to me?

He continues, each word dragging those dark feelings to the

forefront of my brain. "He's the threat, Aria. Remember that. He wants to own you and will do anything to get you there with him. Get the fuck out of that house right now. Run."

"He's the threat," I say, repeating it over and over again, freezing at the front door as I hear Ewan.

"Aria?"

Shivers run through my entire body, and I nearly drop the phone when I hear him say my name again.

My heart begins to race as I hang up on Tobias, and my eyes widen as I turn around. He tilts his head at my stance, furrowing his brows. "What's wrong?"

He planned this; he knew I'd need to come to him to see Jason and made me drink that water. Tobias is right. I need to run.

"Talk to me. What's wrong?"

Ewan steps towards me, and quickly, I spin on my heels, throwing the door open and sprinting as fast as I can while I ignore him calling my name.

I know he can't follow me with Jason in bed–he's not that irresponsible.

My sock-covered feet pound the floor as I run, hearing Ewan yelling in the distance. I take a left down the sidewalk and cross the street, a car nearly crashing into me and swerving last second.

I fall onto my knees and get back up, falling again, realizing whatever Ewan gave me is rushing through my system, and I'm weak. I don't think I felt this way before. Did I? This is Ewan who made me like this.

Ewan drugged me.

The burning feeling of betrayal has me vomiting on the ground in the middle of the road just as someone reaches me. Large hands move my hair from my face as I continue to empty my stomach.

Everything goes blurry, and I cry and sob and scream against the concrete until I feel myself slipping away into darkness once again.

29

ARIA

"Wake up, Aria."

I feel a warm set of lips press against the nape of my neck, sending shivers through my body, causing me to pull the duvet over me more. I can't open my eyes; the sun blinds me when I try.

"Wake up before I fuck you awake."

My eyes ping open and I twist in the sheets, facing an extremely handsome, shirtless Tobias with messy hair. "Tobias...what are you—"

"I haven't been inside you in weeks. Do we need to have the talk right now? You passed out when I found you last night." He tucks a strand of hair behind my ear, his eyes searching my face. "I just have one question for you." He shifts, pinning me beneath him, his large frame overpowering my fairly slim one. "Did you fuck him?"

"Of course not," I reply, frowning at him. "Why would you think that? I just went to see Jason, showered because I was filthy, and left.

"You showered?" he asks, eyes narrowing. "With him?"

"What? No. I would never do that to you."

"What would you think in my position? If I had gone to an ex's house with my phone turned off?"

His venomous words should be ripping through me, but instead, I feel myself *dripping* as his mouth lowers to my neck. I struggle to reply or even think of a logical explanation as his tongue runs up my throat.

"What would you do, Aria?" he whispers against my ear, our surroundings heating up, the anticipation between us thickening just like his cock straining in his boxers. "Do I need to fuck the image of him out of you?"

"I..." My words are cut off as Tobias nudges my legs apart, dragging kisses down my chest, leaving trails of wetness down my stomach with his lips, stopping at the waistband of my underwear. Every single hair rises, swirls of heated pleasure running up my spine as his palms press the inside of my knees, spreading my legs further apart.

"I missed how good you taste, Doctor. I'm so fucking mad at you, so I'm going to eat your pussy and stop just before you come, and then I'll fuck your ass."

I moan softly as he pushes his palms up higher on my thighs, his thumbs pressing against my pussy.

My body reacts to him as he massages around my clit, my thoughts clouded, nerves exploding, heart racing. My body is begging him to please me in ways my fingers can't. Weeks of pleasuring myself to his voice, to his commands–it's all minuscule compared to having him here, gliding his warm tongue over my clit.

I try to tug his hair, but he groans in dissatisfaction and flips me over onto my front. He spreads my cheeks and licks my ass until I'm moaning into my pillow. I arch my back to push my ass against his face, tensing everywhere when his tongue slips into the tight hole and swirls.

A slap to my cheek has me yelping, and he pulls back, stroking himself a few times before lining up with my back hole. "Take a deep breath."

I don't do it on time before he forces his cock so hard and fast into my ass, I bite down on my lip until it bleeds, screaming as he pushes my face into the pillow.

"Such a tight ass," he growls, easing out to the tip and thrusting back in. "So tight and so *mine*."

I'm full of him, so full and overwhelmed, but the tightening coil at the base of my spine enjoys the feeling of him fucking my ass, loving the way he pushes my face further into the pillow and thrusts deeper and faster until the headboard slams repeatedly off the wall.

Just before my orgasm hits, he pulls out of my ass, panting so loudly, I don't need to turn around to know his chest is rising and falling fast, or that his heart is racing.

"You don't get to come yet," he warns. "Turn around."

I kneel in front of him on the bed, tears burning my eyes. Tobias wipes one from my cheek and forces his finger into my mouth. "Can you taste the way you cry? What kind of tears are they, Doctor? Happy, sad, or tears of terror?

I can hear faint echoes in the distance, coming from all directions. My head snaps to the left and right, searching for the noises. They get louder, and Tobias looks around too, then at me.

"Can you hear them?" I ask, and his brows furrow, sucking in his bottom lip as he follows my eyes around the room.

He frowns in confusion. "What can you hear?"

I try to focus, tilting my head as the echoing chimes become more ear-piercing. I feel my heart beginning to race, and not in a heated moment type of way. Instead, I feel like I can't breathe. "It hurts," I say, covering my ears with my hands. The noises are so high pitched, I think my brain might explode.

"Aria, look at me." I refuse, shaking my head as I feel liquid pouring onto my hands, and I begin to scream. "Aria!" Tobias shouts over me, shaking my forearms until I open my eyes. "I can hear it too," he says, taking deep breaths, gesturing with his hand for me to copy him.

I do, in through my nose and out through my mouth, repeating the actions until my heart rate starts to settle and the painful noises start to soften. I lower my hands, expecting to see crimson on my palms, but there's nothing.

"You can hear it?" The chimes become deep, like a drum being blasted with a heavy palm repeatedly. "Where is it coming from?"

The drumming sounds form into a melodic song, and I feel the intense need to raise my hands in the air, shutting my eyes as the beat of Amber Run's song *I Found* takes me far away. I rise from the bed, and the house becomes dark, colorful lights lining the floor as I follow them into the bathroom. I'm floating, the floor coming away from me as gravity fights to keep me down, making my way to the floor-length mirrored wall.

"What's happening to you?" Tobias asks, tilting his head. "Do you feel okay?"

"I feel so...happy."

Tobias follows behind, and I can see from the reflection that he's watching me, enjoying the way my hips move as I dance around naked. "I like it when you embrace it," he says, walking to me and grabbing my hips. "If you embrace it, we can share it."

His lips press to mine, and I melt into the kiss, my fingers digging into his hair as he lifts me onto the sink.

"Share it?" I question him, panting against his mouth, feeling his swollen head press against my entrance. "I will share anything with you."

"Anything?" he repeats, the music vanishing to silence but our heavy breathing. "I want you to share yourself with me then, Aria."

I nod, and he grins at me, easing his tip through my slit; the sensation of not having him inside my pussy for weeks has me gripping onto his back muscles. Each inch he shoves into me makes me gasp and dig my nails into his skin.

He stops and pulls out of me, making me wince. "Wait," Tobias says, his voice shaking. "Are you sure you're okay?"

Looking completely lost, he furrows his brows. "I'm fine," I assure him, digging my heels into his thighs so he enters me again.

"Are you..." His words get strangled in his throat as I roll my hips to him, sheathing his cock to the hilt.

His momentary restraint breaks, and he rapidly sinks into me with his teeth attached to my shoulder, sucking and kissing the raw skin before crashing his lips to mine.

"Faster," I blurt out as his thrusts get more intense, burying deep into me, hitting that sweet spot that has me moaning into his mouth. His grip on my ass is a little painful, but I pay more attention to his cock pummeling into me, relentlessly unleashing as he pulls us away from the sink and fucks me against the tiled wall.

My hand flies up to curl around his throat, and I apply more pressure the closer I get to hitting my euphoric state, grinding against his solid shaft as he moves his hips into mine. "Harder," I moan, my back slamming against the wall as Tobias does as I say.

"Fuck," he drawls, sweat coating our bodies as his lips press against mine once more, his tongue pushing into my mouth and running along my own.

I feel overwhelmed, a mix of happiness, pleasure, and warmth filling me. "Tobias..." I try to tell him something important, something I've been wanting to say for weeks now. "I think I..."

"Do you still take your pill?" he cuts me off, his hands moving to behind my knees and carrying me out of the bathroom while I continue to grind against him, stopping a few times against the hallway walls. "Do you?"

"Yes," I breathe, wrapping my arms around his neck and pushing a hand through the hair at his nape, tugging the strands so he lifts his head to look at me.

Pale green eyes stare back at me, and I fall into a deep trance as Tobias lowers me onto my bed, looking down at my exposed body with his cock pumping in his hand. "Bend over." I watch his hand move up and down his length, my eyes tracing the designs of his inked, muscular body.

I'm not sure if I'm hallucinating or what the hell is going on, but Tobias' appearance keeps changing before me. One second, he has tattoos, and then they vanish. His eyes keep flashing between green and blue, confusing the life out of me. His form ripples, and

I screw my eyes shut, opening them again to see Tobias leaning over me.

"I want to come in your ass. Bend over," he says more sternly. I listen, shifting so I'm on all fours, watching the headboard in anticipation. "I have something to keep you still," he explains, leaning over me and grabbing a box tied to the corner of my bedpost. He tugs at it, and a restraint comes into view with a cuff attached.

He grabs an exact replica at the other corner of the bedpost, pulling the restraints until he's able to cuff my wrists. I wince as they snap back, my body jerking forward. He grabs my hips, and in one swift movement, he's fully inside me as a whimper drops from my mouth. "Retractable," he says, bending over so his chest is to my back, flicking the tight cords. "You're going nowhere."

How did they get there?

He rolls his hips against my ass, and the angle has him filling me more, my teeth gritting with each thrust. I've done anal plenty of times, but it isn't my favorite. I only tried with Ewan, and he was always slow and gentle, not the way Tobias is nearly ripping me apart with how hard he's screwing me.

I wince as he pulls out of me and flips me, and my mind is warping as he grabs my throat with strobe lights flashing behind him, my arms above my head, crossed in this position. He leans forward, kissing me deeply as he enters me once more, his cock swelling as my walls start to clench around him.

"Fucking perfect," he groans with each thrust, his teeth sinking into my shoulder as his muscles tense all over, both hitting our highs with force. I shake my head, blinking as my mind plays tricks on me and I see Ewan hovering above me. I feel comfort, enjoying his hands now running down the length of my body.

"I love you, Aria." He looks down at me filled with appreciation and lust, making me internally swoon. "I fucking love you."

I'd know that voice anywhere. The emotions that flood through me relax me in ways I've not been able to for a while now. He always makes me feel safe, at ease with myself when I feel like I'm drowning.

My eyes close as I sink into the comfort of knowing he's here with me.

"I love you too, Ewan," I moan out, gripping his back muscles as my orgasm reaches its peak.

He halts all movement, his body shaking above me as he leans up, my high vanishing. "What the fuck did you just say?" Tobias snaps at me, his face contorting into something evil. I wince as he jerks out of me, growling, "Ewan?"

I'm speechless, the cuffs tightening as I try to move, watching Tobias step off the bed looking completely demonic. "No, Tobias... I mean you!"

"Bullshit. I should've known you were still screwing him."

I try to move again, and the restraints nearly snap my wrists. "I promise you, I'm not! I swear, I haven't gone near him in months!"

Shaking his head, Tobias turns and boots my mirror, shards of glass shattering across my floor. "I fucking trusted you!"

I can't handle this, my body shaking with fear, rejection, and confusion. My sobs come out strangled as I attempt to free myself from the restraints that have my anxiety building. "Please, Tobias. Take these off me so I can make this right."

"I've fallen for you, something I, as the fucked-up weird kid, could never do!" My heart breaks as I see his eyes brimming with tears, obvious rage flowing through him as he kicks something across the floor and punches my wall, denting the plaster.

He turns to me, fuming. "I can't lose you... I won't."

"You haven't, Tobias. I swear," I cry, wincing as I try to reach him, the cuffs snapping me back into position. "Please, believe me."

"I trusted you, Doctor. I showed you the threat, and you leapt into his fucking arms. How can we ever be together with him walking around? You have no idea the lengths I've gone just to make you fucking happy!"

He strides over to me, leaning down so both palms settle beside my head, ducking so his lips touch my ear. My heart nearly ceases, his hands running between my breasts and wrapping around my throat. "You're mine. Remember that. I need to take care of the threat since you won't."

I gasp as his mouth presses against mine, claiming me as his. I try to chase his lips when he shoves himself away from me, grabbing his clothes and leaving the house.

Gasping through my tears, I try to force one hand to the other to free my naked self. I cry, my face coated with tears. I turn on all fours, my arms no longer crossed above my head, and I use all the strength I have to reach the buckle with my index finger, but my arm flies back into position. A shooting pain runs up my shoulder. I fail, burying my head in the pillow, and I scream, my heart racing at an unsteady pace.

He's going to hurt Ewan.

What have I done?

I CONCENTRATE on the light flashing on my alarm clock for the next hour, attempting to block out my surroundings that keep mocking me.

Hearing the door slam, I bury my head into the pillow more, sobbing as I struggle with reality. Between the chimes, flashing lights, and Ewan appearing as my boyfriend, I can't take it. I don't know what's real anymore.

"Aria?" I hear Gabriella call my name, listening to her heels clicking along the hallway. "Are you home?"

She gasps as she opens my door, finding my naked body strapped to the bed, glass shattered across the floor, bloody fist marks from Tobias hitting the wall next to the dent.

"What the hell happened?" She hurries forward, ignoring my bent over, naked state as she unbuckles me, throwing a comforter over my exposed body. "Are you okay?" she asks, looking around the room then to my swollen red eyes.

"Tobias." I choke out his name, sobbing into Gabriella's shoulder. "I hurt him. He..."

"You're cold." Gabs lifts me from the bed, her arm wrapped

around my back as she helps me into the bathroom, turning on the shower. "Did that asshole hit you?"

I shake my head, my thoughts getting mixed up with what's going on. I hear the chimes again, and I bury my head in my hands. "Make it stop," I beg, the sounds getting louder. "Please," I say once more, grabbing Gabriella's shirt, saliva running down my chin.

She searches my face then uses two fingers to pry open one of my eyes, getting a good look at my pupil. "What are you on?"

"Nothing," I reply, the room starting to spin. The butterflies in my stomach have me seeing the flashing strobe lights of the fairground. I reach my hand out, feeling the wind between my fingers as the speed picks up on the ride.

"Faster," I whisper, the sensation lifting me higher as I start to smile.

I feel a painful sting to my face, and Gabriella is growling at me. "Snap the hell out of it!"

I place my palm to my cheek to ease the raw skin, dropping back against the wall. "Did you just fucking slap me?" I snarl, my rage building.

"I'm calling your mom, Aria. This has gone too far." She shakes her head, concerned, pulling her phone out and tapping away on the screen.

"Mom. Did she go on the rides too?"

She ignores me, placing the phone on the sink as she lifts me from the ground, carrying me into the shower. My body isn't stable enough to hold my own weight right now. Gabs sits me down on the small marble corner seat within the cubicle, soaking herself while she heats my body with the warm water, keeping her hands gentle on my slim frame.

"Ewan has been on the phone with me for days on end, worried sick about you. Your mom too. I think this thing with Tobias needs to end. You're unwell."

My eyes widen at his name, and I grab her hands. "I love Tobias."

"No, you're being controlled by him. There's a massive difference between strong emotions and feared mental submission."

I want to hit her, but a part of me is fighting that urge. "You don't even like me. If you care about me, you would want me to be happy." I let go of her hands, shifting away from her. "Who are you?"

"I'm not the threat here. This is," she says, tapping the side of my head. "I need to find out what's—"

"*Ewan* is a threat... Ewan *is* a threat..."

I repeat this chant, no matter how many times Gabs tells me to stop. Even after she dries me and carries me to my room, dodging the glass, she's dressing me, and I keep the words going like a broken record until I hear the chimes again.

I hear Gabriella's phone ringing, and she settles me on the couch so she can answer it. "Hey, yeah, she's here. Ewan said she ran out of his house in the night and Tobias found her. I don't know what the hell is wrong with her. Meet me at the hospital? Okay, see you there, Doctor Miller."

I frown at her addressing Mom as she always does, and she grabs my jacket, kneeling in front of me while she pulls the leather up my arms. "Where are we going?" My words come out slurred, and I lick my dry lips, fighting the urge to bring up my empty stomach.

"We're going to get you help, Aria. We all love you, and we're going to get you better." Our eyes meet, and I feel a weight lifting from my shoulders, my eyes brimming with tears as I grip her hand in mine. "I know you don't feel like yourself, but I'm never leaving your side again."

My jumbled thoughts become a little clearer, slowly nodding in agreement, and both of us freeze as we hear the door open before slamming shut.

Dad stands in my living room, staring down at my pale face. "What has she taken?" he asks Gabriella, helping her lift me from the couch, each one tucking an arm under my shoulders. "My God, Aria. You're skin and bones."

Concentrating on the chimes remaining at a soft tempo, I

close my eyes and focus on the voices around me, but everything is muffled.

I don't realize we've already gone out to the car, my dad buckling me in. All I see are flashing lights, feeling a heavy bass rattling through my body. Although my mind is hazy and everything seems to be playing in reverse, repeating, slowing down, I try to keep a straight face as Dad drives us to the hospital.

I'm surprised he's here. Being a busy man, tackling every case he can before retirement, he barely has time for his own family.

If they think I'm crazy, and I reckon they already do, I'll be admitted, sent to an institution.

The chimes painfully start to pierce my ears, from my house all the way to the hospital. I keep playing Tobias' words in my head: *embrace it*. Every time I close my eyes and try to do exactly that, the bell-like sounds fade into something soft and relaxing, releasing me from my torment momentarily before exploding once more, causing me to silently wince.

Embrace it... How do I do that?

With my head on Gabriella's lap, her hand stroking my hair, I watch the clouds in the sky, counting every time we pass a lamp post or traffic light. "Where's Tobias?" I ask, looking up at her in panic. "I hurt him, Gabs. I just slept with Ewan."

She shakes her head. "No, you didn't. Forget about Tobias too; he's not good for you." Her reply is clipped, causing me to frown and shift my position to move away from her. She sighs, · tucking her hair behind her ears. "Don't look at me like that. He's been nothing but bad news ever since he came into your life."

"Where are we going?"

"I just want the doctors to run a few tests on you." Her palm lands on my hand, rubbing her thumb along my skin. "Then we can go home and watch movies, okay?"

I nod, lacing our fingers together while I stare at the back of Dad's headrest. I hum *I Found* to myself, my head tilting to each side as the beat plays quietly.

When we reach the hospital parking lot, Dad helps me as we follow Gabriella through the corridors of the ER, the bright lights burning my eyes. "We can just take her to ward four; it's quiet anyway. Doctor Miller is meeting us there," Gabriella says, looking down at her phone screen as we head to meet my mom.

I feel my stomach twisting, and no matter how much I try to hold it back, my body heaves, and I double over. Bile, and barely any of it, splashes across the floor, the taste rancid, stinging my throat as my eyes water painfully.

Reality seems to keep freezing, causing us to glitch to different parts of the hospital. Every time I feel like I'm back to normal, pressure builds in my head, and the blip in my brain restarts.

Fear...something I don't often feel. Being confident and powerful in my head has always gotten me through the day. I'm terrified of how I'm feeling.

Is this what it's like to be afraid of your own thoughts?

I've never been the type of person to depend on anyone, but right now, I want Tobias—I need him. I know he's mad at me, but I know I can fix this, whatever is going on between us.

They think I can't understand them, their disgusted expressions telling me that these people do not enjoy my company. By the looks of it, they would rather be somewhere else.

I can't run. I try, but I'm held in place, like there's glue on my shoes, sticking me to the ground. The world spins, and I feel butterflies as I topple.

I feel a pinch on my arm, a young nurse next to me trying to stick a needle in me. Wincing, I try to pull away from her, but I'm being held down, my heart rate accelerating. With all the hands pressing down on me, I'm suffocating.

The chimes. They are multiplying around me, the flashing lights blinding me as I begin to scream.

Until I feel a stab in my thigh, another sting follows as my eyes slowly close.

30

ARIA

"Addiction can drive people down different roads."

"But she isn't an addict. Someone did this to her," I hear Gabriella reply to the doctor, raising her voice with each word. "Her boyfriend did this."

"Assumptions are also something that shouldn't be thrown around so lightly. If that is the case and you have proof, then he needs to be reported. My job is to make sure the patient's health is seen to. I need to run some more blood tests," the man replies, followed by a door closing and someone muttering under their breath.

Keeping my eyes closed, I listen to every word.

"Did you get little Jason to our sitter, Ewan?" I hear my dad ask, and my heart starts to race at the memories flooding me. "He'll be excited. She hasn't seen him in a few months."

"Yeah," he replies. "I didn't even get a goodbye when he ran into the house."

My parents have staff who work in the manor, and one of them, an older lady named Francis, bonded with Jason throughout our relationship. She would babysit him when we went out for date nights, and he always hung out with her at the house when I went to see my mom and dad.

Wait. Does that mean Ewan is here? Tobias didn't find him?

I'm weak. I've been drifting in and out of sleep for hours. Every time the doctor tries to speak to me, I can't grasp what's real and what's not, tumbling back into a deep, dark hole in my mind. I listen to my surroundings, the clock ticking so loud, it hurts, water running from the sink across from my hospital bed because Gabs can't seem to go half an hour without washing her hands. Mom complaining that she wants to go home, Dad telling her to shut the hell up.

There's one voice I want to hear, one person's face I want to see, and I know after my slip-up, Tobias will be done with me.

Why does it hurt so much?

"She should know," I hear Ewan say to someone. "I don't know why you're shaking your head like that, Dolores. Can you stop being stuck up for one minute? She's your fucking daughter, and all you keep doing is complaining that you want to leave."

"Watch your tone, young man," my mom snaps at him. "I didn't raise her to become some junkie—"

"Don't you dare speak about her that way!"

My eyes ping open in shock at Ewan raising his voice. Blurry vision welcomes me to the hospital room. Everyone's crowding my bed, perched in chairs as Mom scowls at him for snapping at her, something she takes from no one.

"Aria!" Gabs says in surprise, leaning over and grabbing my hand as a sign of comfort. "How are you feeling?"

Croaking, I try to speak, but it turns into a coughing fit as Ewan also leans forward and pats my back, offering me his bottle of water. I shake my head, turning away from him as my eyes meet Gabriella's honey-colored ones. "What's going on?" I ask with a break in my voice, trying to clear my throat once more.

"I'll explain soon. You've been asleep for over twenty four hours. Tell me how you're feeling."

Mom stands from her chair, shaking her head at me in disappointment as she walks out, my dad following her, begging her to stay and hear me out. "What's her problem?"

"She's being her usual self," Ewan says, leaning forward, his arms on the railing of the bed, expression unreadable. "How do you feel?"

I want to ask him what happened between us. I want to know why I have a memory of us sleeping together, and it frightens me that an enormous part of me has no idea if that scares me or if it brings me relief.

One of the doctors comes in, pulling out his pen from his clipboard. "Ahh, you're awake, Miss Miller. Can you both give us a minute?" He gestures to the door as Gabriella and Ewan give me one last look before leaving. "It's good to see you with a little warmth to your face. You've been quite pale." He smiles at me, tucking the clipboard under his arm. "How do you feel?"

"My head hurts."

He pulls down the rails on each side of my bed, adjusting the speed of the IV drip. "You were dehydrated when you came in. We'll let this run through your line and disconnect you," he says, bringing a chair closer and crossing his ankle over his knee. "Now, tell me what's been going on."

"Nothing." I don't know what else to say. In all honesty, the past few weeks have been strange. Right now, it seems to be the first time I've been able to think clearly enough to form a full sentence that isn't mumbled or rehearsed. "I don't know. Everything is slow and fuzzy."

"And how long have you been taking unprescribed Clozapine?"

"Clozapine?" I echo him, tilting my head in confusion. I narrow my eyes to slits to try to look at the paperwork. "What do you mean?"

"You had high levels of it in your system." He looks at me, placing his pen on his clipboard. "For someone who has no mental health issues, I'm deeply concerned, Aria. We've had a check over your heart, but we may need to do further scans to ensure there isn't any swelling of your muscles. Your blood pressure was extremely low when you were brought in. It still is, but not in any way dangerous." He sighs. "Why were you taking it?"

"Are you sure it's Clozapine?"

"We did a full blood panels yesterday, and you have a high level of it in your system. We will need to keep you admitted and monitored for a few more days."

I gulp and nod, saying the word to myself.

Clozapine—one of the strongest forms of antipsychotic medication. It's used only when everything else fails for people with schizoaffective disorders and extreme levels of psychosis. So why the hell is it in my system?

My lips are moving, but no sound comes out, my heart plummeting while he stares at me. A few moments of silence follow, and I clear my throat. "I didn't...I didn't know I was—"

"I understand." He stands, noting something on his clipboard. "I'm going to go over your observations and let you get some more sleep."

"Okay." I feel tingles crawling up the back of my neck, a cold sensation trailing down my cheeks as all the blood drains from my face. "Can I ask Ewan to come in?"

He nods, settling the paperwork on the seat next to him and getting Ewan's attention. "Take a seat."

With Ewan staring at me, I see him take in my pale face and watering eyes, giving me a tight smile. "Are you okay to sit with me?" I ask.

He agrees, resting his arms on the edge of the hospital bed as the doctor checks my temperature, my heart with his stethoscope, my blood pressure, writing down the results. "Still low. I'll get another IV bag sent in once this is done. I'll need to arrange an ultrasound to make sure the baby is okay."

I choke on air, my hand gripping Ewan's with a harsh hold. "Baby?"

———

"HEY," Ewan groans, stretching from his slumber and looking around the room, then at me. "Have you just woken up?"

I nod and smile. "Just a minute ago."

"You're looking more alive. Do you still feel nauseous?"

I shake my head and twist the bedding in my fingers, looking down at my flat stomach and wondering how the hell a baby is in there.

"You didn't need to stay here with me."

He shrugs, standing and walking to the foot of the hospital bed while he stretches his arms above him. My eyes drag down the length of him, averting my gaze to the wall when he notices. "I don't mind. Jason's staying at your parents' place for a few days anyway."

"I'm surprised they even showed up," I say, rolling my eyes and tucking my hair behind my ear. I look at him, chewing down on my bottom lip as I see how deflated he is. "Thank you."

"What for?"

I raise a shoulder, fighting back yet another flood of tears. "I...I just don't know why you're still here."

"I already told you, I don't mind," he replies, pulling his hat on to control his wavy brown hair.

I shake my head, causing him to frown at me, his face full of confusion. "I mean with everything. We split up, and you're still helping me– why? Why do you allow me to run to you whenever I need you?"

Sitting on the chair closest to the bed, he leans his elbows on the edge, running the pad of his thumb along his bottom lip a few times while he thinks. "Look, Aria. I've been in love with you for years, and nothing I do, or you do, will ever change that." I stay silent, my eyes searching his face, wanting him to continue. "I made some really, really bad mistakes when we were younger, and I need to live with that. But if you need me? Of course, I'm going to be here for you." He grabs my hand, cupping it between his. "I know all this is pretty fucked, and I know you're scared, but no matter what, I'm with you the entire way."

I smile at him as a tear falls down my cheek. "You've wasted so much time trying with me, Ewan. I appreciate it, but I refuse to drag you into all of this with me. You and Jason deserve to find someone who isn't some idiot like me."

"Lies," he says with a chuckle in his thick Scottish accent, and my eyes drop to the top of his chest tattoo poking up from his collar. "Aria Miller has always been good enough for me. But that's not why I'm here. I'm here because I care about you and I'm worried."

"I'm pregnant," I whisper, pressure building behind my eyes. He nods slowly.

"And it isn't yours." There's sadness in my tone. "How can I be with you since I was a teenager and fall pregnant by someone else?"

"Hey," he says in a comforting tone, taking my hand. "Don't cry. I'm here regardless."

"Why aren't you running the other way?"

"Everything you've done for me and Jason, what kind of man would I be to leave you to do this by yourself?"

"It's not a favor for a favor, Ewan. I wanted to help you with Jason because he's a part of you," I reply. "I don't even have a clue what's going on in my own life, so it would be wrong of me to drag someone else into it." I pull away from his hold on my hand, leaning forward to hug my knees. "I'm just a lost cause now. Jason and you deserve better."

"If you ever speak about yourself like that again, I'll hunt that bastard down myself and hang him from a bridge." I huff at his threat, and he stands abruptly. "He's lucky I'm not out hunting him down right now."

"Why are you blaming this on Tobias?"

His eyes narrow, and then he huffs. "Gabriella didn't tell you?" When I shake my head, he pinches the bridge of his nose. "Your boyfriend is on medication. A heavy dosage at that. One of those being Clozapine."

"You think he drugged me with it?"

"I don't think. I *know* he did. Gabriella is already working on a report to hand over to the cops."

My body goes stiff, and I have an urge to yell at him, but I stop myself. Because it makes sense. Everything. The fact Tobias even takes that drug in the first place. Everything just clicks.

I feel sick at the idea he tricked me so badly.

Did he switch out my pill? How the hell did he get me pregnant?

In all honesty, I'll be in disbelief until I have my scan. It could be a false positive, or maybe I'm far along and Ewan is the father. But I've had my period recently.

I hug my knees tight and swallow hard. "I'm scared."

"I know, baby. But we're all here for you."

Hearing a knock at the door, we both snap our heads in the direction of it cracking open, a nurse popping her head in to let us know visiting hours are almost over. I turn to Ewan, giving him a tight smile as I note how angry he's getting. "You should go. Get a night of proper sleep and message me when you're awake."

"Okay," he responds, standing and pulling on his jacket and shoes, shocking me as he leans down to place a soft kiss on my forehead. Tingles run up my arms and my neck at the contact, and I do my best not to show it affected me by hiding my blush.

As soon as he's gone, I pull out my phone from under the pillow, fully intending on confronting Tobias and telling him to get the hell out of my life, but my blood runs cold when I see the notifications.

TOBIASWORK

Ten missed calls.

TOBIASWORK

I know what's happening, and please don't be worried. I can fix this. Come and meet me at the underground footpath next to the hospital. Don't be mad at me. Everything I'm doing is for you. You'll understand when I explain.

TOBIASWORK

I love you.

"Oh my God, Aria!" I jump out of my skin, dropping my phone as Gabriella blows through my doorway with my work laptop to hand. "Look," she continues, settling it on my lap. I scan the words on the screen, my eyes widening at its contents.

"You did it. Ivy got accepted into the new trials thanks to you! She flies out to Denmark on Wednesday, but because of everything going on, they've allocated your assistant Margaret to go with her. But Aria... She got in!"

"Gabriella," I begin, choking on my words. I'm in shock, to be honest. I didn't think they'd accept her, but with extensive research and working my ass off, I put up a good enough fight to get her accepted. By the looks of the plan, she has a high chance of a better quality of life.

She hugs me, and we both cry tears of joy, laughing in delight at the incredible news. I reread the last part, congratulating me, Aria Miller, for putting my whole heart into this.

"See, *this* is who you are. *This* is why you need to fight against everything that's going on. There are loads of children just like Ivy who need someone to fight for them, and you are one of the few who goes above and beyond. But look, it worked! And you have an email from her mom too, thanking you a thousand times."

My chest swells with the feeling of pure satisfaction, the reason I love my job. I look at my best friend, the joy in her eyes and the way she is so proud of me everything a person can ever hope for. It's not often you come across an individual who cheers you on, cries with you for your successes. She's not just my best friend; she's like my sister, and I love her.

"Can you come to the ultrasound with me tomorrow?"

She snorts, closing my laptop. "I was coming anyway."

31

ARIA

"**I**'m going to fucking kill you."

I roll my eyes while Gabriella yells through the phone at me, cursing at me for slipping out of the hospital. I have countless missed calls from her, Ewan, and my parents, all trying to find me. I only responded to Gabs because I thought she would understand my plan and why I need to do it.

She doesn't.

"Are you trying to get yourself institutionalized? You're being monitored, Aria. You sneaking off without telling anyone isn't going to help you keep your job secure either." She raises her voice with each word, and I fight the urge to hang up. "Everyone on our ward thinks you're having a mental breakdown as it is, so running off isn't winning you any points."

I ignore her because she's right, but if I sit around and plead that I'm innocent in abusing something as dangerous as antipsychotics, I will regret not trying this.

I had messaged Tobias when Gabriella left to go get me something to eat. I told him I'd meet him, that I wanted answers. He called me. His tone was very low, each word that left his mouth coming across as apologetic because he knows I know what he has been doing to me for weeks.

"He won't hurt me," I say, wrapping my jacket around me tighter, feeling the coldness of the November weather. I can see my bursts of breath, feel the icy air filling my lungs as I make my way down to the underpass next to my place. "If he wanted to hurt me, he would've by now."

"Are you fucking listening to yourself? Look at everything that asshole has done...and you are still that delusional to think he won't hurt you?" I hear Ewan in the background, a door closing as he greets Gabs. "She left the hospital to meet him."

I stop in my tracks, my eyes shutting momentarily as I hear his protests and curses spewing through the phone. "I'm hanging up now."

"No! Aria, it's me," Ewan says, causing Gabriella to huff and tell him she's going to call my parents. "Where are you?"

"I need answers," I tell him, stopping and sitting on a small wall about five minutes from the underpass.

"And you think it's safe to go see him? Come on, Aria," he sighs. "You're smarter than this. Please tell me where you are. I'm heading to my car now."

"Do you trust me?"

I hear him exhale deeply, probably running his hand through his hair and dropping his head. "Yeah," he replies quietly. "I don't trust him. What do you expect to happen?"

"I'll be fine."

"Hang up," I hear a deep voice behind me, *his* voice, and all the confidence evaporates from me, replaced by instant fear that has all the hairs rising on the back of my neck. I stand, turning, and I'm met with the bluest eyes burning into me. "Hang up. Now."

"No, Aria, don't hang—"

Tobias whips my phone out of my hand, hanging up on Ewan. "Took your time," he says, giving me a smirk as he steps forward, tucking my phone into his back pocket.

"Give me that back," I snap at him, reaching out my hand. He shakes his head at me, taking my arm and walking us into the underpass.

His grip is firm, and I try to squirm away from him the best I can. He stops when we have made our way to the other side of the path, where it's dark and secluded. "You're hurting me."

Tobias releases my arm, turning me to face him. "We don't have much time," he begins, and I frown at him, stepping back as he attempts to take my hand in his. "You're afraid." Tilting his head at me, he takes in my shaky posture and my watering eyes from fear. "No, no, no, Aria... Don't be afraid of me." He cups my cheeks in his palms and rests his forehead against mine, my body rigid. "Please don't be afraid of me. I'm the last person on Earth who would harm you."

"You're a monster," I state, finding enough courage to shove him away from me. "I can't take it anymore, Tobias." Panic takes over him, and all the blood drains from his face, his lips moving, no words leaving his mouth. "Clozapine..." I nod my head as his eyes widen. "Yeah, you asshole!"

"You needed help. I was just—"

"No! You have fucked my life up so badly, the last thing I need is your help. I just spent days in the hospital trying to flush all of it out of my system."

He stays silent, and rage builds up around me so intensely, I throw my hand at him, slapping him hard enough that his face jerks to the side, his glasses falling to the ground.

Taking in deep, heavy breaths, I try to stay calm as his eyes darken, narrowing to slits as he turns his face to me. He backs me against the wall of the underpass, crushing his glasses under his shoe as his nostrils flare with fury.

"I deserved that," he says, making me flinch as he tucks my hair behind my ear. "But if you ever hit me again..." He leans in, his mouth inches from mine. "I won't let it slide. I'll cage you for the rest of your life and feed you my cock." He presses his lips to my forehead, my eyes fluttering shut for a moment. "We need to go."

"I'm not going anywhere with you," I say as he turns, causing him to freeze in his steps. "You can't drug me, leave me tied to a bed, mess with my life, then expect me to just forgive you."

245

"I gave you those pills to help you, Aria. You were stressed out, and it was the only thing I could think of to help." He huffs, impatiently tilting his head to a car parked under a streetlight in the distance. "Move."

"Gabriella said the medication was yours. Is that right?"

The silence is killing me. He's not even looking at me as he tries to stay calm.

"Say it to my face, Tobias. Say you drugged me with it. Clozapine is an antipsychotic medication for—"

"I know what they are." Interrupting me abruptly, he blows out his cheeks, watching me. "I know what they fucking are."

I cross my arms in front of me, my fear washed away by the building anger, that annoying part of me battling with my mind to just go with him. "Were they yours?"

I don't know why I so badly need a confession, maybe to make myself feel better and not question what everyone else is saying. I need him to admit that he's a bad person. It would make it easier to leave him.

"If I tell you, will you hurry up and get in the fucking car?" I watch as he chews on his bottom lip in frustration, his nose scrunching up. "They didn't work on me and it's because I'm *not* sick, Aria. There's nothing wrong with me and there's not a thing that you, my parents, or any fucking doctor says will change that."

"You drugged your own girlfriend, Tobias. You swapped them with my birth control pill just so—"

"No, I didn't. Why would I switch them with your fucking pill?" he questions me, taking a few steps until he's in front of me again. "You were drinking heavily. I covered every bottle you bought, right down to the milk, coffee filters. I had to pretend I had gone home so you wouldn't notice."

My jaw tenses, my twitchy hand trying its best not to slap him again. "And you claim you're not sick? Do you know what happens when you drink alcohol with that type of medication?"

"Of course I do. Why do you think I wasn't drinking before?" he replies, shrugging.

"Are you kidding me?" I yell, shoving his chest once more, causing him to back away. "I'm done. Stay the hell away from me." I turn away from him, storming down the path as he catches up to me, circling his arm around my waist. "Let me explain," he says breathlessly, resting his forehead on my shoulder while I slap his hands, giving up after a long minute. "Don't leave."

With a trembling lip and tears falling down my cheeks, I place my hands over his on my waist, interlacing our fingers so I can pull his arms away from me. I turn to him, watching him chew on the inside of his cheek as he blinks rapidly. "I'm still dizzy and my migraine won't go away, and my blood pressure is so low. And it's all your fault."

"I was helping you," he repeats, this time quietly. My eyes shut as the words fall from his mouth as if they are nothing, my heart accelerating. "I meant it when I said everything I'm doing is for you." His palms press against the sides of my face, and he dips his head until the tips of our noses touch. "I love you, Aria. I will do *anything* for you."

"But you can't," I sob, dropping my head to his chest as I allow the flood of tears to fall. "You can't love me the way I need you to." I wrap my arm around him, and he holds the back of my head as silence hangs between us. "You don't hurt people you love the way you've hurt me."

My body shakes in his arms, trying to distract him with my tears while I attempt to get my phone from his back pocket, failing as he pulls us apart and grabs my hand.

"Come with me." He looks hopeful, lifting my hand to his mouth and kissing my knuckles. "I won't force you, but if you're coming, we need to leave now, or we'll miss it."

I'm not sure of what he's capable of, and because a toxic side of me likes seeing him again, I don't push him away when he presses his lips to mine, kissing him back as I feel myself sinking against his body.

I'm a traitor to myself. I woke up next to a sleeping Ewan earlier and felt safe. Now, I'm wrapped up in a psychopath who just drugged me and got me pregnant, and I'm letting him kiss me.

"Miss what?" I ask against his mouth, his fingers lacing through my hair.

He doesn't reply. He just holds my small body against his large frame, towering over me as his tongue rolls along mine, kissing me hard. I groan into his mouth, feeling his teeth nip my bottom lip before pulling away.

"If we get the boat to Ireland, no one will find us." I stare at him in disbelief, holding my breath as he nods at me, agreeing with himself. "Yeah, that way, no one can stop us from being together. Don't you see what they're all doing? They are taking you away from me. I don't let go of what's mine."

"I...I don't have my passport."

"I do. It's in the bag I packed." He grabs my hand and walks us to the car. I stay completely silent, thinking of ways to get out of this but not doing anything that would make him react. "I went to your place the other day, and you were gone. I figured one of those jerks got a hold of you. So, I came up with a plan, a way for us to be happy without me having to kill Ewan. By the time I got back from arranging everything, you were taken to the hospital."

He opens the passenger side door and gestures for me to get in.

"I can't leave," I protest.

"Sure you can," he replies, groaning as I shake my head. "Get in the fucking car, Aria." His snappy tone makes me jump, resulting in me settling in the passenger seat and buckling my belt while he slams the door. "I have a hotel nearby. We can go there until the next boat."

Okay, think, Aria. Think of ways to get out of this. I could grab the steering wheel while we're driving, but that could harm the baby. Oh God, I can't do anything without my phone–unless I try to steal his? Would he hurt me if I tried? Would he hit me? Should I tell him I'm pregnant, or will he do something to the baby?

I look at him, his glasses long gone, a hard look on his face, and decide not to mention the fact I'm carrying his child. I'll tell him eventually, but only when I'm safe.

WE REACH the hotel half an hour later, a small bed and breakfast situated next to the water, a ten-minute drive from Stranraer's boat terminal.

He helps me out of the car, and I can't contain my trembling as he makes his way through the reception, my eyes on the lady, begging her silently to help me. She takes no notice, typing away on her computer with her glasses falling halfway down her crooked nose.

"When did you get discharged?" he asks as he opens the door for me, pulling my jacket off my shoulders.

"I didn't."

Frowning, he takes off his own jacket, placing them both down on the chair next to the door. "What do you mean, you didn't? My girl is becoming ruthless."

I don't respond, because my eyes are glued to the beautiful hotel room: a four-poster bed with roses spread across the bed.

Is he trying to be romantic? While trying to kidnap me?

"It's the only room they had left," he says, as if he can read my thoughts. "I'll put your bag in the bathroom so you can shower and change."

I watch him nervously walking around, not giving me any eye contact and fumbling with the straps of the bag. He turns his back to me to place stuff on the bed, and I spot my phone again.

Hugging myself, I swallow.

"You should probably get out of those clothes, since they're wet from the rain."

I need him to take his clothes off. I need to get my phone back.

Yes, he's very evidently mentally unwell. Yes, he needs help. And yes, I know he has done some awful things to me. But I can't just erase my feelings. The butterflies flutter in my core as he looks at me, thinking my comment about undressing is for something sexual.

"Do you think we have time to?" he asks, walking to me and stroking his knuckles down my arms. The tingling feeling goes straight between my legs, making my breath hitch.

"Time to what?"

He bites on his bottom lip, reaching for the strap on my shoulder and slowly pulling it down. My breathing becomes uneven, my legs crossing from the intensity of his touch alone. His cheek grazes mine as he whispers in my ear. "Do we have time to fuck?"

"Under one condition," I say, pressing my hands to his chest as I walk him back to the edge of the bed, making him sit down. "Tell me everything you've done to me."

He groans as his hands grab at my hips, pulling me to straddle his lap. "Hmm, no. I don't think I will."

I shrug, attempting to stand from him, yelping as he pulls me back down. "You want me?" I ask, wrapping my hands in his hair and tugging it so I can nip at his neck.

"More than you know," he replies breathlessly.

I grind against him, taking a deep breath and hoping he buys into it. I press my lips to his, taking full control as my tongue pushes through his parted lips and runs along his.

He breaks away from the deep kiss after a few minutes, both of us panting.

"Tell me you're not mad at me."

"I'm not a liar," I reply against his lips.

"Just...tell me..."

Moving my hips against him has his words broken. I feel his cock hardening, and I sense my plan starting to vanish as my emotions take over. I'm desperate for him, all of him, and I know it's wrong, completely dangerous, making me want him even more.

I whimper as his mouth attaches to my throat, sucking on the skin as his hand trails up my spine, grabbing the nape of my neck, his lips moving to mine. "I do love you, Aria." He stops my movements, seriousness taking over his face. "It might be different, but I feel for you in ways I've never felt before. Tell me it's enough."

My heart shouldn't be breaking for him. My body shouldn't be reacting to him. My mind needs to turn back on so I can put a stop to this clouded judgement. I know, deep down, who I love, who I want, and who I should be sitting on right now. He's currently looking for me.

The realization has me pausing.

"Why do you have those meds, Tobias?"

He shakes his head, looking to the side. "I don't want you to be afraid of me." I watch his throat bob, swallowing hard. "Everyone fears me, but you don't look at me the way they all do."

"Who?"

"Everyone," he responds, looking back to me. "You spent a brief moment in my world, you've experienced a fraction of the things I feel on a daily basis, and you couldn't handle it." I feel my eyes watering, sucking in my raw bottom lip as Tobias continues, my heart breaking in two. "I don't want to talk about me anymore."

"Fine." I shove his chest so he lies down on the bed, positioning myself above him so I can feel him against me once more, my hand firmly gripping his throat. "Are you going to fuck me or not?"

Please let my plan work. If I can just slip my phone from his pocket and run to the bathroom, I can get help. I can get Tobias help too.

"Hmm, I love it when you're demanding," he says, rubbing his hands up my thighs, raising his hips to press his hardness against me. "Are you going to ride my face, Doctor? I haven't had my tongue in your pussy for a while."

I allow him to pull my shirt off and unclip my bra, butterflies going wild in my stomach. Between my legs is soaking, only building as he sits us up and kisses me, my mind shutting off.

Oh, God. I need to stop before I give in.

I allow him to consume me by kissing me hard. We get as far as our pants coming off before I stop us. "Wait here," I demand, his fingers about to curl into my panties to touch me. "Give me a minute."

I manage to slide my phone free from his pants without him noticing, thankful it's dark. I kiss him until he's lying on his back, seeing how hard he is in his boxers.

I keep the phone hidden as I rush to the bathroom.

32

ARIA

T hree minutes.

That's how long I've been sitting with my back against the door, staring at the flooring of the expensive bathroom. My face is coated in silent tears, painful whimpers silently strangling in my throat as I cover my mouth so Tobias doesn't hear me.

I look down at the screen of my phone, rereading my sent message to Gabriella.

ME

> I'm at the Corsewall Lighthouse Hotel with Tobias, but we leave in two hours. Please, hurry. I locked myself in the bathroom. Please don't call me.

GABS

> I'm at the police station now. Hang tight and stay in the bathroom. We're coming for you. I love you.

I'm broken, feeling like a traitor for tricking Tobias into thinking I was going to have sex with him.

This is it; this is the moment I get him the support he needs.

He may be criminalized for kidnapping and everything else, but at least he will get the proper treatment for whatever mental disorder he has.

I truly believe Tobias has a form of psychosis; maybe he's even a full-on psychopath who tricked me into feeling sorry for him. We will find out soon, but either way, roaming the public is a hazard to himself as well as everyone around him.

I need to help him.

I hear Tobias at the door. He tries to pull down the handle, knocking on the door when he realizes it's locked. "Aria?"

"I'm coming," I answer, my words getting stuck in my throat. I can't stop the sob I inhale, my bottom lip shivering. "Give me a minute."

"Why are you crying?"

The back of my head hits the door, my vision blurring with the tears pooling in my eyes. "I'm not."

"Bullshit." His voice is no longer above me; he must've slid his way down on the opposite side of the door. "Talk to me."

"I'm just so tired, Tobias."

"With me?" he asks. "Are you tired of me?"

My body shakes, hugging my knees to my chest, checking the time on my phone. Six minutes have gone by. I tuck my phone under the mat in the middle of the floor, hiding it from him.

This is most likely my last moment with Tobias before he's arrested, and although I'm terrified of one side of him, the other side has me standing, unlocking the door, and opening it to him as he quickly gets to his feet.

He takes me in with a nervous look, frowning at me in confusion as my lip trembles and tears fall, hugging myself as I walk until I'm in his arms. I settle my cheek against his chest, listening to his racing heart. His hand rests on the back of my head, holding me to his large frame.

"Aria..." Tobias tries to look down at me, but I keep my eyes squeezed shut, shaking my head as I wrap my arms around his waist. "Did I make you cry?"

"Yes," I reply, burying my head into his chest more. "I'm not afraid of you. I'm afraid of who you've turned me into." He sighs in response, and I feel his cheek on the top of my head. "It was supposed to be *just* sex."

Releasing a breathy laugh, he tightens his hold on me, lifting me so my legs wrap around him, walking us to the bed. He sits on the edge, so I straddle him, holding my face in his hands. "You're stronger than before, Aria."

I shake my head, my face screwing up with the ache in my chest.

I shouldn't be feeling so much heartbreak, using our final moments together to weep to him, wanting him to hug me one last time. It hurts, my heart yearning for us to run. It feels like a knife slowly piercing my skin until it's buried deep in my chest, causing me to lower my head on his shoulder and cry harder than ever before.

"We need help, Tobias," I gasp out, tightening my arms around him. My words are almost incoherent, but he holds me closer in his arms. "I love you," I say quietly, uttering those three words for the last time. "I need you to know that."

He pulls back, wiping my tears away with his thumbs. "What's going on?" he asks.

I rest my forehead against his, my heart and mind having a war. "Kiss me," I beg, running my fingers through his hair while he frowns at me. "Please."

This is torture. Not only are they taking forever to get here, but I'm also so close to telling him to run, to hide from everyone coming after him. I don't want him to hate me, but I know he will when he finds out I've completely backstabbed him. I want them to burst through the door, but also, I want to lie in his arms and forget the world.

I need help just as much as he does.

I see the image in my head of his future, bright and safe, his mind calm. I keep myself together, remembering that although I'm doing this for myself and everyone around me, I'm also doing this for him.

Tobias kisses me, pressing his soft lips against mine as we both deeply inhale through our noses. I melt against him, trying to ignore everything else going on in my mind and just focusing on him—us.

I may be confused with everything, and I may be insane for allowing Tobias to warp my mind while still sitting here, kissing him, enjoying his hands holding me, but I don't regret it. Meeting him has been a whirlwind, and he tests my patience more than Ewan ever did. I care for Tobias, enough to do what's necessary so he gets the help he so desperately needs.

"Distract me," I say demandingly against his mouth, fastening my hold on his hair between my fingers. "Ask me something."

He looks confused, but he clears his throat and tucks my hair behind both ears, stroking my cheeks with his thumbs. It feels good, something I'll try to remember. "What do you want to do when we get to Ireland?"

My lip starts to curl in once more, fighting back another surge of tears. "You tell me."

He thinks to himself, a smile playing on his lips. I search his features, memorizing his deep dimples, how long his dark lashes are, his defined cheekbones. "We don't need to get jobs for money. I have plenty. Unless you want to, of course. I guess we can just enjoy being together." His lips gently touch mine, and I feel myself falling apart inside. My jaw tenses as I plaster a fake smile on my face, another tear slipping down my cheek. "Stop crying, Aria. Please."

"I got Ivy into the trials. She leaves for Denmark in two days."

His face lights up, genuinely looking pleased for me as he shows his perfect smile. "I knew you could do it. You should be proud of yourself. I sure am."

"Thanks," I reply, grimacing slightly. "You know I care about you, don't you?"

"Kind of." He laughs a little, his teeth whiter than white. "I'm sorry I've been quite difficult. I shouldn't have done what I did to you, and for that, I truly am sorry." He rests his forehead on mine, and my breath hitches at his shaky tone. "Trying to love someone and fight for control, it's harder than it sounds. Forgive me?"

The knife buried in my chest is now twisting, a sharp pain rendering me speechless.

Why can't he be like this all the time?

I contemplate telling him I'm pregnant, that we created a precious life growing within me. But for some reason, I can't seem to pull together the words while I stare into his hopeful ocean blues.

My heart completely sinks as I hear sirens blaring outside. Tobias raises his brows and looks to the window, the red and blue lights flashing through the frosted glass.

"Shit. Aria, you need to hide," he says quickly, lifting us from the bed and holding my waist. Turning back to look at me with fear in his eyes, he grabs my face, kissing me hard and pulling away to look at the flashing lights getting brighter. "They must be here because you ran away from the hospital. You need to run." I stare at him in disbelief, shock slapping me that he thinks they're actually here for me. "Run!"

"Tobias, I..."

He rushes around the room, tossing me my clothes and throwing his own on, then our shoes. I'm silent, staring at him pacing the room with his hand running through his hair in frustration.

He looks terrified.

"I can't lose you," he begins, cupping my cheeks in his palms with blazing eyes. "I promise I won't let them hurt you."

"No, Tobias," I cry, my hand shaking as I reach up and stroke his cheek. "You—"

I scream, jumping back as the door is kicked open abruptly. Tobias grabs my arm and guards me with his back to my front, protecting me from the flood of officers storming into the room.

Tobias grips my hand in his, backing us into the wall as the group advances towards us. "Don't you fucking dare touch her!" he threatens, raising his forearm as one of them strikes him. He grunts with each land of the long, black baton, doing everything he can to keep me safe.

It's breaking my heart even more that he thinks they're here for me, protecting me from a threat that doesn't even exist. "Tobias." I try to grab his attention, but he moves away from me and lands a harsh punch across one of their faces, flooring them. "Tobias, stop!"

He's overpowered, tackled to the ground. I stay in the corner and wrap my arms around myself as they kneel on his back, sobbing as I fall to the ground. "Aria...run!" he shouts in a panic, managing to get free and grabbing one of their batons, cracking it into an officer's ankle.

I hear a taser, but he's still fighting back, throwing punches and biting into one of the officer's faces, his mouth covered with blood when he looks at me in desperation.

A tall one approaches me, gripping my forearm and tugging me. I hear Tobias yelling threats at him, telling him he will kill him if he touches me, rip his head off if he hurts me, then silence as a taser sticks into his neck, flooring him.

I smack my palm over my mouth, seeing blood covering Tobias' face, gasping out sobs as the ringing in my ears overtakes any sounds around me. I can see him struggling under the mass of bodies, his eyes begging me to run.

Guilt is flooding me. I did this.

I'm thrown out of the room, and I collide with the wall opposite the door, my head hitting the hard wood of the floor. Another deadly threat from Tobias, a few snarls from him being beaten, and more officers storm into the place, fully padded with protective clothing and shields covering their faces.

Is this all necessary? He is one man; surely, all these officers are wasting their time?

"Aria!" I hear Gabriella yelling, rapid footsteps echoing up the hallway as I look up at my panicked best friend. "Oh my God, are you okay? Why are you lying on the ground? That fucking bastard hurt you, didn't he?"

We both look to the room, the sea of yellow and black uniforms battling, and we notice Tobias standing, his face now fully bloodied as he bares his teeth. He throws his fists around like he's enjoying it, yelling at them to let me go, or he'll snap their necks.

Emergency health workers appear, holding bags filled with equipment as they rush to me. Everything is blurring, my head starting to pound with exhaustion. I hear Tobias yelling, things smashing.

"Are you okay?" Gabs asks, wiping away my half-dried tears, moving my hair out of my eyes. "You did the right thing. I can see regret written all over your face."

"I just want him to get help," I say, my lip shaking so much, I have to bite down to stop it, dropping my head to her lap while the paramedics kneel beside me.

After nearly an hour's worth of health checks and observations in the back of the ambulance, Tobias is still inside the hotel.

"Ewan is in the hospital," Gabriella tells me. "There was CCTV footage of Tobias hitting him over the head before he came to meet you, leaving him with a gash down his head and face in the middle of the street."

My eyes widen. "Is he okay?"

"Don't worry," she replies, smiling weakly. "He's got a few stitches but was worried about you. He even tried to leave the hospital without getting his wound closed up."

My shoulder slump. So many bad things keep happening because of Tobias, and now, he has attacked Ewan, and I know I've done the right thing here. It shouldn't have ever gotten to this point in the first place.

"Can we go?"

On cue, the double doors of the hotel burst open, Tobias cuffed at his hands and feet as he's carried out by a group of officers, blood covering everyone, everywhere.

"Aria!" he begins to yell, struggling in his shackles as his eyes stay on mine. "Let me fucking see her!" He's hit once more, and I wince, looking away. "I'll find you."

"You can fuck right off! The baby doesn't need a waste of space like you!" Gabriella screams at him, making all the blood drain from my face, my eyes widen. "You deserve to rot in a cell!"

He ignores her words, his crimson face in total shock as his stunned gaze doesn't leave mine. He stops fighting back, his body relaxing as his eyebrows furrow. He doesn't attack the officers who stand him up or retaliate when one pushes his head, shoving him into the car.

His once aggressive blue eyes are now filled with something...broken.

33

TOBIAS

They took Aria from me.

I knew the second the cops filled the room that it was game over, that I'd lost her. I tried so fucking hard to save her, but I couldn't overpower them.

They took her, and now I'm trapped in a damn cell with gashes and bruises all over my body.

Ewan survived. One of my charges is assault against him, but I wish he fucking died.

I gulp and stare at my hand. She's pregnant. My doctor is growing a life inside her, one we both created, and I can't be there for her. She'll be afraid, lonely, and I need to get to her. I need to be there for my child and my woman.

Emptiness is a strange feeling.

It makes me want to feel something. maybe pain. Maybe guilt. Maybe the way someone's heart stops beating long after I've strangled them.

Well, the last one didn't work. My cellmate stopped breathing an hour ago, and I don't feel any different.

Where is the remorse, the worry of taking one's life?

The guy across from me, separated by bars, hasn't taken his eyes off me. He's Scottish too, like most inmates in this holding facility. I'm not sure what he wants to say to me, or maybe he's scared.

No idea why. It's not like I can break through the bars and kill him too.

It was a silent kill. My first kill. It should've been Ewan, but I settled on taking my anger out on this one. His accent was enough to trigger images of Aria and her ex all over each other, and I needed the feeling erased.

My fingers have marked his throat, his eyes open. I kick his foot, checking to see if rigor mortis has settled in. He's still floppy, but his skin is paling, but all I do is sigh and sit against the wall with parted legs, balancing my elbows on them.

"Is he dead?" the guy across from me finally asks.

I raise a shoulder. "He hasn't had a pulse for nearly an hour."

"Fuck," he swears, stepping away from the bars.

I want to tell him to calm down, but he has vanished into the back of his cell. Being dramatic in this situation isn't going to do him any favors. The guy at my feet is already dead.

Justin was my only call–he called me an idiot and said he would fly over right away, that he'll tell my mother some bullshit story until he can get me out of here.

But I have other plans. And it starts the second a guard walks by, noticing the dead inmates on the ground. He alerts the others through the radio and stupidly unlocks the cell.

Before he can pull out a taser, baton, or whatever else they keep on them as guards, I grab him from behind and use all my strength to twist his neck until I hear the sickening crack.

He drops to the floor just as I'm tackled to the ground.

34

ARIA

'American bedlamite kills two while being held in custody'

The headline glares at me from my hospital room. As if stuck in a bad dream, I turn off the screen and fight the tears that have been falling all day. I pace the room, wiping my cheeks, waiting impatiently to be discharged.

Ewan leans forward on the small sofa. "You good?"

I stop pacing. "Yeah. We're safe. That's all that matters." I smile at him, the fakest ever. "If I think about it, I cry, and I'm so fed up with crying."

He nods, and I look at the staples and stitches on his head and a little on his face before I sit on the edge of the hospital bed. "I'm really sorry he did that to you. He thought you were trying to break us up."

He snorts. "I guess I was, in a way. I wanted you away from him the second I found out you were dating him."

My head turns to the door opening, Gabriella trailing in with Jason. He grins when he sees me, carrying a Get Well Soon balloon and a single red rose.

"Are they for me?" I ask excitedly.

He grins and hands them to me, hugging me so hard, you

wouldn't think he was only ten years old–although he does act a lot younger.

He takes the couch next to his dad and asks me if I'm sore, to which I reply with a shake of my head. "I'm just tired and need a load of sleep."

"You could sleep at home," he suggests. "Dad can make you a cup of tea."

Ewan messes up Jason's hair while he slaps his hand away. "Stop it, Dad!" he whines, shifting along the couch to put some distance between them. "You said you miss making Aria tea!"

He narrows his eyes at his son.

Gabriella settles beside me on the bed, dropping a sandwich on my lap. "The food here sucks. Thank me later."

"Hey, did you not say you had a video call with Ivy's mom today?" she asks.

"Yeah." My eyes flicker from them to the window, the sun already starting to vanish behind the trees. "She's bringing up a lot of fluids, but they said that's a good sign. Her energy levels have risen too."

"And what about the baby?" Ewan adds in, screwing his eyes shut when Jason's face lights up. But before he can ask questions, Gabriella tells him to come with her to get candy from the vending machine.

"Sorry," Ewan says.

I'm thrown off guard, fighting back the emotional fear of loss, making me stare at him in silence for a beat too long before finally answering him. "I have a scan tomorrow."

"That's good. Gabriella going with you?"

"No, she's been called into work all night and doesn't get off her shift until ten minutes before my appointment," I reply, walking over and sitting down next to him on the sofa, my knee bumping his.

When Gabriella returns, we chat for the next hour, mostly about Jason's school, his friends, and how much he beats Ewan in his computer game. I always feel so relaxed when I'm with them. I almost forget the last few months of us not being together, enjoying the peace and quiet in my head.

Gabriella goes to start her shift when a nurse comes in with my discharge letter and informs me when my follow ups are. She reminds me of my appointment tomorrow and tells me to come straight back if I still don't feel one hundred percent.

"Time to go, buddy," Ewan says, patting Jason's shoulder as he stands. "We can grab food on the way home."

Groaning, Jason turns off his game and runs to put on his sneakers.

"I think you should come home tonight. I don't like the thought of you in that apartment by yourself."

"I'm actually excited to lie in my own bed, but could you drive me?"

Jason puts his two hands together. "Please come home. Pleaseeeeee."

Giving him false hope isn't right, so I mess his hair and grab my purse while Ewan picks up my bags.

I give him a faint smile and follow them out of the room and down the hallway, coming to a halt when I spot my mom standing at the entranceway.

Oh, boy. Here we go.

"Ewan!" she begins, her eyes narrowing at me momentarily. "If you need Jason taken care of while you're working, come to me. He doesn't need to see Aria in this state. I don't think she's fit to be around him anyway. Seriously, you should do the both of you a favor and cut her out of your lives. She's nothing but a knocked-up junkie."

Before I can speak or shout, Ewan side-steps in front of me, his fists clenched at his sides. "A knocked-up junkie? Do you hear yourself? Don't speak about her like that, especially in front of my son."

He shakes his head, and I can feel the anger radiating off him, making me place a hand on his shoulder to try and calm him down.

"Yes, *your* son, not hers. Why do you even let her see the boy?

You aren't together, and truthfully, you could do way better than someone who hasn't got her life sorted out."

"Aria has helped me raise him since he was a baby. She will *always* be in his life. You should be ashamed of yourself," he says, turning to Jason and ushering him out to the entrance with Gabriella before he looks over his shoulder. "And she's not a fucking knocked-up junkie."

"She won't be for long; I have her scheduled to deal with the issue tomorrow. You should go, find someone who would take in a halfwit with a kid, no future, no money. I was wrong before. Aria is better off without you. Both of you."

"How dare you speak to him like that!" I yell at her in the middle of the hospital's reception.

Her hand smacks me across the face, and it takes me a few seconds to realize my mom just hit me.

"No, fuck this. Aria, come on." Ewan takes my hand, scowling at my mom, my silence continuing. "What Aria does with the baby is her choice, not yours!"

Without saying a word, I let Ewan lead me out of the hospital to his car. Gabriella gives me a worried look. "What happened?"

"She slapped Aria," Ewan tells her. He pulls open the passenger car door for me. "Get in." His voice is shaking with rage.

"Are you okay, Aria?" Jason asks. I nod, giving him the best smile I can muster.

"Jason," Ewan starts, opening his door for him too. "Hop in."

He listens, Ewan closing it before taking a deep breath and gripping the steering wheel.

"She hit you?" Gabriella asks in disbelief, leaning forward between the seats. "Can I go back there and kick her ass?"

"Yeah!" Jason calls out.

Ewan turns to me, his voice low. "She said she has you scheduled tomorrow for what I can only presume is a—"

I cover his mouth. "I know."

"I'm never going to let anything happen to you again," he says sternly. "Ever."

He has no idea how much my insides are jumping right now, a flock of butterflies threatening to blow through my ribcage. It's not as if this feeling is new; I've never not felt this way about him.

Telling him I want nothing more than for him to protect me might give us all false hope for our relationship, so I stay silent.

BRUSHING my hair in the mirror, I ready myself for my appointment, hoping I'll finally have some sort of good news in my life. I want them to be healthy. That's all I can wish for right now.

Last night, we didn't go straight to Ewan's. We got fried pizza then went back to take the dogs for a walk in the park. It kept my mind off everything, something I guess Ewan intended. It worked, and I'm grateful.

It was good to lie on the couch with the dogs on each side of me, nice to fall asleep easily for the first time in so long. I woke while Ewan was carrying me to the spare room, and I'm not ashamed to admit I missed his scent, the musky cedarwood filling my nose. I missed the comforting feeling of him being so close to me.

"Are you ready?" Ewan asks through the door, having come back from dropping Jason off at school.

I open the door to him running his hand through his hair, spinning his keys around his finger. I say goodbye to the dogs, following Ewan to his car as he pulls a cap on to tame his wild hair.

Since dying my hair brown, I've been missing my blonde hair, but he told me last night that he prefers me with any hair color, so I have no desire to please anyone.

The drive is silent, but it's a peaceful silence I feel comfortable in. I watch the sky, the trees, passing them all as we drive to the hospital. He pulls into the parking lot–closest space to the entrance of the maternity building.

"I get it if you want to do this part yourself. I'll try to reply to some work emails and keep myself busy."

I play with my fingers on my lap, nervous, hating I'm doing all this on my own. "Can you...can you come in with me?" I ask, not taking my eyes off my hands. "I have a feeling it's going to be bad news, and I don't want to be on my own."

"I don't want you to get the wrong idea, Aria."

"I'm the one asking," I say, and he nods slowly. "I know this might be weird for you, so I get it if you don't want to. It's just..." I feel the words strangling in my throat as a lump begins to build. "I don't have a clue what I'm doing. And, *God*, I keep fucking crying."

I wipe away the tears falling down my cheek, feeling Ewan's palm rest over my hand. "Hey, it'll be okay. I'm here for you. Same with Jason and Gabriella."

Watching the way this man looks at me, comforts me, breaks my heart.

"Have you ever tried?" I blurt, my vision hazy from the pools building in my eyes.

He tilts his head in confusion, pulling his hand away from me, leaning his elbow on the steering wheel and waiting for me to clarify.

"To find someone else?"

"Why does everyone think someone needs to be with someone? No, I haven't tried because I have no reason to. I know we are done; I really do, and that's my own fault. But the idea of being with someone else hasn't even crossed my mind, and I'm sorry I did that to you before. It's my biggest regret."

"Do you think I'm crazy? For wanting to keep it?"

He sighs, leaning forward and catching me off guard by tucking my hair behind my ear. The touch is so soft, so tender, that my eyes flutter shut. "Not at all. I know you're going to be a fucking awesome mum, and I'll be here for you both, no matter what."

"But Tobias is a... He... The baby might end up like him."

"Kids aren't defined by who their parents are, Aria. You

should know that by now," he says, staring deeply into my eyes with a soft smile on his lips. "You're nothing like your mum, and thank fucking God for that."

I giggle, feeling some tension disappearing from around me. "Thank fucking God," I repeat his words. My smile falters, and I chew on my lip. "I'm just worried. Gabriella thinks I should lie and say it's not his."

"I don't think lying to him is a good idea, to be honest. I mean, you do whatever you feel is right. But as a father, and someone who's had someone ripped away from me because of lies, and I know she's going to boot my balls for saying this, but I disagree with Gabriella."

"Even if they're a psychopath who kills people?"

"Debatable," he replies with sarcasm, his dimple showing as he drags his tattooed hand down his face. "Just don't let other people make decisions for you, okay? You do you, and I'll be here."

"Okay," I reply, fighting back the smile as tears start to fall again. "Will you come with me then?"

"Lead the way."

The waiting room is cool and bright, with lots of pregnant women with their bottles and cups of water, some smiling at me. I feel strange, as if I'm in the wrong place. I have no bump, and I might not even have a baby waiting to be seen on the scan. What if it was a false positive?

It makes me feel like I have a heaviness in my chest, slowly suffocating me while Ewan taps his hands on his lap.

Before, the idea of becoming a mother scared me. Sure, I helped raise Jason, the ultimate stepmom who devotes her life to him. I'm not blood-related, nor am I even with his dad anymore, but he'll always be like a son to me. Sitting here now, with my hairs raising every time I see a happy couple, I fight back my tears and focus on my breathing.

"Aria Miller."

I hear someone call out my name, and I don't even give Ewan a chance to ask me if he should stay. I grab his hand, ignoring the little shocks in my palm as we walk into the room, my heart beating through my chest with such a force, I think I might pass out.

I should feel uncomfortable in this position, lying on my back while the midwife preps me. Ewan keeps his eyes on mine, giving me a tight-lipped smile. The scanner can't see much, so she needs to do a transvaginal ultrasound. Nerves take over completely as I reach for Ewan's hand and screw my eyes shut.

His thumb strokes over the top of my hand while she talks me through what she's doing.

"Have you had any bleeding or cramping?" I shake my head as she prods me with the ultrasound stick, my eyes now fixed on the screen.

Ewan stays silent next to me, but I can see from the corner of my eye that he's intently watching too.

"Ahh," she starts after a few torturous minutes, moving the screen so I can see better, Ewan leaning into me to see too. "So here we have the sac, and right here..." She clicks something on the computer, making her screen turn different colors as a little blip appears.

I muffle a gasp, and I hear Ewan let out a deep breath he must've been holding. I feel relief, the rush of emotions hitting me square in the face. I cover my mouth with my palm, my other hand grabbing Ewan's sleeve. "Is that..."

I'm lost for words, more tears falling down my face as she moves the probe around, seeing my beautiful baby from a different angle. "According to what measurements I can make out, we are looking at a little over four weeks."

Clearing her throat, she looks closer, then she smiles. "You're early, but everything looks okay so far from what we can see," she says. "We'll arrange another ultrasound for twelve weeks."

I try to nod, my cheeks wet.

She hands me a tissue, my hand still tight in Ewan's as she smiles. "Congratulations."

35

ARIA

Sleeping next to Gabriella is starting to get to me, the non-existent room between us making me unable to get comfortable.

It has become so infuriating, I'm now sleeping on the couch with the dogs next to me. I don't have it in me to take the duvet from her, so Ewan's blanket will have to do.

To be honest, I haven't been able to sleep, overthinking everything.

I have a disciplinary hearing for work in two weeks, giving me time to rest and get my head straight. I've written them a long letter, explaining my rocky road the past few months since meeting Tobias, apologizing repeatedly for my ridiculous behavior and being blind to the type of control my ex-boyfriend had over me.

I just want to go home and get on with my life, not lie on this freezing couch and worry about my career.

"Why are you not in bed?"

My eyes find Ewan, the glow from the lamp in the corner of the room shining on one side of his face. "Gabriella moves too much," I respond, sitting up and dropping my head to the back of the couch, staring at the ceiling before finding his curious gaze once more. "Where are all the spare duvets we had? It's freezing in here."

He crosses his arms at his front, his inked bare chest tense. "Go to sleep in the bed. I'll take the couch."

"You aren't doing that gentleman stuff with me. We both know you hate sleeping on the couch."

He sits on the coffee table in front of me, leaning his elbows on his parted knees. "True, but if you want the bed, take it." I shake my head at him, and he huffs. "Fine. Do you want toast and a cup of tea?"

I can't fight the smile building; he knows how much I love tea and toast in the middle of the night. I nod at him, and he gets to work in the kitchen while I scroll through different news articles on my phone.

Most of them talk about Tobias and his mental health after his mother released multiple statements about him not being well, and I agree with her. He shouldn't be in a jail cell. He needs to be helped.

Surely they can't keep a man with his mental issues locked up? It will only be a matter of time before he does something stupid, reckless, losing himself completely.

Well, he already has by killing two people. Their faces have been all over the news channels, making me feel nauseous that Tobias could commit such a heinous act.

"Any more news on Ivy?"

Ewan hands me my mug of tea, settling himself next to me. I thank him with a smile, sipping at the hot drink. "I checked her stats earlier; everything seems fine. I emailed my work to ask if I can fly over, but it depends on this hearing."

He nods, bringing his own cup to his mouth, and I can hear him gulping. "You can go sleep in the room if you really want to. I'm going to head to the gym anyway."

"Please tell me you turned the heated blanket off?"

He laughs, slouching on the couch, legs parted. "Nope," he says, smirking at me as I shake my head. "It's cold outside. Of course I'm keeping it on."

"I definitely don't want to share a bed with you then."

He frowns at me, the corner of his lip twitching in amusement. "Maybe *I* don't want to share a bed with *you*."

"As if," I say, tossing the blanket off and standing. I spy the tattoo on the side of his neck, freshly done, a row of dead roses along his collarbone. "When did you get that?"

He looks down at his bare chest, a little lost. I walk until I'm between his legs, moving his head to the side so I can get a good look at the details.

"While you were in America. I got one at the top of my leg too, kind of identical to those."

"Can I see?" I ask, my curiosity getting the best of me.

I've always loved Ewan's body–each muscle is defined, slightly tan with tattoos covering him. Although he has my name on him, many others are also dedicated to me. A picture of myself, Ewan, and Jason as stick figures holding hands on his calf, drawn by Jason himself—my favorite.

He gives me a look, moving away from my exploring hands. "Really?"

I'm going to pretend he didn't pull away from my touch, and I'm also going to ignore the sinking feeling taking over me.

"Is it high up? Oh my God. You didn't get your *bits* tattooed, did you?"

"Bits... So fucking PG of you, Aria," he laughs, his hands accidentally touching the sides of my knees, causing me to nearly buckle from the shock running upwards. "It's at the very top of my thigh, near my cock, and unless you want to see it, I can't show you." He points to the stairs, biting his lip to hold back his humorous moment as I scowl at him. "Go to bed."

I nibble my inner cheek. "Can I tell you something?"

"Tell me while I get ready," he says, following me up the stairs and into the bedroom.

I climb onto the bed, the thick duvet I've missed cuddling into covering my body, tucking myself under it while Ewan gathers his gym bag and packs it. The dogs jump up, rolling into balls at my feet. "I'm sorry for being a bitch to you all the time."

He halts his movements, staring at me. "What are you talking about?"

"Since we split up. I cut you out. I just want to say I'm really sorry."

"No need. I had a lot of making up to do," he replies, zipping his bag up and placing it on the bed. "This is good. I like the whole friendship thing we have going on. It's better than the back and forth before."

"Friendship," I repeat, my mouth all of a sudden drying up. "Is it normal to be friends with your ex? What if you get another girlfriend?"

"I mean, I don't plan on it, but you had a boyfriend, remember?"

I plaster a smile on my face when I finally look at him, trying to hide my negative energy, raising my brows as he lies on his side at the bottom of the bed, leaning up on his elbow.

"Yeah," I reply with a giggle, averting my gaze to the TV on the wall above Ewan's head. "Just please don't flash your new girlfriend in my face."

"I wouldn't. I highly doubt I'll ever be in a relationship; not anytime soon anyway. But would you care?"

"Oh, you two!" Gabriella shouts as she walks past the room, slamming the bathroom door behind her. Her voice is echoing, faint, but we can still hear her. "I better not hear you two, or I'll go to my parent's place to stay."

"She's very dramatic," Ewan says, rolling onto his back, slinging his forearm over his eyes. "Do you remember when we walked in on her and the fucking dog lead guy, the one who gagged her?"

I pinch my lips together to hold in my laugh, but it bursts out, and he follows. "On my coffee table! What about when she walked in on us in the tub? And I was under the water, sucking your..." I stop myself, feeling the atmosphere shifting, causing me to drop my head and stare at my fingers. "Sorry."

He gently taps my thigh, making me look up at him through my lashes. "We have a lot of memories together."

"We do," I reply, sucking in a deep breath. "How can we be friends?"

"I think it's already working better this way. It'll be better for Jason and the baby."

Jason *and* the baby. I know he's right, and I know I have a very muddled-up mind, especially over the past few months with Tobias. But I can't shake the feeling coursing through me, the ice-cold liquid in my veins.

"So, do you think this is it between us..." I stop and look for my words. "Do you think we're fully over?" I ask, nervously playing with the corner of the duvet, keeping my eyes on the tattoos on his torso. "After ten years, this is it?"

"Aria...you had a *boyfriend*. For both of us, it should be over. Why do you look so upset?" He leans forward and captures a stray tear falling down my cheek, attempting to tip my chin so I look at him, but I turn my head to the side, holding myself together. "Hey..." He moves into my line of sight, cupping my cheeks with both hands. "We had a good ten years, didn't we?"

I nod, trying to smile through the tears, resting my forehead on his. "We did. I can't believe it's been months since we broke up. It feels like years too."

"I know. Nothing changes with Jason, I promise you. Is that why you're crying? Is this not what you wanted between us?" he asks, rubbing his thumbs under my eyes to catch each tear, tucking my hair behind my ear. "We can stay friends."

I nod, although I want to do the opposite. I want to bat his hands away and climb onto his lap—to kiss him. I want to wrap my arms around his neck and never let go, to beg him not to believe me if I say the love isn't there anymore, because I'd be lying. I want to tell him it has always been him and always will be. But I don't, because he's right.

We did have a good ten years, amongst all the arguments. We were a family of three. We had fun–a lot. Vacations abroad, camping trips, romantic dates, weddings, parties, we did it all together. Ewan is the type of partner who goes above and beyond, although he was always working hard to make up for his mistakes from when we were eighteen. He really was a good boyfriend.

I truly am jealous of his future, because I know there's a massive chance I won't be in it. In fact, that empty feeling alone has me dropping my head forward, resting it on his bare shoulder, relaxing into the feeling of his hand curling around the nape of my neck. "I love our family."

"We're always going to be a family. You, me, Jason, and the baby. I'll even help you arrange visits so Tobias can see his kid. Just because we aren't together doesn't mean we can't be there for each other, okay? Just like next week. I'll be there with you during the hearing."

I smile at him through my blurred vision, dropping my head back down onto his firm shoulder, my body trembling against his.

I do love you. I will always love you.

36

ARIA

One hour and ten minutes.

That's how long I've been sitting in this courtroom, Gabriella on one side, Ewan on the other. The judge has so far discussed what will be happening today with the lawyers, describing the potential charges against Tobias. She has named the witnesses, then the defense witnesses—Tobias' mom and Doctor Blythe.

"It'll be okay, Aria." Gabriella squeezes my hand, running her palm up my arm in an attempt to comfort my nerves. I smile as best I can, but it doesn't reach my eyes. Then, I'm facing forward, ready for Tobias to be brought out.

"Bring the defendant, Tobias Mitchell, in," the judge roars, her wig perfectly curled, glasses falling down her nose. "Keep him restrained."

I feel all the blood drain from my face as the door opens, and then my hairs rise on the back of my neck when I hear the rattle of the chains. I grip Gabriella's arm as four guards drag Tobias out, his hands and feet cuffed, hooked to a leather band around his waist. My nerves betray me, causing my eyes to water at the sight of him being manhandled, men shoving him down by the shoulders so he sits next to his lawyer.

I can hear him grunt, the white t-shirt tight against his back, clicking his head to the side and rolling his shoulders.

Holding my breath, I try to keep my eyes forward as Tobias turns to look through the seated crowd. "Where is she?" I hear him ask, making my heart sink as an officer holds his shoulder as he tries to stand. "Let fucking go of me!" he snaps, shrugging the man off him before raising his cuffed hands to point in his lawyer's face. "You said she would be here."

I slouch a little, keeping myself hidden in the sea of heads at the back of the courtroom, the judge silencing Tobias with a knock of her gavel on the table.

I flinch when they explain Tobias snapped the guard's neck, caught on CCTV, and I avert my eyes when the video plays. Apparently, Tobias is in denial and refuses to acknowledge it's him in the footage, even though he sits down next to two bodies and looks straight at the camera with a dead look.

Tobias shouldn't be in prison. He should be in a facility that will look after him, get him the help he needs. He should be pleading insanity, but my heart sinks, knowing he's not going to.

He's pleading innocent, so it's going to a full trial with a case built against him. This also means that one day soon, I need to sit in the witness box, point to Tobias when asked, and explain in detail everything he did to me and how I got the phone to contact Gabriella.

How do I explain to this room of people that I used my body to get the information? How can I look Ewan in the eye and say those words?

I'm not ready, but I don't think I ever will be. I keep reminding myself I'm doing this for him, but I know he won't see it that way. I need Tobias to understand.

Two people I'm eager to hear speak are Tobias's mom and Doctor Blythe, the only people who are here to defend him. Apparently, Doctor Blythe believes Tobias is a victim to his own mind, that his impulsive behaviors stem from his disconnection from reality.

My eyes drift to the back of Tobias' head throughout the next hour, and I grimace at more details.

The prosecution stands and gives one last statement. "We truly believe Tobias has no feelings towards Miss Miller, that his true motives were to manipulate her into a sexual relationship before drugging her, resulting in manic episodes and forced pregnancy."

Ewan tightens his hold on me, my eyes dropping to stare at our hands.

"Giving him any access to the public would be detrimental to all. We will fight the case to make sure he's never released and able to cause this catastrophic pain again."

"Aria!" he calls as he stands, and I stop breathing, watching as he shoves off the guard who tries to sit him down. If he wasn't cuffed at the ankles, he would be right next to me right now. "They're lying! I would never do that to you, I promise. I'm not like that motherfucker next to you! I would never do anything to come between us!"

"Silence!" the judge calls, my heart accelerating as I keep silent, Gabriella throwing her arm around my shoulders.

"No, I won't stay fucking silent! She's carrying my kid, and I have the right to fucking speak to her!"

His eyes burn into me, blazing, panicking. Tobias grabs one of the guards who comes at him and headbutts him, making everyone in the room gasp except me. The officer covers his nose, blood seeping out, and Tobias is overpowered as security swarm him.

"Aria!" he calls out once more. "Let me talk to my fucking girlfriend!"

"I need to go," I say to Ewan and Gabriella, feeling like I'm going to vomit everywhere. "I can't watch this."

All three of us stand as Tobias is lifted from the ground, his lip burst open. "If I find out you've touched her, I'll kill you, do you hear me? I'm going to fucking kill you!"

My eyes widen at his threat, Ewan's fists and jaw clenching,

Gabriella shoving him back to make him move. I keep my head down, trying not to make eye contact as Tobias once again resists.

"She's mine. No one else can have her!" he continues, swinging his cuffed fists around. "She's mine!"

Gabriella closes the large wooden double doors behind us, muffling Tobias' threats to kill Ewan. We can still hear him yelling.

Hands grab at my face, my eyes opening to see green eyes staring back at me. "Are you okay?"

I shake my head at them both, sucking in my bottom lip to try and hold back my tears. "He's not—"

"Aria?" a woman calls my name, poking her head out of the doors. She looks the same age as my mum, grey hair gelled back into a neat bun, wearing dark purple, office-like dress with kitten heels.

She's American.

"Yeah?"

She nervously steps towards me, fiddling with her purse in front of her. "I'm Violetta Mitchell, Tobias' mom."

I hug myself, pulling away from Ewan and seeing the distraught look taking over her.

"I don't have a lot of time, I need to go back in. But I really need to sit down and speak with you about my son. Can we meet up?"

"He shouldn't be here," I say, pointing to the door. "Tobias needs psychiatric help, not to be sitting in a jail cell where he'll lose himself even more."

"I agree." She sighs, completely exhausted. "Once they read over all of the paperwork I've provided from his clinic back home, Tobias will be transferred to a facility. I promise."

"I need to go."

"I'm sorry," she adds. "Truly. I hope you will allow me to see my grandchildren."

I nod, my jaw clenching.

Tobias has his mother's eyes, but she has something different in them. I shouldn't trust her, and I have no idea why. "When can we meet up?"

Noticing my expression, Gabriella steps forward. "I really need to get her home. It was nice to meet you, Violetta."

"Of course. You are very beautiful, Aria. I hope you will one day forgive my son."

She hands me a card with her number and doesn't wait around for a response. She rubs her hand on my shoulder, turns, and walks back into the courtroom.

GABS

Are you sure you're ready to go home?

ME

Yeah, I've been signed off from the psychiatrist, and I start back at work next week. I need normality. I can hopefully join Ivy in Denmark now that Tobias has been caught, so my job is safe.

GABS

Still a dick.

I GIGGLE at the last message, tossing my phone on Jason's bed as I finish tidying his room.

"You keep standing in my way, Aria. I can't see the TV!" he whines, trying to play his video game. I toss a cushion at him, making him huff and pause whatever he's doing. "Are you really going back tonight? Can't you stay longer?"

"Nope, this is you and your dad's place, Jason. I have a house," I reply, making him pout at me. "It'll go back to the way it was before."

"But Dad seems so happy with you home," he sighs. "Can you stay one more night? Please? We can watch a movie and eat loads of food."

"I only live twenty minutes away. It's not like you won't see me," I laugh, sitting down next to him as he shakes his head. "You'll understand when you're older."

"I'm *ten!*"

"Older, older," I say with a smile. "I'll stay tonight, but I'm going home tomorrow, okay?"

He jumps up and hugs me, a massive grin on his face. "I love you, Aria."

"I love you too, little guy."

I finish tidying up the house, hearing the front door opening and Ewan shouting he's home. I feel strange, like an emptiness begging to be filled as I walk out of the kitchen, melting a smidge when I see him smiling at me.

"Hi."

He pulls his cap off. "Hey. Did you see the news?" he asks, swiping through his phone as he walks toward me. I shake my head, and he stands next to me so I can see the screen: the court case has been adjourned due to an insanity plea. "On the radio, it says he's being transferred in three days. Have you called his mum?"

"I've no idea what to say to her, but I will."

I read the article, seeing a statement from Doctor Blythe that Tobias isn't deemed fit to stand trial, that he is to be taken to a holding facility half an hour from here.

I feel my insides twist as I read he's being sent back to America next week at the request of his mother so he can be institutionalized there.

Psychosis, schizophrenia, anxiety, antisocial personality disorder, and many others have been mentioned in the reports, but none have been solid on what exactly Tobias has. He also suffers from psychogenic nonepileptic seizures, and once, he experienced one while driving, having his license revoked after crashing into another car.

Fear riddles me that my child may have what Tobias has.

"I thought you were leaving today. I was going to drive to your place to pick up Jason."

"Oh. I just came here when I picked him up from school," I nervously lift my shoulder. "I can go now if you want? Jason's dinner is in the oven. I'll just..." I trail off, walking back with my thumb over my shoulder. "I'll pack my things to take back with me. It's better you don't have a wardrobe full of my clothes."

"Okay," he replies, leaning his elbows on the stair banister as I ascend them slowly. "Do you need a hand?"

I shake my head, turning and quickly running, calming myself as I walk into the room and grab a suitcase from the wardrobe. "Why do you need to be so complicated, Aria?" I ask myself, huffing and dropping so my back hits the side of the bed, feeling the carpet beneath me.

I look at the open wardrobe, every hanger in use, boxes of jewelry and shoes at the bottom. I left so much because I truly believed there would be a day I'd come home, but not like this.

I've disregarded the love between Ewan and me, accepted fake love from some psychopath who mistreats me in every way possible. Yes, I care about Tobias in ways I shouldn't, and I truly believe he cares for me, but not in any sort of healthy way. We have no future together.

From this moment forward, I'm focusing on myself and myself alone. I don't need Tobias, and Ewan doesn't need someone like me messing with his head on a weekly basis. I need to focus on my job and finish paperwork so I can fly to Denmark to be with Ivy.

I get to work on packing, feeling a tug on my heartstrings when Jason stands at the door, staring at the half-packed suitcase. I smile at him, and he runs off, slamming his bedroom door behind him.

"He'll be fine," Ewan says, walking into the room and handing me a cup of tea. "He's just gotten used to you being here, that's all."

"None of this should even be happening; it's not fair on him. I should've stayed at my parent's house."

"Your mum would have ended up killing you," he replies, lying on his front on the bed, my back against it, his forearm touching my shoulder. "Did you message her back?"

Oh, yeah, Mom saw on the news Tobias had confessed to drugging me, admitting it was his fault I became delusional, and not to neglect the fact that because of the medication, I may have skipped my pill and become, you know...pregnant. She apologized, saying I should know to stay away from people like him, that I'm to come with them to Barbados.

I nod at his question, and he slides down to sit on the carpet next to me, shoulder to shoulder, both staring at the half-empty wardrobe. A heaviness in my chest has me leaning on him, and I feel his chin on my head.

"I told Jason I'd stay one more night. But if you want me to go, I will."

He huffs, twirling strands of hair around his fingers before our hands interlock. "This is really messing with my head."

"What is?"

After a long moment of soft touch, he releases my hand and moves to his feet, running his fingers through his messy hair. "I think once you go home, we need to stop all of this. No more staying over at each other's places. No more holding hands and cuddling or whatever the fuck is going on right now."

I feel my heart stopping, and I stand. "Why are you saying this? We already agreed to be friends."

"How can I be friends with you, Aria?" He walks until his fingers are in my hair, palms to my cheeks, causing my breath to hitch and my heart to race. "You've no idea how much I want to hold you, kiss you, drag you to bed and..." His nose nudges mine, our lips dangerously close, his emerald eyes hooded as hot bursts of minty breaths hit me.

My hormones are battling with every bit of sense I have, and I ache for him to lean in, close the space between us, and kiss me. The urge is so strong, it's physically painful, my breathing unsteady while every nerve ending explodes.

I watch him with a heart-shattering look, truly seeing how caring he is and how much he has changed. It would be even more confusing for Jason, and Ewan really should be with someone he can have a clean slate with. He should be happy and not worrying about when I'm going to argue with him about the past.

It's not him; it's *me*.

I wish we were destined for each other, but not all love can overcome the past. Maybe I should have told him how I felt instead of putting on a mask, the indifference driving a wedge between us.

I love Ewan, more than I can ever show him, but, and this is a *huge* but, if I loved Ewan as much as I keep telling myself, then why do I crave Tobias so badly?

I feel Ewan's lips ghosting over mine, looking for permission, and I so badly want to give him it.

"I...I can't," I stutter, pulling away from him, instantly missing his touch as I rummage to close the suitcase and get my shoes on, feeling Ewan's gaze burning into the back of my head.

"Aria," he sighs, and I dodge his arms trying to stop me as I walk past him. "Don't leave."

"You deserve better," I tell him, before kissing his cheek and walking out of the house with a heavy heart.

37

ARIA

"She's put on weight too! The doctors are happy with how she's progressing. She hasn't had a seizure in a week either."

I grin, my eyes dancing as I balance my chin on my fists, my elbows leaning on my desk. I've been on a video call with Ivy's mom for the past hour, discussing how she has been, her progress, how much more energetic she seems.

"That's amazing news. I'm proud of her, and you! You're a strong family, and she's lucky to have you all. How is Denmark? Have you been able to go out and about?" I ask, my eyes going from the well-kept mom to Ivy in the bed next to her. "I hear they have good food."

"William is flying over this weekend, so maybe I'll get to explore. I'm not able to take her out just yet." She turns to Ivy, smiling. "But that's okay. We have plenty of time, don't we, sweetie?"

She runs her fingers through Ivy's blonde, curly hair while she attempts a nod, her giggling music to my ears. They both seem so cheery, even though I know deep down, Ivy is still fighting a horrific battle. Her mom is doing an amazing job of holding it together.

It goes to show you can appear as the happiest of people but be battling something so life-changing.

"I'm just waiting on my forms to be finalized, and then I can get a transfer over for the last four weeks. I need to transfer some of my own details over to the midwives there too," I say, sipping on my decaf coffee.

Her eyes widen, tilting her head. "Your own details?"

This is where I break the whole doctor-patient barrier. Ivy's mom and I speak a lot–emails, phone calls, and a few times, I've gone out for coffee with her. I feel comfortable telling her my news, but maybe I'll skip the part that I was impregnated by a psychopathic killer who drugged me and just keep to the basics. After all, she doesn't follow the news. Unless she does, and she's just being respectful by not bringing any of it up to me.

"It's still very early," I reply, watching her eyes go even wider. "I'm due in the summer."

"Wow, congratulations! Can we give Aria a clap, Ivy?" She mimics her hands moving together, and Ivy tries to follow, her shaking body making it hard, but she's determined, cheering as she manages to get them to hit together once.

"I need to go now. I have a meeting at two. I'll email you about my arrival and keep in touch in the meantime, okay? I'll see you both soon."

She waves, holding up Ivy's hand to aid her in doing the same before I smile and end the call.

"Aria, there's someone on line four for you," my assistant Natalie tells me. "He didn't give me a name."

"Thank you," I reply softly, lifting the phone and pressing the button to put whoever he is through. "Good afternoon, you're through to Aria Miller at the genetics department. How can I help you?" The line is silent, and I mute and unmute, attempting to hear something. "Hello?"

The line goes dead, and I frown at the phone before calling my assistant. "Was there a number attached to the call you just transferred to me?"

"No," she responds politely. "I'll ask for one if they call again."

"Did they say who they were calling for, which patient?" I ask, looking through my files for upcoming appointments I may have missed.

"He just asked for Aria. I'm sorry, I'll ask for them next time."

It's not unusual, so I write it down on my sticky note and attach it to my board beside my desk. It's very colorful, with fluorescent pinks, blues, and yellows, each marked from low to high-risk patient cases.

At the very bottom, I have a space saved for me: all the signs of mental illness Tobias has shown and any that can potentially be passed down to our children. I've ordered many books, researched, and even have a doctor lined up to evaluate them when they're old enough.

I've left many voicemails with Tobias' mom, but she hasn't once responded to my pleas for help, for an insight as to what Tobias was like growing up and if there's anything I should look out for.

I could speak to Tobias, try to do my own digging, but with him being locked up and awaiting transfer to the States, I don't see it as possible. He leaves tomorrow, and I've stayed off social media, hidden myself away in my office or at home for the past week. I've done everything possible to hide from the annoying press trying to get an article on the girlfriend of the psychopath, Tobias Mitchell.

It was a stretch even getting my boss to allow me back into work after cancelling my disciplinary meeting and offering me all kinds of support.

Ewan has been checking in with me, but he's more so constantly asking Gabriella how I am, maybe to try not to overstep since I left his house. I want him to message and call me, to reach out, but I understand the barrier and why we need the space.

I search for the file of my next patient, a nine-year-old girl with Rhett's Syndrome. She has recently transferred to Scotland from Wales and desperately needs treatment as she enters the plateau stage of her illness.

As rewarding as my job may be, it's hard to see so many battling something I don't. I want to do everything I possibly can to help.

Maybe that's why I'm so drawn to Tobias.

———

WALKING home is quiet for once, no reporters swarming me for information or groups of people doing their shopping. It's late by the time I finish up at work, and I'm desperate to go to sleep.

I have my headphones on, listening to the soft tones of Muse playing *Madness* while I keep myself wrapped up in the falling snow. Each footstep is on beat, and I feel all my worries seep away for the duration of the song.

My peace is interrupted as my phone starts to ring, cutting off the music through my headphones. I frown, seeing an unknown number calling me. "Hello?" I answer. "Who is it?"

"I've missed your voice."

Tobias' voice echoing in my ear has me stopping in my tracks. "Tobias?"

"I don't have a lot of time, Aria. I need to see you. I'll send you the address, okay?"

"What—"

"I need to see you," he repeats. "You're pregnant, and I'm..." He trails off before speaking to someone about how they have two hours, that they need to be quick. "I'm sorry for doing all of this to you, but I couldn't help it. I love you, even if you think I'm incapable."

"Why are you out?" I ask, reaching my door and unlocking it. "You're supposed to be locked up."

He lets out a breathy laugh. "I have my ways. Come meet me. We don't have a lot of time."

As soon as he says the words, a message comes through that I have two missed calls from Ewan, then another, then one from Gabs.

"I can't let you leave, Tobias. You need the help they're giving you. I can drive you back, *me and you*, and you can talk to me about it all."

"After everything I've done, you still want to help me?"

I try to reply, but he's cut off by someone telling him to hurry up and Tobias telling them to fuck off.

"I killed two people, Aria, and it felt good."

All the blood drains from my face, unable to reply as he chuckles on the other end of the phone. "I had all the control. And they're dead now. I did it for you, so I could get to you and our child."

The line goes dead, and I fall back against the door.

I feel myself falling apart at the seams, battling with every throb of my heart and disagreement spiking from my mind. "Shit," I mutter to myself, dropping my things on the floor as soon as I get into my apartment.

I stay in this position for what feels like hours, but in reality, it has only been minutes. My phone has been ringing. My parents, Ewan, Gabriella. I've gone over every scenario possible, ways to get him back to the station, but I've come up empty.

I have the address in front of me, a message from an unknown number with nothing else. I almost call the cops, but after the first two rings, I hang up. My mind is going so crazy right now that all I want to do is scream.

If he leaves, I won't see him again. If he leaves, he might hurt someone else. If he leaves, he might hurt himself. But...my main worry, one irritating me, is that Tobias will be gone from my life entirely, and that doesn't sit well with me.

I'm going to go get him, drive us to a hotel to talk and urge him to go back.

I'm not sure he's even there anymore. He sent me the address an hour ago, and it's going to take me about an hour to drive there. I hurry around my house while I throw warm clothes on, leaving Gabriella a note not to worry about me, that I'll call her soon, sticking it on the refrigerator.

I'm trying to ignore every voice in my head to turn around, to not walk to my car in the freezing cold, unlock it, and start the engine. I don't turn on the radio because I know it will be filled with Tobias. I'm curious, though–is Justin with him? How did he escape? Did he kill anyone else?

These are all questions I'll ask him directly...if he's still there.

The closer I get to the destination, the more my nerves get the better of me. I'm speeding, yet everything is going too slow, especially with the snow getting heavier. I'm trying to control my breathing but failing, worried sick that he's not there anymore, that I've missed him.

The satellite navigation in my car directs me left, onto a narrow, dark road that takes me deep into the woodlands. It's twenty minutes of my full beam guiding me, freaking me when my tires slide in the snow, the mixture of rain now making it like a deep slush.

My foot eases off the accelerator as the three-floored, wooden cabin comes into view at the top of the never-ending, uphill road. I can hear my pulse, feel it beating away in my neck as I see a black, old-fashioned car parked out front.

I stop when I'm close enough, my chest tightening as I run through the cold, sliding a few times. I make my way up the wooden steps, bang my fist on the front door, noticing the soft glow of the fireplace through the glass.

"Tobias?" I call out, banging my fist even harder, panic rising. "Tobias! Are you in there?"

I yelp as my body is slammed against the glass panels of the door, a razor-sharp blade pressing against my neck as someone whispers in my ear. "You shouldn't be here."

Whoever it is, isn't Tobias or Justin.

The large man grabs my hair and twists me around, the holding facility's staff badge in my face. I try to run, but the air is forced out of my lungs as his boot connects with my back, sending me catapulting down the steps and landing in a heap on the snow.

"No..." I try to beg the man to stop, covering my body to protect my baby as another heavy boot lands on my side. "Please," I cry, turning and crawling on my front, grabbing at the snow to help me move.

"Why did you need to come here? Now you know what I did. You can't tell people I helped them and cause me to lose my job...my family!" he roars, and once again, the air is knocked out of my lungs with each painful blow.

I struggle to catch my breath, wheezing as I cough, spluttering saliva onto the ice beneath me as I try to get away from the evil man.

"Please, I'm...I'm pregnant. I won't...I won't tell anyone. I don't even...even know what you did," I stutter as my body trembles, doing everything I can to make him stop. "I just came to meet..." I start to heave, unable to finish my words. He hums, and I get to my knees in an attempt to catch my breath, my clothes soaked through and frozen, my hair matted to my face. "I'll drive away and...I won't say anything... I...I swear."

"I can't take any chances."

He raises the blade in his hand, my eyes widening at his darkened ones. "No, please!" I shriek, lifting both my arms to protect myself, crouching down to brace for impact, readying for whatever pain I'm about to endure.

I hear crunching sounds followed by a horrifying gasp, and warm drops of red land on me, splattering the white snow around me. I look up, falling back in relief as I see Tobias behind the man, the blade wedged deep in his chest with Tobias' hand wrapped around his.

"Are you okay?" he asks, tossing the man's body aside like it's nothing, dragging deep breaths as he searches me for injuries. "Aria?"

I don't say a word. My head starts to spin, and I feel my body weaken as I fall forward, my face landing in the snow as everything goes black.

38

TOBIAS

She sleeps so beautifully.

Even if she's covered in another man's blood.

My fingertips gently trace her lips, desperate for her to wake up and let me kiss them. Or wrap them around my cock. Or see them move and sound the words that keep replaying in my mind.

I want you. I need you. I love you. You're a good person. We belong together. We're going to be a family. Let's run away together. I want you. I need you. I love you. You're a good person. We belong together. We're going to be a family. Let's run away together. I want you. I need you. I love you. You're a good person. We belong together. We're going to be a family. Let's run away together. I want you. I need you. I love you. You're a good person. We belong together. We're going to be a family. Let's run away together. I want you. I need you. I love you. You're a good person. We belong together. We're going to be a family. Let's run away together.

Like a mantra. Her voice. Her breathy voice in my ear when she's nowhere around. It has become all I can hear, and I'm not sure if the words are from my memories, or if my mind is playing tricks on me.

The fact she's here, lying unconscious before me, shows she cares. She came for me, and now, I have her.

She'll wake. I'll tell her we can work through these issues. I can see past the fact Ewan has been all over her the past few weeks despite her carrying my child. I can forgive her.

I will forgive her.

My phone buzzes on the table beside me. I glance over to see my mom's contact flashing up before I roll my eyes and reject the call.

My gaze falls on Aria again, and I wrap a strand of brown around my finger, tsking at the change of color to try and defy me.

She could have any color of hair, and she'd still be mine.

Her clothes are wet, the flames from the fire doing nothing to dry her, so I leave her there and look around the shack. Justin found it while we were looking for somewhere to hide out until we formed a plan. He wanted to leave right away, but I couldn't leave without my doctor and unborn child.

The owners are dead. Justin threw their bodies into the lake nearby, weighted them down enough that when their bodies float to the surface, we'll be long gone.

Grabbing another blanket, I check outside. Justin left a while ago for the meeting with the guy helping us escape, but he has been gone a few hours. I was supposed to go after my contact back home arranged it all, but I have more important plans.

Her eyelids flutter, her brows furrowing, and I replace the blanket with a dry one while I watch her slowly wake.

I need her to smile at me, to tell me she's happy to see me.

And then, we'll leave this place for good.

39

ARIA

I feel a hot sensation on the side of my face, hearing the sound of wood crackling in a fire, and I can smell it too. It doesn't hurt when I move, but it's uncomfortable on my side, and I feel a hand on my arm as I try to sit up, opening my eyes to see Tobias' concerned, mesmerizing ocean blues.

I don't jump in surprise like I should.

"Don't move. Just lie down until you're fully awake," he says, tucking my messy hair behind my ear, the dents of his dimples deepening. "You've no idea how good it is to see you."

I flinch away from his soft touch on my cheek, causing him to sigh and kneel next to me. I'm lying on a soft, beige corner couch pushed up towards the massive fireplace, probably to heat up my frozen body.

Tobias looks different–stubble, no glasses, messy hair making him look exhausted, yet he's still as handsome as ever, even while wearing a hoodie and sweats he probably stole off someone.

"You..." My mouth runs dry, seeing images of the man's body falling to the ground next to me. My eyes open wider as I look at my hands and then to Tobias, specks of blood covering us. "You killed him."

"I had to," he responds with a shrug. "He was seconds from killing you."

I throw the blanket off my body and stand with a slight wince, looking down at him. "But you *killed* him! Who was he?"

"Just a driver for the facility. Justin paid him to help me escape during the transfer." He looks at his new phone then tosses it on the table next to the couch. "We've got time to disappear."

"Who's we? And he's not *just* a worker. He was a human being with a family, and you took his life, just like you did with the two people you also killed!"

He doesn't seem to care. All he does is stare at me.

"You could have just injured him to stop him."

"He was about to kill you, Aria!" He huffs, shaking his head. "I acted on instinct, and I don't regret it."

"Of course," I reply sarcastically.

Stepping back, I make my way through the open-floor plan room, stopping in the kitchen, scrubbing the crimson stains on my hands vigorously in the sink. It burns, the harshness of the brush making my skin raw.

I know Tobias can hear my rapid bursts of breaths, the gasps that fall from my lips as I try not to break down and grip the sink. I don't know why I keep making these ridiculous decisions, having it in my head that I, the woman he drugged and messed with, could talk Tobias Mitchell into going back into custody.

I haven't been myself at all this year, and it's ever since I met him.

"Aria." He draws out a sigh, his hand finding my waist as I stare at him in the reflection of the window above the sink. "Please don't be mad at me."

"Mad?" I retort as I spin around, knocking his hand away from me. "Do you want me to list off everything you've done to me? I *should* be mad. I shouldn't be standing here, trying to help you once again!" I shove at his chest as I walk by him, standing by the fire, trying to heat myself up as my soaked clothes cling to my skin.

"Then why are you here?" he asks, standing beside me as we both stare into the dancing inferno.

"You killed people, Tobias. You shouldn't be allowed to walk freely." I pat down my pockets, turning to look at my surroundings. "Where's my phone?"

"There's no signal out here."

I cross my arms, snarling at him. "Where is it?"

He walks until his chest is to my face, his breathing uneven as his nostrils flare. "Why're you here?"

I try to hold my stance, keeping my chin up. "You need to go back," I say, feeling my heart starting to accelerate at his closeness. "You...you're dangerous."

"Are you afraid of me?"

"No," I respond quickly, confidently, watching him nod. I don't flinch as he tucks a strand of hair behind my ear with a shaky hand, and I keep my eyes on his, the intensity in the small act alone making me falter.

"I should be," I say breathlessly as his fingertips graze down my neck, his thumb pressing on my chin to part my lips.

"I missed you."

I slap his hand away, even though, deep down, I want him to continue. "You can't use fake words on me to change my mind. You need to go back, and that's why I'm here."

His hands are moving up my arms lazily, slow strokes that have my eyes fluttering, and I don't stop him. "Fake words," he repeats with a sliver of sadness. "You really don't believe I care for you, do you?"

Even through my cold, soaked coat, his touch is annoyingly electrifying. "No," I whisper. "You can't feel that way about me. It's..." My throat begins to tighten and I tense my jaw to stop it from trembling. "The way you've treated me. It's impossible."

"It's not, Aria." Both of his hands reach up to my face, and I feel my eyes water as he takes a deep breath. "I do love you. It might not be the same way you feel it, but it's a raw emotion that's strong enough for me to know exactly what I want and what lengths I'll go to to keep you safe, you and our baby."

I cry, allowing my tears to fall down to his hands on my cheeks. "This is all just a game to you."

He leans in and presses his forehead to mine, my fingers curling around his wrists, holding him to me. "What can I do to prove to you it's real?"

"Go back," I croak through a sob, feeling my knees buckling. "Go back with me now, and I'll believe you."

"I'll never see you again," he replies, his jaw clenching. "I can't."

With a surge of anger, I move away from him and march out to the coldness as I breathe out bursts of foggy air. I bow my head, my body shaking as every emotion floods me.

I feel an immense amount of rage. I'm so angry at Tobias for becoming my assistant, for getting close to him to a point I'd feel this strongly about him. It's driving me insane that he has done so much to me, yet I still can't look at him without feeling butterflies. I want to walk in there and punch him hard, but then I'd feel bad and probably apologize.

But I also feel confused. I have everything back home with Ewan. I could have a life. Yet, I'm standing on this porch of some random shack with my psychotic ex who escaped custody.

Lastly, I feel my heart shattering at every passing moment between us. I know it's wrong, but I wish we met under different circumstances. If he wasn't challenged in ways I can't explain, we could have been something special. I truly believe he cares for me, but love? I find it hard to believe someone like him could feel that way about anyone when he admitted to me he liked killing.

Love. It's quite a dangerous thing, isn't it? It can have so many effects on someone, positively and negatively. However, is it really possible for someone to love two people? To be drawn to the wrong person? I know for a fact Ewan would make me happy, safe, and we'd be a solid unit for both our kids. But with Tobias, we have no future–he's going to end up in jail for the rest of his life.

It's quite sad, actually, that the man opening the door behind me and staying silent while I sob into the coldness has no chance of a proper life. Yet, when he's with me, he's good at keeping himself balanced. When I'm not there, he's somehow capable of murder.

"There are clothes upstairs that will fit you," Tobias tells me, leaning his elbows on the banister beside mine, glancing at me sideways. "You're going to get sick if you stay in those. They're soaked."

"I'm not getting changed here."

He takes a deep breath and tugs at a strand of brown, forcing me to look down. "You have that guy's blood splattered over your face and hair."

I gasp and cover my mouth, rushing into the lodge with Tobias trailing behind.

"When he'd hit you, did he hurt you?" he asks as I make my way up the narrow stairs to the first floor, flicking on the lights to find the bathroom. "Will the baby be okay?"

"We're fine," I reply without looking at him, feeling my soul leave my body when I stare into the mirror at my harrowing image.

I lose my footing and grab the sink, looking down at my clothes and then to my reflection once more, not waiting a second to start stripping in a flustered manner.

I'm not caring that Tobias is standing in the doorway, keeping his eyes on the wall so he doesn't look at me as I remove every single piece of clothing. I stifle a sob, leaving them in a pile on the floor and standing in the shower, turning on the cool water.

I grab the nearest soap, rubbing off every spot of blood in a hurry, grimacing at the thin trail of red running down the drain as I shampoo my hair, all while Tobias stands with his back to me in silence.

"This is your fault," I say, searching for a bottle of conditioner. "I can't believe you killed him."

"I'm sorry," he replies quietly. "But I was protecting you and our child, something I will always do."

I turn to face his back. "Sure," I reply mockingly, rinsing the conditioner through my hair, noticing the mirror steaming up.

"Aria." He turns to face me, and my breath hitches. I fully expect his eyes to drag down the length of my exposed body, but he keeps them trained on mine through the glass, gulping down whatever lump has gathered in his throat.

"Don't let them feel alone. That's when it gets dark and the voices start." He taps the side of his head, seeming to be struggling with this. "Control means everything."

"What voices?"

He shuts his eyes and runs his palm down his face. "I can't talk about this while you're naked, Aria. It's distracting."

I huff, wiping down the steamed-up glass so he can see me properly, caught on each other's gaze, the annoying organ in my chest beating faster as the silence between us becomes torturous. With our eyes glued, I tip my head, daring myself to say the words, the feeling of desire multiplying drastically.

I take a deep breath, not sure if I'll regret it, but the words tumble out anyway. "Take your clothes off."

He's taken aback by my request, frowning at me before pulling his hoodie over his head. I try not to gawk at him, but it's useless. Tobias' body is a work of art, the curves of his muscles shadowing his slightly tanned skin, rippling through his shirt before he pulls it off.

My favorite part of him is his defined back, so when he turns to pull his pants down, my eyes don't fall from it. I'm ashamed to admit I feel a twinge of exhilaration between my legs, that my mouth feels dry when I should be running for the hills.

Memories flash before me–my fingertips running down his spine while he pummels into me, feeling his hot breath on the sensitive skin of my neck while I grab at his powerful shoulders.

"Are you going to let me touch you?" he asks, knocking me from my daydream. I watch as he walks until he's behind me, his bare chest to my back. I try to control each breath that leaves my lungs, but I'm struggling, facing forward. "I'll make it feel good. I'll be gentle."

I feel the warmth of his body pressing against my back, his strong arms wrapping around me, holding me while the water washes away our sanity and the dead man's blood. My mind is a million miles away, yet it's clearer than ever as I lace my fingers in his. I haven't had this in a while, the butterflies going wild. "Keep going."

I know enjoying this moment is wrong.

I know enjoying Tobias' body against mine is wrong.

But as wrong as it should feel, and how insane I must be for wanting to keep his body attached to mine, I push aside those thoughts while I enjoy this, before it's ripped away from me, before reality settles back in and I need to accept that this...is wrong.

"My father was like me before he died, so there is a chance I pass on the gene to our kid," he tells me.

I inwardly wince, tightening my hold on his hand. "How did he die?"

He drops his head so his nose buries into the crook of my neck, making me shiver under the hot water. "He hung himself."

I release his hands and turn in his arms, wrapping my body around his, telling him I'm sorry about his father. We stay this way for God knows how long, Tobias explaining he did have a good childhood, homeschooled because he couldn't handle school.

His dad was unpredictable with his mood swings, always confused and talking to nothing. Finally, he was diagnosed with a bad case of schizophrenia. He took his own life when Tobias was sixteen, and his mom married Doctor Blythe a few years later.

Blythe got him a position in the hospital, believing he was under control with the new medication he was prescribed. That was, until he met me.

Tobias holds me close to him, his chin on my shoulder as he explains he *was* in control, but he started to feel things that were new to him, and he had no idea how to work with them. He stopped taking all five of his meds so he could be good enough for me after Gabriella let him know he wasn't.

She was only looking out for me like a best friend should. She must've noticed something was off with Tobias when we started getting together.

He struggles to keep going, becoming a little agitated. I look up at him, droplets of water falling from our faces, my eyes flitting from his to his lips, having an inner battle.

"Don't do something you're going to regret," he warns me. "You've absolutely no idea how much I'm holding back."

"Then don't. Don't hold back."

I want him to kiss me, because if he doesn't, then I need to kiss him, and then I have to admit to myself exactly how much I want him—need him. I watch him bite down on his bottom lip, letting it drag until it's free. He must be having the same feelings as I am, wanting this so badly and trying to not think about the consequences.

Tobias knows exactly how my body works, every position and angle to be in so my body reacts to his touch in a certain way, how fast and hard I want it just by the intensity of my nails in his back. He has made it his mission to learn how to drag out each orgasm, making me writhe beneath and above him.

But why is he shaking his head and stepping away from me?

"I can't."

"You can't?" I cover my nakedness, watching him as he rinses off the suds on his body and leaves the shower. He wraps a towel around his waist, silent. "Tobias?"

"One of the last times we were together, you called me Ewan and said you loved me. It's all I keep hearing, and they mock me, Aria." He points to his head, tapping at it. "They mock me about you, and I can't stop them."

I'm speechless, watching as he leaves the bathroom without saying another word. I remember that moment, the image of Ewan above me so clear that I truly believed it. But if he didn't drug me, then that wouldn't have happened at all.

I follow after him with a large towel wrapped around me, stopping in the doorway of a bedroom while he sets aside clothes for us both. "If you're going to leave me, you need to do it before

Justin gets back. He isn't a fan of you, and I'm not in the mood to bury his body as well."

"You're disgusting."

"And you're *still* fucking here!" he shouts as he turns to me, making me jump back. "You know how bad a person I am, and you're still fucking here. Get off your high pedestal, Aria, and stop acting like—"

Against my better judgement, I launch myself at Tobias and crash my lips over his, catching him off guard as he falls back onto the bed, taking me with him.

"Don't ever speak to me like that again," I warn against his mouth as his hands grab at my hips, straddling him. My lips are on his once more, sighing as he returns the passionate kiss, his hand on the back of my head.

My warning seems to have turned him on, feeling his hard cock pressing against the annoying barrier of the towel. Thankfully, Tobias unravels it from me and tosses it aside. My body tingles at the proximity of our bodies, keeping our mouths magnetized as we become one.

Every nerve within me is exploding from his touch, his hand keeping a tight grip in my hair while the other roams the length of my body, grabbing at my breasts and ass, my tongue running along his as I groan into his mouth.

Tobias flips us, making me gasp as his hand cups between my legs, leaning down and sucking on my nipple harshly just as he shoves two fingers inside me, causing a strangled whimper to drop from my mouth as I arch my back.

"Will you regret this?" he asks, running his tongue up my throat. He curls his fingers as he works against the sensation already building, bursts of breath heating my neck. His fingers vanish. "You have no idea what regret is, Doctor." He pushes his cock into me so deep, I choke. "Don't make me show you."

I shouldn't enjoy this. I shouldn't move with him. Kiss him back. Become needier, wetter, louder.

This is my reality, one warped, messed-up, and extremely disturbing existence that comes with a heavy price.

My entire life.

So why am I writhing beneath him while he fucks me senseless?

Why am I moaning so loud, anyone in a fifty-mile radius can hear me?

What is making me so insane that I want this?

Tobias wraps his arms around me while he flips us so I'm above him, riding his length as he groans. I want to hear him grunt my name out as he feels immense pleasure, to tell me how much I mean to him, even if it's in a way that makes absolutely no sense.

I love the way my body tingles when he grabs my throat and slams me down on him, running the large hand up the side of my face and gripping my hair. I love the way our bodies join, sweating, slapping, swallowing each other's moans as we search for impending euphoria.

I'm losing myself with him, and there's nothing I can do to stop it. My mind is battling my heart and my hormones, numbing itself from the pain this destruction most definitely will cause.

"This is wrong," I say shakily as Tobias runs his palm up my spine, pushing against each vertebra until he grips the nape of my neck. Our hips meet relentlessly, bodies grinding in sync as I drop my head to his shoulder, heat building everywhere. "I shouldn't be doing this."

"Then why are you?" he groans against my ear, yanking me back by the hair to look at him while I ride his cock, my walls tensing around his thickness. "Why the fuck are you here, Aria?"

With Tobias pressing his raw lips against my collarbone, each suck and bite of my sensitive skin sends shocks to my core. I try to form a sentence, trying to ignore the burning sensation at the bottom of my spine as he pulls harder on my hair to elongate my throat.

"You..." I lose my words, feeling a wave of pleasure shooting up my inner thighs. "You told me to come."

He releases his hold of my hair, and I look down at him as

both of his hands grip my hips, making me grind against him slow and hard. "Do you always come when I tell you to?"

Feeling him bury deeper, hitting that sweet spot, I throw my head back, my fingers digging into his shoulders. Strangled whimpers leave my mouth as I ride him faster, my breathing uneasy as my heart rattles in my chest.

"Yes," I moan, my hands moving to cover his as he thrusts upwards to meet my movements. Gasping for a deep breath, I lean forward and grab him by the throat, making his blue eyes light up as I tighten my grip.

I shriek as he pulls himself up, flipping me on all fours. He positions himself behind me and doesn't wait a second to shove inside me again. I gasp with each thrust, gripping the bedding as I try to stay in position, his relentless thrusts driving into me.

He grasps a handful of my hair, his chest meeting my back, pulling my hair until I can see in the mirror in front of us. "I want you to watch yourself come," he rasps in my ear, keeping his movements steady and hard.

I hold my eyes on my own, my mouth wide open, giving him an opportunity to push two fingers in, pressing on my tongue as I moan. The erotic feeling of watching myself with his fingers gagging me, fucking me from behind, has me struggling to hold back the fire.

Sucking in his bottom lip, he picks up the pace. I hold my breath as I feel it...the building, the clenching, his cock pummeling into me like a hammer when the surge of electricity explodes within me.

"Fuck, Aria," he blurts as he begins to throb inside me, filling me just as the pinnacle of my orgasm has me seeing flashes of white mixed with stars, ultimately falling apart as his name falls from my lips in a whimper.

40

TOBIAS

My doctor is lying beside me, full of my cum, marks on her throat that prove my claim.

And she's carrying my child.

Ewan doesn't have a fighting chance.

Because she's mine forever now.

41

ARIA

Waking up hours later, the room barely lit from the glowing fire downstairs, I feel a slight ache between my legs, my body full of goosebumps as the breeze blows in from the window. I fully open my eyes, feeling a heaviness around my waist, looking down to see Tobias with his arms wrapped around me, sleeping peacefully.

It's the first time we've had clothes on in hours.

I enjoy these moments, having time to run my fingers through his soft hair and watch him relax, not staring at him and wondering what thoughts are jumbling in his head. I run the pad of my finger along his jawline, tracing up and down his cheekbone and pulling away as he stirs in his sleep. A muscle in his face tenses and his dimple dents in, lips parting slowly.

Why does he need to be so challenged?

Why does he need to be a murderer?

"Stop touching my face," he groans as I run my thumb along his bottom lip, making me giggle. "What are you doing?"

"I like your face," I admit, laughing again as the corner of his lip curls up. "It's nice to look at."

"It's even better to sit on."

I slap his back playfully, and he shifts so he's beside me,

pulling me into his arms as my head settles on his chest. I continue my exploration, tracing the ridges of his powerful muscles.

"Can I ask you something?"

I nod, and he holds me closer to him.

"If it's a girl, can we call her Lucy?"

I look up at him, my heart crushing and warming at the same time. "Lucy?"

"Yeah. Or we can double-barrel it or something. It's your call. I remember you told me if you ever had a kid, if it was a girl, you wanted her middle name to be Gabriella. Why not something like Luciella? I haven't been able to stop thinking about that name."

I can't stop the smile pulling along my face, my body warming that he'd even consider names in the situation we are in. Why is it making me warm, seeing a fatherly side of him?

"I like that," I agree, repositioning myself so I'm straddling him, his hands on my hips. "What if it's a boy?"

"I don't know." He thinks, pushing his tongue into his cheek with narrowing eyes as he looks around us. "We could call him something like Colton or Ayden?"

"No," I reply, pressing my lips to his and leaning back up, my chin on my fists, elbows resting on his chest. "What about Kayden?"

He thinks for a second then shakes his head. "I'll meet you halfway and say...Kade."

I bite my bottom lip to try to conceal my grin, my eyes failing me as they dance. He notices my happiness, making him smile too. "Kade it is. Kade or Luciella Mitchell."

"I love them," I say, and he nods, clutching my face in his hands.

"I love *you*. You're everything to me. Are we forever, Aria?"

I should say no, but I smile. "Do you want us to be?"

"I love you more than life itself. I'd die for you if I had to." His expression drops. "Will you show me how to be a good dad?"

My heart breaks for him in a way it shouldn't. "Of course."

He pulls me in so his mouth connects with mine, quickly but softly, our tongues in sync, groaning as I lower myself onto him. Only the sound of the crackling fire downstairs can be heard as we take it slow, our heads tilting to deepen the passionate kiss. The moon is shining through the window, making it easy to see the ocean blue of his eyes when I pull away.

"Aria..." He moves my hair away from my face, and I melt at how vulnerable he looks. "You're everything to me, you know that?"

I nod, because although he's dangerous and unpredictable, I know I mean a lot to him.

"You're going to leave, aren't you?" he asks. "You're going to say this was a mistake, blame me, then fuck off out of my life."

I grimace at his seriousness as I sit up, his entire demeanor shifting to something unrecognizable from the happy father-to-be he was before. "What?"

"Come on, Aria." He moves to wrap his arms around the small of my back, sitting up, kissing me once on the lips. "Be honest. Are you going to run away with me? We can hide until everything dies down and be a family, the three of us."

I search his anxious face, my heart sinking at his hopefulness. "Tobias, I..." I'm stuck on what to say, my words falling silent.

"Look, I know things are pretty fucking crazy right now, and that's my fault, but I really want this with you. I want a chance at this. Let me at least try, Aria."

"You need help, Tobias, help I can't give you," I respond with a wrench in my throat. "Me being here and feeding into this obsession you have isn't making anything better. You can't feel those types of emotions, you really can't. If you come back with me—"

He abruptly shoves me to the side, making me yelp as my body hits the mattress. Tobias stands, running his hand through his hair as he paces the floor. "I'm getting really fed up with people saying that shit. Who the fuck are you to say what I can and can't feel? Do you think I like worrying about you every single fucking second? Do you think I enjoy watching you have someone like Ewan near you?"

I get to my feet, heart hammering in my chest. "If you just let me help you, then maybe we have a chance."

What am I doing?

"You really think there is a chance for us?" Tobias closes the distance between us, his hands in my hair. "I've killed people, Aria. Everyone around me thinks I'm insane."

When I don't say anything, he can read my response through my facial expression, that I might agree with everyone else.

He screws his face up. "You know I'm not." He steps away from me, his rapid blinks and clenching and unclenching his fists having me backing away. "You know I'm not," he repeats before he slaps himself across the face, hard. "She fucking knows I'm not." He slaps himself again. "Get away from me, Aria."

"What?"

His fist slams against the wall. "Leave!" he roars at me, making me jump. I frantically put on my clothes while he hyperventilates in the corner of the room, muttering under his breath.

I stand in the doorway, seeing him relaxing a little. "Tobias?"

He doesn't respond, but his knees hit the floor as his head falls into his hands. "I can never be with you, can I? We can never be a real family because of me."

Feeling the crushing sensation in my chest, my lip trembles. "We need to think about our child, Tobias. We can't be on the run with a baby. Let's try to work something out, find out what your options are," I lie, attempting to keep him as calm as possible. "I'll do anything I can to help."

I kneel next to him, my hand on his back, rubbing in circles to comfort him.

"What are my options?" he asks, turning to face me with bloodshot eyes. "What can I do?"

"Come back with me, get the help you need. It's the first step to you getting better."

He shakes his head and drops it onto my shoulder. "I can't, Aria. They'll lock me up, and I'll never see you again. Is that why you're here, to take me back?"

I shake my head. I feel his panic, his hands in my hair as his forehead rests against mine, uttering *no* repeatedly. I'm not sure what's happening, but the quick bursts of breath and rapid blinking starts again.

"Why did you come then?" I hear his voice breaking, and he loudly gulps. "Fucking hell, Aria. You're messing with my head so damn much."

I curl my fingers around his, urging him to move away from me, my lips parting at his watering eyes. "We can do this together. We can prove to everyone you aren't a threat," I say, flinching as his head snaps up at me abruptly.

I stand back from him as he grabs at his dark strands, watching as he tries to control his breathing, his face reddening.

"Are you okay?" He looks like he's losing it, like he's about to blow the fuck up. I need to get the hell away from him. I watch as he slaps the side of his head repeatedly in rage, keeping my eyes on his as I move to create more distance between us. "Tobias?" I falter in my steps, undeniably scared of this version of him. "Are you okay?" I repeat.

"Am I okay? Of course I'm not fucking okay. You're trying to take my kid away from me, and it's not even born yet! How did Ewan even put up with you for so long? Oh, wait..." He hits the side of his head harshly and walks until he's in my face, spittle running down his chin with blazing eyes. "He looked elsewhere."

"Stop it," I beg him, taken aback by his outburst. "You need to calm down, Tobias. I'm not taking anyone away from you, and I'm not with Ewan."

I wince as he grips the sides of my arms, pulling me to his chest as he whispers maniacally in my ear. "You're taking Aria away from me, Doctor. And I will kill everyone close to you if you do. I will destroy everything around you if you keep Aria from me."

Every single ounce of blood leaves my face, shivers taking over me as darkness consumes his eyes. "Don't do this."

"Maybe Ewan will be my first target." He shrugs dismissively, scrunching his nose, his fingers bruising the skin of my arm as I struggle to free myself. "Is that enough to convince you to stay?"

I try to tell him to release his hold, that he's hurting me, but he's completely gone from the room; although his body is right in front of me, he isn't here. I'm not sure who the hell this is, but he's scaring me, hurting me, and I feel obliged to raise my knee as quick and hard as possible to strike him between the legs.

He falls to the ground in a grunt, and I run in panic, leaving him in a heap as I search for the bedroom down the hallway. I slam the door shut, my heart racing as I push a dresser in front of the door. I feel tears falling down my face, fear for my unborn baby coiling in my gut as I hear his footsteps coming closer, Tobias' voice urging me to stop being this way.

I cry out as he begins to pound against the door, the dresser rattling with each hit. My body shakes, panic rising within me as I search the room for something to defend myself. "It's me, Tobias. It's Aria!"

"No," he shouts, the dresser moving aside as the door flies open. I scream and move to the opposite side of the room, hugging my hands to my chest. "Aria loves me. Aria would never leave me. You..." He paces until he's in front of my shaking form, pointing in my face. "You are not the woman I'm in love with. You need to be taught a lesson, Doctor. No one takes what's mine."

"Tobias, please, stop this. I am Aria! You're scaring me," I whimper, reaching forward and grabbing his face. "Look at me!" I yell at him, his emotionless expression making the blood run cold in my veins. I slap him, hard, attempting to knock him out of whatever trance he's in.

He doesn't react. All he does is move my hands away and steps back. I watch as his jaw clenches, his eyes searching the length of my body. "I want her back."

Both our heads snap to the side in the direction of a door opening, a voice yelling at Tobias.

Justin's voice.

Tobias' words from earlier rattle in my mind, that Justin isn't a fan of me. The relief that fills me is quickly replaced with immense fear, enough to make my tears fall faster, my body to shake harder.

Tobias huffs, running his hand down his face in frustration. "Fucking hell."

With his fingers curled around my wrist, not painfully but enough to show force, he tugs me out of the room and in the direction of Justin.

"Wait, no... You said he doesn't like me." I panic, trying to pull away from him dragging me down the steps into the main room. "Please, let me go."

He releases me, blocking me from running out of the room by colliding with his chest. Justin has his back to us, setting aside a shovel, a torch, money, and an axe from a rucksack. I feel myself die inside, my breaths coming out in hard bursts as his whistling halts.

Panic starts to rip through me as Tobias pushes me towards him, and as soon as his hazel eyes land on me, he shakes his head. "You're an idiot," he tells me.

I turn quickly to Tobias, my eyes pleading with him. "Don't do this," I cry. His face darkens, his eyes void of all emotion. Bile stings my throat, vision blurring as my heart accelerates to an unhealthy pace. I open my mouth to beg, to somehow make him snap out of it, to make him realize it's me, but he jerks his neck to the side in dismissal. "Please, Tobias," I whimper.

"Can't believe Aria actually showed up. Dumb bitch."

"This isn't Aria," Tobias says, and I stop breathing.

"Can we get this over with? We can just torture the information out of her, or maybe just kill her," Justin says. "The only reason we're still here is your little infatuation with the whore." He looks at me with disgust, waving his knife around. "Tell him where Ewan is so we can get to it already."

Ewan?

My confusion makes Justin laugh. "You didn't really think we were going to leave without dealing with your boyfriend, did you?"

I feel a tear trickle down my cheek as Tobias smirks at Justin, chortling and rolling his shoulder with his rapidly blinking eyes on me again. "She is a whore, Aria isn't. Ewan isn't any of their boyfriend."

"Whatever," Justin retorts, shaking his head at his manic friend. "So, Aria isn't Aria. Then who the fuck is she?"

Tobias releases me ever so slightly, frowning at Justin, who backs away. "I don't know who the hell she is, but she isn't Aria. And I'm not leaving until I have her!"

When he turns back to me, I see the faltering in his expression, *my* Tobias trying to push through, to snap himself out of whatever is going on. "I need Aria," he tells me, lowering his voice to a desperate whisper. "You have no idea how much I need her. Do you at least know where she is?"

Justin wiggles his finger next to his head in a circular motion, rolling his eyes, referring to Tobias as a lunatic behind his back before sliding off the counter.

I shake my head when he pushes me for a reply, wincing as he pulls my hair tighter, anxiety riddling me as Justin approaches on the left, swinging the knife in his hand. "*Or*...we can just kill you," he says with a shrug. "I don't mind. Then we can leave already."

"The baby," I whisper, my lip quivering as I flatten my palm over my abdomen protectively. "Tobias...the baby. Please, let us go."

"Who cares if she's pregnant?" Justin asks Tobias in disgust, grimacing at him. "Just kill them both so we can be on our way. You don't need them."

I feel my heart sink as Tobias shakes his head, sniffing, the anger on his face evident. "Aria's carrying my child, *not* her. It's not mine."

"Why are you doing this?" I ask, tears streaming down my face. "Please snap out of it, Tobias. Please."

Justin flips a knife in his hand. "Can we kill her and leave? The cops are probably tracking her car."

"Tobias..." Whimpering with a shaky bottom lip, I feel immense fear, the feeling multiplying as Tobias stays silent. "It's me."

He shoves me forward. "Kill her."

As soon as the words drop from Tobias' mouth, my brows knit together in confusion, and before I can even respond or beg him, I feel a sharp, painful sting just above my hip, blistering shocks travelling down my leg and up my side.

I look with wide eyes and a shuddering body, seeing the knife piercing through my skin, shoved in until the hilt, followed by Justin's lips coming to my ear. "You don't deserve to be a mother anyway."

He pulls the blade out abruptly, making my body horribly convulse and fold. I gasp, my breathing completely halted as I drop to my knees, holding my hand to the gaping wound.

Tobias stands back, his eyes wide as he looks from me then to Justin holding the bloody weapon, running his finger up the soaked metal, coating his skin in red as he inspects it.

"Tobias," I choke, attempting to lean forward and grab his hand for help. "Please."

Time stands still, and I see my entire life flash before my eyes for the second time before I hear sirens, and both of them vanish.

42

ARIA

Beeping, voices, and a trace of the familiar sound of Ewan's soft snores gradually build from an echo. Distant chatter and someone crying has me opening one of my eyes with effort, the dryness of my mouth and lips uncomfortable, the ache of my entire body making me grimace loudly.

"Aria!" I hear Gabriella call out my name, her big, brown, broken eyes on me, the little lines of red showing she hasn't slept and has been crying for *far* too long. "Ewan, wake up!" She looks behind her and kicks his chair, having him jump up.

Tears brim my eyes, and I allow them to fall as they both embrace me carefully, dodging the stitches bandaged up. I'm so *sore*, my body full of goosebumps as I realize I'm safe.

"Where's Tobias?" I ask, wincing as I try to sit up, though a shooting pain going up my side has me settling back down. "What happened?"

"Someone stabbed you. Who was it?" Gabriella asks, moving my hair out of my face. "Was it Tobias?"

My eyes flit side to side, trying to gather my memories. "Justin," I whisper, making her frown.

"Justin?"

"He...he stabbed me."

"Mother fucker," Ewan blurts, tensing his fists and standing. "I'm going to fucking kill him. How did he even get to you in the first place?"

I brace myself for Storm Gabriella, staring at my fingers. "Tobias gave me the address."

"And you *went?*" she snaps at me. "Are you fucking kidding me? Tobias has killed people, drugged you, drove you into insanity, and you still went to see him? Are you actually serious right now?"

They both look so disappointed in me.

"Gabriella," Ewan says, "she's only just woken up."

I give Ewan a tight smile as he sits down on the edge of the bed, settling his hand over mine. His tired eyes and messy hair hold my gaze.

"You're safe, and that's what matters. My mum called and said she's going to keep Jason while we're on watch," Ewan tells me, tilting his head behind him.

Officers wearing luminous yellow vests stand in the doorway, on guard, protecting us. "Everyone thought you were kidnapped, so anyone who is a witness or involved is on watch. There have been cars outside the hospital and our house," Gabriella says to me. "You've been out for two days. The doctor said there weren't any vital organs ruptured, so you're good."

My eyes widen. "The baby."

"They are sure it's fine. The wound is too far to the right to cause damage." She grins at me, and I feel my body relaxing, a deep breath releasing as I look down at my barely noticeable, swollen baby bump. I smile at Ewan as he mirrors it, squeezing my hand.

Gabriella quickly runs out to tell the nurses I'm awake, and one comes in to check me over, informing me the doctor said I need to go for a meeting with the midwives.

"I told Ewan he can go with you, if that's okay? I need to sleep; I've been awake for *two days straight*, waiting patiently for you to wake up," Gabriella says, yawning and rubbing her hand down her tired face.

Ewan was with me for the first scan, and we both agreed he'll be there for the rest. Would that offer still stand when I tell him I slept with Tobias again after refusing him? I hope so. I can't bear the thought of losing him.

But it's selfish. He needs to know.

"Only if that's okay," Ewan adds when I don't reply, leaning his elbows on the bed, his tattoos straining under his tense muscles. I spot my name on his bicep and smile, nodding at him.

We sit for the next hour, chatting and watching *Still Game* on the small screen in the corner of the white hospital room. I laugh a lot, which hurts. I listen to these two idiots verbally abuse each other over who my child will love the most. Gabriella tells him she will buy the kid everything they could ever want, and Ewan tuts at her, calling her a spoiled rich girl.

I don't know why I'm crying, but I am. I have these two with me, both by my side, and I love them so differently but so strongly.

"I need to tell you guys something." I slept with Tobias. Again. And I've betrayed Ewan and myself and this child by doing so. "I..." Words fail.

A nurse pops her head in, telling me a porter is coming to take me to the meeting in five minutes. I sit with my head on Gabriella's shoulder, watching the rest of the episode with Ewan's hand in mine.

"Ready?" the nurse asks with a huge grin, clipboard in hand, moving aside so the elderly porter can wheel in the chair.

I nod, Ewan and the porter helping me into the wheelchair and covering me with a hospital blanket. I wave to Gabs, her head already dropping to the chair to nap.

Ewan's hand falls onto my shoulder as he nods to the officers standing guard, squeezing me, showing me support as we make our way two floors down to the meeting room. He makes small talk with the porter, talking about some sports game and how disastrous the score was.

I stay silent, listening to my pulse as I feel myself start to panic.

Ewan walks ahead to open the door for us, and I spot the stick figures of me, Jason, and Ewan tattooed on his calf, making me smile. "After you," he says with a hand gesture, smiling. They wheel me into the room, helping me up onto the chair as the midwife greets us and sits down, powering up her computer.

I'm nervous; although Gabriella said the baby wasn't harmed, I won't fully believe it until I hear those words from the midwife's mouth.

"Okay," she begins, clasping her hands. "First off, how are you feeling?" I shrug a little, giving her a tight smile. "The good thing is, the uterus wasn't punctured on impact, and when we scanned you, there were no issues. You were unconscious before, so we wanted to speak to you in person. Everything looked perfectly healthy." She pauses for a moment. "I do apologize, but in the previous scan you had, not everything was detected," she says, looking from us to the computer again. "You're a little further along, so we were able to get a better look this time."

Ewan and I look at each other, my heart racing, synchronized beats throbbing in our laced hands.

The doctor smiles. "You're having twins."

43

ARIA

I feel the sweat running down my back, the thump of my heart rattling my chest. My hands shake as I sign off on the statement for the investigators. Four hours of questioning, repeating myself, crying, and allowing them to talk down to me about my relationship with Tobias, I eventually ask to be excused, my lawyer agreeing as he locks his briefcase next to me.

Tobias is now being charged with assault against Ewan, theft, breach of prison, and not two murders, but *three*. I disclosed the whereabouts of the worker's body and sent the officers to the lodge that was burned to a crisp, the body along with it.

If not for the worker's dental records, they'd never have been able to identify him. Justin is being charged with attempted murder against me and my babies, but both of them are ghosts in the night, vanished from the streets, spotted rarely over the past few weeks.

My car was found near the shack, and a trail of footprints was traced to a nearby motorway, where it ends. All my wheels were punctured, my windows smashed, my phone, purse, and any money I had gone.

For apparently being rich, Tobias robbed me of everything. My bank was emptied, all my accounts at null. That's a separate issue being dealt with. A random man was seen at an ATM at the border of Scotland and England, lifting as much as possible from my bank. Justin, a day later, maxed out my credit card at the same bank machine.

I haven't even bothered to get a new phone. I'm happy with using Ewan's old one and having the people around me I need.

Ewan offered to pay my half of the rent, and to be honest, I couldn't refuse him. My parents would never help, so I wouldn't lower myself to even ask. He has been my saving grace, driving me to work when the police escorts forget, hiding me from news reporters, staying over when Gabriella has a late shift, chatting on the phone with me in the middle of the night when I can't sleep.

"We will be in contact, Aria," the investigator says, raising his eyebrows at me and folding up his paperwork. "We will have a patrol car outside your house. I know you get escorts to work and back, but we can't take any chances of them coming after you. I believe Tobias Mitchell will strike when we least expect him to."

I nod once, feeling the tingles run up my spine, my nerves still shattered from the way they spoke to me. I think I might burst out crying as soon as we walk out of this room. "Thank you," I reply, making my way down the narrow hallway and out of the police station to the busy main road.

"Oh, and congratulations on the news," my lawyer announces behind me, tilting his head down. "I'll let you know what happens next and just...be safe." He walks away, giving me a tight smile mirroring my own.

I'm still a bit sore, but the doctors were happy to discharge me the second week, giving me strict orders to rest but not stay in bed. After plenty of relaxing, I wanted to get back to normal and feel somewhat useful.

I see Ewan pull into the parking lot after ten minutes of waiting in the snow, and I feel all the butterflies replace the twisting tension in my gut. It's ridiculous that I can even feel this way, considering I've been with him every day for the last three weeks.

He knows what happened.

And for some reason, he's still here.

The four of us have been kind of inseparable. Gabs, Ewan, Jason, and I all binge movies and series while the school is off for their break. The dogs have loved sleeping in my bed, curling up at my feet every night.

I've not heard a single word from Tobias, and I'm ashamed to admit I intentionally didn't block him from my phone for a week so I can contact him if I need to. But my better judgement has finally kicked my ass and made me see sense: I have no reason to speak to him. I mean, he told Justin to kill me, which could have killed his own babies.

Our twins.

It took me nearly a week to even talk about the fact that I'm having twins, and Ewan had to speak to my parents for me because they went crazy, calling me irresponsible. My mom even went as far as calling me an idiot for wanting to keep them. She's adamant I should abort them and move on with my life.

But they are my life. She can stay away from us.

To say Ewan lost his cool is an understatement, but whatever he said worked. I received a long apology message sent to Gabriella's phone, my mom asking for my forgiveness.

I haven't replied.

My head is all over the place, but I know the way I feel as soon as I sit in the car, Ewan's hand in mine while he asks me how it went. It's something I need. Wanting something the way I craved Tobias and his wicked ways somehow dominated what I actually needed, and I need myself more than anything. My babies need a healthy, safe, and above all, sane mother.

"Jason wants to stay with Francis tonight. Gabriella is off work, so do you still need me to come over?"

Yes. "No," I reply, clipping my seatbelt in. "Aren't you fed up with sleeping on the couch? Go home and get a good sleep, maybe go have a drink with your friends."

"You know I hate drinking," he replies, indicating his car to turn right. "I might go out, though, maybe go for a long run. Are you sure you don't need me?"

I smile at him, nodding, and focus on staying calm while I feel like crying. "You deserve time away from me," I say after a long pause. "I'm surprised you're still helping me."

He rolls his eyes, turning the music up loud and continuing to drive until we reach my place, parking at the gate. "I forgot to show you this," he says, pulling out his phone. "Tobias' mum made a statement yesterday, asking for her son to come out of hiding."

Violetta also added in her statement that she sends all the love and well wishes to me.

EWAN DOESN'T GO ANYWHERE. As soon as he drops me off at my apartment, he's back within an hour with food, a heat pack, and a few candles, since my lamp is still broken.

Gabriella sits with us for a while, all three of us talking about the last ten years and how we think our lives will be once the twins are here. She's on her fourth beer, teasing Ewan when he says he doesn't want to drink.

They used to play drinking games, way before she hated him. They were friends who got along, but when it came out that Ewan cheated years ago and he lied to my face in the present, she lost all respect for him.

So the fact they're laughing together now is huge progress.

She stands and stretches from the couch we're all sharing. "I'm going to bed. Please don't fuck on the couch. And please don't be naked when I come for my midnight coffee."

My face heats. "Shut up."

"You act like you haven't walked in on us before," Ewan says, laughing. "Your couch is safe."

I know this friendship thing is working, but the undeniable chemistry between us is still there. I still feel butterflies going crazy when I'm around him, when he touches my hand or when he's close. I smile when I see him looking at me, forgetting all the mess for a split second.

Why can I not just move on? Why can I not forget about him and accept this is over between us, that we are done?

It's ridiculous. One minute, I'm all over Tobias, then next, I'm staring at Ewan, wishing I could have forever with him.

When the movie ends, Ewan makes a bed on the sofa, and I go to my room, but I can't sleep.

Going to him is irresponsible. We've agreed to be friends and work out things along the way, but I need him. I want to lie in his arms and fall asleep.

But that would lead us both on, right?

But it's not misleading. I miss him, and he makes me feel safe.

My heart wins the inner battle, and I shove aside my bedding, my bare feet padding along the floor as I make my way into the living room. I see Ewan on the couch, the blanket dropped to the floor, his legs spread out and his arms above his head. I watch him intently, my hormones going crazy at him only in boxers, his tanned skin defining his abs and tattoos all over.

"Ewan," I whisper his name, moving his leg so I can sit on the edge of the couch. "Ewan."

One of his eyes opens slightly, and he groans as he stretches. "Hi."

"I can't sleep. Can I lie with you?"

He tilts his head at me but shifts to reposition himself, giving me space to lie down next to him, facing him. I can see he's struggling with where to put his hand, kind of floating above me. Feeling my heart race, I cuddle into his chest, bringing his hand down around my side.

Is it normal to cry from happiness in this position? I can't stop the overwhelming feeling hitting me like a tidal wave. "What's wrong?" Ewan asks, moving my hair out of my face as I look up to meet his pale greens. "Why are you crying?"

Swallowing the lump in my throat, I shake my head. "I just hate everything," I let out a sob, my lip trembling. "And I'm so scared I'm going to fail these kids, Ewan."

"You couldn't fail."

I nod, my eyes closing as he runs his thumbs up to my cheek, catching my painful tears. "I always thought if I was to ever have kids, they'd be with you. But..." I struggle to finish, burying my head in his chest again as my body shakes. "I'm so sorry I didn't forgive you sooner."

"That's my own fault, not yours," he replies, holding me against him. "We both know if it wasn't for you, I'd have messed up on the parenting front. You taught me everything. You're not going to do this alone, Aria. I'm going to be here, a father figure in their lives, like you did with Jason. I know we aren't together..." He leans back to look at me, his jaw tensing at my tear-soaked face. "But I'll be here."

I keep my eyes on his, my hands on his chest as I shift so I'm level with him. My breathing is uneven, and I have an urge to close any distance between us.

"You don't need to," I whisper, my eyes falling to his lips then back to his tired eyes. "I don't want you to feel obligated to."

I can feel his heart starting to speed up under my palm on his chest, his pupils dilating. "I want to," he whispers back, gulping. "Kade and Luciella are the names you said you liked?" I nod at him, remembering telling him in the hospital my favorites if there's one of each. "Well, together, we will give them an awesome life, right?"

I lean forward, my hands gliding up his hard, tattooed chest and into his hair, my nose against his, waiting for his reaction. "I miss you," I sigh, hooking my leg around his frozen form, his eyes searching my face. "I really miss you."

As soon as his hand rests on my hip, I give in and press my lips against his, enjoying the millisecond of closeness before Ewan pulls away, his touch leaving my body. Dread fills me as I watch him, his brows furrowed with a dumbfounded look. "You can't do that, Aria. You can't seek me out for comfort."

Hurt and completely embarrassed, I stand from the couch, pulling my shirt down to cover my panties.

"I thought..." I trail off looking at the wall above him as I chew on my lip. "I'm going to bed."

Before I can walk away, Ewan sits up and grabs my hand,

staring at me as he runs his thumb over my skin, sending shocks through me. "You know if we kiss, it won't end there. I just can't, Aria."

"I get it." Against my attempts to stop it, a sob falls from my lips, making him cock a brow and pull me between his legs, his hands on my hips.

"Why are you crying?"

"I'm pregnant and sad and lost and I miss you." I sniff and look away. "You don't want me anymore."

At risk of sounding manipulative, I can't look at him. I'm selfish. I'm being so selfish. He wipes the tears sliding down my cheek with his thumb and gives me a warm smile when I eventually meet his gaze.

"I still think you're the most beautiful person in this world, and being pregnant just amplifies it. I just think it will mean a lot to me and nothing to you."

"It isn't like that," I reply. "I just..." I trail off once more, feeling a pressure in my chest. "I don't know."

"You can't kiss me then hop into bed with Tobias when and if he ever shows up." He shakes his head, running an inked hand down his face. "I want you to be sure before you do something like that. Okay?"

"Yeah," I muster a reply, my throat dry, eyes watering. "Can we go somewhere? The three of us? I need to leave town, and I want to be with you."

"I have leave for the next two weeks. I'm sure I can work something out with Jason's school to do work at home. Where do you want to go?"

"The caravan?"

He smiles, a glint in his eyes. "I forgot we had that. Fine. We'll go tomorrow."

Relief fills me, and I lower my head so hide the tears that keep coming.

"Can you...can you lie in bed with me? I don't want to be alone."

He smiles warmly, nodding, lacing our fingers as he walks us to my bedroom. I climb under the duvet, waiting for him to get in before resting my head on his chest. It feels safe, being here with him. I miss Ewan, miss the way things used to be.

Running my fingers up his arm, I trace his thick veins before settling my palm on his chest, snuggling into him. He presses his lips to my forehead, an act that has me blushing as his chin rests on my head. "Goodnight, Aria."

I grin, hiking my leg over him and feeling myself breathe as he holds me in place. "Goodnight."

I struggled to sleep before, but now, I easily fall into a dream. For the first time in weeks, I don't wake through the night. Instead, I'm met with Ewan's morning wood, causing him to run for a cold shower.

44

ARIA

Jason is excited we're on a family trip. He has talked the entire way about what we'll be doing. Board games, movies, walks along the beach. Three hours of driving, and we reach the caravan site.

Ewan unloads the car while I unlock the door, Jason running into his bedroom. It's huge for being a caravan–a sitting room, kitchen area, dining corner, a small bathroom, and three good-sized bedrooms.

Once we're settled, I drop onto the sofa.

"Can we play this?" Jason asks, holding up the game called Frustration. "I want to be red."

Ewan decides to be blue, and I choose yellow. We sit side by side, his arm slung over the back of the couch with his knee bent, resting his foot on the seat. "I'm pretty sure Aria is terrible at this game," he says with a laugh, Jason giggling with a grin. "It's okay. I'll maybe let you win."

I slap his leg under the table. "I'm going to ruin you," I warn him, narrowing my eyes. He raises a brow at me, smirking. "I'll win fair and square," I add in.

I don't.

Three games later, and I'm starting to realize I'm shockingly bad at this.

Jason and Ewan seem to have ganged up on me, knocking me off the board whenever they can instead of knocking each other, making me huff and slouch away from them.

At noon, we decide to wrap up and walk to the stone-filled beach, watching Jason throw rocks into the water while Ewan stands behind me.

I'm silent. I like how silent it is.

"I want to protect you all," he tells me. "I'm not going to be much against someone like Tobias, but I want you to know I will do everything possible to keep you all safe."

"You already are," I reply, gesturing to our surroundings. "This is safe."

"Barely."

I huff. "I'm terrified of enjoying this, worried this is all too good to be true. I've always had you and Jason, but I feel like I could lose this at any moment."

"Yeah." He glances down at our hands before he reaches for mine, lacing our fingers. It's a small act that has me struggling to hold it together. "Do you think we have a chance?"

My gaze moves to him. "After everything? You would be with me?"

"Of course I would. But we can go slow, as slow as we both need. We can focus on helping Tobias."

I frown. "Help Tobias?"

"You said he needed help because he's mentally ill, and going by how dangerous he is, he needs it."

I gesture to his head. "He hurt you," I point out.

He shrugs. "If the guy has lost touch with reality and his only focus is you, then he will do just about anything to have you."

"Are you really saying all of this?" I ask, turning in his arms. "Why are you all of a sudden Team Tobias?"

"I'm not. I just know he's struggling, and with how much you care for him, I need to help too." He looks over at Jason, the little one still throwing stones into the shallow waves. "When we get home, I'll tell my mum to take Jason until this blows over, just to make sure he's safe."

My eyes flicker to Jason looking for crabs in the rock pool. "That's probably for the best. I don't know how to help Tobias anymore, even if I do..." I stop myself. "Sorry."

"Don't be," he says, taking a deep breath. "I know you love him."

"Can I say I love you both?"

He gives me a warm, genuine smile. "I know you do."

"Aria! Look at how far I can skip this rock!" Jason yells, breaking me away from Ewan's intense gaze. "It goes so far!"

I smile at him, wiping my tears away with my gloves. "I bet I can beat you!"

I don't.

I can't seem to skip a stone even once, yet Ewan and Jason have them skidding across the water like it's the easiest thing in the world.

The sun starts to set, the coldness creeping in more while I make food for us before sitting around the table. As a family, we watch a comedy, giggling away at Jason asking far too many questions.

"Am I getting a little brother or sister?" Jason asks.

Silence follows, my heart racing as I look from Ewan to Jason, unsure of how to explain the situation. "Umm," I start and stop, gawking at the miniature Ewan staring back at me, waiting for my reply. "I'm having twins, so there are two."

"So I have two brothers?" He sounds so happy, his face lighting up with glee. "Woah!"

Ewan and I haven't properly discussed any of this, just that he'd be there for me like I have been for Jason, but what do I even say at this point? Yes, I would say Jason is like a son to me, and no matter what, I will treat all the kids equally, but would he understand?

I freeze as he leans down, whispering to my nonexistent bump since I'm still extremely early. "You're both going to be my best friends. I love you guys already." He smiles at me as he sits back up. "You're going to get *so* fat, Aria."

Ewan spits out his juice just as Jason stands and runs into his room. His father is trying to cover his mouth to stop from laughing, his body shaking next to me. "Sorry," he sputters. "You have to admit, that was a funny one from him."

I roll my eyes at him, gathering everything off the table to clean up. "He isn't wrong, though. I can already feel my breasts getting bigger." I huff as I fill up the sink, running the water. "And I have stress zits."

He leans his elbow on the counter next to the sink. "I think you look hot."

"You would say that," I respond, shouldering him. "Don't try to make me feel better by lying to me."

Drying my hands on the dishcloth, I lean against the counter opposite him.

"I'm not lying. You're beautiful," he admits, biting down on his bottom lip. "And I love you."

"Loving me and being attracted to me are two different things."

"I'm attracted to you, Aria," he says, taking a step towards me, my heart rate increasing. "I'm ridiculously attracted to you."

"You're probably saying all this because you haven't had sex in a while."

He laughs, playfully glaring at me before clasping his hands on each side of my waist. "Four months. But I'm not trying to fuck you, Aria."

Before I can stop myself, I breathlessly blurt out, "Why not?"

"If we have a chance and are taking things slow, that kind of means no sex, I think."

"I don't believe you haven't been with someone else since we broke up," I say, shrieking as Ewan lifts me onto the counter, settling between my legs. "I think you're lying again."

I don't really, but the look on his face has me smirking and holding back a laugh. "Does that make me less of a man?" he asks, running his hands up and down my thighs, distracting me.

"Because I don't want a quick fuck. I already know who I want."

"Let's say we have never met before, and I'm a random girl at the bar. Would you take me home and fuck me?"

"Yes," he replies instantly, shrugging. "As I said, you're hot."

I stare at him, running my tongue along my lips while my eyes drop to his. I feel so much stirring inside me, making me want to slam my thighs together to ease the tension, and I want nothing more than to have Ewan closer to me. "Will...will you kiss me?"

"Do you want me to?" he asks, leaning in until his nose nudges mine. "Is that what you want, Aria?"

My breathing has become uneven, my body nearly shaking from want, need, anything that results in Ewan and I becoming one.

I have an urge to push my lips against his, but Jason is possibly awake. I don't think I can hold myself or my hormones back, but before anything can happen, Ewan drops his head to my shoulder, huffing.

"This isn't taking it slow," he says, shaking his head while I grip his shirt from the back, holding him to me as I hook my ankles. "We have plenty of time for this, if this is what you want. I just want you to be sure, because as soon as I kiss you, I don't think I'll be able to stop."

I don't want you to.

"Okay."

He helps me down, the corner of his mouth turning up, walking us to the couch to watch another movie. I'm curled up in his arms, feeling safe, feeling *everything*.

I fall into a light sleep, fully aware of my surroundings as Ewan moves from under me, turning off the tv and telling Jason to go to bed. He hooks his arms under my legs and shoulders, carrying me into the main bedroom at the end of the caravan. I feel him tucking me in, and I reach out to grab him as he pulls away from kissing my forehead, the small act overwhelming me with emotions. "Sleep in here with me."

"Come on, Aria. I don't think that's a good idea."

I pull him, begging with my eyes. "I just... I don't want to be alone."

I see him gulping, hear it, waiting for him to stop being in his head. "Fine," he says, stepping back, my eyes widen as he pulls his shirt over his head and tosses it aside. The slight glow of the lamp defines each muscle, his tattooed body walking towards the door to close it.

I can't take my eyes off him as he climbs in next to me, facing me. "Tomorrow, we'll start to think of a plan to help Tobias, okay? We can't hide forever."

I nod, pulling the duvet up to my chin. "Thank you for being so understanding. Most guys would walk the other way if their...*you know* got pregnant by someone else."

He smiles, reaching for my hand and lacing our fingers, resting it between us as we face each other. "You always stayed by my side throughout everything with Jason. Even when his mum failed him, you remained patient and mature about it all. You love my son like your own, and I'll be the exact same with the twins."

"You will?" I ask, eyeing him, feeling my heart swell. "You'll love my kids too?"

"I told you—no matter what, I'll be here for you all. If we don't find a way to be together, then I'm still going to be here."

I smile, him mirroring it as his eyes start to close. I feel like I could cry, but not sad tears. I want to wrap myself around him and stay there forever, make promises we will keep, expressing exactly how we feel.

I could tell him now—it's now or never. Those three words he hasn't heard from me for months. They never changed their meaning, not once have I felt any less towards him.

"I love you, Ewan," I say, the words falling from my mouth so naturally, my eyes watering. "I've never...I've never stopped loving you."

His eyes open, staring at me through his dark lashes. Everything around me becomes a blur as I lose myself in the moment, my lip trembling as I move forward, my knees hitting his.

"Say something," I urge him to speak, to not just stare at me with a dumbfounded look.

"You had a boyfriend," he eventually responds, his breathing uneven like my own. "You—"

"I know..." I try to cut him off, reaching my hand up to rake my fingers through his messy brown hair. "I know."

"What do you want then?" he asks, and I stay silent, desperate for him to kiss me as I move my body even closer to his, the heat between us unbearable, the intense chemistry sending my mind reeling. "I need you to tell me."

"I want you to kiss me already," I say with a laugh. "I really want you to kiss—"

As soon as Ewan's lips softly press against mine, time stands still. It's not a deep kiss, nothing more than our mouths connected, but it's enough to completely take my breath away. We stay like this for a few moments, consumed in each other as his hand reaches up to cup my face, humming as he tilts his head, his tongue running along my lips until they part.

"I told you," he groans into my mouth, our tongues moving in a steady rhythm as my leg hikes up his hip. "I told you I wouldn't be able to control myself if I kissed you, so we need to stop."

"Shh." I silence him with a hard kiss, enjoying the way his hand explores every part of my body, traveling from my hip to my ass, squeezing it, making its way up my spine to grip the nape of my neck just as I feel his hardness against me.

I suck on his tongue, and he swallows my moans as I grind myself against him.

"I need you," I say truthfully, dropping my hand between us to the waistband of his boxers. "Can I have you?"

He doesn't answer me. All he does is pull me to him, kissing me once again with more desire, groaning his approval as I reach into his boxers and run my fingers over his hardening cock.

"Aria," he moans into my mouth, pulling away from me as he drags his wet mouth down to my throat, sucking on the skin there while his fingers trail down my ribs, pushing his hand into my panties to feel how wet I am.

"Fuck," he growls, swirling his fingers around my clit, making me arch my back for more contact. I try to drag his face back to mine, but he stops entirely, pulling away from me.

The absence of his touch against my skin makes me want him more. I try to straddle him, but he grabs my hips. "Stop."

I frown and sit up, staring down at him as we both pant. "Stop?"

"I can't fuck you," he admits, making my heart drop a thousand feet. "It's too soon."

He shifts me off him, standing from the bed as I get to my knees, holding the duvet to my flushed skin. "Ewan, we're adults."

"No, it's not that. Tobias is still out there. If I sleep with you, I can't watch you fall back into his arms when he shows up."

I grimace at his honesty. "I won't."

"You don't know that," he responds, wiping his hand down his face, trying to catch his breath. "What if we go back, and he's there? I can't fuck you and then sit around like an idiot. I'm sorry. I want this to work, but only if it's me and you. I won't be able to handle anything else."

My lip quivers, my heart twisting painfully. "I'm sorry," I say quietly, feeling an immense weight on my chest as I drop my face to my hands. "I'm so sorry."

"No," he sighs, sitting on the bed next to me, wrapping his arms around my shoulders and pulling me to him. "It's not your fault, baby. I just need to know you're fully into this, that's all. When Tobias is found and you still feel this way, maybe it's best if we try then?"

I nod, crying into his chest with his hand rubbing up my back. My world is a rollercoaster at the moment, and I have no idea when I'll get off, but my babies deserve a happy ending.

We *need* it.

45

TOBIAS

Where the fuck is she?

I check the cameras in her house, and she's not there.

She's not at work. Not at one of the stores she gets groceries from. Not walking in the fucking park with the dogs she shares with that fuckface Ewan.

I'm losing my goddamn mind. Someone has taken her–my fucking doctor.

And since the reporters have put it out everywhere, and Aria decided not to tell me, she vanished with my kids.

Twins.

Two of me.

Justin sits in the car beside me as we follow Gabriella. She's on the phone, completely unaware I'm preparing rope to tie her wrists with while Justin comments on her ass.

Not that I'll look.

"Who do you think she's talking to? She ghosted me. What if she has someone else keeping her bed warm?"

I shrug. "Why do you care?"

He snaps his head in my direction. "You have me following

the best friend of your baby mama, and you think you can ask me that? Why the fuck do you care if Aria has moved on?"

"She hasn't," I snap, seconds from strangling him. "Pull towards the sidewalk and get this over with."

"I thought I should let you know, just in case she tells you. I stole Aria's purse and emptied all her accounts. She also had some questionable videos on her phone, but I deleted them so you won't get your cold little heart broken."

My teeth grind to dust as I fist my hands. "Stop talking before I tie you up and throw you off a damn cliff."

"Just thought you should know," he mutters, following Gabriella as she turns into the park for the shortcut to their apartment.

Once we grab her, we have one more stop to make. My contact gave me more than enough information on Kaleb, Aria's fling from years ago. He hurt her, so I'm going to hurt him.

The plan is slowly starting to work–I have a few things left to do, but my main focus right now is tracking Aria down while watching Justin cover Gabriella's mouth with chloroform and drag her into the trunk.

46

ARIA

The drive home two days later is quiet. Ewan and I have kept our distance while touching and sleeping, but we can't seem to take our eyes off one another. It makes me feel like a kid, to be honest, having your crush so close to you, even talking to you, getting the flutters.

We weren't supposed to leave yet, but we got anxious and decided it was best to take Jason to Ewan's mom's house and figure out our next steps. Plus, Gabriella hasn't replied to me in over twenty-four hours, and no matter how many times I send a text to say it's Aria using Ewan's phone, I get no reply.

Jason is asleep in the back of the car, and Ewan has kept his attention on the road for the past three hours while I read reports emailed to me by Doctor Shique.

"I'll just drop you off. I need to take Jason to my parents' house," Ewan says, pulling up next to the sidewalk. I look up to see Gabriella's bedroom light on, making me smile. "I'll call you when I drop him off, okay?"

I nod at him, giving Jason one more look over my shoulder, a warmth filling me. "I enjoyed being away with just the two of you. It was fun and relaxing from everything going on here," I admit, making his dimple dent. "Thank you."

"We'll do it again," he responds, leaning over and kissing my cheek, making me melt. "Maybe this time, you'll beat me at Frustration."

I raise a brow. "Depends on if you mean the game," I joke, watching Ewan narrow his eyes at me with a smirk. I grin at him, my bottom lip between my teeth as I get out of the car, grabbing my bag from the trunk and tapping it for him to drive.

I can't wait to lie in the tub and relax with a charcoal face mask on and a cup of tea. Then, I'll tell Gabriella she's a bitch for not replying to me.

I'm excited to see her, tell her everything that has happened between Ewan and me. She will probably roll her eyes when I tell her I can still feel Ewan's lips on mine, that I still feel his presence all over me, but deep down, she will love that we connected.

Unlocking the door, I drop my bag on the floor. "It's just me!" I call out, walking into the kitchen and grabbing a glass of water, sipping it as I walk around the quiet house. "Gabs?"

Her room is empty, so I turn her light off and go to the bathroom, starting to run a hot bath with a hint of lavender bubbles. Walking into my bedroom to grab my towel, I gasp, the glass slipping from my fingers and smashing across my floor as Tobias stands from my bed, an unrecognizable look on his face.

"Was it worth it?"

"Tobias?"

My voice falters as he approaches me, crushing the glass under his heavy boot. Each horrifying step he takes throws me back two until I'm falling against the door. My heart nearly blows out of my chest as all the air leaves my lungs, making me feel faint.

"How did... No," I say, completely out of breath. "You need to leave!"

He shakes head. "I couldn't find you." He sucks in his bottom lip, releasing it with a curious look. "I was worried."

"Please don't hurt me," I beg him with a croak in my throat, tears already rolling down my cheeks as I cover myself instinctively. "I'm pregnant with your kids."

"What? Why would I hurt you?" he asks, tilting his head,

looking hurt by me pleading for our lives, dropping his confused gaze to my hands doing all they can to protect our babies. "I *want* my kids to be safe, Aria. Why would you even say that?"

"You need to leave," I repeat, biting my lip to hide how terrified I am. All my hairs are rising, my spine straightening as he looks at me with some form of adoration. "Please leave."

I gasp as he reaches a hand forward, flinching, preparing myself for his strike. But instead, my body tenses from his soft touch against my skin. The pad of his thumb runs along my cheekbone, his fingers in my hair. "I'm disappointed. You tried to run away with him. Why won't you run away with me?"

"You're dangerous."

"Dangerous," he retorts, sighing, running a finger and thumb over his eyebrows. "How do I show you I care about you? What will make you believe me when I say you literally mean *everything* to me?"

In all honesty, I have no idea what Tobias could possibly do to make me believe him. He has done so much to me, to my life, and no words or actions will ever take those awful memories away.

I stare into his eyes, the different shades of blue clustering together. "Tobias..." I trail off, huffing, biting my thumbnail. "You need to listen to me, and you need to let me finish, okay?" He moves his head up and down in a slow nod, shifting his weight to the edge of the table so his knees are close to mine. "I'm a scientist and I help people; it's what I do. But when I met you, I had no idea you were broken in ways that are irreparable. I intentionally shrugged off so many signs because of my feelings for you. I risked my job countless times and ignored my instincts to run the opposite way."

My blunt words burn him. "I know what you're going to say," he responds, chewing the inside of his cheek as he stares at his feet, hands clasped as his elbows rest on his parted thighs. "I know *exactly* what you're going to say."

"Then let me say it."

He nods, keeping his eyes on the ground. "Okay," he replies quietly.

See, this is the side of Tobias that pulls me in and wraps around my heart; the other side of him just breaks it.

"Up here," I point to my head as he looks up at me through his dark lashes, "is one of the most dangerous parts of a human being. It can play tricks on us, make us think things that aren't real, make us feel things we don't." He shakes his head, averting his eyes back to the floor. "I do believe you care about me, Tobias. But it's dangerous. You've even killed people."

"I did that for you."

"That's even worse." I keep my tone as soft as possible, even though I'm exploding inside to scream, to run, to hide. I just want Tobias to understand he needs help, that running away is the worst thing he can do. If I can talk him into seeking out some sort of help, I can keep him safe.

"Why would I want to stare at four walls for the rest of my life? To be drugged up on a cocktail of whatever the fuck they can throw at me? How can I have my own kids visit me in a place like that without them ending up like me?"

My heart breaks for him, watching his eyes glaze over. "But being out here isn't good for you."

"You're good for me," he responds, reaching forward and cupping my cheeks in his hands. "I don't feel that void when I'm with you. I don't feel like I need to hide who I am, which is what I've been doing for years. Just stop fighting me, please. All we need to do is get out of here, and we can be free from all of this, be a family."

I tense my jaw, holding back tears as I see one slip down his cheek. "I deserve to be happy," I say, watching his eyes search my face with a broken frown. "You terrify me, Tobias. I can't be with someone who can flip at any given moment, especially with kids around."

He sighs, thinking for a long moment. "If I turn myself in, will you forgive me?"

My spine straightens at his seriousness, and I'm lost for words as my mouth moves but no sound comes out. "Will you give me the chance to be a good father?" he adds.

Moving my head up and down in silence, I feel my heart racing even more, his shaking hands still on my face.

"Then I'll do it."

What?

"You will?"

He nods, leaning forward to rest his forehead against mine with a tense jaw. "Promise me you won't leave me there to rot, that you'll stay by my side."

"I promise."

He sighs once more, dropping his head in defeat, keeping his hands in place. "Fucking hell."

"I'll help you. I promise I will," I tell him, tipping his chin to look at me. "Okay?"

"I'm drowning in every way possible, Aria." Tobias holds my face with such delicateness, I nearly melt at his touch, begging me with his eyes as he lowers his lips to mine. "All I want is you. I need you." I pull back before his mouth connects with mine, making his hands drop to his knees. He looks at me in confusion. "You said you'd forgive me?"

"I...I..." Standing, I stare down at him. "I'll go call the station for you."

He narrows his eyes to slits at me. "Aria?" I ignore him, walking around the couch and heading for the kitchen to grab my phone. He stops dead in the doorway, frowning at Ewan's old phone in my hand, the background a picture of us three at the beach.

Before I can press the call button for the cops, he swipes it out of my hand, dodging me trying to take it from him while he searches its contents.

"Why are Ewan and Gabriella your only contacts?"

I freeze my movements, watching darkness take over his eyes as they flit from me to the screen, reading the messages I've been sending to Gabriella.

My entire body goes stiff, because I know he's reading about me telling Gabs I kissed Ewan and that something happened.

Another message that I feel happy, then a string of texts of me asking where she is and why she's not answering.

"Tobias, please just—"

"You cheated on me," he spits. "You fucking cheated on me!"

No, I'm losing Tobias to the evil that haunts him, and I have no idea how to bring him back.

Tobias' fist slams against the kitchen wall over and over again, denting the surface, blood splattering around it with each hit he throws. My body flinches with each blow, my shoulders tensing.

"Fuck!" he roars, slapping the side of his face, panting as he settles his hands on the table with his head down. "They're his, aren't they?"

I tilt my head at him, backing into the corner of the room. "What?"

He slaps his palm on the table with force, making me jump as he spins on his heels, stepping until he's in my face. "He got you fucking pregnant, didn't he?" he yells at me with fire in his eyes, slapping the side of his face once more. "You let me think they were mine so I didn't know you were cheating on me, you fucking—"

"Stop it!" I interrupt him, shoving at his shoulders, his rapid blinking completely out of control as he seethes through each breath. "Stop letting it overtake you!"

"Overtake me? It's you. It's always fucking you!"

I watch as he runs frantically in his own mind, his fingers raking through his hair, eyes wide as he takes deep breaths. "Tobias, try to calm down, please."

I scream as he launches the phone at my kitchen window, cracking it. "I can't calm the fuck down; don't you get that? You want him." He turns his back to me, shaking his head. "She wants him. They aren't my kids; they can't be."

I sideways glance at my knife block, unsure if I will need to go as far as defending myself by inflicting pain on him. "I haven't slept with Ewan in a long time, Tobias. You're the father, I promise. Please just try to control your breathing and look at me." I move towards him, my hand on his shoulder, turning him. "Focus on me."

With a snarl, he looks me up and down, his entire form shaking with rage. "I love you enough to accept what we need to do. That way, we can all be together forever."

"What?"

He pulls me out of the kitchen and down the hallway, stopping at Gabriella's bedroom. "Sit on the bed," he orders, and I comply, watching him pull apart her wardrobe in a hurry. With my heart racing at an unhealthy pace, I gulp down a painful lump suffocating me. "They should do it."

My eyes widen as he turns, two long cables in his hand while he checks the sturdiness of the curtain pole. "No, Tobias. No. You don't want to do this."

"I do," he responds, knotting them both with large loops big enough to wrap around our necks. "You can go first, then I'll go. Or we can do it together." I jump from the bed and try for the door, but he grabs me once more. "Stop fucking fighting this."

"I don't want to die!" I scream out, kicking my legs as he tosses me back on the bed. "Please!" I cry as I bury my head in the duvet, my body heaving while he stands on Gabriella's stool, positioning the cables side by side. "Tobias, please. I want my kids to have a chance at life."

"Our fucking kids. *Ours!*" he corrects me, snapping at me with wide eyes, delusional to his earlier accusation. "This is not up for negotiation, Aria. Stand up."

My nerves are taking over, but I need to protect my babies. I grab a pen from Gabriella's bedside unit, driving the point into his bicep before making a run for it.

Somehow, I manage to make it to the bathroom and lock the door while Tobias groans in pain, yelling at me to get back.

I rest my back against the door, breathless, tears soaking my face. "Oh my God," I say to myself, covering my mouth as I hear Tobias' footsteps advancing, passing the door to enter the kitchen down the hall, returning seconds later.

"Aria, you need to open the door right now. You're ruining

everything." I stay silent, my body shaking as I weep for my life. The sound of him busting open the door touches my ears as he leans against it to mirror my seated position. "It's the only way. I don't want the other side of you coming out and making it worse. She's evil and hates *everything* about me."

The other side of me?

Why the hell did we need to leave Dumfries? Why did I not tell Ewan we'd just stay there forever? I was in heaven, happy, carefree, and now, I'm in a living hell as I hear Tobias taking deep breaths to try to control himself.

"My mom told me you were beautiful, that she understands why I'm so in love with you. She told me I should never stop fighting for what I want. And that's *you*, Aria. I want you in ways that make me... I don't even know how to explain it."

"If you loved me, you wouldn't try to kill me," I snap.

Silence follows as I wait for Tobias to calm down so we can talk.

I hear him let out a deep breath. "It won't be long now."

Frowning, I sit forward, my eyes widening as soon as I smell it. *Gas.*

"What are you doing?" I ask, rushing to the window, but it's locked. "Tobias!"

"I do love you, Aria. I wish I was normal so you could actually be with me, but I'm not. I've never even been close to it." His voice echoes in the room, soft and calm. "But you saw something in me that made me enjoy life for the first time ever, even if it was only for a few months. It won't hurt. I promise you'll pass out before I light it up."

I gasp a cry, grabbing a hand towel, rolling it up in a panic and stuffing it under the door to block any more gas from leaking in. "You can't do this!" I yell at him, my breathing erratic. I use another hand towel, soaking it in the tub then holding it to my face, pacing the bathroom while I press a palm to my stomach.

"You need to just sit down and let yourself fall asleep."

"Stop it!" I cry through the wet rag, every single nerve in my body exploding with fear. Then, I hear it: the flicking of a lighter as Tobias coughs.

I have one last chance.

Unlocking the door, he falls back as I open it and jump over him, dropping the hand towel as I make a run for it.

I manage to grab my keys and unlock my car, climbing in, completely out of breath, tears streaming down my face.

Before I can close the door, my heart sinks as a hand full of dried blood stops it. "Aria!" Tobias calls out, curling his fingers on the metal as I scream, trying to yank it shut and failing as he throws it open. "I'm trying to save you from her!"

He grabs my hair, pain surging through me while he pulls me from the car and slams my back against it. He cups my face in his hands, blood trickling down his arm where the pen is still lodged, something he doesn't seem bothered by. "Come back to me, Aria. Don't let her control you."

"No one is controlling me but you! You're a psychopath!"

He chuckles, biting his lip. "And you loved me anyway. You *and* the doctor did. Or you still do. I'm confused with you both." He presses his lips to my forehead, inhaling deeply. "Okay, let's go."

Dragging me to the back of the car, he looks at our surroundings, the neighborhood in darkness with no one out to see what the noise is.

"Get in," he orders me as he pulls the trunk open. "Now." I struggle, trying to get away from him as his hand tightens in my hair, sending shocks of pain through my scalp.

I whimper, doing as he says, climbing in and curling up as he slams it shut. My heart needs to slow before I pass out, which is probably a good thing at this point so I won't feel what pain Tobias is about to inflict on me.

"I'm so sorry," I tell my babies, my hands wrapping around myself. "I'm so sorry I failed you both."

I've never thought about dying. Well, *I have*, but not at my own hands or someone else's. I always thought I'd be an old lady, lying in my bed, my children and grandchildren surrounding me, feeling like I accomplished something by living my life.

I wanted my kids to have a life, and that's about to be taken away at the hands of their own father.

And now? I'm regretting everything, everything from the point of meeting Tobias Mitchell.

I care about him a lot. I know he has his issues, that he needs help, but at this point, he's truly irredeemable in my eyes. The dark side of him is far too powerful for his softness, the part I fell in love with. I wish I was stronger, that I was able to fix him, to make him see sense.

All I can do is lie here and hope my family and friends know how much I love them, that no matter what lies ahead, I will fight until my last breath.

The car comes to a halt, my hand pressing to my mouth as I hear chattering, my pulse quickening.

Footsteps crunching on stones make their way to the back of the car, my entire form freezing as it opens wide, my blood running cold at Justin smiling down at me. "It's about time you both got here."

He isn't gentle. I yelp as he grips my wrist and yanks me out into the cold. There's a snow-covered woodland surrounding us, hiding us. Tobias is standing with his arms crossed at the entrance of the small, abandoned building of an old animal shelter. I recognize it; it has been closed down for years in the middle of nowhere.

The woman next to him makes me freeze.

"Aria, dear, it's good to see you again," Violetta says with a smile, opening her arms for some sort of embrace. I flinch as she approaches, making her stop in her tracks, looking from me to Tobias. "She didn't agree?"

Tobias shakes his head. "I didn't ask. Just take her inside."

Ask what?

They walk me into the foul-smelling building, mold and grass growing on the walls and floor. I whimper as I enter a room filled with bright white lights, my eyes widening at the sight before me.

Five large, caged kennels line the opposite side of the room, set up with drips hooked to each one. My heart sinks when I see Gabriella shoved into one, sedated with whatever they're pumping into her.

For some reason, Kaleb is in the one beside her, also sedated.

"Gabriella?" I sob out with a gasp, bile rising in my throat. "Gabs?"

Tobias comes up behind me as his mom and Justin walk in front of me, grinning. His hands rest on my hips while I stand frozen in place, holding my breath as he lowers his mouth to my ear.

"Which one do you want, Doctor?"

47

TOBIAS

Where the fuck is Aria? Where the fuck is Aria? Where the fuck is Aria? Where the fuck is Aria? Where the fuck is Aria? Where the fuck is Aria? Where the fuck is Aria? Where the fuck is Aria? Where the fuck is Aria? Where the fuck is Aria? Where the fuck is Aria? Where the fuck is Aria? Where the fuck is Aria? Where the fuck is Aria? Where the fuck is Aria? Where the fuck is Aria?

I can't stop it.

48

ARIA

Darkness looms in Tobias' eyes, glaring at me from across the room while his mom tends to the pen lodged in his arm.

I feel it, the demonic presence of his dark side filling all my senses, like unpredictable waves surrounding him that are only looking to cause carnage. The evil wants to be known, to be feared, and since all I can think of is how we are all about to die, he's succeeding.

Each step he takes while he angrily paces makes me shiver–the way he twitches his neck to the side, blinks at a rapid speed, and ultimately looks emotionless, like a receptacle full of death and hatred.

I'm sitting on a wooden chair in the corner of a bright room, my hands bound in front of me with a red cable tie. Tobias had pushed me into the dog crate next to Gabs but took me out before sitting me here.

Every time his eyes land on mine, he clenches his fists and averts his drained gaze to the ground barely a second later. Every time Justin walks by me and intentionally kicks my chair to frighten me more, he glares at him before he falters.

He's fighting himself.

The crates are large...for dogs. But for human beings? Tiny. Both Gabs and Kaleb have their knees to their chests, wincing in discomfort with black tape over their mouths to keep them quiet. Gabriella is whimpering for her life, her eyes begging me to run every time Tobias and Justin turn their backs.

It's pointless. We're in the middle of nowhere, surrounded by woodlands. If I do manage to get away, they'll catch me.

Violetta huffs, breaking me from my blank stare at the white wall. She throws down the bloody gauze from stitching up Tobias. "I still think this is a bad idea. If we leave now, we can catch the next boat and be out of here. She..." Her eyes land on mine, strangely looking concerned. "She doesn't want you anymore. We are wasting time."

"Agreed," Justin says, shoving his hands in his pockets. "He doesn't listen."

Tobias glares at Justin, who raises both hands in defeat.

Kaleb starts kicking at his cage, trying to shout through the tape on his mouth. Each blast of his foot vibrates in my ears, and my headache worsens. I close my eyes when I see Justin lift the keys from the table, twirling them around his finger. "Why is he here again?"

"He disrespected my girlfriend." My eyes open once more, staring at Tobias while he confidently smiles at them with raised brows. "No one messes with her."

"Girlfriend," I hear Justin mutter under his breath, followed by a snort.

Before I can say anything, Gabriella's phone beeps in Justin's hand. "Found him," he says in excitement, lifting the screen for Tobias to see. "He said he's just home from dropping his kid off, that she and Aria can pick him up in twenty minutes."

My eyes widen at Tobias shoving his jacket on, keeping his gaze off mine while he packs a hammer and chains into a bag. "Don't you dare touch him!" I warn Tobias in a sneer, my nerve endings exploding. When he ignores me, I push myself off the chair and shake in my rigid stance, begging him to look at me. "Please."

Justin comes at me, shoving my chest so I fall back in the chair with a grunt.

Tobias narrows his eyes at him. "Don't do that to her."

He lifts his hands in defense, his brow raised. "Whatever, big guy. Can we go now?"

"Don't lay a finger on her." Tobias looks over at me without making eye contact, and then he tilts his head to Gabs. "But if the other one starts being a nuisance, you can just kill her," he tells his mom before pointing at Kaleb. "Keep him alive for me. I want to teach him a lesson for speaking to my girl the way he did."

She nods once, her head dropping. "You really don't need to hurt them."

He sniffs, tossing his bag over his shoulder. "That's up to the doctor."

She huffs and crosses her arms as she sits. "Torturing the people she loves will push her away from you. How do you expect her to let us raise the children if you've killed everyone around her? Winning her trust is what you need to do, and even at that...it's close to impossible."

My shoulders tense as Tobias drops a heavy fist onto the dog grooming table in the middle of the room. "I won't leave her! You don't get it. I can't lose her."

"You already have," she replies in a low tone, blunt, matter-of-fact.

"Stay the fuck out of it," he tells her with a pointed finger. "You don't know her like I do."

I need him to listen to his mom. "Tobias..." I stop my words just as she widens her eyes at me, shaking her head while Tobias drops his. I take her wordless advice, keeping silent.

He's finally done it, though. I'm officially terrified of Tobias.

The rope I was once comfortably holding is now thin and weak, hanging on by a single thread, threatening to snap. Tobias owns that thread... *My* life, *my* unborn babies, *my* final breath and vulnerability. He owns it all, no matter if I agree to go with him or not. *He* controls what happens next.

"Hurry up!" Justin yells from the reception down the narrow, cold hallway. "I told him they were picking him up like ten minutes ago."

I close my eyes, my chin shaking as I hold back tears. They are going to drive to Ewan's place, he's going to walk out thinking it's me, and he'll be met with a pair of vicious animals.

"Please don't hurt him," I beg Tobias, but he ignores me yet again as he leaves the room, slamming the heavy door closed behind him. I gasp out a weep, dropping my face to my bound hands.

"I tried," Violetta says after a few passing moments of my cries filling the room in broken echoes. "I really did try."

I gulp, my eyes drifting to Gabriella still tied up with her mouth taped. "So did I."

"You need to understand, Tobias is my baby boy," she says, standing from the chair and slowly walking over to me. "I'm his mother and my job right now is to keep him alive and safe."

"Alive and safe?" I let out a breathy laugh. "He's definitely not safe. He's wanted for murder and now kidnapping. He's not even safe from himself. If he succeeded earlier, we would all be dead."

"Meaning?" she asks, tilting her head with a frown.

I wipe my eyes on my sleeves. "He tried to kill me, twice."

She doesn't flinch. "Tobias won't kill you."

I chuckle again. "First time, he wanted us to both hang ourselves." I watch her face drop, her lips parting as fear washes over her. "And then he tried to blow my house up with us both inside."

"You're lying."

I shake my head. "I wish I was."

She drops to her chair, twisting the pendant of her necklace between her thumb and finger. "My son was going to kill himself?"

I nod. "Ten minutes before, he agreed to hand himself in under the condition that I stay by his side."

She presses her palm to her mouth, closing her eyes as a tear slides down her cheek. "He did?" she asks with a croak, her lip quivering. "He agreed to turn himself in?"

Nodding, I say, "We can help him, Violetta. You can let us out, and we can keep him safe from himself."

"He will never forgive me," she says, pressing her palm to her chest. "He's all I have."

"I'm pregnant with your grandchildren, and the chances of us surviving this with me denying Tobias are slim." I move forward, taking her hand in between mine, the plastic causing painful friction against my wrists. "I won't doom my unborn babies; I will get out of this. Please...please, help us?"

The corner of her mouth turns up ever so slightly as she strokes the back of her fingers down my cheek. She takes a deep breath, and I get to my feet as she stands. "My son is a good person. He was taking a cocktail of different things that helped regulate most of the issues he faced daily, but—"

"But he stopped them when he met me," I finish her sentence, remembering Tobias telling me he'd stopped his meds because he wanted to be normal. "He told me."

"His stepfather was monitoring his behavior around you at work, but Tobias had lashed out at him for some reason. He broke his ribs with one punch. They never really formed much of a relationship over the years. Roderick... You know him as Blythe."

"Yeah."

She nods, rubbing her hand down her face the same way Tobias does. "He is very unique, Aria. I have had many specialists observe him since he was young. He's a trickster, and a really good one at that. He intentionally manipulated their results so they couldn't diagnose him. He always told me he didn't want a label, that he didn't need one because he wasn't different."

She clears her throat and continues.

"When Tobias was a teenager, his father taught him to compartmentalize his emotions, arrange them in a way that protects them from each dissociation. He was able to protect things like empathy, love, fear, and anything that rendered him powerless. As he got older, I watched him fight against himself to keep them safe, to make sure they didn't get lost. He was terrifying to be around."

I look over at Gabriella and Kaleb, both sitting with their mouths taped and their hands bounded, watching, listening.

"I don't know how to explain it. There are parts of him that aren't even in touch with reality, that don't even know who I am. They only come out when he's blinded by rage. I have no idea who he is right now. He's not my son...not the real Tobias." She sighs, looking down at her fingers in her lap. "He has to be inside that vessel, Aria. My son needs to be there...somewhere."

Her body is trembling, but she keeps going.

"He has a lot of things going on, but I don't know if it's really him, or if he's tricking us into thinking it. Blythe thinks he's a psychopath trying to play a game with everyone, even you. But I believe each part of him has a different disorder."

"I think Blythe might be right, and if he is... Tobias is a good actor." I walk over to Gabriella's crate, leaning down to her and curling my fingers over hers as they grip the bars. I turn back to Violetta. "Tobias is going to torture my friends, isn't he? Until I agree to leave with him?"

She moves her head up and down slowly, wiping her eyes with her fingertips. "Where will you run to if I let you all go?"

I feel a wave of relief hit me, making me breathe deeply as I turn to her. "You will let us go?"

"Only if you promise not to call the cops. Let me get my son out."

I sigh. "He needs help, Violetta."

"I'll help him," she says, nodding as she lifts the keys from the table, picking up Tobias' hunting knife and cutting my hands free. "You need to injure me so he doesn't know I let you go." She hands me the knife, molding her fingers over mine on the handle. "Make it look believable."

"I'm not stabbing you," I retort, moving away to unlock the cages. Kaleb doesn't even wait for my help or to unbind his hands. He scurries out and runs from the room without a word.

I help Gabriella out, cutting her hands free and carefully

removing the tape from her mouth, embracing her as she cries into my shoulder. "We're going to be okay," I tell her as she weeps, her body shaking.

"We are never getting boyfriends again after this," she says with a sobbing laugh, her arms tightening over me. "We need to go."

I turn to Violetta, and she nods. "Make it look believable." She gestures to the knife in my hand. "Just don't kill me. I'm all he has too."

I freeze as she takes my hand and presses the point just above my hip to demonstrate. "If you stab me right here, I'll survive."

I grip her wrist, paranoid she'll hurt me, but before I can say anything, banging has our heads snapping to the side.

Tobias kicks the door open, dragging Kaleb behind him, dropping him on the ground with his eyes set on the knife pressing against my hip, my hand on his mom's wrist, and Gabriella gasping, backing away.

"What the fuck are you doing?" he shouts at his mom, closing the distance as the knife drops to the floor, grabbing her by the throat and shoving her against the wall. "You're trying to kill her!" Slapping the side of his head, Tobias fumes, a fire burning in his eyes as his face reddens, veins sticking out from his neck, rendering him completely unrecognizable.

"I wasn't!" Violetta cries out, her voice croaking from the pressure on her throat. "P...please."

Gabriella and I back away, our eyes on the door, hands gripping each other's arms. As soon as I see Violetta struggling to breathe, I let go of Gabs. I brace myself, gritting my teeth as I run for the blade on the ground.

His foot crushes my hand just as I reach it, and I scream in pain, moving away from him as he lifts the weapon and presses it to his mom's throat.

"No!" I yell, jumping forward to grab his arm. "She wasn't going to hurt me!"

He stays silent, heavily breathing through his nose while he growls at her. "Get in the crate." He throws her aside, slamming it shut while she whimpers. "You as well, Doctor."

I don't argue back. I slowly get into the cage. "She wasn't going to hurt me, Tobias." He's still not looking at me, his eyes dark, the whites bloodshot.

Taking a deep breath, he closes his eyes and pulls Kaleb to his knees, kicking him until he's in front of me. Before I can question what he's doing, he slices the blade across his throat, cutting through flesh and muscle, blood shooting all over me, splattering across the floor. The eardrum-blowing scream coming from him is like an animal being tortured, making me feel dizzy and sick as I fall back, my feet sliding in the crimson liquid filling the floor of my crate.

I scream, covering my mouth with my palm as my eyes bulge at the lifeless body in front of me, blood pooling around him.

He just killed Kaleb.

"Tobias," his mom cries. "What have you done?"

"I did what was necessary. He hurt Aria years ago, so this is my revenge." He grabs Gabriella and kicks her legs, making her kneel in Kaleb's death.

"Don't do this," I beg him for what seems like the hundredth time today, Kaleb's blood coating my face, my fingers turning white from my death grip on the crate door. "You don't need to kill people! She's my best friend!"

"Last chance. Are you or are you not going to give me Aria so we can leave?"

Before I can reply and say yes, Gabriella stops me. "Aria."

Gabriella's lip is shaking, her face drained of any color as she stares at me.

"Aria...listen to me," she orders, and my eyes meet hers. "The twins are your priority, always, and they're even mine." Her voice breaks, and I feel my heart starting to race even more, twisting, shattering. "I love you more than anything, and I've had the best years with you as my best friend, as my *sister*." Tears burn my eyes, gulping down a solid lump in my throat as I shake my head, my face contorting with impending grief. "I need you to be strong. I need you to get out of here and give your babies the best lives ever. Don't give it all up for me, please."

"No," I whimper, feeling my heart suffocating. "Please, no. I need you, Gabs."

"Just don't find someone funnier than me, okay?" She laughs, but I just feel a knife digging deeper into my chest. "And don't you *dare* steal my clothes."

With a racing heart and tears streaming down my face, I grit my teeth, desperate for Tobias to stop this. "Don't," I plead with him once more. "Please remember you chose Luciella. Your daughter will be named after the person under your grip."

His eyes don't meet mine; he doesn't even flinch at my words.

"Be strong," Gabriella tells me. "I love you."

49

ARIA

Soon as he goes to cut her throat, I scream in panic.

"Don't! Let me talk to you in private," I blurt out, thinking of anything and everything to save her as she attempts to slap his face and push herself up, water splashing over the blood-soaked floor. "Aria... Umm, she wants to talk to you, in...in private."

I know it's me saying those words, but everything is going in such slow motion, it takes me a second to realize. All I can hear are my erratic bursts of breath and the pounding of my heart, rendering me deaf to everything else.

His blank glare regards me as a stranger as he looks me up and down before he snarls.

Tobias tosses Gabriella to the side, sending her sprawling next to Kaleb's corpse. She pants desperately into the ground, her palms holding her up ever so slightly with shaking arms. He raises a questioning brow, crouching down to my level. I stay completely frozen, overcome with both relief and fear. "What did you say?"

Gulping, I look at his hands, elbows resting on his knees; large, experienced, deadly.

I see his middle finger shaking, like a tremor...something he never had before.

Looking up at him, I chew on my bottom lip. The ocean blue of his eyes shines through ever so slightly, the dilated pupils making it nearly impossible to see how beautiful his eyes really are. *Will they be the last thing I see?*

He breathes heavily through his nose. "I don't like to repeat myself, Doctor."

I nod, my brows knitting together as I tell myself this is the only way to save my best friend. "Aria... She wants to talk to you." I look down at my fingers hooked on the crate door, ashamed of myself for feeding into this strange obsession of my apparent dissociation. "Away from everyone," I continue without looking at him, my eyes lifting to Gabriella begging me with her desperate gaze.

"No," Gabs chokes out in a groggy, broken tone. I can hear it twisting in her throat as she tries to sit up but struggles from her shock. "Aria, *no*. Don't you fucking dare."

I feel the tightness in my chest worsening a little as I hear Violetta's whimpers from the cage next to me, pleading with Tobias to stop all of this, that he can't kill his own children because he'll never forgive himself. My shoulders tense as he snaps at her that he would never harm them, that she's to shut the fuck up.

Against my better judgement, I look at him, trying to stop tears from falling. "You want Aria, don't you?" He nods in response. "If you kill Gabriella, I will never forgive you. *Aria* will never forgive you."

He sniffs, looking down at Gabs and running his hands through his hair as he drops his head in frustration. My heart nearly blows through my chest as he leans forward to unlock my cage, dragging me out.

"Get in," he orders Gabriella. She complies, crawling through the puddle of blood as quick as her weakened body can push her before Tobias kicks the door shut and locks it.

"If you hurt her or those babies, I will fucking destroy every part of you, Tobias!" Gabriella threatens as he grabs my hand and tugs me out of the room. "Do you hear me?" Her voice is still echoing down the hallway, my heart breaking at her weeping, pleading for him not to hurt me.

He's taking carefully controlled, deep breaths while I follow him, ignoring Gabriella's threats. I get why she's losing it, I really do. This is reckless and dangerous, but what else was I to do? Let her die?

Seeing Tobias lodging the blade into the back of his pants, my eyes widen as I realize I can possibly get us out of here. I just need to somehow get the knife and find enough courage to kill him.

Could I even do that? To save everyone, I need to.

"I want her," Tobias tells me as soon as he slams the door of the small, messy office, pinning me to the wall by the shoulders and glaring into my eyes. "You can't keep her from... You can't... Not from me." I hear his voice breaking, an audible gulp as his hands leave my body and press against the wall on each side of my head. He blinks fast, his jaw tensing, struggling to hold up this act. "I really need her."

A minute passes with him staring at me, searching my face as I struggle to say anything, overwhelmed with horror. I flinch as he pushes off the wall and turns his back to me, running both of his hands through his hair. My eyes drop to the blade poking through his hoodie, and my fingers involuntarily twitch as I work out how I'm going to do this.

I don't want to hurt him.

I care about him, regardless of all the horrible things he has done. I can't turn off my feelings for him, but I need to kill or at least badly injure him so he stops before he kills someone else.

My adrenaline is through the roof, keeping me from passing out from shock while I keep my back glued to the wall. He killed Kaleb. He covered me in blood then was about to kill Gabriella, all so I'd leave with him.

He's a psychopath.

"It is me, Tobias. I am Aria. You don't need to do all this."

He grunts, sitting down on the edge of the desk, looking

exhausted, faint purple bags under his eyes. "I have no other option. I refuse to force you to be with me, so it needs to be your choice."

"Threatening to kill the people I care about so I leave with you is forcing me." I sigh as he drops his head, my chest tightening. "You tried to kill my best friend," I whimper, holding the back of my hand to my mouth, still against the wall. "You killed Kaleb..."

"He lied to you and broke your heart." He scoffs, looking up at me. "He's lucky I didn't torture him."

"He lied about having a girlfriend over five years ago. I wasn't heartbroken."

"Still fucked you," he retorts.

I shake my head and drop my hand. "And that right there is one of the many reasons why I can't be with you," I say, crossing my arms as rage rips through me, hoping he can't sense how equally terrified I am as I step forward and point to my chest. "I'm Aria. I'm the person you apparently love. All I ever wanted to do was help you, and you've just made it worse!"

Raising my voice isn't going to help, but I feel so mad, pent-up anger sizzling at my fingertips as they dig into my palms. This man drives me insane. He's dangerous, psychotic, and a pathological liar.

"I don't know what else to do," he replies in a quiet and broken tone, his head down once more. "I can't control you, no matter how hard I try."

"But you *do*. Look around us," I say, tossing both my arms out to the sides as he looks up, the darkness dimming in his eyes. "This is control. And I don't like it at all. Love doesn't do this, not real love."

"You control me too. I'd do anything you say." He stops me from interrupting him with a huff. "Anything except letting the cops get me and becoming brainwashed until I die. I'd rather be on the end of a noose than be without you."

"Then let us go."

He shakes his head. "I can't."

One more step forward. "Why the hell not?"

He sucks on his bottom lip, his dark lashes lowering. "Why can't you come with me? What's stopping you?"

"If I ran around killing people, became toxic and possessive, drugged you, would you still want to be with me?"

"That's not who you are," he replies, merely a whisper before groaning into his hands. After a few seconds, he lets out a chuckle into his palms "The doctor, though, maybe she would be like that."

"This needs to stop, Tobias. I'm me, there is only one of me, and she's starting to get sick and tired of this psychotic obsession."

Our eyes meet as he snaps his head up, the blues now in full bloom. "That's..." He struggles with his words, shaking his head once. "Fucking hell. I've messed it all up, haven't I? You're going to let Ewan raise my kids, and..." He trails off, shaking his head once more as he shoves a stack of papers off the desk. "Fucking hell. How come he gets everything?"

"You killed people." He doesn't reply; he just shakes his head and launches something off the wall, something I don't seem to react to. "Will you let us go?"

"No, I already said I can't. Justin will be here with Ewan soon anyway."

I feel my soul leave my body, my teeth grinding. "But why not? And what are you going to do to Ewan?" I ask, walking until I'm in front of him, making him lift his head to look up at me. His eyes are wet, his face as white as snow. "Do you want to hurt them all just because you want me? Do you want to lose me even more than you already have?"

"Of course I fucking don't. You don't get it; I have no choice." His face twists, tensing his jaw as he looks to the side, grimacing. "I can't even look at you."

"Why?" I ask with a frown.

"You have another man's blood on you."

My eyes widen, bile rising up my throat. "What?" I ask shakily but he ignores me. I start erratically wiping my sleeve down my face while my stomach turns, painfully scrubbing the material against my face. Kaleb's blood is already starting to dry on my skin, and as soon as I realize it's there, I can smell it. "Oh my God," I say as I wipe harder, my sleeve streaking crimson.

Tobias huffs, standing from the desk and pulling his hoodie off, handing it to me. I try to ignore the flash of abs that appear. "Use this; it's damp from the snow." I stare at the black material in his hand, stepping back and shaking my head. "Hurry up and use it, Aria."

Aria.

I know I shouldn't, but hearing him say my name and not calling me "doctor" makes the tension around me calm a little. He's not full of rage, or even clenching his fists to hold in his anger. He's relaxed, sitting against the desk with a soft expression on his face, and, if anything, he looks nervous.

Tobias looks like he's hurting, struggling emotionally.

He won't hurt me.

"Okay," I say with an uneasiness in my voice, my hand trembling as I take it from him and use it to clean the blood from my face and neck while he stares at his boots. Putting it down on the desk behind him when I'm clean, I glance at him, seeing his bloodshot eyes, the dimple that seems to permanently dent his cheek, his lip secured between his teeth. It makes me sigh and stand back until my body is against the wall once more.

"What happens now then?"

He shrugs. "We wait on Justin to bring Ewan."

"And what do you plan on doing to him?" The words feel like poison on my tongue, making me nauseous. "You're going to torture Ewan until I agree to go with you?"

"I don't know," he replies, taking a deep breath. "I want it to be me who makes you happy, not him. Do you know how it feels? To be me? To be told every fucking day that what you feel isn't real, that it's fake? I try, Aria." I see his chin quiver, and he sucks his bottom lip into his mouth to stop it. "I try to prove it, and it gets blown up in my goddamn face."

Closing my eyes for a long second, I calculate how idiotic I am as I walk to him, resting my trembling hand on his shoulder. "I need you to stay calm and tell me what you feel." My other hand lands on his other shoulder, and I see him tense. "Do you still feel mad with me here, like this?"

He gulps, releasing a harsh breath, trying to stand. "No."

Try harder, Aria. The blade is so close.

Looking up at him through my lashes, I press against his shoulders until he sits back on the desk. "Tell me why I should go with you."

My heart races, trying to keep myself together while I use seduction to get the knife from him. I'm also fighting against the butterflies fluttering in my stomach from being so close to him, close enough to see his hauntingly handsome features I refuse to admit I've missed. "Give me reasons why I shouldn't be afraid of you."

"Because I don't feel that part of me when I'm with you. I'm not perfect by any means, but I don't have the urge to lose it when I'm with you. I feel very...protective of you. I can keep you all safe," he responds, my body going rigid as he lifts a hand and tucks a strand of brown hair behind my ear, leaving his thumb to rest against my cheek. "Do you feel anything for me anymore?"

"Of course I do," I whisper. "But I don't feel safe around you. You just tried to kill Gabriella, you *did* kill Kaleb, and then what happened back at my apartment..."

I feel the fire burning all over me as he drops both of his hands to my hips. The sensation is wrong, forbidden, and I shouldn't be exploding at the simple touch, especially when he pulls me between his legs and drops his head on my shoulder. "I'm sorry. I'm so, so fucking sorry, Aria. I don't want to do this. I don't want to take you or your friends and hurt them just so the girl I love wants to be with me." I hear him choke on a low sob, his body tensing. "This isn't me. Please believe that."

"How do you feel when I do this?" I ask him, changing the subject and running my fingers through his hair, feeling the tension in his muscles under my palm start to lessen. "Do you feel calmer?"

"Yeah," he responds with a mumble and a slow nod. I close my eyes, continuing to run my fingers through his hair while he takes steady breaths, his fingers curling around my hips before completely snaking around the small of my back. "Please come with me."

I don't answer him. I physically can't. Feeling tears welling up and falling down my cheeks, I try to keep my own breathing calm when my eyes fall on the blade poking out from under his shirt as he leans forward, pulling me closer to him.

His breathing is becoming heavy, hot bursts of breath hitting my face. "I don't want to hurt you." His nose nudges mine, tears sliding down his cheeks and puddling at my fingers. "I don't want to hurt our..." He stops, more tears falling with a sharp inhale. "I'm so sorry I fucked up. I wish I could take it all back and be good for you."

I drop one of my hands from his face, resting it on his chest, feeling his heart racing against my palm. "I said I'd stand by you, I swore I would. I still mean it. All we need to do is walk out of that door and get in the car. You can take responsibility for your actions and show our kids you aren't...you aren't the monster everyone paints you to be."

"Do you think I'm a monster?" he asks, his voice breaking with each word. "I don't want to be."

"You just need help, Tobias."

"Could you ever love me again?" he questions me in a heart-breaking tone, his dimples denting while he waits for my response. "Will you let me be part of their lives?"

I don't respond to him with words. Instead, I take a deep breath and press my lips to his, catching him completely off guard as he falls back to sit on the desk once more. We both inhale deeply, groaning in approval as our lips part, moving our tongues in sync, savoring the feeling of something that will never ever happen again.

Because I need to kill him.

I can taste our melded tears each time our lips connect, his murderous hands sliding up my arms, along my collarbones, ending with one in my hair and the other comfortably around my throat as he tilts his head to the side, slanting his mouth, our lips parting once more.

My fingers grip at the material over his chest, and Tobias pulls away from the kiss, making me chase his lips to reconnect them in a desperate plea to keep going. He stands, not breaking contact while he grabs at my thighs, spins, and places me on the desk, standing between my parted legs while I accidentally moan at his hands moving up to my hips.

I'm using my tongue as a weapon, distracting him with each stroke, nearing my end goal.

I just keep getting side-tracked, becoming consumed by him, being completely devoured by a psychotic killer, and I'm enjoying it. This is so wrong...

Focus, Aria.

"I have no idea what you're doing," he says into my mouth, moving his hand to wrap his fingers around my throat again, applying a minuscule amount of pressure to pull us apart. "What are you doing?"

He doesn't give me a chance to reply, his tongue delves back into my mouth while my hands explore his body. I push my palms up his toned chest, ending with my hands wrapped in his hair, tugging a fistful that causes him to groan against my lips and push himself more between my legs, his hand tightening on my throat.

He's a killer.

He just tried to kill your best friend.

"Does this mean you're leaving with me?" he asks, his tone full of hope, smiling against my mouth even though I haven't replied. His fingers pull down the zip of my jacket, and he yanks it to the ground, wrapping his arms around me possessively. He grins at me, pulling down my bottom lip with his teeth until it pops back into place, kissing me again. "You're giving me a chance?"

He isn't Ewan. He's a psychopathic murderer.

I try to pay attention to our mouths moving together while I trail a hand down his back, lowering until I feel the cool metal. I gasp into his mouth and freeze my hand there, basking in the moment before I end it all.

"I won't let them cut the babies out of you, okay? I promise."

I abruptly pull away from him, feeling my eyes nearly bulging out of my head. "What?"

Pushing his hand through my hair, he cups the back of my head and pulls me to him again, the tip of his nose brushing against my cheek while he breathes over my mouth. "Trust me, I won't let anything happen to you. I promise I won't hurt Gabriella or Ewan. Just come with me and let me look after you. I swear to you, I won't do what I did at your place ever again."

He crashes his lips to mine, consuming me while my mind explodes at his revelation. "They'd die," I manage to say through the kiss. "I'm not even in my second trimester."

He looks lost as he pulls back, his lips swollen, face flushed, breathless before he hardens his expression. My hand falls away from the handle as he shifts me further onto the desk. "I won't let them. Just tell me what I can do to have this. This right here is what I want more than anything."

I can feel the metal once more, and my heart nearly drops that this is our final moment.

"Will you hand yourself over to the cops? That's all I'll ask of you," I question him one last time as my fingers carefully wrap around the handle. "Will you?" I push for an answer as his brows furrow, searching my face with his head tilted.

My blood turns ice cold, painful shivers running up my spine.

He caught me.

When he drops his head to my chest, both of his hands move to my stomach, making my lips part and gasp in surprise. "You two have the strongest mom ever, and I know she'll keep you both safe, safer than daddy ever could." He removes one hand, twisting it around his back to grab my hand on the handle of the blade. "But Mommy needs to put Daddy out of his misery now." I hold my breath as he wraps his fingers around mine, pulling the blade free before directing it to press against his spine. "I love the three of you, and I always will, no matter what anyone says, no matter what anyone thinks they know about me. Everything I did, I did because I thought I was doing right by you."

I feel a twist in my gut, my heart nearly stopping, any form of breathing seizing. "Tobias," I choke out his name.

"There are four bags of money buried at the nearby beach. Dig where the painted red stones are and give our kids the best life...one I couldn't."

I grit my teeth to hold myself together. "How do I bring you back? Tell me what I can do instead of this. I want this side of you, not the dark side, not the dangerous side."

Tobias releases his hand from mine, looking up at me through his dark lashes, his electro-blue eyes watering as he stares at me before pressing his lips to my forehead, lingering for a few seconds. "I am who I am, and I can't change that." He sighs and audibly gulps. "I'm tired, Aria. I wanted to give you the world, not destroy yours. Just...just do it."

I gasp out a sob, my body shaking in his arms, moving my other hand so I have two on the handle for more power behind the deadly thrust.

"Promise me they'll know who I am, the real me, the one you once fell in love with."

I nod, our noses touching as our foreheads meet, tears falling down both of our cheeks, my face contorting in ways it never has before. "I'm sorry I couldn't do more to help you." Each breath shakes as I try to stop myself from hyperventilating. "I'm so...s...so sorry."

"You tried."

Closing my eyes, I take a deep breath and press my lips to his one last time.

50

ARIA

Freeing ourselves from a toxic relationship is hard, but it only ever seems to be the good memories that burn into our brains, breaking our hearts and driving us to the brink of insanity.

We should be wondering why instead; why was the relationship bad? Why are we reducing ourselves to nothing when we should be basking in greatness, that we are free from the clutches of the devils that haunt us?

"You're everything to me."

"Are we forever, Aria?"

"I love you more than life itself. I'd die for you if I had to."

"Will you show me how to be a good dad?"

I'm trying to push myself, tightening my grip on the handle of the blade, but I'm overwhelmed with so many emotions, I can't see or think clearly.

There are so many memories with him that are crushing me.

But they are all memories I shouldn't be thinking of. I should be thinking of all the things he has done to me. But no, all I can think about is the good side while I contemplate wiping him from the Earth, from my life—*forever.*

Tobias Mitchell is hot and cold, the assistant, the dimpled

psychopath, the dark-haired asshole, the guy I fell in love with when I should have been running in the opposite direction.

And now, I'm sitting with him between my legs, his hands in my hair, my lips fused to his, seconds from driving a blade into him.

I want to save him; I want him to want to be saved without having me as a possession. The few and limited positive qualities he holds aren't enough for him to have a normal life with me or his kids, but enough that he can live, to get help, treatment, anything that doesn't require him to be six feet under.

Can I *really* kill him? Am I capable of that type of heinous act?

With lungs screaming for oxygen, I feel the burning sensation in my chest, in dire need for them to fill, but I'm frozen in time. My twisted, traitorous heart begs for the dark love consuming me, pleading with me to give into it, to embrace it.

And my mind is exploding with every passing second I have the knife pressed to Tobias' back, my fingers twitching as I brace myself to take someone's life...to take his life.

His breath whispers against my pale skin, his lips grazing my neck. "Breathe. You can do this. Do it for both of us. All of us."

I feel myself imploding with a suffocating heart and a reeling mind urging me to continue, but it's as if our possessive souls are interlocking, dark meeting light, existing side by side, and I drop the blade with a painful sob catching in my throat. "I...I can't do it."

I'm not a killer.

"Do it," he orders me with a touch of anger, his hands tightening around me until I feel my lungs start to scream. "You need to."

"Why?" I sob, tears burning my eyes. "I can't hurt you. I can't."

Tobias huffs in frustration and pulls away from me, gritting his teeth. I can see the shift, the rage, the confusion. "How can you protect our kids if you can't take out the biggest threat, huh?" He slaps his palm against his chest, trying to control his breathing. "Me, right here. I'm that. How can I trust you to protect them?"

And just like that, gentle Tobias is nowhere to be seen. I feel my heart twisting in my chest as I watch him, his stance changing to defensive, his fists clenching at his side as he blinks.

Gulping a painful lump, I lower my voice to a soft whisper. "You need to calm down."

"You don't get to tell me what to fucking do. You're nothing to me. All you ever were was a good fuck gone wrong."

I frown in confusion, trying to mask the hurt. "Gone wrong?"

He nods, prodding the inside of his cheek with his tongue. "You weren't supposed to get into my fucking head." I stay silent, watching him have yet another inner battle with himself. "She's tricking you. She's tricking you," he says repeatedly as he paces the length of the small office, my body freezing as he bends down and grabs the blade from the ground. "Take her back. I need to take her..."

Grabbing me by the arm, he drags me out of the room, ignoring my pleas as he pulls me down the narrow corridor and tosses me onto the floor next to Kaleb's lifeless body, his eyes wide open next to my face.

I scream, pulling myself to my knees and scurrying away until my back hits the wall, my heart nearly blowing through my chest at his blue lips and paling skin.

"Aria!" Gabriella yells, and I snap my head in her direction, panicking, her face pressed against the cage door. "Are you okay?"

I nod once. "Y...yeah."

"Did he touch you?" she asks with tears streaming down her face. She looks relieved as I shake my head, her eyes closing as she releases a breath.

Tobias chuckles as he steps over Kaleb's lifeless body, leaning against the table and crossing his ankles. "Did I touch her?" he repeats Gabriella's question with a scoff. "She kissed me and loved every minute of it. Right, Aria?" He watches us both shaking, silently sobbing. "I gave her a chance to kill me, and did she? No, I'm shocked we didn't fuck, to be honest." He rolls his eyes as I mouth *sorry* to Gabs. "The two of you are pathetic..."

Before he can continue his verbal torture, the sound of an engine echoes through the room, the small, rectangular window slightly ajar. My pulse quickens as the sound of snow crunching underneath car tires comes to a stop.

A door slams, followed by uncontrollable coughing and Justin telling someone to stop bleeding all over him.

Ewan.

All my hairs rise, a sinking feeling settling in my chest, an over-whelming sense of dread that makes me feel nauseous.

"Ahh, perfect timing," Tobias says with a smile before raising a brow, regarding me as I press my palms to myself protectively. "I trust you aren't dumb enough to try anything."

I stay silent, trying to hold myself together as he leaves the room.

Faint voices can be heard, but Gabs' muttering makes them impossible to make out. "We're going to get out of here, I'll make sure of it," she says as I slide down to the floor, my back to the wall, legs bent as I clasp my hands over my shins. "There must be a way out."

"He said they want to cut the babies out of me."

I don't look at her, but I can see in my peripheral vision that she's nodding in disgust, her chin trembling as tears fall down her cheeks. "She told me." Her head tilts to Violetta in the cage next to her. "Disgusting."

Narrowing my eyes at his mom, I try not to jump up and slap her through the bars. "You knew?"

I scowl at her as Justin and Tobias round the corner to the corridor, my heart dropping as I see Ewan slouching in between them, blood streaking his face, one eye swollen shut, shirt ripped with obvious deep slash marks down his chest. They pull him along the floor by his elbows, his feet dragging behind him.

His left eye widens as he lifts his head. "Aria!" he yells out as soon as his bloody gaze falls on me, but Tobias' grip on his arm stops him from lunging forward, his voice panicked. "Are you okay?"

"She's fine," Tobias answers with a huff as they get to the middle of the room, dropping him in front of me. "Get this over with already."

I crawl to him, overlooking the mix of blood on the ground while my hands wrap around his, my eyes taking in every wound on his face and deep cuts to his chest. "Oh my God." My palm shakes as I lift it to his cheek, being careful not to touch the gaping gash on his forehead with blood pouring out of it like a red river. I snarl at Justin, looking proud of himself. "What did you do to him?"

He shrugs, glancing from Tobias, to me, to Ewan. "He tried to hit me with a hammer, so I returned the favor...and more."

Ewan's body is shaking, and I can see Tobias out of the corner of my eye, glowering at the two of us on the floor. Tightening my hand around his, I run my thumb over his skin.

"Aria, get the fuck away from him," Tobias orders, but I shake my head as we both scurry back to the wall. "I mean it... Move away from him now before I make you."

Ewan grunts in pain as he moves in front of me, sitting with his back to me, his hand curled around to hold mine, the other wrapping around my back from behind, protecting me in any way he can. "I got you," he says with a groan. "I won't let him hurt you."

Tobias laughs, *really* laughs. "What the fuck are you going to do? Look at you."

I watch him take a step towards us, and I brace myself, closing my eyes, my grip tightening on Ewan's hand and his ripped top.

"Can't you see?" Gabriella blurts out, sneering at Tobias as everyone snaps their heads in her direction. Her fingers curl around the metal, eyes blazing with hatred. "That right there." She tilts her head at Ewan and me, smiling at Tobias vindictively. I can see the fear in her eyes as she tries to distract him from attacking us. "That is what normal people call true love, not this obsession you have with her. You will never have Aria, you will never have happiness, and you will *never* be a good person." She laughs, flattening her lips to a straight line. "Never."

My entire body tenses, my eyes wide as I try to move, but Ewan holds me down. "Gabriella...no. You're just going to set him off." I see Tobias' fists clenching, his nostrils flaring as he looks from us to Gabs.

She scoffs. "No, fuck him!" She points a finger at Tobias, full-blown raging, losing her marbles. "I'm fed up with your bullshit! You're lost, so lost that you think Aria can save you. Trust me, I feel for you in ways I shouldn't, but you don't deserve a happy ending with my best friend. You deserve to be locked away for the rest of your life. Those babies deserve a chance at life without you."

I know she's saying most of this to keep him from coming for Ewan and me, but the fire I can see burning within, the dark energy blowing around him, has me fearing for her life.

"What the fuck did you say?"

Gabriella smirks, giving me a quick glance. "You heard me."

She's suicidal.

I try to move again, but Ewan tightens his hold around me.

She's trying to divert the attention to her to save us.

"Aria is mine," Tobias tells her with a red face.

She looks at us then back at Tobias, cocking an eyebrow. "Clearly."

"Gabriella, stop it!" I yell at her, but she ignores me.

I freeze as Tobias lunges forward, but Justin stops him with a hand to his chest. He smirks at him, raising his brows. "I'll do it." He pushes away from Tobias, narrowing his eyes at her, and I watch in horror as he twirls the key to the padlock around his finger. "Anything else you want to add? Maybe you want to suck my cock one last time?"

She sneers at him and spits in his face.

I close my eyes and hold my breath while Justin chuckles to himself, wiping his face with the back of his hand. "You really are a fucking bitch."

As he approaches her cage door again, I rush to my feet, sliding momentarily in Kaleb's blood. "Don't!"

My words are useless, especially when Tobias grabs me, dropping the blade in front of me. He wraps his arm around mine from behind, trapping me as Justin yanks a thrashing Gabriella out of the cage. "Please, leave her alone She's just—" I'm silenced, Tobias' palm tight over my mouth.

I can see Ewan struggling to get to his feet, coughing up blood on the floor.

Everything is happening too fast, but also in extreme slow motion.

One second, Justin is pulling her from the cage, Violetta yelling at him to stop as he grabs her by the hair. Then, he kicks her behind her legs so she drops to her knees before him.

Ewan falls on his front, choking and groaning as he too shouts something at Justin.

I'm struggling against Tobias' grip, his palm harsh over my mouth, muffling my screams.

Justin pulls out a hammer.

There's blood already coating it–Ewan's blood.

I try to move forward as he raises it above his head, my heart tripling in speed, screaming as loud as I can against Tobias' hand. He shushes me and steps back, my eyes falling to Ewan pulling himself up on the table.

He'll save her.

He has to.

But as the hammer drops down on her skull, the silence is deafening as the thud reverberates around the room.

Immediately, my chest caves in, all the oxygen leaving the atmosphere, a high-pitched ringing shrieking painfully in my ears. My temples throb with pressure, flashes of black and white lights everywhere. My entire life turns upside down, the room chaotic but silent as my heart drops, breaking, twisting, my eyes screwing shut tighter than ever before. I stop fighting against Tobias, my body limp in his arms as a strangled scream dies in my throat.

No.

No. No. No.

I open my eyes, the blood draining from my face as I watch him deliver repeated blows. Gabriella's body falls to the floor as I tremble uncontrollably, wincing with each swing of the hammer. Two hits, three, four, and a fifth one before I bite down on Tobias' palm as hard as I can until he releases me.

I lose my footing as soon as his arms unravel from me. There's no sound, not even from the thrashing heart in my chest, threatening to stop at any given moment as Kaleb and Gabriella's blood mixes together in a deep red puddle at my feet, my eyes unblinking, my body paralyzed as shock overwhelms me.

All those times we sat in bed and watched tv, listened to music, festivals, traveled, laughed, smiled, cried, everything you'd do with your best friend flooding me until I go blind. I gasp and drop to my knees next to her, my body shaking as I watch hers heave helplessly.

"No," I mutter as my lip quivers, my hands trembling as I hold her face, her bloodshot, fluttering eyes fighting to stay open. "No."

Justin laughs behind me, and I see red, gripping the blade from the floor and scrambling to my feet. I don't even need to think twice before driving the blade right into the back of his neck as forcefully as possible. I pull it back and strike his shoulder again and again as I scream at the top of my lungs. He falls to the ground, my body on top of him, relentlessly thrusting the blade into him until my arms grow tired.

His blood is covering me, but I don't stop, even as I feel the crimson liquid making my fingers slide on the handle.

I'm blinded by rage, desperate to end this carnage.

A hand grasps my shoulder, and I decide to finish this once and for all. The adrenaline has me turning and driving the blade into his side as hard as I can, feeling each layer of muscle splitting as the knife buries deep into his body.

I open my eyes, and it isn't Tobias.

"Ewan?" My face twists as he looks down at the knife impaled in his side. "Oh my God!" I catch his weak body, lowering him to the ground, settling his head on my lap. He's gasping, attempting to fill his lungs. "I thought you were... Oh my God!"

"Ru...run," he spits out, his bloodied teeth clenching.

Gabriella's body is heaving next to me, Ewan tensing in my arms, both of them watching me. I reach over and take her hand in mine, completely stuck on what I can do to save them.

"What do I do?" I cry out, growling at Tobias, who's sitting with his arms crossed, unbothered by the scene before him, even at his close friend butchered on the floor at his feet. "We need to call an ambulance!"

"Why would I do that?"

I look between Gabriella and Ewan; both are fighting for their lives in my arms. If we get them help, they can survive.

Taking a deep, steady breath, tears streaming down my face as my heart shatters into a million pieces, I make a deal with the devil. "I'll go with you."

Ewan groans in pain next to me, trying to shake his head, but there's no time.

"Call an ambulance and I'll go with you. You can have me, but only if you call an ambulance. *Now.*"

Tobias straightens, his brows furrowing. "You mean it? You'll leave with me?"

I nod. "But you need to call for help right now, Tobias."

Ewan's hand snatches mine in a tight grip, his eyes burning into me as Tobias leaves the room with his phone pressed to his ear.

"Wh...what are y...you doing?" Ewan's words break, crimson sputtering from his lips. "No...you..."

I smile at him, tears coating my cheeks as I lean down and press my forehead to his. "I love you so much, and I always will, always have. Jason needs his dad, and I need you to live. This is the only way."

He shakes his head, face contorting. "N...no, A...Aria."

I sob, clenching my teeth before I press my lips to his, the small act astronomical in this moment. "We ran out of time, Ewan."

He tries to shake his head, attempting to drag in deep breaths while coughing uncontrollably. "Pl...please don't leave...leave me."

"Let's go," Tobias says as he enters the room. "They're on their way." I turn to look at him, his dark side seeming to have been suppressed somewhat as he unlocks his mom's cage and pulls her out. "You can stay with them until the paramedics get here. I've dragged you through my shit for long enough."

"You want me to stay?" she asks in shock.

He nods then reaches over and grabs me. "Come on."

I pull myself from his grasp, pressing my lips to Gabriella's forehead. "I promise I'll see you really soon. Don't rent my room out," I whisper to her, my lips touching her head once more. "I love you. Be strong."

Gabriella isn't struggling anymore, but if the paramedics get here fast, they can save them both. They need to. I refuse to believe anything else.

This is really happening; I'm saving them by handing my life to Tobias and risking everything. But what else am I to do? Jason needs his dad, and everyone needs Gabriella. I *have* to do this.

Ewan is begging me, but all I can do is give him an apologetic smile, not caring that Tobias is hovering behind me as I move forward and press my lips to his one last time. The grip on my shirt yanking me back breaks the goodbye kiss within a second.

I don't look back as Tobias takes my hand and pulls me out of the room.

I don't look back as we leave the abandoned building. We climb the snow-filled woodlands, flashing red and blue lights and sirens appearing at the bottom of the hill.

I can't look back.

As soon as we make it to the top, nearly twenty-five minutes later, Tobias stops to catch his breath. "You okay?"

I sneer at him, snapping. "Is that a joke?"

He doesn't answer me, but he does take my hand, pulling me along the snow. I'm not shaking with how cold it is, or the bitterness of the ice biting my skin, but I'm rattling with the blazing inferno ripping through me, like really bad, unwanted adrenaline.

We reach the edge of a cliff, and Tobias stops, looking over to me. "Do you even know where we're going?" I ask him.

He stays silent.

I laugh in disbelief.

"For the record, I told him not to hurt anyone." He turns to me, a sincere look in his eyes. "I told him we were just going to threaten them, that's all."

"You were going to hurt Gabriella before...before he did that." I cross my arms, my lip trembling again. "He hit her over the head with a...with a..." I cover my mouth as I struggle to finish the sentence. "Oh, God."

He takes careful steps towards me before throwing his hands up in exasperation. "I didn't want anyone to get hurt."

I cry into my hands, my face twisting. "I stabbed Ewan." As I turn to Tobias, my eyes widen in shock. "I stabbed him. And I...I killed Justin."

"It was self-defense," he says, reaching up with both hands to cup my cheeks as I shake. "Ewan was an accident, Aria."

I accept defeat, giving in, craving my last chance for comfort. I drop my head to his chest and let it all out, screaming into him, allowing myself to feel all the emotions surging through my body, ripping my heart from my chest.

It hurts. The images are burned into my mind.

"I'm the same as you now."

His body tenses, looking down at me with a frown. "You're nothing like me."

I shake my head, wiping my eyes. "I am."

Flashing lights start to surround us, and Tobias lets go of me abruptly, twisting his body, seeing the red and blue coming from every direction, the faint sound of sirens growing louder.

"Shit," he blurts out and grabs my hand, both running in the snow with no direction. "Fuck!" He halts at the cliff, looking down to see the thrashing waves pelting off the rocks. "You can't jump, can you?"

"I'm pregnant, Tobias. Plus, no one would survive that."

He swears to himself, running his hand through his hair as the lights become brighter, sirens blaring from the forest surrounding us.

He freezes, looking over his shoulder at the cliff then back to me. "You hate me, right?"

I tilt my head. "What?"

He closes distance, taking my cheeks in his cold, wet hands, moving the hair out of my face. "Tell me you hate me, that you want me dead. Just say those words." Tobias looks over my shoulder, the sound of dogs barking making me hold in a sigh of relief. "The babies are better off without me, and so are you. If it were up to you, you'd want me completely out of the picture, right?"

"If it were up to me, I'd make sure you got the help you desperately need," I reply, reaching up to grab his wrists.

Pressing his heated forehead to mine, he closes his eyes. "Just say it. Please. You want Ewan to be their dad. You want to raise them with him because he's a good person and you love him. Please, just *say* it."

I see a tear fall down his cheek, his pulse racing in his neck as I reach up to hold him. "Look at me." He does, and his swollen red eyes and pale face tells me everything I need to know, especially since he keeps looking behind him, his suicidal stare on the cliff. "Why would you rather die instead of getting help?"

The dogs barking grows louder, and I can hear footsteps crunching in the snow, torches shining on us, voices yelling but still too far away to make out what they're saying.

"I don't want them to see me like that, the way I saw my own dad."

I close my eyes and sigh, moving my other hand to the opposite side of his neck. "It won't be like that."

"I need you to just..." He stops, screwing his face up. "You don't need or want me. Say it!" he screams through a sob that rips from his throat before lowering his voice to a whisper. "Please."

"No."

A close, loud bark has Tobias pulling away from me, backstepping as he takes quick breaths. "I can't do it, Aria. I can't do that to them." He raises his hands up as I try to grab him, edging closer to the cliff. "Ewan is a good dad, and you're going to be an amazing mom. I'm just Tobias, the guy who'll break their hearts every time they come to visit me."

"Tobias..."

"I won't do it to them." He dodges me when I try to grab him again, one final step from the edge of his demise. "I'm dangerous. I'm the bad guy. I'm fucking insatiable when it comes to pain, and I can't help it. But I do love you."

He freezes and drops his hands, tears falling down his cheeks. "I have no idea how to be normal for you. I lied before. I just wanted to hurt you. You weren't a good fuck gone wrong; you are...were...the best thing that ever happened to me."

The cops are right behind me now, shouting at us to raise our hands, to freeze, to get down, to step away from the cliffside while I stare at Tobias' blue eyes shining in the moonlight, his sadness making me falter and panic.

"I want you to be their dad," I say in a heart-breaking tone, watching him get a millimeter from the edge. I panic. "You've done horrific things, Tobias, you really have, but that doesn't mean I don't love you."

"What did you say?"

I step towards him, urging myself to say the three words that go against every sensible thought in my head. "I love you."

"She just said she loves me," he says to himself. "She...loves me."

He smirks, but it falters, his expression changing to something serious as he steps towards me and grabs my face, pressing his lips to mine.

He pulls away from me, the corner of his mouth tugging up as his dimples dent in, his ocean blues dancing. "Thank you for loving me."

I gasp as he throws himself backwards just as an officer collides with my body and pins me to the snow-covered ground. My arm reaches to my front to protect myself.

"Tobias!" I release an ear-piercing scream. "Tobias!"

I manage to drag my head to the side, watching the scene

unfold before me. I can't believe that after everything we've been through, all the sick, twisted games, the heartbreak, murder, the infatuation to own every part of me, this is it.

I sob, closing my eyes momentarily as relief floods through me, consuming every inch of my body as Tobias stops resisting the officers.

EPILOGUE
ARIA

Five Years Later

"Aria Miller, this year's medal recipient, is being recognized for her outstanding work and contributions to the fields of pediatric medicine and genetic science, and her exceptional research in collaboration with multiple organizations. Most recently, she founded a charity focused on mental health awareness. She worked extensively on the discovery of new genetic mutations that affect the mitochondria. By doing this in such a short number of years, she not only has generated more jobs for research but has saved thousands of lives around the world."

Clapping fills my ears. I straighten my pencil skirt, taking deep breaths while I stare at my fingers twisting in my lap. A hand curls around them, tightening, running his thumb over my skin in comfort.

"You've got this. I'm so proud of you," Ewan tells me, pressing his lips to my temple as Doctor Shique continues speaking to the hundreds of people in the dark theatre hall.

"She had been relentless with her research, month after month, year after year. She worked harder, harder than I had ever seen anyone work, only to be told no, over and over again. Did that stop her from going on to create the new *Gemgene* trials? No, of course it didn't."

Each time the crowd surrounding us breaks into applause, my heart beats faster. Perspiration forms along my forehead, the room growing far too hot as I listen to him praise me.

"I've had the pleasure of working alongside Aria for many years now, and when I tell you she is a fighter, incredibly determined, and an inspiration to survivors all over the world, I mean it."

The room grows silent, and I squeeze Ewan's hand, my nails digging into his palm, resisting the urge to get up and run for the hills. "I can't stand up in front of all these people."

Anxiety riddles me daily, to the point that I haven't gotten up on a stage and spoken in years. Sure, I've sat in busy meeting rooms week after week, but only after hours of hyperventilating that usually resulted in me bringing my lunch up in the toilet once finished.

But at this moment, with hundreds of eyes on me, I don't think I can do it.

I go to therapy every single week since that horrific night, practicing different methods to help me relax when my mind is on fire. I haven't touched alcohol in years. I don't need it, Kade and Luciella definitely don't need their mom drunk every night.

"I'll be proud of you either way," Ewan says, lacing his fingers in mine. "But as soon as we get home, I'm ripping that skirt off you." His mouth is close to my ear, and I clench my thighs. "That's a promise."

I smirk and slap his torso as my eyes flit to Jason, the sixteen-year-old with an attitude who, thankfully, doesn't hear his dad's crude statement. My hand momentarily trails the outline of the deep scar on Ewan's chest, the one he kept hidden for years before finally letting me trace my fingertips along it, telling him he should embrace the fact that he survived that torturous night five years ago.

We both should.

We have only just become official. I wanted a break from any type of relationship to focus on myself, on the twins, on Jason and Ewan as we co-parented over the years. It didn't stop us from warming each other's beds often, and he basically lived with me for the first year so I could help him with his physio, both healing the other mentally, emotionally, and eventually...physically.

I sold the house and moved in with him a few months ago, and we are due to move into a larger one on the waterfront, in a small town not far from where we grew up. I refused my inheritance when my father died two years ago and told the investigators where Tobias buried his bags of money, which, after a long battle with the law, were returned to his accounts.

I refused his money too, but that didn't stop him from putting a chunk of it into savings accounts for the kids, which means they'll set for life when they're old enough. He even set a savings up for Jason, filling it with two-hundred grand that'll become available to him in a few years.

But for now, I want to make my own success, my own money. I want to show the kids I can do it all without any help.

Life, after years of heartbreak, havoc, and craziness, is good.

I'm happy.

It has been wild and crazy, filled with hardships and struggles, but I've finally gotten to a place where I feel safe and, well...happy.

"Now, without further ado, I would like to introduce you all to Aria Miller."

Ewan kisses my cheek, releasing my hand to clap alongside the crowd. "Smash it," he tells me with a wink. "You can do it."

Nodding, I bite my lip with nerves as I stand from my chair, looking around at everyone applauding. I make my way to the stage in slow motion, violin music playing overhead. I accept a gentleman's hand to help me up the steps, positioning myself under the spotlight as Doctor Shique grins at me.

"It's good to see you again." He lowers the purple ribbon over my head, the golden medal heavy against my chest. "You deserve this."

"Thank you," I reply with a smile just as the music starts to lower, every nerve ending exploding as I glance at the audience now getting to their feet, cheering. My eyes find Ewan, and he nods at me proudly, making me dig deep and internally puff my chest for courage. "Breathe, Aria," I mutter to myself, taking a deep breath in through my mouth and out through my nose.

Doctor Shique backs away, allowing me to stand at the podium in the middle of the stage, tapping the microphone.

"I...I, um, I honestly have no idea what to say." I look down at the medal, feeling my eyes watering with pride. "Oh, God, my mascara is going to run," I say, the crowd laughing with me as I use my fingertips to wipe away the stray tears. "I don't think I deserve this. There are many researchers out there, especially in this room, who deserve it more than me."

I see a lot of heads shaking with smiles on their faces, disagreeing with me. I shift on each foot, my heart racing.

"There's one person who always believed in me the most, even when I failed." I take a deep breath, and find Gabriella's parents in the crowd, giving them a nod before I continue. "I met her when I was in college, and we were inseparable ever since." My voice breaks, and I swallow down a lump. "We traveled during research; we were always together. We were roommates. We were like sisters, and I honestly still feel lost when I wake up in the morning. I think I always will."

Her beautiful face flashes before me, her wide smile, her hazel eyes dancing with glee, mouthing to me to keep going like she always does, guiding me through every step in life. *Her smile will brighten the skies forever.* It's what's engraved on her headstone, and it's true.

I miss her.

"And I...and I..." Struggling to continue, I take a deep breath, gulping before I keep going. "I know she's looking down on me right now, questioning why..." I release a single laugh. "No, not questioning. She's screaming in disgust as to why I'm wearing my hair this way or why I'm wearing her white shirt."

They laugh again, some wiping tears from their eyes, especially her mom.

I stop, grasping hold of the podium. "I...um, I have her to thank for everything I have, because she always pushed me. Even up here," I point to my head, my nostrils flaring as tears fall, "she still helps me. She always pulls me from my nightmares, holds my hand, gives me a kick up the behind when I falter or when I feel like giving up."

I hear a few sniffles in the crowd, and Ewan wraps his arm around Jason's shoulders. "Gabriella... She saved me, and I hope she knows she did. She saved my children and the man I love. Everything I am today is because of her."

I look down at the medal once more. "I have her to thank for this." I raise it, my lip trembling. "I'm going to continue to make her proud every moment of my life, right up until I see her again, because she's my best friend, forever and always. This...this belongs to her."

The crowd stands, clapping once again as I lower my head, trying to compose myself.

My gaze remains on my trembling fingers, taking deep breaths as Doctor Shique appears beside me, his hand circling on my back. "We're all proud of you," he tells me, and before I can turn to leave the stage, he stops me. "There's someone else who wants to congratulate you."

I look up at him in confusion and wipe my tears with a tissue he offers, seeing him glance over my shoulder with a grin.

Turning, my mouth drops, blinking several times as Ivy Dermot, the now thirteen-year-old girl holding a bouquet of white roses with a massive smile, rises from her wheelchair. An aide walks alongside her as she takes careful steps towards me in her leg braces.

Her mom and dad stand behind her, applauding with proud tears in their eyes, nodding and giving me the thumbs up.

"What..." I stop, shocked, speechless.

The little girl I met all those years ago.

The little girl I travelled the world to save.

The little girl who gave *me* the drive to continue, fighting every single day even after her body started to give up, she's...walking.

My mind is moving in slow motion. After years of physio-therapy and treatment for her symptoms, the trials stretched out for three years, saving her, she's here...and she's *really* walking.

I glance at Ewan over my shoulder. His eyes are wide, and even Jason has his hand over his mouth. They know how important this moment is for me.

As soon as she reaches me, I drop to my knees in astonish-ment, my hand clasped to my forehead, *completely* lost for words as she straightens her arms, handing me the large bouquet of flowers.

Using every ounce of strength in her fragile body, she wraps her arms around me, making it all worth it.

"MOMMY, WHERE ARE WE GOING?" Luciella asks as she skips alongside me.

"To see our father, stupid," Kade replies to her in a bratty tone. When I narrow my eyes on him, he shakes his head. "She's asked like a thousand times, Mom."

"She was only asking. She's excited."

I roll my eyes at the five-year-old twins who couldn't be any more different from each other.

Lu—Luciella—is a miniature version of myself, with curly, platinum blonde hair, dark blue eyes, a few freckles on her face, polite and sweet.

Then, there's Kade. He looks exactly like his father, with dark hair, blue eyes, dimples, longer lashes than anyone I know. While his looks and sometimes boisterous attitude might come from Tobias, everything else comes from Ewan. I mean, I guess he has been the one to raise him from birth, so it's only natural.

The sun is beaming down on us as we walk hand in hand. Annoyingly, the press is here, like they always are when one of the workers leaks I'm visiting. This time, with the kids with me, I want to yell at them to give us some privacy.

Kade lifts his middle finger to them.

This is their first visit with him. After years of therapy and isolation, he finally got accepted for face-to-face visitation once a month. It has taken a lot for me to give in. Ewan and I had a lot of talks with the kids, trying to prepare them. I'm nervous, having Tobias out in an open space, around us, but several psychiatrists and doctors have certified that, with close security, he is allowed to spend one supervised hour with his children.

There's only so much I could do to prepare five-year-olds for this, but going by the video calls, I reckon they'll be fine. However, I won't put them in a position they aren't comfortable with, so if they appear on edge or want to leave, then we will.

If Tobias steps out of line, intentionally sabotages his meds, or gets into any sort of trouble, any contact with me will be cut. Ever since he was given the all-clear for visits under good behavior, he hasn't stepped out of line once. The specialists at his mental institution even say he's like a different person, all things considered.

His lawyer is still in contact. Mr. Vize was his defense, managing to stop Tobias from getting the death penalty and securing a plea deal of insanity, saving his life. The next appeal is in a year, this time to have him transferred closer to home. So far, I don't see it going well, especially since Mr. Vize just adopted two kids and has been working on fewer cases.

The first year of his sentence, I didn't hear a word from Tobias, making me wonder if I'd ever see him again. But when he finally was taken off suicide watch and underwent numerous therapies, the specialists started to notice a change.

They were able to break through the cracks of his mind games. Tobias feared the idea of being heavily medicated, of being a vessel, but he's the complete opposite, as if his daily treatment suppresses the evil I experienced first-hand.

The first time I saw him after so long was two years ago, and I felt my heart stop. His once ocean blue eyes were sunken in, dark purple bags under them. He was thin, the handcuffs sliding up and over his elbows. No words were spoken; he just sat opposite the glass pane, staring at me, drinking me in after so long, ignoring me as I tried to speak until he was taken away an hour later.

His mom is serving an eight-year sentence for aiding a criminal, and that's all I know or care to know. Justin is dead, and Tobias took the fall for it to protect me.

Over the last month, in an attempt to prepare the kids to see Tobias, we were granted video calls for half an hour every two weeks, his therapist staying glued to his side. I could see his eyes light up each time they laughed or asked him ridiculous questions. I knew that, at times, he was staring at me. I could see the way his throat bobbed, and his fingers fidgeted every time I smiled.

After we check-in and have been searched, we follow the receptionist down a long corridor filled with windows that look out to the family area, the kids still arguing over who gets to hug him first. My eyes widen at how beautiful the place really is. There's artificial grass, trees, benches, a small pond, and sandboxes for the kids.

My heart nearly drops when I see him sitting at a picnic table with his back to us. A young woman is next to him, pointing around them while he nods. I can see the muscles have built back up along his shoulders, his sun-kissed arms leaning against the wooden table.

The guard searches me one last time before swiping his badge, the first set of doors sliding open. "You have one hour, and if there are any suspicious activities or sexual contact, you will be removed, and visitation privileges will be revoked."

I try not to frown at the sexual contact comment while I look between the kids then back up at him with a raised brow.

He talks into his radio, telling whoever it is that Tobias Mitchell's visitation begins in three...two...one.

The second door opens, and his head snaps in our direction, lips parting. He looks better. He looks well, healthy.

The kids try to pull from my hands as we make our way to

him. "Are they allowed to hug him?" I ask the therapist, who nods and lifts her paperwork, resting her hand on Tobias' shoulder before going to join one of the guards.

I'm about to let go of their hands, but I can see Tobias is nervous, so I hold them tighter. For a split second, I look between them as they stare at him, Kade moving behind my leg. Luciella glances up at me with a smile, her finger in her mouth.

I look up at Tobias. "Okay?"

He takes a deep breath. "Okay," he replies with a short nod.

"Do you want to go see him?" I ask Luciella, and she nods enthusiastically before she runs at him, followed by Kade.

"Daddy!" they yell in unison as they launch themselves at him, both wrapping their arms around his neck. The smile pulling across his face, causing his dimples to dent in deep, makes my heart swell, and I tear up. "Mommy took us on a *huge* plane!"

He holds them tight, burying his head into Lu's shoulder, then Kade's, messing his hair while he smirks at him. "It's good to finally meet you two," he says with a sniff, trying to keep himself together, holding them even tighter. "You're both so big."

"I'm five!" Lu says with a massive smile. "Kade is five too."

"Wow," he replies with wide eyes. "Five is a cool age."

I bite my lip to stop it from trembling, my eyes flitting to the therapist I've had weekly calls with, and she gives me a thumbs up.

Watching them converse easily, I take a seat at the picnic table, nervously playing with my fingers. The kids eventually run to the sandpit, and Tobias looks over his shoulder at me, shoving his hands in his pockets while he takes careful steps towards me. "Hi."

I smile as I look down at my fingers. "Hi."

"What do you think of the place?" he asks as he looks around, his blue eyes dancing under the bright lights.

"It's beautiful," I reply, glancing at our surroundings, the little speakers playing sound effects of wind, quacking ducks, chattering people, anything to make it seem more realistic. "They said you helped design it?"

"Well, I gave a few suggestions." He nods, taking a seat beside me as he watches the kids throw sand at each other. "I wanted it to be perfect for them. I wanted it to be different."

I turn my head to look at him, smiling. "It *is* perfect."

Tobias smirks, his eyes searching my face. "You seem to get more perfect every time I see you."

I blush, shaking my head. "You said you'd stop saying stuff like that."

Laughing, he rolls his eyes. "I guess I can't help myself." He leans forward and moves a strand of curly blonde hair behind my ear. "Especially when you're so close to me." He huffs out his nose and leans away from me. "Shayla..." He looks over at his therapist. "She wants me to do this exercise where I say exactly how I feel, so I want to try it with you, okay?"

I nod, looking from the twins to him. "Of course."

"First, I want to say sorry. I don't mean for falling in love with you, but for all the havoc that came with it. I lost...I lost myself often, and when I did, I wasn't me. I let myself fall into a dark hole, and every time I tried to get out, it got deeper. I should have listened to you and gotten help before things went as far as they did. Maybe I wouldn't be incarcerated in a mental institution for the rest of my life. Maybe I'd have a chance at a happy ending with you and our kids." He glances at Kade and Lu, the corner of his mouth tugging up. "But I can see how happy you all are, and that's enough for me. If Ewan is your forever, if he is the one who can show my children the right path in life, then I'm happy too."

"Really?" I blurt out.

This is the first time Tobias has ever mentioned Ewan without losing his head–the name was a trigger for him for years, landing him in solitary confinement. But to hear the name fall from his lips in such a positive way... It's making my eyes water.

"Don't get me wrong, I wish it was me, but I can see he gives you all something I can't."

"What's that?" I ask.

"Happiness," he replies with a shrug. "And I've recently found out that happiness means more than anything. Yeah, if I was given the opportunity..." He lowers his voice to a whisper. "I'd happily find one of the broom closets in here and fuck you senseless." My eyes widen, and I snort out a laugh.

We both burst out laughing, and the kids snap their heads in our direction, grinning as Kade whispers something to Lu, making her giggle and toss more sand at him.

"But you're okay?" I ask him, serious, my eyes burning into his. "You're really okay?"

"As long as you and the kids are, then yeah." He nods, shrugging as he stands.

"Ewan asked me to marry him."

He tilts his head. "Do you want to?"

"I still haven't given him an answer."

"Marry him."

A frown pulls across my face. "What?"

"Marry him. Go live your life and raise our kids. Make sure he makes you happier than I ever can, but just know, once I'm out, I'm coming for you."

He swipes a tear sliding down my cheek. "Will you?"

"Yeah. I'll wait forever if I need to, because you're mine."

I gulp and look away, but his voice brings me back. "Do you want to help us build a sandcastle?"

I bite my lip, putting my purse down on the table, walking side by side with Tobias until we reach them, kneeling and trying to act like a normal family, even if it's only for an hour.

Kade and Tobias keep looking at each other, and it's so strange to see the mini version of him. I can see him trying to psychoanalyze the twins, looking for any signs they are like him, but in all honesty, they are still far too young.

"I think you need to look out for Kade," Tobias says as we pack up, his voice serious. "I just have a feeling he's going to be..." He searches for the words, glancing at his son. "He's going to be a handful."

"Well, you can help me. We'll be back next month anyway." I pull my purse up my shoulder, resting my hand on his. He turns it in my hold and smiles down as his fingers lace with mine. "I'm proud of you," I continue. "I'm really proud of you."

He frowns, confused. "After everything I've done, you still care. I don't get it at all."

I tighten my hand over his before letting go, Kade and Luciella jumping on him. "I guess I can't help myself," I say with a smile.

Wrapping his arms around them both as he stands, he lifts them into a big hug. "Be good for Mommy, and I'll see you guys real soon, okay?"

"I love you, Daddy," Lu and Kade say in unison, causing me to clench my teeth to stop my tears.

Tobias opens his eyes to look at me, still holding the kids to his chest. "I love you both so much. Even Mommy."

It's strange. Years ago, I had no idea how much he would change my life, for the good and for the bad.

When I first met him, I never thought I'd fall in love with him, a relentlessly psychopath, ignoring every single red flag that came my way. I should've taken a step back and paid attention to the signs my assistant had issued.

But I didn't, and I can't turn back time.

He overtook every part of me, consumed me, and I let him.

I was taken into the arms of the devil and exposed to a world I didn't belong in. With a desired thirst and need for destruction, our demons danced, and I lost myself.

I lost myself in him.

And now, I'm found. We *both* are.

THE END

ABOUT THE AUTHOR

Leigh Rivers is a Scottish Biomedical Scientist who has ventured into the world of writing dark, morally gray characters with roller-coaster storylines to drive her readers wild.

When she isn't reading, writing on her laptop, or gaming until ridiculous hours, she dances at the pole studio, goes to the gym, and walks her four dogs with her two sons and husband.

If you liked this book, you'll possibly enjoy The Edge of Darkness Trilogy, where you follow the story of Kade Mitchell and Stacey Rhodes.

Find Leigh:
  Instagram: authorleighrivers
  Facebook: authorleighrivers
  Join her FB reader group: Leigh Rivers Dark Romantics
  Email: leighriverspa@gmail.com

ALSO BY LEIGH RIVERS

The Web of Silence Duet
Chokehold
Broken Realms Series